Atasya

S.G. ROSE

☾

We are all wanderers on this earth.
Our hearts are full of wonder,
and our souls are deep with dreams.

A Gypsy Proverb

ATASYA

Published in the USA
Available on Amazon
Inquiries: *atasya.s.g.rose@gmail.com*

ISBN: 9780984248216

☾

For the One who has given us stories to tell
and songs to sing in the darkness
and in the light.

☾

Love and gratitude beyond measure
to my beloved husband,
without whom this book would not exist. . .
my dearly devoted family and friends,
who helped, encouraged and believed. . .
and to Princess Peep, who found her way
over the river and through the woods
back home to my heart.

☾

These are the tales of the vagabond children of YaH ~ passionate souls bound by blood with hearts attuned to the deep wisdom of nature and the Heavens. Those remembered within these pages followed The Spirit of the Wind (*Balval*) to places few are called to go.

Magic flowed through their hands, creating a living tapestry woven of fibers both silken and coarse, dyed the colors of autumn beneath the sun. A single shimmering cord of celestial origin, the *'higher Kintala,'* runs through it, but can be seen only by those who seek it.

When the time arrived for the outsiders to leave this world, they draped their story over a dusty dreamscape with the prayer that a kindred heart would come upon it and their passage through this world not be forgotten.

For a great many moons, countless travelers passed by the treasure that lay beside the way, until the day an old storyteller's feet found the path. Her curious eye did not miss the glint of gold beneath a blanket of long-fallen leaves, and when a breath from Balval swept them away, the tales of the weaving became hers to tell.

☾

The characters and storylines within this book are fictitious and do not portray any person, living or otherwise, with the exceptions of the "little moustache man," (Hitler) and Sabella, an extraordinary woman who was a high wire performer in a German Cirque during WWII.

Glimpses into historical Romany[i] culture and tradition are based upon research, but as the Roma did not encourage reading or writing and relied upon a verbal telling of their past, literary sources are extremely limited. Historians believe that this explains why more was written about the persecution of other groups during the Holocaust than of the Roma, who suffered equally.

Towns, cities, and locales have been loosely based upon actual places, but others are imagined. There are no maps for the journey within.

The fable of *"The Princess and the Snake"* in Part One has been adapted for this book. The original author is unknown.

The Romany/Gypsy language varies greatly among different regions and tribes. The names, words and phrases in *Atasya* were gathered from multiple sources. In an effort to be consistent, a general rule of pronunciation has been applied, where emphasis is placed on the next to last syllable. It is hoped that the footnotes and the Glossary at the back of the book will be helpful to the reader.

The term 'Gypsy,' was commonly used in the timeframe of this book. No disrespect is intended.

Introduction

$\mathcal{J}$'ve always held to the romantic notion that a measure of fiery Gypsy blood runs through my half-Serbian veins, but I knew little about the history of the Roma until I followed a leading to write this book.

My eyes were opened by a study of early Romany culture and the persecution they have suffered for being who they are. An estimated half a million Roma were killed during the Holocaust and a brutal history of slavery came before that.

Only when I abandoned the modern, stereotypical portrayals of Gypsy life could the ten-year journey of writing *Atasya* begin. Visions of the magnificent landscapes through which their caravans traveled came next, and it was there that I wandered into the lives of Renata, Tamás, Nadya and the others. I was allowed to tag along under the condition that they be free to paint their own pictures, sing their own songs and tell their own tales.

Gypsies are master storytellers and almost always choose song and dance over sad soliloquies, though the latter cannot be completely avoided. They prefer nature and adventure, passion and romance, magic and the supernatural. All the things fairytales are made of.

Many signs were sent while I was writing the first three parts of *Atasya*, but the most memorable was an enchanting encounter with a 92-years-young lady on a riverside walk. She made me guess her age (it was impossible), and I told her she was an inspiration. She said her name was Romni and that she was a writer and storyteller. I exclaimed with great surprise that I was writing a book about Gypsies, and a few days later, at her invitation, we ate gelato in her little cottage and chatted about miracles, perseverance, re-inventing yourself, her career as an entertainer, and how we both talked to God all the time.

This world is a supernatural place, but the magic is lost on many. Our capacity for such experiences is determined by desire and I have learned to leave plenty of room for the unexpected.

Continued…

My childhood dream of running away with the Gypsies has come true. Raconteurs, singers, musicians, dancers, and artists at heart, we readily go where our imaginations take us. There are treasures hidden beneath the mossy floor of the Slovenian forests, among the tangled roots of the Redwood Giants, and in many other places within these pages. I hope you find them.

It's with joy that I share *Atasya*, (the Gypsy word for both 'yesterday' and 'tomorrow'), where Now is Forever beneath the boughs of an enchanted willow tree, gems fall from the edges of Charos, and celestial beings take on unexpected forms; where blood oaths are eternal, and even in the face of great evil, true love never, ever fails.

S. G. Rose

Contents

Description

Disclaimer

Dedication

Introduction

Table of Contents

Atasya

Part One

☾

Slovenia

Mid to Late 1800s

(

Chapter One
~ Mirno ~

"Things have a way of their own, proclaimed the Gypsy...
it's simply a matter of waking up their souls."
Gabriel Garcia Marquez

I was born at the lake's edge and here, with a carpet of daisies at my feet, I shall live out my days. The waters are sweet and I have blessed them with floating lilies, darting minnows, playful frogs and sparkling dragonflies. When travelers come, I whisper a welcome and offer the shade of my arms. Their thirst is safely quenched, for the streams that feed the lake have been purified by passage through ancient stone caverns nearby.

Summer days find me leaning out over my shimmering liquid mirror gazing at my reflection, while soft breezes tease and tangle my hair across the water's surface. I linger there from dawn 'til the first star winks in the sapphire sky, and after my children have all gone to sleep and the moon floats upward through the canopy of stars, I bathe in its silvery light. Only then do I surrender to waves of melancholy and weep at the memory of his touch in the sun.

While many visitors have praised my virtues and partaken of my grace, his was the one soul I knew at first sight, as he did mine. Love came easy, each of us being exactly what the other needed. He came to me often at first, sharing his adventures and dreams while I listened and gave him rest. Thus restored, he would gain strength for each new quest, and when the day came that he wrote his name on my heart, I was secretly pleased, for I wanted to be his alone.

His way was to come and go, so this he did, trusting in my favor and confident that the shade of my boughs would be waiting whenever the roads brought him back – for it was always so. I could not follow him, of course, for limits have been placed upon my powers and I must care for those I've given life. Before he arrived, I hadn't known anything was missing, but once I knew his love, I found myself growing restless without him. I would search the horizon from dawn 'til dusk, and only his return filled the emptiness. Other voices and places called him, and as often as he came to me, he always left again, with never a promise of when he might return.

I've lived at the lake so long now that my toes have taken root and inched their way down the little hill and out into the shallows where the polliwogs tickle them in the spring. My longing for him does not ebb, but others are dependent upon me and I cannot allow myself to shrivel or die in sorrow, so I hold my feelings inside. I have learned to be content with where I am planted and am grateful for all that flows to me, for I have seen that of everything I've birthed, love is the only thing that does not die.

My eyes are growing dim but I will forever look to the hills with hope. His memory is grafted into my heart, and hidden there, he is a part of me forever.

Winter is on its way and frost clings to my boughs. Soon my kingdom will slumber and I shall bow to the bitter wind. Not all of us will survive the storms, and because you ask what I have seen in all my years, I shall tell you while I can.

*W*ithin my view lies the small Slovenian village of Mirno. In the beginning of things, people drew together for their collective safety and survival. Then, some chose to settle down and build a community. Mirno is such a place. The name means *'peaceful,'* and not only does it signal to outsiders that they can hope for refuge, but it's a constant reminder to the citizenry of what they themselves ought to be.

I shall always see Mirno as it was back then – home to hardworking folks who took pride in their trades, were sustained by the work of their hands, and who raised their offspring to be the same. Their bodies were hardened from work, but their hearts were soft.

Those who sought to live among them were generally welcomed and aided in friendly fashion with the expectation that they would earn their keep. There wasn't enough to go around if they didn't, and the less industrious would find themselves back on the road in search of a more prosperous settlement where less effort was required to survive. When no kinder place was found, the prodigals would return, ragged, repentant, and anxious to work harder should grace be extended to them again. There was always a need for more hands, so after receiving a stern lecture on fortitude and faithfulness, they'd be given a hot meal and a second chance.

It would be a grave understatement to call Mirno and the surrounding countryside 'picturesque.' Of all regions in the land, it has always been the most blessed. Mild weather and rich soils yield bountiful crops, both domestic and wild, and even those with no land of their own can still forage for herbs, roots, berries, and mushrooms to take to market, while their children sell wildflower bouquets garnered fresh from the meadows.

Back when Mirno's story begins, the hills and dales were sprinkled with thatched-roof cottages posing on squares of vivid green. Humble homesteads where laundry flapped in the breeze and cats lapped up spills at milking time; where chickens pecked in kitchens and yards, and ducks patrolled ponds with their downy, wobbly hatchlings parading behind.

Like coarse stitches on a rumpled patchwork quilt, low fieldstone walls meandered through lush pastures where sheep, horses and cows grazed together compatibly with no apparent desire for escape. It was strong backs and calloused hands that piled the stones and built the houses and barns. There were fields to plow, livestock to be tended, wood to be chopped, water to be pumped, gardens to plant, crops to harvest and preserve. Work took priority. Everyone from young to old had a job to do, and complaints were seldom heard. That was before electricity and other modern distractions, of course.

You can still reach the remaining farms by narrow dirt roads that wind through the landscape and alongside rivers which often disappear and re-emerge elsewhere – sometimes within caves or in the canyons of the Wildwoods, where deep gorges and treacherous channels churn the gentle flow into raging rapids. The rush of sudden power makes the waters forget their humble beginnings. They grow cold and their proud roar echoes through the imposing stone walls. Given time, an unchallenged force can carve whatever path it wills. No wonder, then (and it always happens the same way) that when they reach the edge of the world, it is their own momentum that sends them over the edge, and there, the ruthless, reckless torrent is dispassionately disassembled in mid-air by an invisible, almighty hand that casts each helpless droplet to its inevitable downward plunge. If not lost to the wind or rocks, it will join the quiet pool below, where rainbows arch in the mist and perpetual thunder bears witness to the fall.

 *B*eyond Mirno, deep forests provide wood for building, cooking, and warmth. My powers end there. The Wildwoods, as they have been called for as long as anyone can remember, are home to primeval magic of both kinds, and some in-between. It was understood by the early inhabitants of this place that no more was to be taken than what was offered. They respected this law, gathered broken branches, and laid their axes only to that which had already fallen upon the mossy floor where the ferns and toadstools grow.

 Should you ever enter the Wildwoods, you must speak only in whispers, for even the birds and insects are hushed there. Though the paths are lovely, they should be traversed quickly with frequent backward glances, for eyes are always watching. Bears and wolves make their dens there, and other creatures no one likes to think about that haunt and hunt, lurk and stalk, and move so soundlessly that their presence cannot be discerned. There's no telling what might be crouching behind that old stump on the trail just ahead – the one with the huckleberry bush growing from its jagged rotting core, loaded with plump red berries begging to be picked.

 In the past, folks usually traveled through by horseback or in wagons or carriages. The Wildwoods do not invite humans to linger, and never after nightfall. Even so, some have. Hunters, lovers, foragers. Had they been wiser and fulfilled their missions quickly with less fanfare, or had they simply continued steadily on to their destinations without stopping at all, they may have been allowed to live.

 To reinforce their warnings, parents used to tell the same gory stories to their children as they themselves had been told. Having your precious son or daughter disappear and never knowing whether they had been eaten by wild beasts or spirited away by phantoms was a curse no mother or father could bear.

 In my observation, there is no such thing as a totally compliant child, whatever its caretakers might believe, and nearly all the youthful inquisitors always find ways to steal off to the forbidden woodlands anyway. There, they gather and dare one another to enter. Participation in the game depends upon individual temperaments and how badly a youngster has been affected by the warnings. The fearful remain on the sidelines to keep an eye out for beasts, ghouls, and winged monsters, while the brashest stride in.

The challenge invariably ends at the sound of a branch breaking deeper in the forest, but the rush of adrenalin seems to give the young participants a sense of power and encourages bravery tempered by caution along with the belief that when they are older, they will be able to traverse the paths fearlessly. It has worked for some, but I am sad to say that I have seen the Wildwoods prove others fatally wrong.

*I*n the old days, the furthest of the farms was over a half-day's journey from town at a brisk pace on foot, and considerably less by horse and wagon, should a landowner be prosperous enough to own them. Most made the trip in once a week to buy and sell.

Mirno's main gateway deposits travelers in the town's courtyard – the heart of all activity. Standing guard on the opposite side is a formidable Gothic church with chiseled steps, arched stained glass windows and tall doorways. The bell tower is studded by a Roman clock, and above it, pointing steadfastly toward the institution's authority to rule, rises an elaborate Italian cross. At the time of my tale, it was the duty of one aging servant of the parish to polish both it and the bell, and to pull the heavy cord at appointed times. The sound is still heard for miles around and is a comfort to the villagers and farmers alike. It signals that all is well and all is the same, thanks be to God and the church. For them to hear it at any other time means the opposite. The prominence of the cathedral declares Mirno to be a God-fearing place, lest anyone have any other notions.

Stone buildings of less ornate architectural styles encircle the plaza and hold gathering places and businesses. Flowers spill from boxes below leaded windowpanes and carved placards hang from forged iron brackets above doors. Alehouse and Inn, Bakery, Candle-Maker, Potter, Woodworker, Dressmaker-Tailor, and Shoemaker. The less genteel trades lie on the outskirts. Narrow cobblestone alleyways extend like crooked spokes from the courtyard hub. Some are lined with the tall homes of well-to-do citizens, and others lead to less ornate buildings that share walls and house businesses whose proprietors reside in the back rooms or upper floors. Signs advertise services now, but in times past, Mirno's populace all knew who lived where, and they called upon the physicians, midwives, barbers, and such when needed.

Everyone went to market, where fresh game, vegetables, fruits, baked goods and handcrafts of all kinds were sold in the square. It was a gathering place where they could drink, eat and enjoy local entertainment, and it got even better when the Gypsies came to town.

𝓜irno reveres the past, and if you were to ask its inhabitants, both then and now, they would answer that life there is as good as it needs to be. Of course, none of them have a memory as long as mine, and I can tell you without a shadow of a doubt that if fortune had not favored the brave, this story would be quite different.

As I suppose is the case in any quaint, historic village, there are things not mentioned on the present day tour. And if you are the sort who gets gut feelings when something is being deliberately omitted, then you have probably already guessed that there is more to Mirno's past than the charming guide in his period costume is telling you.

𝓑ut I have said enough for now. Dusk is upon the lake and solace calls me. Should you wish to know more truth of the past, ask the old-timer who sits at the end of the tavern bar. If his mug is empty, he can be bribed. Keep your voice low. If he agrees to your company, he will lead you to a table in the corner where, after the barmaid has brought the ale, he will solemnly cross himself as though his words could hold the power to unleash the same horrors again. His account always begins the same, and the rest you must judge for yourself.

"It was a moonlit night so lovely as never to have invited such an unholy thing. While everyone slept, an ancient evil crept into town. Only one soul caught the uneasy shift in the wind and sensed what the others did not, and that person's end was…well…too awful to tell."

Further on, the details will be too disturbing for him to divulge without more ale and a beef pie. His claim that Mirno has taken nearly a century to recover from the assault is true. He was just a boy when he was told the story by an old woman who lived it firsthand.

Poor fellow. Nobody believes him and they all think he's crazy.

☾

Chapter Two
~ The Vrag ~

*"Be sober, be vigilant; for your adversary the devil, as a roaring lion,
walketh about, seeking whom he may devour."*
Yeshua

The Vrag was not in a hurry. He preferred to maintain a low profile until he had gained a full understanding of what lay before him. He was assured that the cacophony of everyday life would distract from his presence, and by the time the prey grew suspicious it would be too late. In the old demon's defense, he was playing by the rules. These creatures had been warned for generations – had in fact weaned their offspring on the stories – but their grave weakness was complacency. A false sense of security had displaced the reverence and vigilance of their forefathers and they had become lazy.

Human nature was pathetically predictable. The Vrag could already hear their desperate pleas as they claimed ignorance to the end. Their memories were conveniently short, and over long periods of time when physical proof was lacking, even great truths invariably disintegrated into fables to be acted out on holidays by children in home-sewn costumes for the amusement of doting parents. The bending of their wills and minds could easily be achieved by applying slow, unrelenting pressure. An inch, a decade, a generation at a time, and he would have them rationalizing away even their most basic instincts. The ones that told them when something was wrong.

Patience had its rewards, and much was at stake in this game of the ages. The Vrag liked to think he was the better strategist, and one move ahead of his adversary, whose methods differed drastically. YaH also desired that the beings should do His will, which He asserted was for their own well-being, but He called upon their hidden virtues and promised them redemption, while the demon preferred using them against themselves. This tactic relied upon them never suspecting that they were its pawns, of course. They had to be convinced that they

YaH *(YAH as in 'saw')* – God, The Creator, O Del
Vrag *(vrAG)* – a chief demon

9

were the masters of their own fates right up to the point where the jaws of his trap sprang shut. YaH would have to help them then. His aid depended upon relationship (the mere thought sickened the demon), and if they did not want that, their Maker would not intrude.

YaH called them 'offspring,' and favored them above all his creations. To Him, they were little lambs to be protected. To the Vrag, and others like him, they were sheep for the slaughter – prey to be hunted, outwitted, captured, corralled, and controlled by any means necessary. He particularly enjoyed disguising himself as one of YaH's enlightened leaders. They flocked to him then.

Though the stage had been set by those before him, the Vrag owed them no debt of gratitude. The unholy hierarchy to which they all belonged was bereft of such platitudes. Threats of what they would suffer if they failed Beng, and the promise of promotion if they succeeded, were what fueled them. Their tireless assaults were paying off and these unsuspecting simpletons now held to the notion that the events and warnings chronicled by their ancestors were myths born of fantasy, not fact. Most of them did not even know how to fight back.

The Vrag hungered for the terrors to come, and in the meantime, he was bored. There was no real challenge here. No worthy opponent that he could see. No new strategies to be devised. It was all ridiculously easy. Stir the pot and slowly turn up the heat. Whisper accusations and shatter trust. Awaken and seduce the darkness within the weak. Gouge a furrow, sow seeds of lust, envy, strife, and division, then feast on the harvest. Choke forgiveness and crush hope. Twist, destroy, confuse, deceive, and manipulate until they were desperate enough to relinquish what it wanted for the return of their so-called peace and sanity. The odds guaranteed that a fair number of them would do his bidding. He just needed to watch and wait for them to come to the surface. The whole lot was pathetic and they were in his way.

So, the assault began. No single incident overtly suspicious at first, but taken as a whole, a disquieting distortion of the usual legato rhythm of life in the Slovenian village.

Crop failures, strange accidents, illnesses, and un-timely deaths. Betrayal, abandonment. The calamities befell almost every household and before long, Mirno's inhabitants were right where he wanted them.

Beng *(bENG)* – the devil

10

Superstition overrode reason and false accusations spread like the plague. Thus cultivated, a nameless, faceless fear took root. Someone or something had to be blamed so that a face could be put on it, and many fingers pointed toward the band of Gypsies who had arrived in the area at the same time the trouble began. While most of the townsfolk coexisted amicably with them, the travelers were invariably the first to be blamed for any unusual or unnerving occurrences wherever they roamed.

To make things worse, winter had arrived, bringing its own customary hardships. The last of the autumn crops had been harvested and stored away in larders and root cellars, and scavengers pecked at what lay rotting in the gardens and fields. Each day was colder and shorter than the one before and by supper it was dark.

Some time had passed since the Vrag had settled in and his intentions had begun to bear their poisonous fruit. Deprived of peace and rest, his terrified victims were in hiding. Evening chores were hurried, animals stabled, shutters locked and doors barred earlier than usual.

As the bone-chilling fog crept across the pastures from the sea and oozed through Mirno's slick, cobblestone alleyways, her inhabitants huddled in their homes, hunched over thin soup and thick brown bread, praying for deliverance from what they could not see or comprehend. During the day they looked to the church for answers but were usually assigned more penance and sent away with a stern reminder to pay their tithes. After dark, only the fools ventured out to numb their worried minds in the tavern, and their number was dwindling.

And so, it was quite disturbing that on one such night, when fear had imposed its curfew and emptied the streets, a small figure, its face and form obscured by a ragged scarf and oversized cloak, was seen darting from shadow to shadow, ducking into doorways and looking furtively over its shoulder before scurrying on.

The frightened little thing was clutching something to its chest and running for its life.

☾

Chapter Three
~ The Ghel from Nowhere ~

"Come, come, whoever you are, wanderer, worshiper, lover of leaving.
It doesn't matter. Ours is not a caravan of despair."
Rumi

$\mathcal{W}$e seldom camp in one place for long. Hundreds of years of slavery, persecution and oppression keep us on the move. Whether we suffer, endure, or escape torment makes little difference, for we are bound by blood to those before us who did, and to be Roma is to be nothing else.

There is no understanding of us in this world, so we make our way through it by staying on the fringes, offering our trades, services and entertainment while otherwise keeping to ourselves. After we pass a few months in any given location, the decision must be made whether to stay or move on, and while several practical factors carry weight, the tolerance of nearby villagers invariably tips the scales.

Our caravan travels within the rain shadow of the Carpathian Mountains. We've been camped near the village of Mirno for almost half a year and are debating whether to stay over the winter. The hunting, fishing, and gathering are good, the weather is tolerable, and there is money to be made in the marketplace selling our wares and entertaining the townsfolk with stories, music, and dance.

Our songs and folklore are a living history. Colorful tapestries woven of fact and fantasy – 'darane svatura and paramicha' – fairytales and fables of magic and the supernatural, shaded by the teller's mood and intentions, and never spun the same way twice.

Wherever we go, *'The Story of Renata'* is the most requested ballad. It is told with music, and only those who lived it know how much is true.

ghel *(ghel, like 'bell')* – girl
darane svatura *(da-RAIN, sva-TOOR-uh* – fairytales and fables of magic and the supernatural
paramicha *(para-MEE-cha)* – fables
Roma *(Roe-MAW)* – Gypsy, Romany, Romani

13

The Story of Renata

One summer, when we were three days by wagon from Budapest, a young woman wandered into our camp.

"Kasko san?" we asked. She was Roma, and understood our language, but had no memory of whose she was, where she'd come from or why she was alone. Either it was the truth or she did not wish to answer and was simply good at keeping secrets. She was in rags and starving, so we took her in, cared for her and she remained with our caravan.

The stranger was prone to straying away from camp and would sometimes return with little treasures which she treated as sacred. She collected these things as reminders of what she's been shown while she was gone.

After a time, when her memories did not return, a name was chosen for her: Renata.

"It means 'reborn.' You are a part of our family, now."

But she wasn't, really. She was different, and we did not know what to do with her. Strange forces called her and she would willingly follow, oblivious to the potential dangers outside the camp. Given the simple task of gathering firewood, she would pick wildflowers instead, or nap beneath a tree, and more than once she was found dancing under the moon while singing in an unfamiliar language.

Fearing that she would meet with harm, the older women asked one of the boys by the name of Tamás, to watch over her. Though he feigned annoyance, he was secretly happy to legitimately do so.

Renata was oblivious to the aura that surrounded her. Her lithe, small-boned body, long raven hair and green eyes gave away her origins, whatever they were. The males of the tribe were drawn to her like bees to nectar, which made the older women protective and the younger ones jealous.

Even before he was assigned the duty, young Tamás had already been spying on the mysterious ghel. He was confused by the feelings that had been awakened within him, so he kept them to himself and played the boyish role. That was before the afternoon at the lake.

Kasko san *(casko-SAHN)* – Whose are you?

Tamás was shadowing Renata from a safe distance that day, when a hare hopped across the path and into a thicket.

Thinking his mother would make a fine stew of it, he dove into the bushes in pursuit. After a regrettable chase, he emerged scratched and empty-handed. Worse yet, he'd lost sight of Renata. Knowing she favored the lake, he ran in that direction, only to be devastated by what he found.

She was not sitting in her usual spot beneath the willow and Tamás hurried to the mound from which the tree grew to better survey the area. There he saw her, floating out beyond the reeds, still as death.

His heart stopped. The fault was his! They'd told him to keep her safe, and if he had not foolishly chased that rabbit, he would have been there to save her! He squeezed his eyes shut and commanded it to be a dream, but when he opened them again, nothing had changed.

He was steeling himself to retrieve her when he saw the tiny ripples around her hands and feet. Overjoyed, he opened his mouth to call out, but something hushed him, so he watched from behind the willow. As if summoned, dragonflies rose from the lily pads, flew to the young woman, and landed softly on her body. Her laughter created a wave of magic that reached the shore, where it washed over Tamás, and made him question, once again, if he was playing a part in a dream.

Whether he was asleep or awake he realized that what he felt for her was love, but that he could never tell her so.

Believing the tree had hidden him from view, he left and did not speak to her about what he had seen that day.

Renata, of course, had known he was there all along, for she felt his soul the moment he arrived.

Days later in camp, the secret longings, jealousies, worries and gentle scoldings continued until it was discovered that Renata was with child, which changed everything.

As usual, questioning her was pointless, but it was believed that our tribe had been called upon to save two lives not only one.

As the months passed and her baby started to wiggle inside, Renata finally felt safe within our familia and told us some of the things she was shown away from the camp. We knew, then, that she had *'The Dook'* – which means *'The Sight'* – and we thanked God for sending her.

*A*nd that is the end of the story as its most often told.

*"B*ut what things did she tell you?"* There's always someone in the audience who demands to know more before they will toss a coin into the tambourine. We are prepared.

"Well, here is something that you shall never forget," the storyteller will say. *"Renata lived in the Now. We gypsies have a word for yesterday and tomorrow: atasya. It the same word because they are both beyond our control. A person has far less sorrow this way. Do you see? It is simple wisdom, but life is better for it."*

*W*hile most Gypsy tales are imagined, or at least heavily embellished for entertainment purposes, Renata's story needed no exaggeration. It was indeed quite true and held more than enough magic and mystery of its own. The only change made (and this, out of love for Tamás) was to the ending, for in the real-life version, not long after the mysterious young woman found them and became a part of their lives, she was gone, leaving her treasures and her story behind.

Atasya *(ah-TOSS-yuh)* – Yesterday, Tomorrow

☾

Chapter Four
~ In Renata's Words ~

*"Be not forgetful to entertain strangers:
for thereby some have entertained angels unawares."*

Hebrews 13:2

I do not know whose I am or where I belong. I cannot remember my family, those I cared for, or those who cared for me, if there were any. If evil befell me and mine, it is best that I have forgotten.

Everything was taken. Everything but Balval, the Spirit of the Wind, who is above all and in all, and cannot be stolen, violated, or killed. He has filled the void and become father, mother, and husband – loving me, teaching me, sustaining me. He led me to these who have sheltered me. My life is His from this moment to my last and I shall belong to no other. I do not expect these new brothers and sisters to understand. It is enough that they are kind.

Balval calls me. He yearns for me and I for Him, like a river for the sea. I open my mouth and His words fill it, strong and sweet, like honey dripping from the comb. They are the food of my soul, my strength, and my joy.

The others want me to remember. They fear I cannot be like them until I awaken from the dreams. But why would I choose such a thing when He meets me there? Let them call me dinilo. It matters not. If I am crazy, let me die this way, adrift in a dream of love that knows no end.

Tamás understands me as I am or tries valiantly at least. He is a dear boy, and quite different from the other males of this tribe. I feel tenderly toward him as I would a younger brother, though he wishes I would see him as a man. Those matters aside, there is freedom in our time together and I can safely be myself with him. I am not as unaware as they think and knew from the start that his mother had sent him to keep an eye on me. Her intentions are good and his earnest,

Balval *(Ball-VAL)* – the invisible Spirit of God, the Wind
dinilo (din-EEL-oh) – crazy

awkward devotion is genuine and endearing. I need a friend to care about me and to remind me that beasts roam the forest, and that it isn't safe to wander there after dark. I have seen the eyes.

Tamás knows I collect treasures, though I have not yet told him of their significance. On the night of a full moon, as we sat by the river and watched it rise huge and orange like a pumpkin in the charcoal sky, he gave me a box to keep them in. I was deeply moved. When I admired the designs etched into the top and the finely tooled clasp, he said that he had asked his uncle, a silversmith, for instruction, and that he intends to be a fine metalworker himself one day. And a musician, of course.

The box might as well have held his precious, beating heart. Had it, he'd have been spared it breaking the following day when Tsura publicly announced that I had a baby growing inside. Romani law demands chastity and Romani boys only marry virgin Romani girls.

With our relationship clearly defined, and the flames of his romantic imaginings extinguished, Tamás and I have relaxed and grown closer. He is a gentle soul, wise for his age, and often grasps things of the Spirit more readily than I expect him to.

As this new life grows within me, I feel a swelling desire to share more, as though the life of the Spirit is growing in rhythm with the child, waiting and wanting to emerge – seeking to know and to be known. Most surprising is that some within my new familia have declared me to be gifted. Balval has said that the gifts are for everyone, and I have told them this repeatedly, but they just shake their heads. Maybe some consider it, but I have learned that *'yes'* can mean *'no'* and *'no'* can mean *'yes'* with these Roma, and I cannot always read their hearts.

Tamás mother and the others try hard. They want to paint a new life for me – one of love and triumph over impossible odds. They have even given me a small vardo which shall be mine and my child's.

The story to be told is that I once had a husband, and we met with violence in our travels. He, my brave Rom, gave his life that I might escape. The offspring of such a man would surely inherit his strength and courage. Best that it be a boy, then. There are moons still to go, and they have already started suggesting names like Guaril and Lash, reminding me that they mean *victor* and *warrior,* in case I've forgotten.

$\mathcal{M}$y child is a girl and I already know her name.

☾

Chapter Five

~ Renata in the Wildwoods ~

Werifesteria: *To wander longingly through the forest in search of mystery.*

More secrets are hidden in the Wildwoods than anyone knows. Those who left them there are long gone now, but if you listen with your heart, you might still catch the echoes of their passage.

For the rare souls allowed in, the only way to travel is by feel, and the forest does not make that easy. Its stoic, ancient appearance belies the fact that it is in a constant state of transformation where death and decay give way to new life, birthed only to be consumed by other hungry life, and so it goes.

This never-ending medley sustains untold numbers of creatures, almost all unseen, from the infinitesimal to the fearsome, whose existence, however brief or seemingly insignificant, is essential to the survival of the whole. In this soft green womb, the air is moist, thick, and heavy with the pungent, primal smells of earth and animal, and the deeper in you venture the more of your other self gets left behind.

The fear of being swallowed keeps many out, but no matter what they say to dissuade me, I belong in that place, traversing fallen trees over lush gullies and dreaming on spongy moss in patches of filtered sunlight while the One who created it all tells me secrets.

How I hear His voice I cannot say, nor can I describe it. I only know that it comes from a hidden place beyond and yet within. It is unmistakable – a song – each note infused with the musician's emotion, and every word a precious truth. He is a God of many colors and moods.

Once, in early spring, when a shaft of sunlight set dewdrops afire in a cluster of Trillium chalices, He said, *"People seek diamonds and pearls. Look, my child, here are your diamonds and pearls!"* And in the summer, as I picked shimmering red huckleberries, He whispered, *"Rubies!"* Gold coins shower down from birch trees in

19

autumn and necklaces of silver rim the brook in winter. The riches are abundant and free. I do not have to go in search of them, labor for them or pay for them. I have only to open my eyes and heart to receive them. These wonders do not last beyond the moments in which they are given, which makes the treasures of the Wildwoods even more sacred.

Perhaps I proved myself worthy of more, but I doubt that, for it seems to me that the Creator's rewards have less to do with worthiness than with openness and willingness, which is how I was led to the ruins.

𝒥'd gone in a different direction that day, away from the stream which I usually kept within my sight or my hearing. There was no discernable path into the forest this way, only little rabbit trails that stopped as abruptly as they appeared. It was a denser, darker stand, with evergreens, beech, alder, and vine maples crowded together, each fighting for its spot, every neck straining upward to drink the light. The ground was dry and hard, and a tenacious shrub with dark green, waxen leaves and white berries dominated the undergrowth. Its vermillion roots wormed their way in and out of the soil like tentacles, threatening to trip me with every step. The first tumble left me with scraped knees and palms, and I kept my eyes on the ground after that. I stopped often to listen, but the place was shrouded in silence, and I remember wondering more than once whether the adventure had been ill chosen. I leaned heavily upon a strong inborn sense of direction, but it was being challenged there.

One can only gauge the passing of time by hunger or thirst when in the Wildwoods, and as I was feeling both, I sat down on a broad, fallen log to rest and eat my lunch of bread, hard cheese, and an apple. Had I been elsewhere in a more familiar part of the forest, my meal would have included a handful of sweet, warm berries and a drink of cold water from the stream.

The day was half gone, and I had no sense of where I was, so I asked, *"Balval, where shall I go now? Why did You bring me here?"* If there was no answer soon, I'd turn back and hope to re-trace my steps.

Suddenly, the flapping of wings filled the air and I looked up to see several enormous ravens landing in the lower branches of the nearest cedar tree. They were eyeing the food I'd laid out on my scarf.

"You'll have to go find your own lunch," I said with a laugh. They countered with a chorus of raucous cawing and flew closer. I don't view black birds as a bad omen. In fact, Roma belief was quite the opposite. But I had the sense that these larger cousins had not come in answer to my request for guidance or as a portent of good fortune. They wanted my food and intended to take it.

One by one they dropped from the sky and landed brazenly on the end of the log, their sleek heads cocked, eyes like polished black stones, darting, sizing me up, strategizing, calculating the strike. A couple I might have reasoned with and shared a morsel, but they kept coming, filling the trees above.

"Sssssst!" I waved my hand, *"Go away!"*

They defied me and another glided down.

I hastily bundled up the remainder of my lunch and tucked it in the pocket of my skirt. Then I shook my scarf and the remaining crumbs in their direction. This caused a momentary flurry of feathers and the largest bird dove on the scraps before the others could reach them. With one swift thrust of its shiny beak, it speared a bit of crust from a clump of lichen, gulped it down, and looked demandingly at me for more.

Emboldened by their leader and spurred on by the noise of the gang above, the ones on the log began making menacing clicking sounds and moving slowly toward me. Leathery talons arched, they picked and hopped their way along the rotting bark, each awkward, jerky step bringing them closer. All eyes were on my skirt where they had seen me hide the food. More landed, and within seconds I was surrounded. Though my inclination was to jump up and run, I knew better. Instead, I covered my head with my scarf, wrapped my arms around my knees and buried my face.

The first stab was to my thigh, and the next to my forearm. The squawking from above turned frantic and the furious beating of wings churned the air around me. Feathers and claws brushed over my body and I squeezed my eyes tight and braced for the vicious assault.

Strangely, it did not come. Instead, the ravens' cries abruptly stopped and they all took to the sky. After a long moment of silence, I lifted my head and found myself looking at the reason why.

Not more than three paces away sat an enormous wolf, white as snow with unblinking crystal-blue eyes that gazed into mine.

I was too awe-struck to feel afraid, and when I finally found my voice, it sounded very small.

"Thank you."

His left ear twitched.

"They wanted my food." I slowly reached into my skirt pocket and found a bit of cheese. As I pulled it out, the beast licked his chops, and I prayed silently to Balval that I was not inadvertently whetting its appetite for flesh. I tossed it in the wolf's direction. He gave it an obligatory sniff, sat down, and continued to stare at me.

The atmosphere had begun to feel strange, and a silence even deeper than the Wildwoods fell. The wolf made a small noise in his throat, tipped his head back, opened his mouth and howled three times. Each primal cry was longer and more powerful than the one before it and they made my heart tremble. After the third howl, his eyes returned to my face as if he was awaiting my response.

I'd heard stories of solitary wolves with mystical powers but had never encountered one other than a sighting on a faraway ridge once in the moonlight. I should have been afraid, but this one had given me no reason for that. I was not sure what my next move should be, so I tentatively began a conversation.

"You're very beautiful."

He tilted his head.

I continued, *"I can see this is your forest. I felt I was led here today, but now I fear I have intruded. Forgive me."*

I lowered my legs slowly to the ground, slid off the log, and prepared to leave, prompting the wolf to stand up as well. He was majestic, and the most feared predator in all the lands my people traveled.

A lone raven scout circled high above the treetops and squawked a continual warning to all creatures within earshot. The wolf shook his powerful body, and the warm, wild scent reached my nostrils.

I longed for the enmity between humankind and wild animals to be undone. I knew the connection I felt came from a deeper place – a memory of how it had been in the beginning before evil had twisted the divine order, but it would be foolish to assume that the wolf understood any of that. The ability to communicate with O Del's creatures had been lost long ago. They were hunted now, and whatever I said, this one had no reason to trust me. I was at its mercy, so I followed my heart's inclination to kneel and open my arms.

As though he'd been waiting for the invitation, the wolf came to me and laid his head upon my lap. After I scratched behind his ears and picked a few remnants of the forest from his coat, the bond was forged. He rose to his feet, ran a short distance away, then turned and looked back. I knew he wanted me to follow him, so I did.

O Del *(oh-DEL)* – God, The Creator, YaH

☾
Chapter Six
~ The Ruins ~

"The angel looked down at me and I heard the words,
'Be wary as a serpent, my daughter, and gentle as a dove.'"

The wolf led me deeper into the Wildwoods than I would ever have ventured on my own, always outpacing me and occasionally disappearing. The first few times it happened, I became anxious and wondered whether I might be following a ghost. If so, having come this far so fast, I would be utterly lost. But when I called out *'Volk!'* (the Gypsy word for his kind) he would always come back, nuzzle my hand reassuringly and then run off again while I did my best to keep up.

At a point, the pathway widened and large, flat rocks appeared beneath the dirt and roots. An embankment with stone steps etched in its side rose on my left. They were overgrown with ivy and moss, and it was evident that the place had been deserted for a long time.

Though my guide was not in sight, I knew to climb the stairway. Halfway up, I was overwhelmed by the sensation that I had done so many times before, and I became so dizzy that I had to sit down.

Such surreal occurrences are not foreign to me. I have pondered their meaning many times but until I figure it out, I must consign them to the same category as my dreams, which often unveil secrets and foretell events.

I've learned the hard way that such things are best kept to myself. People are often unnerved by my stories and continue to look at me strangely even after I have changed the subject. Then, the rumors begin.

Once the disoriented feeling eased a bit, I ventured up the remaining steps where I found the wolf waiting at our destination.

Before me stood two stone pillars and an iron gate. Inside, the statue of an angel presided over a small courtyard and behind it were the crumbling remains of a building. The gate hinges were corroded with rust and I was barely able to open it wide enough to slip through.

The wolf had gone around and was lying in front of the statue, panting contentedly. Though covered by a layer of dirt and moss, the winged statue was strikingly beautiful and lifelike. I wondered who had inspired it. The figure was dressed in a flowing robe and her wavy, waist-length hair framed delicate features. Her arms were outstretched over an altar, palms open in blessing. In her left hand was a dove, and in the right, a small snake, both carved in exquisite detail. Her expression was one of such compassion that I felt moved to bow my head.

Why had I been led here? So that I could tell the others of this place?

"*No.*" The voice was firm.

Why then?

While I pondered the question, I began absent-mindedly brushing the dead leaves, sticks, pine needles and cones from the altar. Had I not been distracted by my thoughts, I would have spotted the dagger in time to avoid injury, but it was hidden beneath the debris, and when I swept some stems away, the blade met my hand.

Roma craftsmen are renowned knife makers, but this one, with its intricately carved handle of bone, was unlike anything I'd ever seen. When I picked it up, it fit in my palm as though it had been made for me, and I was so entranced by its beauty that I did not notice that I was bleeding until I saw the crimson drops upon the altar.

What had this place been? I hoped to find an answer within the ruins – something to tell the tale – so I began exploring the rubble, climbing over rotting timbers, reaching into nooks and crannies, and moving stones to peer beneath them. The wolf's interest matched my own and at one point his keen sense of smell led me to vines bearing tiny, ripe blackberries, which I hungrily plucked and ate, while marveling at how he could possibly have known they were one of my favorite things.

The feeling I experienced on the stairs had not completely passed. It was as though the place had been waiting for my return. Suddenly, I was overtaken by a great weariness, and decided to lie down on the grass at the edge of the ruins. There, I fell instantly into a deep sleep. The last thing I saw before the dreams began was the wolf's eyes as he stood guard beside me.

*J*n the first dream, the forest was young and I was on the lane with Volk. He'd come to me when I was orphaned as a child and had been my companion and protector ever since. We'd been foraging most of the day and were on our way home.

Flowering thyme spilled over the edges of the staircase and cascaded down the hillside in fragrant purple rivulets. Wild roses climbed the pillars on either side of the gate, and just inside, the statue of my mother greeted me. From there, a path led through the garden to the front door of the stone cottage my parents had built.

"For you, my Dai." I said, as I added a spray of wild honeysuckle to the older offerings upon the altar.

I walked to the cottage, went inside, and placed my basket on the table. I'd lived here all my life and every inch was filled with articles made by my parents' hands and my own.

I had a distinct memory of my father proudly proclaiming, *"We're a family of artists, Miri."* The words were attached to a misty image of little me, happily bouncing along in a large wooden cart, snuggly tucked in between hand-woven rugs, pottery, and a quilt made of scraps I'd helped my mother trim. We were on our way to market, and I'd been promised sweets if we did well.

The next winter, my Dai got sick and then she wasn't there anymore. After that, Dati was always sad. He made the angel statue and a beautiful dagger for me and that's where my memories of him end.

I'm grown now.

It's late in the afternoon and Volk and I have been gone since morning, so I decide to take a short nap and start dinner when I wake up. I hang my cloak on the hook by the door and lay down on my mattress. After pulling up a blanket, I pat the place next to me, which is Volk's cue to settle in, and together, we drift off.

Before very long I hear hushed voices outside. People seldom visit and I prefer it that way. I try to sit up but am unable to move my body. Am I dreaming? I've heard of such spells and am terrified. By straining hard, I can make out part of the conversation through the window above my head.

Dai *(D-eye)* – Mother
Dati *(DAH-tee)* – Father

27

"We'd better not let that other one over there see what we're up to. It has wings. I hate the ones with wings."

The response was caustic. *"Moron! That's only a statue!"*

"We can't be too safe. I've heard of such things holding power. I swear her eyes followed me when we walked past!"

"Well, we'll destroy it too, then, after we've killed the thing in the house. Will that make you happy?"

"Maybe we should wait on the killing until we get what we came for. If we don't return with it, we'll be the ones who'll die, and it won't be swift."

I had to awaken Volk! I summoned every ounce of my will to form his name, but no sound came out. I fought, and the spell slowly weakened, but when I was finally able to stand up, I saw my body still asleep on the bed! I had no time to dwell on the impossibility of the scene and made my way soundlessly across the room to the window nearest the door where my garden hoe was leaning against the wall. I could use it as a weapon.

I peered through a tiny portal in the lace curtains and saw two men in long, hooded robes standing a few paces from my front door. I also become aware of a persistent vibration, like the hum of crickets in a dry field on a hot day. I could not tell whether it was coming from outside or in, but it was the sort of sound that could drive a person mad.

The men turned in my direction but gave no indication that they had seen me. I drew back in shock, for they were not fully human. While the top half of their faces was handsome, the remainder was savage and evil. Rows of thorny teeth jutted from black orifices and below the sleeves of their robes, blistered reptilian claws twitched with impatience to shred their prey. I was as repulsed by the hatred that dripped from their speech as I was by their appearance. The more dominant of the two snarled with every word. The other one was in fear of him.

"She'd better have it inside. We don't dare go back without it."

"It's here someplace. They hide it."

The underling pulled up his mask. *"We should cover up. Show her only our best face. Maybe if we say we're travelers and ask for the kindness of a drink or a meal she'd let us in."*

"Why waste time when we can just kill her?"

"It was only an idea. I have them, you know."

"You're worthless. That's why he puts me in charge. Let's go."

The moment had come and they walked toward my door. I grabbed the hoe but it did not move, and only then did I comprehend that I was not in my physical form. What if they got in the house and killed my body on the bed? How could any of this be happening?

I screamed again from the bottom of my soul, "*VOLK! Pomagaj mi!*" and this time he heard. The door flew open on its own and a blur of white fur and bared teeth streaked past me. He reached the walkway in one bound and tore into the demons, taking them by surprise. Their defense was vicious, but they were no match for the speed and strength of my protector.

I buried my face in my hands. The noise was horrific – like the battle was being fought in Hades itself. And then, it was over.

When I dared to look, it was not Volk standing over the demons' remains, but a man surrounded by a light so bright that I was forced to shield my eyes. Blood as black as tar dripped from the knife in his hand, and he thrust both arms up to the sky, crying out victoriously in a language I did not know. Then, he vanished and the weapon fell from empty air onto the stones at my feet. I was astounded to see that it was the dagger my father had made for me. I picked it up and Volk's howl reached my ears from deep in the forest.

*W*hen I awoke, the cottage was stifling. I threw off the blanket and the sleeping wolf beside me opened a curious eye.

I'd napped far longer than planned. The nightmare was burning in my mind and I was sick to my stomach. I could recall every horrifying detail and was afraid to move from the bed. What if the demons' bodies were lying outside?

When I finally gathered my wits, I rose and walked slowly to the door. It was standing wide open, though I distinctly remembered having closed it behind us when we came in earlier.

Volk roused himself, stretched and came to my side. Pausing briefly at the threshold, he walked outside, sniffed the ground at the place of the battle and bounded off into the forest in search of dinner. The only thing marring the stillness was the strange buzzing sound.

Breathing deeply to clear my head, I walked to the courtyard and found my angel as serene as always, arms reaching, hands open, ready to bless. I told her of the dream and how frightened I'd been, but her expression did not change. I needed her to comfort me or to interpret its meaning but she only listened.

A gentler, wiser, more patient mother had never lived. When my Dati told me she had to leave because her time on Earth was over, I understood a little better, but I still missed her every day. That was why he made the statue in her likeness. So that she could be near us forever.

My Dati was Roma and he could do everything. His fiddle still rested on the mantle and I kept the dagger he'd made for me in a belt at my waist. I could still remember the day a peddler came to the house claiming he had discovered bones deep within a cave high in the mountains and that they held supernatural powers. Dati believed in magic so he traded for a small one and it later became the handle of my knife.

My Dati had been gone for a long time. I couldn't even remember his face anymore. I wished I had a statue of him, too.

Something was still off key. I'd been trying to ignore the strange feeling since I'd awakened, but it was growing stronger, along with the unrelenting hum. The light seemed different too, as though everything was washed in amber shadow. I felt like a stranger in a world that looked like mine but wasn't.

Reasoning that a routine task might help me feel normal, I began removing the older offerings from my mother's altar. As I reached for a bouquet of withered roses, something moved beneath it, and I jerked my hand back just in time to avoid the deadly strike of a viper. Having missed its mark, it spun and slithered up the statue and coiled itself in the palm of her left hand. Immediately, a dove cooed from its perch on the rooftop, flew down and landed softly in her other hand. As I watched, they both turned to stone and I heard the words, *"Be wary as a serpent, my child, and gentle as a dove. Awaken, now."*

When I opened my eyes, the wolf was lying beside me in the grass and the strange buzzing sound had stopped. All was as it had been before I'd fallen asleep. As mysterious as this current reality was, those of my dreams were even more so, and I knew they had been just as real.

((

Chapter Seven
~ The Discovery ~

"You have been chosen.
A calling rests upon your life."

*H*owever disturbing certain aspects of my first experience had been, the desire to return to the ruins was strong, and before the old women of the caravan became worried about my safety, I slipped away to go there as often as I could.

Volk always anticipated my visits and would be waiting for me at the forest's edge. We were easy companions from the start, both young, strong, wild at heart and hungry for an adventure. I would have followed him to the end of the world and should I have needed saving he would have sped to my rescue.

I never thought about how or when those mystical days together would end, but there is a last time for everything, and perhaps it's best that we don't know when that will be. In the meantime, for those with searching eyes and listening ears, the world is full of wonder. We are all playing our parts in a grand production which began long before we set foot here and will continue long after we are gone.

I'd brought food to Volk's liking that day, and he knew I had it. *"For lunch,"* I laughed, as he nuzzled the pocket of my skirt. *"And water,"* I shook the flask hanging from my belt. *"Will you find berries?"* I could have sworn he nodded before we headed into the woods.

With no stopping but to gather a few wildflowers, we reached our destination by late morning. Once there, I placed my bouquet on the altar and walked to the grassy area where the dreams had overtaken me on our first visit. I'd arrived at the conclusion that the place was enchanted, and that souls from the past had come to tell me their stories. My strong inborn curiosity would not allow me to ignore the possibility of residual evidence, so I searched for clues every time I came.

I spread out the bundles of food – smoked sausage, apples, cheese curds and bread. Volk swallowed his share of the meat in seconds, and I immediately regretted not bringing more. I took one small bite of my portion and gave him the rest.

Suddenly, he lost interest in the food, ran to the far edge of the clearing, and looked upward expectantly. I saw nothing at first, but then they emerged from within a cloud – shimmering pillars of light filled with an array of pulsing colors. As they descended, they formed into small orbs, and surrounded Volk. There were far more of them than he could fend off, presuming a wolf could fight them at all, and I watched anxiously, part of me ready to grab a stick and run into their midst, and the other part knowing that if a wolf could not overcome them, I certainly had no chance of doing so.

Volk was alternately leaping up in the air and rolling on the ground while the lights spun and danced around him, and with great relief, I realized that he was not fighting – he was *playing.* When the happy greeting settled down, the spheres reassembled into tall, slender flames and began to move in my direction. Volk ran to me, his thick coat shimmering, and when I put my hand on his head, his fur crackled with energy. He smelled like the air after a thunderstorm.

"Volk! What are they?"

The voices answered as one. *"Have no fear."*

"Who…what are you? What do you want?"

In answer, a vision began to form in my mind and I was shown what had happened in the clearing long ago.

A house was under construction and a cornerstone had been set in place. Night had fallen and by the light of a full moon, a young woman entered the clearing. After a quick look around, she fell to her knees and began to dig alongside the cornerstone. When the hole was deep enough, she placed a bundle in it and pushed the dirt back in place. Then, she bowed her head for a moment, stood up, and disappeared back into the forest.

The vision ended and the voices spoke. *"You have been chosen. A calling rests upon your life."*

I remembered the dreams on my first day in that place.

The lights spoke again. *"While on Earth, we protected that which you are about to find. It can never be allowed to fall into the hands of anyone or anything with impure intent."*

Was that what the demons in my first dream had been after?

The lights grew brighter and taller. *"Guard it with your life. The Chosen are shown the way."*

Then, they shot upward into the clouds and were gone. Volk let out a disappointed whimper and looked at me woefully.

During the encounter with the lights, particles of divine energy had begun to flow through my bloodstream. For the first time I could feel the innerworkings of my body and the intelligence within every cell. I knew, somehow, that this awareness was our Creator's intention for us, but that humans had gone numb. The glorious sensation was now fading, and although I tried desperately to hold on to it, I could not. I stared at my hands and watched as the last sparks left through my fingertips and helpless tears sprang from my eyes.

I sat in the same spot for a long time, praying for the lights to return and when they did not, I headed for the cornerstone with Volk behind me. It was the only thing left intact within the rubble. I scraped off the moss, removed the loose debris from around it, and began to dig.

The ground at the base of the stone was bone dry, and I was scooping out sand when my fingers touched the package.

"Volk! It's here!"

I pulled out the bundle, brushed it off, and untied the cording. Inside was a book, its leather cover darkened by age. We Romany women did not know how to read, but I knew it was the treasure I'd been called upon to protect. I asked O Del to give me a sign and though there were no birds in the sky, a white feather floated down onto my lap. I tucked it between the pages.

It was time to go. I went to the altar, picked up the dagger and wrapped it and the book in my scarf. I asked for the angel's blessing and felt it rest upon me.

Like always, Volk guided me out of the Wildwoods. Good as I was at traversing the forests and fields, and as many times as we had been to the ruins together, I had never once been able to find my way there or back without him.

A few days after that, everything changed and I was not to see my beloved Volk again. There were nights, though, when the moon was full and I could not sleep, that I heard him call. His voice was unlike any other. Powerful with an edge of melancholy and deep longing. On those nights, I would light a lamp so he could find me and watch for him to emerge from the darkness.

Sometimes I'd make it 'til dawn, but most often, my hopes of seeing him would melt into dreams and I would awaken in the morning, disappointed in myself for having slept through his possible return. Something else deeper told me, though, that he would never let that happen.

Chapter Eight
~ The Promise ~

"They call it 'young love,' but it's only the hearts that are young.
Love, itself, has no age."

SGR

Tamás was thirteen when Renata came. He had never seen such a beautiful creature and was smitten from the start.

She did not know her own age, but the women guessed her to be twenty or so. Gypsy ghels were married young, and it was assumed she had been, too. Tamás had no hope for a match with her, so hid his feelings and became her friend and brother instead. As soon as he finished his own chores, he'd tag along on hers, and they would steal moments to sit by the river or within the birch tree grove where she would sing secrets to him and he would play tunes for her on his violin. The magic would fall, then, and her words and his notes would weave together in a way of their own and she would laugh at his surprise when it happened.

"See, Tamás, you just need to let Balval move through you. Let go. It's much easier than trying on your own. Open your heart and your mind. Our willingness – that's all the spirit of O Del needs. We don't have to understand everything, and we never will. But how beautiful it is to be the instrument, the cup, to taste the sweet wine poured in and out of us as we yield." She would close her eyes and sway back and forth as she sang, sometimes blissfully tearful, always smiling – and he would be entranced and imagine his head upon her breast.

"Ahhh...yes, Balval, the Wind. Here he comes! He's speaking! Can you hear him, Tamás?"

And the boy would close his eyes and open his ears and try with his whole being. He did not want to disappoint her, *or* Balval.

"Do you?" She was somewhere else, presumably with Balval, and was asking from that other place.

"*I...I think so,*" he lied.

She tested him. "*What do you hear?*"

"*I'm...I'm not really sure,*" he stuttered. "*Uhhh...music?*"

And she'd look at him tenderly, knowing he would do and say anything to please her.

"*The songs are always within us, Tamás. They are there from the start. O Del says we are loved more than we can ever imagine. He has plans for us, and they are always good. He likes your violin-playing, by the way, and says you will be a great gilabno someday.*" And she'd laugh, tousle his hair, and kiss him on the forehead, which would thrill him, and he'd pick up his fiddle and let the notes praise her and O Del.

There were times when Renata swore him to secrecy beforehand and shared a bit of something she remembered from her life before, like the color of the vardo that had once been her home, and the sunflowers she had painted on the walls; how the smell of the river made her happy, and the startling fact that she possessed a book.

Tamás feared for her concerning this last confession, for the Roma held fiercely to their traditions, and reading or writing was strictly forbidden. Anyone showing an interest in such things, particularly females, risked swift and harsh punishment. Maybe that was why she had been alone and wandering. Perhaps she was an outcast.

On the way back to the camp one day, when her belly was swollen to a frightening size, she said something that confused him.

"*Tamás?*"

"*Yes, my sister?*" It helped his lovesickness to call her that.

"*My child will be here soon, and I need you to give her something for me. Can I trust you to do that?*"

He wondered how she could know her baby was a ghel and why she couldn't give the child whatever it was, herself.

"*Yes, of course, but I...*"

She stopped, turned to face him, took his hands, and squeezed them tight for emphasis. He knew he should not thrill to her touch and struggled to hide it.

vardo *(VAR-doe)* – wagon
gilabno *(*gil-AHB-no) – traveling musician

36

"It is a sacred trust, Tamás, and Balval has told me that it is to fall upon you. You must guard my child, for she will be given a mission and Beng will seek to harm her. I no longer have a father or husband, so O Del has become these to me, and He shall be her father as well."

Tears glistened in her eyes and although it hadn't been very long, she looked much older than when they'd first met. The lithe, fearless, talks-to-the-wind Renata, he knew very well. This desperate, heavy-with-unborn-child woman gripping his hands, made him nervous.

She sensed everything, and he should have known she would read his face. Relaxing her grasp, she brought her emotions under control. She did not want to frighten or overwhelm him, but time was running out and she needed assurance.

"Do you swear?"

She knew something he did not. Though he didn't understand how her gifts worked, he knew better than to question them. If he or the others at camp needed to know something, she would tell them, and if not, wild horses couldn't get it out of her. So, he pledged what she asked, not because he believed in himself, but because *she* did.

"I swear," he promised.

~

𝐿ife's path is short for some and long for others. The passionate vows of one's youth inevitably meet crossroads of fate, and even if the boy had stopped to consider what he would do if called upon to keep his promise, he could never possibly have imagined the part he would play in the story that was soon to unfold.

☾
Chapter Nine
~ A Ghel ~

*"The world is indeed full of peril...but still there is much that is fair
...and though love is now mingled with grief, it still grows
perhaps the greater."*
J.R.R. Tolkien

Once a Romany girl reached womanhood, she gained a small measure of power in the otherwise patriarchal society: the ability to contaminate the males. Cleanliness rituals were strictly observed, and extreme precautions were taken to protect the men from being 'polluted' by female blood. Births took place away from the central area of the encampment and were followed by forty days of purification, so Tamás staked out a hiding place nearby Renata's wagon and assured her he would be close by when her time came.

Though her labor was long, Renata did not cry out. That didn't surprise Tamás. She was strong, and Balval was with her. Of that he was certain. The Spirit who gave them songs would watch over her.

When Tamás heard the infant's cry, his heart leapt. Then came Tsura's voice, *"A ghel!"* After a while, the women exited the wagon, his mother last.

"Go home to your husbands. Everything is fine," she said. *"I'll be back after I fetch more water."*

Tamás watched the various-colored shawls dissolve into the darkness and then ran to Renata's vardo.

"Sister?" He whispered.

"Tamás! Come in!" She answered weakly.

Were he to be discovered with Renata, they would declare him 'mahrime' and he could be expelled from the tribe. But young boys seldom stop to consider consequences over impulse, and rules had never applied to Renata anyway. After one quick look around, he abandoned

mahrime *(MAH-ree-MAY)* – contaminated, unclean

everything he had been taught and scrambled soundlessly up into the candle-lit vardo. There, he found her, pale and exhausted upon her bed, holding the tiny bundle, her eyes brimming with tears of love.

"Look at her Tamás! She's a miracle! Just as O Del promised."

He knelt by her side and peered at the cocooned infant, who'd been deftly swaddled by the midwives. The round, ruddy face below a feathery tuft of jet-black hair, eyes shut tight against the world, perfectly sculpted lips making tiny sucking motions, and he was too overwhelmed to speak.

"Her name is Nadya." Renata's voice was so faint he had to lean close to hear her. *"When she's older, she will have a calling. You won't forget what we talked about, will you Tamás?"*

"I promise," he assured her emphatically, *"I will do what you asked."*

"The box you made for me...it's hidden in the front of the vardo under the bench...keep it safe for her. Take care of her, Tamás."

And then he saw the blood, and Renata's face changed, and he realized that everything was not as his mother had thought. He screamed for her, and seconds later she was there, alarmed to see him, but too concerned about Renata to be angry. She pushed him aside and commanded him to run and get his aunt, the eldest midwife, and to tell her to come quickly.

*"GO, SON! **RUN**!"* Her face was ashen and her voice a fierce whisper as she shoved him out of the wagon. *"And tell no one you were in here!"*

With all his young strength and speed, Tamás leapt from the vardo and tried to outrun Balval, but the Spirit that held power over life and death had already carried away the boy's first love.

~

$\mathcal{T}$here was no comforting the young man. Nothing could be said or done to lessen his pain or to close the hole in his heart, nor could any of them comprehend the depth of his sorrow. The baby was his only connection to Renata, and the helpless little thing was being wet nursed, coddled, washed, and fussed over continually by the women, who sent him away on meaningless errands whenever he came near. Every time he heard the little one cry, whatever frail defense he had managed to build against the grief would crumble.

His beloved was gone. She'd bled to death and they'd buried her body by the tree at the lake where he'd first believed. This time there was no magic in the air, the dragonflies mourned, and the lake was filled with the tears of the willow.

Tamás spent the late autumn days away from the camp in one of his and Renata's favorite hideouts, the birch tree grove. There, he sat numbly listening. For what, He didn't know. The voice of Balval that she so easily heard? A melody from within? Any scrap of evidence to prove she was with him still and that he would one day be able to feel again, live again, play again, and become what she had foretold.

The music, the magic and his faith had all died with Renata. The same notes that had leapt from his soul to dance for her now disintegrated in mid-flight, their ashes drifting aimlessly down into the soggy blanket of decaying grey skeletons beneath his feet. In life, the same leaves had clung bravely to lush green boughs that had sheltered and sighed above them. Was she sighing and sheltering him now? Why couldn't his eyes see as hers had? Why couldn't he hear?

He took his fiddle with him everywhere, not because he could bring himself to play it, but because it had been in his hands since he was four. It sat beside him like a faithful dog, and laid on his lap like a trusting cat, waiting patiently for its broken-hearted young master to find a way through the darkness. When he did, it would not judge his passion or his pain, and would be grateful only for his touch. It would cry all the tears he could not cry and speak all the words he could not say. And in the years to come, when this season of suffering was a melancholy memory in the heart of a strong man, the scars of loss would bring only tender remembrance and the two would tell 'The Story of Renata' the way no other voices ever could.

☾

Chapter Ten
~ Nadya ~

"Life is either a daring adventure or nothing at all."
Helen Keller

They told me, when I was small, that my mother was too beautiful for this world, and that the same wind that brought me carried her away to Charos in the sky. When I asked why it would do such a thing, they said it had its own reasons and did as it pleased. It was wild and came from the mouth of O Del and it might just as easily sweep her back to us some other day. Stranger things had happened.

I feel her near me and have dreamed of her. There have even been times when I thought I saw her, but I cannot be sure of that last thing.

Whatever may be, I am not alone, because just as it was given to her, she passed to me *'The Sight,'* which our people call *'The Dook.'* Because of this, they say I must always be good, and grow smart and strong, and listen to the Earth, the stars, and the voice of O Del without arguing. For I will be given songs to sing and stories to tell and mysteries to speak. So, I try to listen, and I am learning to hear as she did. Sometimes I share what I know with them – but not everything.

Tamás says I have my mother's eyes, her hair, her heart, and her gifts. My name is Nadya, which means 'Hope.' I am a child of the forests and fields, the caravan is my family, and my home is everywhere.

I am Roma.

Charos *(CHAR-os)* – Heaven

$\mathcal{N}$adya was not old enough to fully understand the differences between her people and the gadje (everyone else). Innocence bloomed on her face, and kindness guided her heart with no shadow of turning at all. She was the darling of the Gypsy band, where no child was an orphan, for they were all raised together by many loving parents.

One day, when they'd gone to the marketplace to sell and perform, a group of village children pointed at Nadya and whispered. She was barely five at the time, and assumed that they were admiring her colorful clothes, so she put her hands on her hips and her chin in the air like the older ghels did when they danced and spun around in a circle as fast as she could so that her skirt would unfurl like a flower. Regrettably, the dizzying performance came to an abrupt, undignified finale when her feet could not keep up.

Tamás was playing his violin nearby and heard the laughter. Seeing Nadya sprawled on the cobblestones, he reached her in seconds, scooped her up, planted her firmly on his shoulders and galloped away before the taunts could wound her spirit. Forgetting her pain and humiliation, she squealed with delight, grabbed handfuls of his thick black hair, and held on tight. His love for his little Gypsy princess knew no bounds and she adored him the same. He was her big brother, playmate and best friend, all rolled into one. She could not imagine a world without him and did not need to.

However wild and free, Gypsy childhood was brief. Marriages were arranged, and by nine, ten or eleven, a chavi would be promised to a chav several and sometimes many years older. Her father would be recompensed with a darro – be it gold coins or a pig, depending upon the wealth of the tribe – and on her wedding day, the adolescent would leave her family to join her husband's. There, under the strict tutelage of her mother-in-law, she would assume the adult responsibilities of the union. This demanded far more from the child bride than from her mate, and she could look forward to serving his needs until death parted them. Gypsy women accepted their toilsome lives without question, and often inexplicably outlived their far less devoted husbands, who were lucky to make it to the ripe old age of forty five.

gadje *(gah-DJEE)* – non-Gypsies
chavi *(shah-VEE)* – girl
chav *(sh-AHV)* – boy
darro *(DAH-roe)* – dowry

44

$\mathfrak{F}$or Tamás' mother, Tsura, life without a husband was even more arduous than with one. She could bear no more children, and up until the time Renata arrived, her boy had been her whole life. Were she not a widow, and she and Nadya not dependent upon her son, a marriage would have been arranged for him long ago. There was talk.

Tamás had been graced with his father's strong jaw line, dark, wavy hair, and good looks. Several ghels had made their attractions to him apparent, and although he was not immune to female flattery, he knew Gypsy women to be competitive, jealous, and fiery by nature and saw no possible way to divide his energies between his mother, a wife, and the little girl who needed him. Until Nadya reached womanhood, he had a promise to keep.

Romany law and tradition allowed for little to no flexibility. It was the glue that held their people together from one generation to the next. Tamás knew that despite his hesitancy, or perhaps because of it, the social pressure for him to marry was going to increase. The mother hens were clucking, and their daughters were eyeing him, hoping to be chosen. It was only a matter of time before Tsura would arrange a match. He hadn't decided what he would do when that happened, so he pushed it all to the back of his mind.

He'd had a brother once. A twin, which was the meaning of his own name. He possessed but one memory of 'Other Tamás.' A watery reflection of someone small who would have walked and talked and looked like him if the fates had been kinder. An equal born to shoulder half the load and endure the harshness of life by his side. In his imagination, the two would have charmed and captivated their audiences with fantastic tales and fiddle duels. Then later, they'd have drunk wine and smoked stolen tobacco out behind the vardos, while dreaming of the day they would become storvandre.

His equally handsome brother probably wouldn't have minded marrying one of the pretty young Gypsy girls. Kizzy, perhaps, who was a good cook and liked to clean. They would have gone right to work making babies, and he, the proud uncle, would be helping to raise his nieces and nephews as though they were his own. He dreamed of the adventures he and his comrade twin would have had and what an impressive duo they would have made. And when he felt weak or

storvandre *(stor-VAHN-dray)* – long distance traveling musicians troubled, he reminded himself of the revelation he had been given as a boy after his beloved Renata had died – that because Other Tamás would always be part of him, he possessed the fortitude of two men. Balval had told him, then, that for the journey ahead, he would need the full measure of that strength, and more.

By the age of eight, Nadya was becoming an exquisite, fine-boned miniature of her mother. Whenever Tamás looked at her, an invisible hand would close around his heart, and if he gave place to the fear that he could fail this child and lose her as he had Renata, its cruel grip would tighten. But he was no longer a child and had learned how to bring such thoughts into submission. He fought off the fear by focusing on the joy of his moments with Nadya and on his deep gratitude for the sacred responsibility he had been given.

The fiercely independent little sprite possessed her mother's gifts, and like Renata, preferred being out away from the camp exploring the fields and forests beyond. Slovenia was a playground of natural wonders for the imaginative child. Endless trails snaked through mysterious woodlands, trodden smooth, according to the ghel, by devious goblins and generally friendly elves – though you dared not completely count on the latter. There were streams to cross, rivers that flowed underground, meadows to dance in, trees to climb, treasures to collect, and distant turreted castles that inspired impromptu skits where she, a princess orphaned after an evil assault on her parents' kingdom, had been bewitched and left to wander with no memory of her nobility until a brave prince (the role invariably assigned to Tamás) rescued her. The spell would then be broken, she would re-claim her rightful throne, and together they would rule over their happy, loyal subjects – humans and talking beasts alike – with wisdom and kindness for the remainder of their days. There were many variations on the theme.

It was on one such excursion that she and Tamás came upon the cave. The thick vines that obscured its entrance allowed only a few shafts of sunlight to penetrate the interior, but after a cursory inspection that yielded no visible evidence to the contrary, they agreed that it did not appear to be the habitation of anyone or anything that they would not wish to encounter.

Gypsies being a superstitious lot, and not fond of the dark, they decided to come back the following day with lamps to explore further. They told no one else what they had found and savored the belief that they were the very first to discover the place. They were wrong in the latter assumption, for entities far wilder than Nadya's imagination were already at work.

Upon their return, lamplight revealed the cave to be much larger than they had thought. On the right side, behind a massive boulder, was a small tunnel through which they could hear the sound of flowing water. Before prudent action could be discussed, Nadya, who was as quick as a fox and just as wily, scrambled inside, leaving Tamás to call after her repeatedly, only to be ignored by the fearless little spelunker. The passageway was not big enough for the young man to stand, so he bent over and slowly made his way down it until he saw a faint glow ahead. The reprove he was about to deliver died in his throat as an enormous grotto opened before him. At its center stood Nadya, arms flung open in welcome, beaming with pride over her discovery.

"Tamás! Look! I knew it was here! It was calling to me! Isn't it beautiful?" She was surrounded by a crop of limestone spires that arose from the floor and others that hung from the ceiling. Behind her, water trickled from a crack in a wall into a pool, and then out again through another channel. Tamás cautiously reached toward one of the stone pillars, and Nadya ran to his side.

"It's alright," she laughed. *"They're like rocks! I already touched them."* She ran her hand boldly over the lumpy surface and gave him the kind of casually superior look that youngsters get when they have ascertained a thing that the adults aren't privy to. Her arrival a moment before his had established her as the expert on caves.

They stayed and explored until the candles in their lamps had burned down to nubs, at which point Tamás insisted that they leave – this time in a voice stern enough that Nadya obeyed. She chattered all the way back to camp, begging for them to return – the next time with food and candles. *"Lots and lots of candles!"*

*J*n the vardo that night, as he was tucking her in, she whispered (for Tsura was within earshot), *"Tamás, I am going to dream about our cave!"*

He kissed her head and whispered back, *"You do that, Princess, and tell me all about it tomorrow!"*

She smiled contentedly, snuggled down into her quilts and within seconds drifted away to places where he could never follow.

☾

Chapter Eleven

~ Treasures ~

"There are some secrets which will not permit themselves to be told."
Edgar Allan Poe

To Nadya's great frustration, she was not given a vote as to where or when the caravan was moving. The cave was no longer within reasonable walking distance and an entire season passed before she overheard a secret conversation wherein one of the seers was telling the elders that she'd had a dream in which Mirno was calling them back. They sounded receptive and Nadya was overjoyed.

This time, however, when the Gypsies returned, things had changed, especially in the marketplace.

A finger couldn't be put on it exactly, but it was not the same friendly, profitable place it had been before. A sour, suspicious aura surrounded many of the villagers and they had few if any extra coins to spend on Gypsy entertainment or trinkets. Only the knife sellers did a steady business.

In the caravan, talk began about whether the seer had been wrong and that they might be better off moving on. So far, most felt they should stay awhile longer in hopes that things would improve. Ultimately, the elders would decide, and they could not be rushed. Nadya didn't want to leave. She loved everything about the area, especially the cave, and often begged Tamás to take her there.

The young man had worries. With each passing day, the promises he had made to Renata weighed more heavily upon his heart. Caring for Nadya was pure joy, but he did not know how or when to execute the other trust Renata had asked of him. The ghel was as unique as her mother, but was she ready? He needed an unmistakable sign and beseeched O Del, Balval and Renata all at the same time to send one.

He did not have to wait long.

A couple of days later, Nadya awoke earlier than usual and came to him by the campfire. Her little brow was furrowed and her eyes were intense. *"Tamás?"*

"Yes, Nadya?"

"I had a dream last night and I don't know what it means."

"Tell me about it."

"A lady came to me, and she said she had something to give me."

His heart skipped a beat. *"What did she look like?"*

"She was very beautiful with long black hair and I knew she was wise."

He considered his words carefully before speaking.

"Did she tell you what it was?"

"No. When I asked her, she said, 'You will see.' And then she said she had to go, and I was sad because in the dream I loved her so much. Was she my Dai, Tamás?"

He thought there would be no harm in her believing so, and answered, *"I think she may have been. Those we love who've gone away to Charos sometimes return to us in dreams."*

"Has she ever come to you?"

"No. She doesn't need to. You are enough." He reached out and drew her close to his chest, so she could not see the tears in his eyes.

"I wonder what she wants to give me? What do you suppose it is?"

"I have an idea. Shall we go to the cave today?"

She happily agreed, and he knew the time had come.

"What's in the bag, Tamás?" The child never missed a thing.

"Our lunch," he hedged.

"No, I mean that other thing," she persisted, pointing.

"You'll have to wait. I will show you when we're in the cave."

"Ooooo!" She loved surprises but guessing them was even more fun. *"It's a treasure box!"*

50

He looked at her in wonder. She was still so young, and this was only the beginning.

They arrived at the cave and checked to be sure no one was in sight before entering. When they reached the deeper cavern, they set their lamps down on what they had named 'table rock' at the center. It was Nadya's habit to position candle stubs around the room, for she loved to see the exaggerated, flickering shadows of the columns towering above them and pretended they were friendly giants arising from their sleep. Today, she did not want to take time for make-believe.

Tamás had not rehearsed what he was going to say to her and tried to buy himself some time by offering her lunch first, but Nadya was more interested treasures than food.

"Alright then," he wondered why he felt so nervous, *"I won't make you wait any longer."*

Nadya sat as still as stone while Tamás pulled out the box. Her eyes rested upon it and then opened wide as she looked at him and asked with breathless anticipation, *"Is it from my Dai?"*

"Yes. As I have told you, she was like a sister to me and I loved her very much. I was a little older than you when she first came to the caravan. But you already know that story."

She never tired of hearing it and had asked him to tell her many times because it made her mother real. *"She gave this to you for me?"*

"Yes. Well, I made it for her and gave it to her first, and then she asked me to give it to you when the time was right. I have kept it hidden for this day, and that hasn't been easy because you know how Tsura cleans!" He rolled his eyes and she giggled with understanding of the overly attentive woman who had borne him and raised them both.

"The other day I asked for a sign and your dream was that sign." His fingers traced the boyish craftsmanship and he smiled in memory of his all-consuming desire to delight his beloved Renata. *"She filled it with her own treasures and made me promise to give them to you."*

Nadya opened the lid, and as he watched her carefully lift out each item and display them on the rock, Tamás thought that she did not seem like a child at all.

A dagger with a carved handle of bone
A small, smooth stone with a hole in the middle
A white feather
An old leather book.

"I wish I knew the secrets of these things," Nadya said wistfully. *"Will you help me Tamás?"*

He heard her mother's voice, *"Tamás, will you help me?"* and knew Renata was there with them.

"Of course," he answered, though he hadn't the slightest idea how or where to begin.

They examined the items in the box, both imagining Renata's hands holding each treasure but neither saying so.

Nadya stroked the feather across her cheek and turned the stone over and over in the palm of her hand. Tamás' face softened in remembrance, and he said, *"I gave her that. I found it in the river. Such stones are said to hold power and it is believed that those who possess them will be protected from evil."*

"I will wear it!" Nadya exclaimed and slipped it into her pocket.

The dagger was the finest craftsmanship Tamás had ever seen. The blade was sharp as a razor and other than a dark stain on the handle which he suspected was blood, it was like new. He did not know more about it than that, for Renata had never shown it to him. There had also been no story about the feather.

Last was the book, and as neither he nor Nadya could read, its contents were a mystery.

The days were growing shorter and it would be dusk by the time they returned to camp, so they agreed that the box and its contents would be safest left in the cave. Nadya knew the perfect spot – a niche in the wall behind where the stream formed a pool. She'd investigated there on a previous visit and insisted she had discovered an ogre's cache of plundered gold (pieces of iron pyrite serving as convincing nuggets). It was almost impossible to get to, and no one would know the box was there but them. As he watched the nimble little girl squeeze through the calcified spires and tiptoe around the edge of the pool,

Tamás felt a surprising rush of relief that Renata's secrets were no longer his to protect alone.

By the following morning, the weather had turned. Wind and torrential rain kept the Gypsies in camp, holed up in their respective vardos, where the men passed the time napping, whittling, and playing their instruments, and the women sewed and cleaned.

Nadya threaded a leather cord through the hole in the stone and tied it around her neck. The weight of the necklace resting against her body made her feel close to her Dai and Tamás.

She was supposed to be practicing her embroidering but was restless and unable to think about anything but the remaining contents of the box.

Most mysterious was the book. She wondered if her Dai had known what it said. She was certain that if her mother were still alive, she would tell her, and that made Nadya long for her even more.

She had been told that reading was forbidden and not to be interested in it, but she was too curious of a soul to follow anyone else's orders without asking a lot of questions, and it didn't matter who they were. She wanted to know the reasons for the rules and for everything else they said, and if logical answers weren't provided, she deduced things on her own. She was still growing and learning and wanted to know everything. It appeared that most of the others had stopped doing both, and they were tired of her always asking, *"But why?"*

She remembered having seen a man in the village walking with a book under his arm. He was near the tall stone building with the bell on top. Other people had passed him and bowed their heads respectfully, so she guessed him to be someone of importance. He would briefly acknowledge those who greeted him but did not stop to talk. Maybe if she could find him, he would help. She began to devise a plan, and fearing that Tamás might not approve, decided to keep it to herself.

☽

Chapter Twelve

~ The Assault ~

"For we wrestle not against flesh and blood..."
Ephesians 6:12

The Vrag had adopted countless personas over the eons and was known by many different names. He was a trickster and master deceiver who played the odds, followed his hunches, and made educated guesses with startling accuracy. His ego and voracious appetite demanded appeasement at any cost, and he was rightfully feared by those he outranked in the legions of Beng. Only his superiors knew that his all-seeing, all-knowing act was a ruse. They knew because they were even more depraved, and the Vrag was theirs to command. Until he managed to outsmart them, his illusions of grandeur were merely demented fantasies.

If intel had not pointed to Mirno as the probable location of the book, the Vrag wouldn't be wasting time and resources on the pathetic little settlement. He had one fully co-operative human working undercover there, but the assignment was taking longer than anticipated, and he was growing more irritated by the day. He could not be everywhere at once, so had posted watchers at strategic points. They reported nothing of significance, which made him distrust them even more than usual.

The disgusting excuse for a regiment that had been assigned to him served only under threat of torment, or in the case of the most stupid among them, the deluded belief that they could rise to greater power in the food chain by secretly plotting against and outsmarting their captain. When they tried, he'd rip them to pieces and eat them alive in front of the others. There were always new recruits eager to step in, but then the Vrag had to train them, and with all the infernal paranoia, threatening and torturing, he was getting no rest.

Lust, gluttony, greed, sloth, wrath, envy, and pride. YaH warned his willful creatures against the destruction these behaviors would bring, so the Vrag knew better than to leave the humans wrestling with right and wrong. It was easier to encourage the belief that neither existed, that everything was grey, and that choices should be made according to their own selfish reasons as dictated by their precious 'feelings.'

The demon salivated with delight when a society that had once honored YaH began to crumble, and there was a long string of them. He was happy to take the credit and saw no point in messing with a formula that worked so well.

Rule number one was never to allow the humans to feel so lost or remorseful that they turned to his adversary, for YaH would reward their repentance with love and forgiveness, patch them up, replenish their strength, give them purpose, and send them right back out into the fight.

No. The Vrag needed them wounded, angry, dissatisfied, stubborn, carnal, and self-centered until he had completed his mission. Then, he would turn them on themselves and leave them to their own destruction. In the meantime, the slow ruin of their insignificant lives was just auxiliary entertainment.

Nurturing the villagers' miseries had succeeded in revealing a good number of weak links whom the Vrag could use. To dissuade them from higher thought or conviction, he was feeding them a juicy diet of anything they craved – whatever temporarily dulled their pain and hushed their consciences. Any light that tried to creep in (and YaH's forces never stopped trying) had to be extinguished, and the best way to do that was to churn up dark clouds of trouble upon trouble. When employing this tactic, the Vrag had to be careful not to overplay his hand, for he had learned the hard way that some humans could be more astute than he gave them credit for. In times past, ardent students of his adversary had discerned the Vrag's presence and evoked YaH's powers to thwart the demon's plans. When word got back to Beng's headquarters, the Vrag's punishment had been unspeakable.

In any case, although the 'mountain-of-troubles strategy' could be a bit of a gamble, it worked so much of the time that the Vrag just couldn't resist. It was too much fun to spin the wheel and watch them bounce around. First, they would be distracted from what was good in their lives, and as problems mounted, they would gradually succumb to the darker side of their natures and be driven straight into the Vrag's waiting arms. Then, he'd soothe the despicable creatures and tell them they didn't deserve their hardships. He'd numb them with the sedative of their choice, discourage any uncomfortable introspection, and dispel any remaining doubts by pointing to the intolerance of others as justification for their misery. After that, their penchant for self-destruction took over and his job was done.

The Vrag's melodrama had been playing for millennia, always with a fresh new cast of characters, and he never tired of watching the show. He liked to boast that he was undefeated and had left no spark of hope alive since his work began.

However, like others of his kind (none of whom shall bother to read pages like these written by souls such as mine), the Vrag's fatal flaw was that he never hung around long enough to notice those who rose from the ashes.

Chapter Thirteen
~ Snakes and Princesses ~

*"Plan, of course, but if you wish to achieve success,
plan mostly for the unexpected."*

SGR

*N*adya's mind never stopped working. A couple of days later when the weather had cleared, she got up early in the morning with the women, and before they could tell her what to do, announced casually that she was going to gather firewood. Tsura stopped scrubbing clothes and looked up from the washtub with surprise. The ghel was a lot like her mother and much more prone to wandering off in a daydream than voluntarily following through on tasks. Perhaps this was a genuine effort and a sign that she was growing up. Tsura decided to put her suspicions aside and waved Nadya off without the customary lecture.

As soon as she was out of sight, Nadya headed in the direction of the village. Her plan was to get there before everyone else so that she would have time to find the man with the book. The Gypsies took the shortest route to market, but it was also the most open, with no place to hide, so she chose the less-traveled path through the forest which converged with the main road not far from town.

The tribe always finished their work before leaving camp, and some arrived at the marketplace before others. The first group came to stake out the best locations to peddle their goods, and the musicians, dancers and entertainers came later when the courtyard was full of people. The children all ran free and were watched over by the tribe in general, so Nadya's plan was to get to the village first, track down the man with the book, mingle innocently with the sellers' children when they arrived, and then gravitate to the performers when they showed up. There were holes in her plot, but it made sense in a ten-year-old's mind.

Nadya had never been through the Wildwoods alone before, but she was not afraid. Her people told many stories, and she had been warned of the Mulo – spirits that wandered in such places at night and noonday – but this was neither of those times. It was a beautiful autumn morning, the dew lay in shining droplets on the moss-carpeted floor, and the forest was just waking up. A rabbit darted out from the brambles and she called to it. Hearing its name, or something that sounded like a name, it froze, stared at her, wiggled its whiskers and tail in greeting, and hopped away.

Further on, she narrowly missed stepping on a puffy, black and orange striped caterpillar. When she picked it up, it curled into a ball and played dead.

"Poor little thing! Don't be afraid! Would you like to come on a walk with me?"

She pretended to hear its affirmative answer. *"Good! Let's go!"* and popped it into the pocket of her skirt. It felt good to have company.

The path led to a shallow stream that you crossed by stepping (or in a little girl's case, jumping) from stone to stone. Just as she was about to leap from the bank onto the first rock, a small movement caught her eye, and she looked down to see a little brown snake with yellow stripes at the water's edge.

"Hello," she said cheerily, and although it did not seem to acknowledge her, the encounter reminded her of a story she'd heard one of the women tell the others when they were preparing food for a wedding. At the end they all looked at one another, shook their heads back and forth and made little 'tsk-tsk-tsk' noises. She didn't understand what it meant, and when she asked, they said that if she always listened to their advice, she would not have to find out. That, of course, had made her even more curious.

mulo *(MOO-low)* – lost souls

The Princess and the Snake

A gentle, kind-hearted Gypsy Princess was walking through the forest one day when she came to a little stream. Just as she was about to cross, she heard a voice.

"Princess! Princess!"

She looked down to see a small snake with bright red markings smiling up at her. She immediately took a step back, for she recognized it to be the kind that though beautiful, was deadly poisonous.

"Why are you afraid of me?" the snake asked in a sad voice.

"Because you could hurt me!" the Princess replied.

"Oh, my dear, why would I hurt you?" it said, innocently. *"Who told you such an awful thing?"*

"Those who care for me. They said to watch out for your kind." She stood her ground.

It dropped its head dejectedly. *"Why would they say such things when they haven't even met me? People can be so cruel. I should have known that I could never hope to make a friend of one as lovely as you."*

The Gypsy ghel felt sudden remorse for judging the snake so harshly and hurting its feelings. She took a tiny step closer and it slowly raised its head again.

"I'm sorry," she said. *"I didn't mean to be unkind. It's just that I must be careful here in the forest. There are many dangers."*

"How well I know! There's no one I can trust and I am so lonely!" the snake said miserably. *"In fact, I came here today in hopes of crossing this stream, for I would like to start a new life on the other side. But now that I see how difficult that would be, I fear there is no way I can make it alone. The current is much too swift, and I would be carried downstream and drowned."* Its voice dwindled off hopelessly.

"Oh my," replied the Princess with concern. *"What will you do?"*

"I don't know," it answered. *"Things would be better over there, but…"* it paused, leaving the sentence up in the air.

"But?" she asked.

"Well, there is one hope," it said tentatively.

"What is that?"

"If you are going across, could you…would you…might you be so gracious as to carry me?" it asked in a pleading voice.

"Oh my! Well, I…I…"

Hearing the hesitation in her voice, the snake immediately recanted. *"Never mind, dear. I see that I have asked too much. I've done nothing to deserve your help and I shouldn't have bothered you."* The snake turned to leave.

"Wait!" she said, abandoning her better judgment. *"I will carry you across, but only if you swear not to hurt me."*

The creature immediately came closer. *"Hurt you? Oh, my dear, how can I abolish your fears? I will owe my new life to you! I would never hurt you and you will have my love forever!"*

Convinced of the snake's sincerity and flattered by its adoration, the Princess told herself that this particular reptile might be an exception to the rule, and she carefully picked it up. Then, because she did not want to risk it falling, she slipped it gently into her bodice where it promptly nestled down with a blissful look on its face.

With the snake curled safely near her heart, the Princess made her way across the rapidly flowing stream. She tiptoed easily from stone to stone, and with each step she felt braver, kinder, stronger and more noble for proving the others wrong.

Alas, the instant she stepped up onto the embankment, the snake sank its fangs deep into her flesh. The poison coursed through her bloodstream and she collapsed in agony. Then, the creature slithered out of her bodice, coiled in front of her face, licked its lips and gazed coldly into her eyes.

With her final breath she gasped, *"Why? You said you loved me and that I could trust you! How could you do this?"*

The snake answered truthfully without emotion. *"I am hardly to blame, foolish ghel. You knew what I was when you picked me up."*

And it turned and slithered away.

~

All Nadya had gotten from the story was that it was best not to pick up snakes, so she ignored the brown one and went on her way.

She felt at home in the forest, knew what berries to pick, and which wild plants were safe to munch on if she was hungry. Tamás had taught her these things from the time she was small. She did not fear the animals, and in fact, her first inclination was to speak to them, but since she could not understand their languages, it was doubtful that they could understand hers, so she sent kind thoughts to their hearts while making soothing sounds, and that usually worked.

It was not the creatures with fur or feathers or scales that you needed to fear the most, but the ones with skin who walked on two feet. It was the humans that Beng was able to use. He had been deceiving them from the beginning, and caused them to do terrible things, whereas animals acted purely on instinct. They did not have to make the decision to be good or bad, which was a constant dilemma for Nadya, who, the older she got, was coming to realize that she had great potential for both.

She was almost through the trees when she remembered the caterpillar. Sitting down on a fallen log, she reached into her pocket, lifted out the fuzzy ball and set it carefully down on the cracked bark.

"I hope you enjoyed our journey. What is that? You wish I would tell your fortune but have no coins to pay me? Do not worry, I shall tell you anyway. Very soon the weather will grow colder, and you will spin a cocoon, and then you will sleep for a long time, and when you awaken you will be changed! You shall not ever have to crawl on the ground again, for you will have wings and will fly in the sky! You probably don't believe me, and I know it sounds impossible, but it is said that none of us can ever know how much our lives will change or how fast! You shall see this come to pass, and you will remember the Gypsy ghel who told you so! I must go now, my little friend. Goodbye!"

Pleased with herself, she walked out of the woods and into the adjoining field, where the sun was considerably brighter. There, the path merged with the lane to town. She would keep to the tall grass alongside, so that if anyone came, she could duck down and hide. A young Gypsy ghel walking alone would seem odd, and if Tamás and Tsura found out she had gone into the village without telling them, they wouldn't let her out of their sight again. If that happened, she would never be able to find out what was in the book.

She waited until a farmer's wagon came by loaded with pumpkins, squash, corn, a pig, chickens and children, and then trotted along behind it, shooshing the youngsters with her finger over her lips so they wouldn't announce her presence. They made faces and stuck their tongues out at her but played the game.

In town, vendors were setting up their wares. The market would soon be full, and before the arrival of the first part of her familia, Nadya had to find the reading man. She surmised that the big building with the bell might be his house and decided to start there.

She had never been so near the structure before and the closer she got, the larger it loomed, rigid and silent. Not the warm, soft silence of the forest, but the cold, stern silence of stone. The only one there was a wrinkled old beggar woman sitting hunched over at the bottom of the steps. Wispy strands of white hair escaped from the ragged scarf on her head. Her patched dress was made of coarse brown material and peeking from beneath the frayed hem were shoes so worn as to provide little or no protection at all. Her bony hands were clutching the top of a cane held between her knees, and a small black pot sat on the ground beside her. Had Nadya a coin to her name at all, she would have given it to the poor thing.

She had feelings about people sometimes. She never knew when it was going to happen, but when it did, she was always right. Tamás had witnessed it and would just shake his head in wonder when it happened. She was having a feeling now.

"Ellow, ghel," the toothless mouth croaked.

"Hello," Nadya answered politely.

"Wot brings ye 'ere this early?"

"I'm looking for a man."

"A man? Wot man?"

"A man who can read books." Nadya recklessly blurted out.

The stooped shoulders straightened. *"Wot did ye say child?"*

Nadya moved closer, leaned forward, and repeated each word clearly and slowly, *"I am looking for the man who reads books. I saw him carrying one near here before."*

Beneath the grey straw eyebrows, the crone's sunken sockets widened to reveal two black coals that locked on Nadya's eyes with such intensity that the ghel could not look away. She instinctively took two steps backward where she would be out of reach of the cane.

"Wot are ye afraid of?" the old woman grinned. *"I know 'im."* Then her voice changed. *"Take care, child. Not all is as it seems here in the 'ouse of God.'"*

This was *God's* house? Up until now, Nadya had thought O Del lived everywhere, but if this was His home, maybe she could meet Him! And if the two of them hit it off, maybe the others from the caravan could come too!

It was a grand house, indeed. The bell tower was so tall that when she leaned backward to look up at it, she almost fell over. On the side facing the courtyard was what she knew to be a clock, a large round circle with marks going around and two big spears that pointed at them. Nadya did not know how to tell time, but she had watched it and knew that when the spears both pointed straight up, the bell would ring many times and villagers would eat their lunches.

The steep stone steps leading up to the cathedral doors were a challenge for a small girl's legs, and when she reached the top and turned around, the beggar woman was nowhere to be seen. It did not seem like she could have walked away that fast, and this struck Nadya as odd. No matter. She was going to see O Del!

The doors were more suited to a castle than a house. The carved wood had blackened over time, and there were big iron knockers in the middle of each – one in the shape of a lamb's head and the other a lion. Nadya stood on tiptoe, reached for the less frightening of the two, and before she could lose her nerve, grabbed the ring boldly and swung it down with all her might. The sound wasn't very loud, for she wasn't very strong, but she prayed O Del would hear it anyway. She waited, her heart in her throat, in the fervent hope that He would answer as a lamb and not as a lion, for no one knew His true form.

To Nadya's grave disappointment, O Del was not at home. This, she was forced to conclude after putting her ear to the door, rapping several more times, and hearing only hollow echoes within. Frustrated, she sat down on the top step and contemplated her next move.

From that vantage point she could see the market filling up in the courtyard. Tsura and a few others had just come through the gate and Nadya immediately felt a twinge of guilt for deceiving her familia. But she had discovered O Del's house! And she would meet Him soon and ask Him her questions! And when she explained why she'd had to be so sneaky about it, He would understand.

Before long, the rest of the Gypsies arrived. Nadya joined the group and stayed near Tamás, twirling to his violin songs, and shaking her tambourine. She imagined how her mother might have danced to his music, because he had told her they wrote many of the songs together.

She was happily spinning, jingling, and imagining, when the spears on the clock both pointed straight up. The bell rang several times before it dawned on Nadya that somebody had to be inside of God's house pulling on the rope. It would have looked suspicious if she were to run off in the middle of a dance, so she made a different plan for the following day when the clock would look the same and the bell would ring again.

Chapter Fourteen
~ Brother Caesaré ~

"Oh, what a tangled web we weave,
when first we practice to deceive."
Sir Walter Scott

*H*oping her excitement did not show, Nadya came into town the next morning in the usual way with Tsura and the others. She offered to fetch food and water and to help them however she could, which meant she would be able to move about freely, and if someone looked for her, they would assume she was elsewhere with others of the group. She would watch the spears on the clock and be waiting at the back door of the church when the bell started to ring. There were fewer worries about being seen there than at the front and she figured that O Del might go in and out that way for the same reason. It was even better than her previous plan, and this time she would not fail.

As the noon hour approached, she slipped into the crowd and made her way to the cathedral, which sat, as it always did, starkly quiet amid all the surrounding courtyard activity. The beggar woman was there in the same spot, too, watching Nadya's approach like a hawk. She lifted a scrawny finger in greeting and Nadya dropped her head politely. She had the uncomfortable feeling that the old lady knew exactly what she was up to.

The Roma did not like cemeteries, and there was one right behind the church. The thought of bodies and bones lying under the ground in neat rows with blocks of stone on top made Nadya shudder. Death didn't make sense. The river and the trees and the flowers did not die. The water kept flowing to other places and changed shapes. The trees and flowers slept in the winter but woke up again in the spring. Why not people and animals? The good went to Charos, she thought, and they could come back to visit in our dreams, as her Dai had done. And the bad people? Did they linger as phantoms like Tsura believed, and try to possess you? Nadya dearly hoped not. Tsura worried way too much.

Tamás had taken her to visit her mother once at a beautiful blue lake where flowers floated on the water and the branches of a big tree brushed the ground. There was no marker for the grave, just soft green grass and little white daisies, but Tamás said Renata would have liked that best, and he would never forget the exact spot anyway. Although it was a magical place where fairies played hide and seek in the cattails, Nadya decided she would rather think of her Dai among the stars, which had no end.

The back door of O Del's house was not nearly as large or fancy as the front, but it also had a knocker. She had already decided to wait until the bell stopped ringing to make her presence known, so she sat down on the stoop and clamped her hands over her ears until the loud clanging stopped. When all was quiet again, she jumped to her feet, grabbed the metal ring, and rapped it sharply on the door. Then she squared her shoulders and waited.

"Child!" An urgent, raspy voice startled the girl. The old woman had followed her and was standing not far away.

"Do ye remember what I said to ye?"

Uncertain, Nadya stuttered, *"I...uh...that this is the house of God?"*

"They call it that. And what else did I say?"

Nadya struggled because it hadn't made sense. *"That things are not as they seem?"*

The woman nodded slowly, *"Yah, child, yah..."* And she hobbled back around the corner.

Nadya could not understand why the ragged old woman cared at all, or what her words meant, but there was no time to wonder, for she heard the sound of a metal bar scraping and the door began to open. She held her breath. O Del!

A round-faced man with a bald head and a long grey beard peered out cautiously, and seeing just a little girl, opened the door wider. He was dressed in a brown robe tied at the waist with a cord, which Nadya thought was strange attire for the almighty O Del. She had been expecting someone more colorful, like the things He made in the world.

O Del was winded from descending the stairs. He assumed she was a beggar, and said, *"Wait here, I'll bring you some bread."*

68

Nadya declined, *"Thank you, but I am not hungry."* Then, covering up her disappointment in the homely individual, she asked tentatively,

"Are you O Del? God?"

He stifled a smile. *"No, child, I am Brother Caesaré. I help take care of The Lord's house."*

"Is He home? The Lord?"

She'd won him over and he softened. *"Well, in a manner of speaking, God is always here, but if you've come for an audience, I'm afraid it isn't possible. There are certain hours for Mass and confession."*

Nadya was not sure what Mass and confession were, but the last thing sounded like confections, which children with money could buy in the marketplace, and she couldn't imagine anything more wonderful than eating sweets with O Del. She highly doubted they would allow a Gypsy girl to participate, though.

"I need to see Him now. This is the only time I could come."

The friar was both amused and intrigued by the child's boldness, so he asked, *"Can you tell me the nature of your business with God – or 'O Del' as you call Him?"*

When she looked confused, he re-stated the question. *"Why do you need to talk to Him?"*

"Oh. I…um…well…it's a secret. I need help with something."

"You can tell me, and I will relay your request," he said.

Suddenly, as though they had just been whispered in her ear, Nadya heard the old woman's words again. Did they apply now? She still did not know what they meant. Was this man not what he seemed? She decided to believe that he was, for he had given her no reason to think otherwise.

"I need something to be read."

"Ah. Well, that's not such a big thing to ask. But do your father and mother know you are here?" He recognized her to be Roma and knew perfectly well that her family had no idea where she was. They staunchly avoided both churches and cemeteries.

Caesaré *(Sez-ah-RAY)*

69

Nadya dropped her head. *"I don't have a mother or a father."* It wasn't a lie, and always gained her sympathy.

"Oh," he said, his kindly face softening even more. *"I'm so sorry. But where are those you travel with?"*

"In the marketplace, and I must not stay long, or they will worry about me. I saw a man walking with a book near here one day. I thought he might have come from this building. Was he God?"

"No, my child, that would have been Father Vincent."

"Does he live here?"

"No, he lives next door," the friar nodded to his right.

"Should I go there, then?"

"I wouldn't advise it. He's an extremely busy man."

Nadya did not know what to ask next and a tear of disappointment escaped down one cheek.

The friar reached out, patted her head awkwardly, and said *"There, there...no need for tears, child. I can help you read whatever it is that needs reading."*

Her heart leapt, *"You can?!"*

"I'll be glad to. Where is it?"

"Oh, it's hidden," she blurted out, immediately regretting her candor.

"Hidden? Ah, of course. Because your people would not approve. Is that right?"

"Yes!" Nadya replied. His understanding made her feel better.

"So why is this thing so important?"

"It was my mother's book, and now it is mine."

"And since you must keep it hidden, how do you propose to bring it here?"

"I haven't figured that part out yet, but I will."

"Alright then, little one. When you have figured it out..." he interrupted himself, *"...and what is your name so that I may address you properly?"*

"Nadya," she answered proudly.

"Well, it has been a pleasure to meet you, Nadya. As I was saying, when you have figured it out, come knock on the door as you did today at this same time, and we will talk again. But not on Sunday. Do you know the difference between the other days of the week and Sunday? I am much too busy then. Now, run along back to your family before they worry. Go with God."

Brother Caesaré made a shape in the air that ended with a small dismissive wave.

Nadya gave a happy little curtsey and said, *"I will be back as soon as I can!"*

She was exploding with excitement. Not only had her plan worked, but she was soon to know the secrets of her mother's book, and O Del's very own bellringer was going to help!

((

Chapter Fifteen
~ Little Lies ~

"Listen to your bones, child. They will speak to ye."

Coming up with a strategy to get the book into town was more difficult than Nadya had imagined. She and Tamás were together so much that going to the cave without him, retrieving the book, hiding it, and then sneaking into town was virtually impossible. She finally concluded that the only way she could pull it off was if she pretended that she did not want to spend as much time with him. The prospect made her feel awful, but it was a temporary deception critical to the mission. Her mother had left her the book because it was important, and Nadya was consumed by the desire to know what it said. Tamás would never have let her do what she was doing, so as much as she loved him, he could not be in on her plan.

She began telling him in her most grown-up voice that she was sorry, but that she did not have time for adventures every day anymore because she had to practice her sewing and weaving and such. She also declared that she was old enough to take up residence in her mother's vardo, which had been used for storage since Renata's passing. She would be spending her nights there too, she said, and no longer needed to be tucked in or told a story. She was too old for that now.

Although he looked sad, Tamás' nodded and said that he had plenty of work to finish anyway, and that he would leave her to her female tasks and interests. As he prepared the vardo for Nadya, his mind was filled with images of the wee chavi in her mother's arms and Renata's last words to him.

He had been faithful. Nadya would forever be innocent in his mind, which is why he never suspected that she was lying to him. Nadya knew it was wrong, but the execution of her plan outweighed all regrettable subterfuge.

She also feigned a fervent interest in berry-picking and made it a habit to venture out daily, slowly extending the length of time she was gone and supplying excuses if anyone commented. This would be her alibi when she made the trip to the cave for the book. She had only been there with Tamás before, but she knew the way well. If she ran, and did not linger at all once inside, she could manage it in much less time than their excursions normally took.

*A*utumn's colors were fading and daylight hours were dwindling. As Gypsy bands do not make a habit of traveling at night, they were spending less time in the village marketplace and more time back at the camp. In the evenings, they ate supper, told stories, played music, danced, and sang, while the children moved from one campfire to another, giving Nadya the opportunity she needed to get away unnoticed.

The thought of making the trip into town in the dark gave her the shivers, but she decided she would wait until the moon was full, for sometimes it was so big and bright this time of the year that you could still see quite well. She would run fast, and not think about mulo. She also had the stone Tamás had given her mother for protection.

No sooner had Nadya devised her strategy than bad weather set in, stalling her again for a couple of weeks. She'd laid the groundwork, though, and when the skies cleared and they went to town, she quickly made her way to the back of the church, where she found Brother Ceasaré raking fallen leaves in the cemetery. He was both surprised and pleased to see her.

"Well, hello there, Nadya! I've been wondering about you. I wasn't sure I would see you again. Have you brought your book?"

"No, I can't bring it just yet, but I will very soon. I have to go get it from where it's hidden, and no one can know."

He raised a wiry eyebrow. *"Ah. They would not allow it."*

"No, they wouldn't. I'm the only one who understands how important it is."

"Do you know when you will be able to bring it?"

"I hope at the next full moon."

"Not during the day?"

"Oh, no. I can't bring it in the day. Someone might see me."

The friar found the girl's grit irresistible. His curiosity about the book was growing, so he made no attempt to talk her out of her plan or even to point out what dangers it might entail. He leaned his rake against the back wall and headed up the staircase to go inside.

Nadya followed him halfway up and asked, *"It will be after supper when I come. Is that alright?"*

"I shall make you some warm milk, then." He smiled.

"I would like that!" Nadya put her hands together in the shape of the steeple and bowed as she had seen the Father of God's house do on the street that first day, and Brother Caesaré did the same before he closed the door.

Nadya's eyes were on the steps as she hopped down, and when she reached the bottom, she looked up just in time to avoid running into the beggar woman. She was startled, and blurted out, *"What do you want?!"*

The wrinkles in the old woman's forehead deepened and she replied, *"What do I want? Ye are the one who wants something, aren't ye?"*

Nadya squirmed. *"I mean, why are you always here?"*

"I am here because ye are here, child." The eyes held Nadya's and did not blink. Then, she stepped aside so that the ghel could pass. Her words never made sense, and Nadya did not feel like she needed help. She had the itchy feeling, though, that the old woman knew things she did not.

"Yer bones," the old woman's words trailed after her. *"Listen to yer bones, child. They will speak to ye."*

☾

Chapter Sixteen

~ The Intruder ~

*"Control is an illusion. Other forces will intervene.
Of that you may be certain."*

SGR

However well-laid, Nadya's plans were entirely subject to the weather. If it rained, she wouldn't be able to get away from camp to retrieve the book from the cave nor would she have moonlight to travel by. When she asked an elder for a forecast, he laughed and said that the weather shared its secrets with no one and enjoyed playing games. He noted, however, that autumn appeared to be lingering. Mornings and evenings were crisp and fog hung in the valley. Afternoons were warm and the skies were blue.

Reasoning that it would be a good idea to check everything out before she went to the cave on her own, and since she'd been missing Tamás terribly, she suggested they make the trip. He happily agreed, and she added that she wanted to keep the visit short so that she would have time to pick berries on the way back. Those that remained would be ruined the next time it rained.

They did not talk much, for Nadya was busy making mental notes of landmarks and how far it was between them. Time was harder to guess than distance. She thought the clock on the bell tower in town was a good idea and could not understand why her people did not keep time.

When Tamás reached for her hand, she pretended not to notice and shifted her basket from the other side to that one.

He filled the awkward moment. *"So, Princess, I see you are wearing your necklace."*

She reached up to touch the stone, *"It reminds me of her. I can feel the power in it, too."*

He replied, *"Good! We can always use more power."*

"Yes," Nadya abruptly changed the subject and replied in as grown-up of a voice as she could muster. *"I'm not a baby anymore."*

He smiled. *"No, you are not. And you've become quite the berry-picker. We will have jam on our bread this winter thanks to you."*

"I'm fast."

Tamás agreed, *"Yes, you are, indeed."*

Nadya continued, *"And Tsura says my sewing is good, too,"* she added. *"She's giving me more mending to do. That's why I don't have time for adventures."*

"Ah," Tamás said, *"Well, something tells me you'll be good at anything you decide to do. Perhaps you'll make me a shirt someday?"*

She blurted, *"And you probably shouldn't call me 'Princess' anymore."* She hadn't planned to say it. She just wanted him to think she was grown up.

Tamás' heart and face fell. *"Really? Why?"*

"Because that was when I was a little ghel and we played pretend, and I am not little anymore."

"Oh."

She knew she had hurt him. She was deceiving the one person in the world who loved her unfailingly and whom she loved the same, but the plan demanded it. She couldn't think about his feelings right now. She would fix it all later, after she had done what she needed to do. Once it was over, he would understand, and then he would be proud of her for being so brave. She hoped.

Nadya had been paying attention to where the hands were on the church clock and was getting a better feel for what hours were and how to keep track of them. No one did that at camp. You got up just before the sun (the women, anyway), made the fire, started breakfast, carried water, did laundry, and made lunch. Then you gathered food, made supper, cleaned up, stoked the fire for the night, and finally, if you still had the energy, danced, and sang while the men drank and played their instruments. Then you went to bed, slept, and woke up to do it all over again the following morning. On market days, the schedule changed somewhat. It also changed when people got married or had babies or died. Gypsies didn't need a clock for any of it.

Nadya was a performer by nature and had figured out early on that there were advantages to keeping the adults happy. When she was polite and obedient, they trusted her and she could get away with more behind their backs. She enjoyed her position as the orphaned sweetheart of the tribe and thought it funny when they would credit themselves for her good behavior. Since the moment of her birth, the strength of Nadya's will had charted her life, and Tamás was the only one who knew the real ghel. That was why her present behavior seemed strange.

As gauged by the rumbling in Nadya's stomach, they reached the cave just before lunch. At the entrance, Tamás gave her an exaggerated wink and ceremoniously lit his newly acquired lantern. It burned spirits, and as the first man in camp to own one, he was quite proud of it.

The instant they stepped inside, Nadya knew something was wrong. *"Shhhh…"* she silenced Tamás before he could speak. *"Listen!"*

He lifted the lantern higher, and they saw it – an immense black mass hunched at the rear wall. It saw them too, and slowly stood up, its yellow eyes murderous in the reflected light of the lantern and its lips peeled back revealing glistening fangs the size of daggers. It let out a guttural growl followed by a vicious snarl, and sprang toward them, covering the distance in one impossible leap.

Nadya screamed and Tamás swung his lantern hard, hitting the beast in the face. The alcohol burst into flames setting its hide on fire, and with an otherworldly shriek, it bolted blindly out of the cave.

The spilled fuel had soaked Tamás' shirt and his sleeve was ablaze. Nadya frantically tore the shawl from her shoulders and smothered the flames, but he had already been badly burned.

Tamás grabbed her. *"Are you alright?!"*

"Yes, just scared is all. But Tamás, your arm!" She exclaimed.

"Candles…did you bring any?" he coughed.

"Yes!" she rummaged in a pocket and shakily pulled out two stubs.

He hastily lit one for each of them and looked at her closely. *"Are you sure you aren't hurt?"*

*"No, but **you** are!"*

"Thanks to O Del, we're both alive."

*"What **was** that thing, Tamás?"*

"Nothing I've ever seen before."

"What should we do now?"

"It's out there someplace nursing its wounds. We're going straight back to camp. And to think you've been out here berry-picking on your own. I must have been dinilo!"

When Tamás meant a thing, he meant it. Nadya knew better than to argue, but even while she worried about his injuries and even before she stopped shaking, she was already trying to figure out how she was going to deal with this latest obstacle to retrieving the book.

Clearly, her plan would have to change. Unless the beast died – and she doubted it was hurt that badly – it would return to its lair. Tamás had not noticed the wads of blood-soaked fleece and the half-eaten sheep's carcass lying in the shadows, and she was not about to point them out.

*B*ack at camp, Tsura responded with alarm to her son's burns and tended to them with her usual drama, efficiency, and admonishments. When she asked how the accident had happened, he peddled the story that he had mishandled his new lantern. His eyes met Nadya's over the lie and she made the appropriate gestures and sounds.

After Tsura finished bandaging Tamás' arm, he donned a clean shirt and the three of them ate dinner in silence. Neither Tamás nor Nadya wished to make up any more tales and they were both lost in their own thoughts. After the meal, Nadya helped Tsura clean up while Tamás smoked and drank enough wine to numb his pain.

"I'm very tired," Nadya announced. *"May I go to bed early?"*

"Of course, chavi," Tsura replied, *"I am feeling the same. Tamás, my son, with those burns, you should rest, too."*

The brooding young man did not answer.

Nadya went to him, gently touched his bandaged arm and looked into his eyes. *"May O Del heal you,"* she said, and she meant it with all her heart. A few more nights and the moon would be full.

Chapter Seventeen
~ The Song ~

"Balval was within her now,
and she was no longer afraid of anything."

𝒩adya tossed and turned fretfully upon her bed. Her mind churned with questions.

"Oh, my Dai! What should I do? There's a monster in the cave and I'm scared to go back! My plan was working so well – I thought you were guiding me! How will I ever get your book now?"

Finally, when no answers came, she forced her eyes closed, curled into a ball like the little caterpillar in the forest, and prayed desperately that a kind hand would reach down, pick her up, and keep her safe through the night.

𝐼t was dark in the dream, and Nadya was walking away from camp. A cool mist clung to her skin, and little puffs of steam escaped from her lips. She could feel the dust between her toes and thought it odd that even though she was barefoot, the sharp pebbles on the pathway did not hurt her feet.

She looked over her shoulder to see slow-moving silhouettes passing in front of dying campfires and had the feeling that no one knew or cared that she was gone. Had she ever existed there at all? Was she a spirit? One of those who roamed in the night? Had she ever been anything more?

She found herself walking faster and faster until suddenly, she remembered that she could step up into the air. As her feet left the ground, she wondered how she could have forgotten such an amazing fact. It had to be that all the troubles of this world weigh you down and keep you from rising until you leave them behind.

Nadya floated upward until she reached the tops of the trees. She loved traveling this way but knew it was dependent upon belief, and that a single doubt would cause her to be earthbound once more. The freedom to fly was about relinquishing all other thoughts to the contrary and accepting that the ability was within you.

The path that led to the cave lay below her, but she felt no fear, for even if the beast had returned, it could not see or harm her in the sky. She felt drawn to a valley beyond, where a lake mirrored the night sky. When she arrived, she touched down near a large weeping willow tree at the water's edge. At first, she could not see anyone beneath the canopy and thought it was the tree that greeted her, for that would have seemed quite natural in such a dream.

"Good evening, Nadya. I've been waiting for you. Come sit with me. Isn't the lake lovely in the moonlight?"

Nadya parted the curtain of branches to see a beautiful woman with long black hair. Iridescent dragonflies formed a living crown upon her head, and her dress was made of shimmering silver fabric that draped as gracefully over her body as the arms of the willow did over the water. It was she who had spoken, not the tree – or perhaps they were one and the same in this place.

The ghel knew instantly who she was.

"Dai!" Renata held out her arms and Nadya ran into them.

"Yes, my precious chavi, but we are more than mother and daughter here in this place. Shall I explain?" Releasing Nadya from the embrace, she gestured for them to sit.

"When it was offered, I came to Earth because I was needed. You followed for the same reason. We all come with a purpose and remain connected to the One who sends us. Even though you may sometimes feel alone, that's an illusion. We are all parts of the Creator and thus, part of one another. It has always been so and always shall be.

"In Charos, our true home, we dwell together in peace because we know and are known. There are no strangers there, nor sadness or even an impure thought, for O Del's love fills everyone."

The picture that formed in Nadya's mind brought a smile to her heart, but questions leapt to mind.

Renata knew what they were and answered. *"For reasons not fully understood by anyone but O Del, once a soul makes the journey here, a veil falls, and many forget who they are. They do not remember where they came from, or why, so they set out on their own and some become lost along the way. They go places they shouldn't go and do things they shouldn't do. They play the parts expected of them, and after a while, they become so empty and weary that they give up and stop searching for the meaning in any of it.*

"Others sense that they belong somewhere else. From the time they are small, they feel like strangers on Earth. They do not stay in any one place for long and must travel many different roads until they find their purpose.

"In dreams like this, we are free from the limitations of human bodies. You have already re-discovered a small part of the power you possess. You can move through the air because your soul has always been able to do so. And now that you have seen me here, you will never have to wonder about me again. I learned much on Earth and did what my soul came to do. After your birth, I no longer needed a human body and returned to my true form. I am alive forever, as you shall be, and we will be together evermore in Charos."

Nadya reached for Renata's hands. They were not rough like a Gypsy's, but soft as rose petals, steady and strong. The love that flowed through them was unlike anything she had ever felt.

"I've brought you a gift," Renata smiled. *"We possess many from the beginning, but others we must ask for. O Del wants to know that we desire them. You would be surprised at how many go unopened. I have always wanted all of them, and I'm sure you do too, but not everyone is ready."*

Nadya was mystified. *"Why?"*

"Only those who decline them can answer that. When you remembered that you could travel in the sky you didn't see many others there, did you?"

"No. Only a few. But it's so wonderful, why wouldn't everyone want to?"

"Because they cannot see beyond the veil." Renata answered. *"It takes the form of a thick black curtain, and Beng, the enemy of all souls,*

deceives them into thinking they can never get past it. The light they so desperately need reaches them only through tiny pinholes, like stars in the night sky.

"But know this, my chavi: things are changing! With each brave heart that pierces the darkness, more light streams through, and one day the veil will disintegrate and there will be nothing but Light on the Earth as it is in Charos. That, dear one, is the reason we come."

"There are some here who like the dark." Nadya said sadly.

"Yes, there are. Beng has children, too. They do not reason as we do. But O Del did not send us without a way to fight what the darkness holds. His gifts are also weapons, and it is one of these that I am to offer you now. Do you want it?"

"Oh, yes!" Nadya exclaimed.

Renata smiled. *"Then close your eyes and open your heart."*

Her voice was a melody, and the words were a song. Nadya did not know the language, but as the sounds filled the air between them, she found them upon her own lips. As each syllable formed, others poured out behind it, like an inner spring. A song of Charos was pouring through her, and she could feel its power.

~

𝒩adya awoke mid-song to the faraway howl of a wolf. Moonbeams streamed through the patchwork curtain of lace scraps at the window of her vardo and cast dappled shadows across the bed. She could still taste the sweet sounds in her mouth and knew the song had changed her. Balval was within her now, and she was no longer afraid of anything.

~

𝒯he gleaming harvest moon did not disappoint its young crusader the following night. Nadya had been singing her song and though she remembered how wonderful it felt to float up off the ground, she had not been able to repeat the experience thus far. She was also upset with

84

herself for waking from the dream before she could ask her Dai about the contents of the box, particularly the book.

As fortune would have it, the caravan was celebrating a betrothal that night. Nadya feigned tiredness and encouraged Tsura and Tamás to attend the festivities without her. By the time they returned, her light would be out and they would think she was asleep.

Nadya cracked her vardo door and listened to their voices fade away. She was dressed warmly, there was a fresh candle in her lamp, and several extras in the posotis of her skirt.

She took the same path as in her dream but her hopes were dashed when her repeated attempts to rise from the ground failed. Perhaps being barefoot was a prerequisite to walking on air. After removing her shoes and knotting the laces together, she slung them over her shoulder and set out confidently again. Regrettably, a sharp stone immediately introduced itself to her big toe and while she was hopping around in pain, her other foot landed on a thorny stick. The next thing she knew she was on the ground, rocking back and forth rubbing her wounds and muttering words she'd been told never to use. The finer points of lift would have to be explored some other time. Right now, she had to put her shoes back on and go do the bravest thing she had ever done.

posotis *(poe-SO-tis)* – hidden pocket

Chapter Eighteen
~ The Vision ~

"'Courage,' said the angel, is not something you muster up.
It's remembering the power of your God."

SGR

*I*gnoring the injuries to her feet, Nadya sang her song softly all the way to the cave and felt no fear whatsoever. Not when she heard a noise in the bushes, or when an owl swooped down to get a close look at her, or even when she heard sounds that might otherwise have sent shivers up her spine. At those times, the song became fierce and strong.

Thusly fortified, she was gravely disheartened when at the very moment she reached her destination, the melody ceased. As hard as she tried to call up the notes, they were gone, and now when she needed them most, she did not have them. Like thunderstorms that roll in to pour rain upon the dry ground and then just as quickly end, the song seemed to have a mind of its own. Perhaps it had done its job, then. But it was much more encouraging when she could hear it out loud.

She shook off a shiver and remembered that her Dai was there with her. Then, she lit her lamp and stepped into the cave. It was silent, and though the smell of death still hung in the air, she did not sense the presence of the beast. On the wall to her left, the sheep's carcass had been finished off and only a few scattered bones were left to mark the spot. The monster was no doubt out hunting more defenseless prey. She would have to hurry before it returned.

Nadya scooted through the tunnel and into the cavern faster than ever before. She was relieved to see her mother's box undisturbed in its hiding place, and quickly removed the book. Having sewn another posotis into the gathers of her skirt for this very undertaking, she was dismayed to find that she'd made it too small. Her error would make everything more difficult, as she would have to carry things in both hands now. She hurriedly wrapped the book in her scarf and hastened back through the maze of spires. Part way down the tunnel she was met by the stench of wet fur and fresh blood. A dragging sound and nightmarish noises told her the creature had returned.

But so had the song! The words were a battle cry and she sang them silently. She extinguished her lamp and crouched in the blackness. Where was the monster? Would it smell her presence and come crawling down the passageway? How bad did it hurt to be eaten alive? And if she weren't its next meal, how long would she be trapped here before it left the cave again?

As the long moments passed, she thought about those she loved, pictured their faces, and imagined what would happen if she were never to return. Tamás could not lose her. He could *not*. She had to live for him. And Tsura, who had raised her, would mourn all the days of her life and blame herself until death alone brought peace. And what about her beautiful Dai? Would Nadya be joining her in Charos soon?

Then, the faces faded and in their place was a reflection of herself. Not as a young Gypsy ghel cowering in a cave, but as a warrior dressed in armor with a sword and shield.

Empowered by the vision, Nadya waited until it had been quiet for a while, re-lit her lamp and moved soundlessly ahead. A fresh kill lay partially blocking the way out – a young stag, its soft brown eyes glazed over in death. Her heart broke for the dear thing. How fast must the monster be to outrun the swiftest animal in the meadows?

If it was waiting in the shadows, it would have pounced on her by now, wouldn't it? Keeping her back to the wall, she skirted the mangled deer and inched forward. Was she just imagining the black mass at the far end of the room where it had been lurking when she and Tamás first encountered it? She strained her eyes and ears. Hearing what sounded like labored breathing, she cautiously lifted her lamp and saw the hideously deformed mound of matted fur rising and falling in sleep. It had exhausted itself in the hunt.

Recalling how it felt to fly, Nadya made it outside in seconds, and once there, ran as fast as her heart and feet would take her until she reached the gates of Mirno.

She was never to know that later that night, when a blood red shadow crept over the moon, another soul would enter the cavern through a secret passage that she and Tamás had never seen.

This soul had no fear of monsters, knew where Nadya had hidden the box, and had come for the dagger.

~

Stealing into the village turned out to be easier than Nadya had expected. Large lamps sat atop tall posts, and deep shadows pooled beneath them where she could hide from the eyes of anyone still on the streets. It didn't take long for her to reach the back of the church, where she ran up the steps, grabbed the door knocker and swung it down three times as hard as she could.

After a brief delay, during which she kept her eyes fixed on the door and not on the cemetery behind her, Brother Caesaré answered. Nadya's flushed cheeks made him suspect something was wrong and he immediately put his huge, bell-ringing hand upon her shoulder and pulled her inside.

"Come in child. You're shaking! I've been wondering what become of you. Saints! Have you run all the way here? Are you alright?"

While everything within her desired the sympathy of the big round man in the scratchy brown robe, Nadya wanted a lecture even less, so she lied.

"I had a hard time getting away and I didn't want you to think I wasn't coming, and it was taking me too long to get here, so I ran." She said it all in one breath and gasped for air at the end.

"Well, I'm glad you made it." He stuck his head outside, looked around furtively, shut the door and pointed down a long, dim hallway. *"This way. Hurry along."*

Flickering lanterns studded the walls and it was as cold inside as out. Nadya had expected O Del's house to be warmer. Brother Caesaré moved fast for his size, and she trotted behind, taking careful note of her surroundings, as all Gypsy children were taught to do should they ever need to make a speedy exit. When the friar bolted the door to his chamber behind them, that opportunity was lost.

Nadya surveyed the room. Stone walls, same as the corridor. Worn wood floor, cracked planks cleanly swept and waxed. (The picture that sprung into Nadya's mind of fat Brother Caesaré on his hands and knees vigorously scrubbing and polishing, necessitated the stifling of a giggle.) Far above her head bundles of dried herbs and other plants hung from exposed timbers, and a tall ladder leaned against a nearby wall to reach them. Pottery dishes, bowls and tankards, racks of glass vials, and corked bottles of assorted brews marched across open shelves. A work bench held various tools and an impressive assortment of knives hung at the ready above a large, stained butcher's block.

The friar's neatly made bed stood against one wall. With its ornately carved head and footboards, it was the most impressive piece of furniture in the room. Beside it stood a tall wardrobe in which Nadya imagined more brown robes must hang and maybe a nightgown. Two rough-hewn chairs sat in front of the fireplace, along with a small table where a loaf of bread flanked by crocks of butter and honey waited. A mug filled to the brim with creamy milk sat on the stone hearth close to the warmth of the flames.

The intermingled smells of stone and cedar, herbs and spices, along with freshly baked bread, was soothing and reminded the ghel of some other place in some other time where she had been safe and happy, but she couldn't remember where or when that had been.

"Are you hungry?" Brother Caesaré pulled out one of the chairs for her.

"Yes. May I sit there?" She pointed to the hearth.

"Of course, child." He tossed another log on the fire. *"Put your things here on the table. Is that the book?"* he nodded toward the bundle in her hand.

"Yes." Ignoring his instructions, she climbed up on the hearthstone and set the book and the lamp down beside her. Then, she reached for the mug.

He raised an eyebrow and asked, *"Butter and honey on your bread then?"*

"Oh, yes, please!" Nadya replied, pulling up her knees and cupping the steaming mug between her palms.

Brother Caesaré swabbed a thick slice of bread with generous amounts of both and handed it to her along with a cloth napkin which she looked at curiously.

Struck again by the girl's fierce independence, he studied her for a moment, then walked across the room, took a bottle of wine down from a shelf, poured himself a healthy measure and sat down in the chair closest to her.

Nadya could not remember when such ordinary food had tasted so good, but her enjoyment was overshadowed by sadness, for the picture of the poor stag's dead eyes refused to leave her mind.

The warm milk soon took effect and Nadya relaxed completely. She did not allow herself to think about the trip home, and instead entertained the fantasy that the bed across the room was hers and that she lived in the safety of O Del's house, and would grow up there, cleaning and cooking to earn her keep and being taught how to read and write by Brother Caesaré.

Her eyelids became increasingly heavy, and just as her head dropped to her chest, the friar's voice cut through the drowsy daydream.

"Child? Do you need to lie down?"

"No!" She snapped to attention. *"I mean, no thank you, I am fine. I'm just a little tired from running so far. I can show you the book now if you like."*

"Please do," he answered.

She unwrapped it and put it in his outstretched hands.

"Saints," he said softly, as he gingerly opened the cover. A feeling that Nadya could not identify filled the room and the air became as thick as the honey in the crock.

"Your mother gave you this book, you say?"

"Yes. She left it for me."

"Well, my child, this book is a great deal older than your mother. It is very, very old. And you know nothing more about it?"

"No." Nadya replied. *"Nothing. Can you read it?"*

The friar stroked his long beard and paused at length while he turned each page. Nadya didn't move. She did not want to rush him and had no idea what to expect. Finally, she could not restrain herself.

"Brother Caesaré?"

He looked up as though he'd forgotten she was there, and quickly wiped tears from his eyes before they could spill over.

"Saints..." He said it like a prayer and continued to pour over the pages in silence.

Nadya pressed, *"Will you tell me what it says?"*

"This book should be in the safe keeping of the Church. To think the Almighty would trust it to a Gypsy..." He shook his head incredulously, crossed himself, and mumbled something she couldn't quite hear.

Nadya was becoming impatient. *"What is it about?"*

"I cannot really explain it, child. Perhaps you could leave it with me and come back another night and we can talk more about it then."

"No! It's my job to protect it. I cannot leave it here." Nadya slid off the hearth and stood tall as the soldier she now knew she was.

The friar's tone turned authoritative. *"I really don't think you'll understand it. It's...it's written for..."* and his voice trailed off as he continued to read.

She did not believe him. *"But I might! I don't have much time though. I can only come see you when the moon is full, and winter will be here soon. There is talk that our caravan may move..."*

"Then please consider leaving it with me for safe keeping!" The friar's failure to hide the desperation in his voice put Nadya on alert.

"I cannot do that. My Dai would not approve."

"Your Dai is not here to be displeased, is she? Didn't you tell me she died?"

"She is not dead!" Nadya exclaimed defensively. *"Not really. Her body died but she didn't. I talk to her and she tells me secrets and gives me gifts."*

The friar's eyebrows arched. *"Secrets and gifts?"*

Nadya knew she'd said too much. This was going downhill.

"I am sorry, Brother Caesaré. *You have been so kind to me, but it is getting quite late, and if my family discovers I'm gone..."* She left the rest to his imagination. *"If I can manage it, may I bring the book back again? And you can tell me more about it then?"*

The friar did not smile. He couldn't let the book be lost to this ragged child and her tribe of vagabonds and decided his best move would be to remain helpful.

"I would be honored. I will look forward to our next visit when we can spend more time. I hope it will be soon. May I at least transcribe a few words from the book while you are here now?"

This seemed reasonable, so Nadya asked for more milk and munched her sticky bread crusts while Brother Caesaré wrote feverishly on parchment for as long as she could grant. Then she wiped her fingers on her skirt, pried the book gently out of his hands, wrapped it back up in her scarf and bid him goodnight. The friar maintained his composure, escorted her out the back, and grumbled fretfully all the way back to his quarters.

O Del answered the child's prayers, and other than a sighting of several unusually bright lights which twinkled in different colors low in the sky, the trip back to camp was uneventful. Even though she hadn't learned much about the book, she'd been able to successfully meet with Brother Caesaré, and would be able to do so again. Back at camp, she slipped into her vardo, snuggled down under her quilt, and fell asleep holding the stone, which had proven its worth again. In her dreams, the murdered stag came back to life and was now white as snow with silver antlers. She was riding on his back and they were flying through the sky as fast as the wind.

~

The friar did not sleep a wink that night nor several others after it. Not even strong doses of his potions helped. When Father Vincent asked if something was bothering him, he said it was only that he'd been up late studying. It was not a lie. He'd re-read what he had written down from the book countless times. Supernatural forces had been set in motion and it was all beyond the bell ringer's comprehension.

Brother Caesaré's brown, bone-weary world had changed. He knew things, now, that would not leave his head. Nothing was what he had previously believed it to be, and he was deeply confused.

To add to the friar's internal battle, the fact that he was keeping a secret from Father Vincent burrowed into his flesh like a thorn. His religion demanded he confess his sin of omission, and if the Gypsy girl returned – which he alternately prayed for and feared – he would have to alert the priest. Father Vincent's powers of persuasion would be far more effective than his own. He cringed at what that would mean for the child but duty to the Church overrode any notions to the contrary.

☾
Chapter Nineteen
~ *The Priest* ~

"Master, there are tares in your field. Shall we pull them up?"
"No, for you might damage the wheat in the process.
Wait until the harvest. They'll be separated then, bundled, and burned."
The Parable of the Wheat and the Tares

𝄐ather Vincent was exactly the sort of individual whom one would expect to pursue the priesthood. Born into an influential Italian family, he served as an altar boy and attended seminary, after which he was assigned to a Slovenian diocese. Mirno was his second post. He did not speak of the first and changed the subject when asked. Brother Caesaré knew nothing about the subject other than that the priest's tenure had been brief and his departure abrupt.

Luciano Cristoforo Abella – re-named Father Vincent by the church – was destined to wear the robes. His well-to-do parents wanted to boast that one of their sons was a priest, and he, the middle child, was the best prospect. Their firstborn was strong-willed, and the youngest, frivolous, while Luci was sensitive, intelligent, and quiet. But still waters run deep, and there was much they did not care to know about the restless currents beneath their boy's seemingly placid exterior.

Luci had always known he was different. Something was coiled tightly inside his mind, and relentlessly sought to unwind and strike. He suffered debilitating headaches for which no cause could be found, and although he did not know it to be unusual at first, he was often able to perceive what others were thinking. When this happened, he could also feel their emotions. While the exercise of this gift wrought insight beyond his years, the weight of it imposed more pain than a child's soul would ordinarily have had to bear. He loved deeply, suffered by the same measure and learned not to talk about either one. Should he dip his toe in those waters, the responses were predictable. The other children would laugh and mock him. His Madre would kiss him and

Luciano Cristoforo Abella *(loochee-AHNO Christo FORO ah-BELLah)*
Luci *((LOO-chee)*

remind him that he was special and chosen by God, and his Padre would tell him men had to be masters of their emotions and inclinations.

He did not want to be special or different. He did not want to come from a rich family, nor did he want to be a slave to God. He wanted to be playing stick ball with the boys in the alley and running wild with no worries or prognostications on his mind.

Knowledge was the key to power. He figured that out soon after his parents handed him over to the Church. The gaining of it did not merely mean applying himself to his studies but watching for and listening to things others missed – the seemingly unimportant and often obscure little details that led to an understanding of what lived in the shadows.

In addition to his keen intuition, Luci learned to read facial expressions, body language and nuances in voice – clues that eventually led to the acquisition of information he would never have possessed otherwise. These skills aided him in many ways, and the sharper they became, the easier it was to surpass his peers.

He made no one aware of his perceptions, which gave him a feeling of superiority. All of this is not to say that he wasn't still a sympathetic young man, for he made a great effort to be so. But had his own desires ever been considered, he would never have chosen a life sentence of self-sacrifice, rigid conformity, piety, and uncomplaining service. There was greater freedom at the top.

Luci's prayers were those he had been taught. The words afforded no comfort, and no one heard or answered. He was alternately amused by and jealous of the peasants who poured their hearts out to him in confession. They left convinced of absolution, while he knew full well that the Almighty had never granted him such power. He despised serving the downtrodden. It should have been the other way around.

Meanwhile, his cool, polished manner kept his congregation respectful, and his chiseled features, jet black hair, fair skin and astonishingly blue eyes effectively distracted his audience from true worship. Luci was no stranger to temptation, and while piously pretending not to notice the unholy desire in a parishioner's eyes, the priest later had them discretely brought to his quarters where he indulged his own dark desires.

It was not a human presence that shadowed Luciano and whispered in his ear. It was an always-reasonable disembodied voice that he could rely upon when his heart confused him. It assured him that he had a higher purpose among the sheep and that he was not one of them. It promised that if he proved himself worthy, he would be exalted. It said that the incident at his first post in Maribor had been an unfortunate slip and if he learned from it and was not caught again, he would go unpunished. Until then, his penance was to feign holiness in Mirno – the last place on earth he wanted to be or intended to remain.

Luci's sights were set on Rome.

Chapter Twenty
~ Tsura ~

"Free will. We'd be spared so much pain and regret without it."
SGR

Tsura's mood was dark. Some days were just like that, and if you asked her what was wrong – which was a bad idea unless you were prepared to listen – she would be more than happy to tell you. No one understood or appreciated her. In fact, they seemed to go out of their way not to show her any love or respect. She could only assume that this was because she spoke her mind. People didn't like to hear the truth. Those who just went along with everything and never stated an opinion – *they* were loved. She, who only wanted what was best for everyone and who would serve them 'til her dying day, was taken for granted.

She'd been beautiful once. The best dancer in the troupe. All the men had desired her, and her jealous husband was secretly proud of it. But youth had fled, her man was dead, and the ache in her bones never left. She went to sleep every night wondering if she would awaken the next day, and not caring if she didn't or did.

Topping her list of problems was Tamás, her darling son. He had never been like the other chavs, which she blamed on the loss of his twin at birth and his father the following season. He was melancholy by nature – a dreamer born with a faraway look in his eyes – and although she knew he harbored many secrets, he never shared them with her.

When Renata died in childbirth, Tsura feared he would never be the same – that grief had broken his mind. He withdrew completely and did not speak to anyone for a long time. Her comforting words fell upon deaf ears and she ached for him to be little again so that she could hold him in her arms and love away his sorrow. Instead, she watched helplessly as he wove a cocoon around his pain. If she knew anything about her son at all, it was that he would not let go of those he loved. They were hidden safely in his heart where he could keep them from harm. There, they never died.

Nadya gave his life meaning and Tsura supposed that was good, but it was hard to imagine how he could give a wife the same attention, and it was past time for that to happen. He was handsome, and an accomplished musician and metal worker – a prize of a husband for any ghel in the caravan. Their mothers were growing impatient, and some had given up and promised their daughters to other men. Tsura had been making excuses, but the truth was that she was afraid of Tamás' reaction should she make a match. She'd brought it up before and the fire in his eyes had been enough to silence her. Then, he'd taken Baro, ridden away into the night and hadn't returned until late the next day. If it weren't for Nadya, he might not have come back at all. When he returned, he did not speak to his mother for several more days. She had begged his uncle to talk some sense into him, but Coz hadn't reported back on the matter, and she could only nag just so much.

Oh, to have been born a man! They had all the power and they knew it. A Gypsy woman's lot was to wash, cook, clean, bear the children and serve her Rom's needs for as long as he lived. Gypsy men often died young, and it was even worse for their widows after that. Tsura was fortunate to have a son who could add a daughter-in-law to their family. She was tired and needed the help.

Nadya could not remain under her wing much longer and matching her to a future husband was second on Tsura's list of obligations. When the ghel was a couple years older, she would marry the man to whom she'd been promised, move in with her new family, and work alongside her mother-in-law.

Whether Tamás and Nadya liked it or not, they had no say in such matters. Tradition could not be avoided forever.

Kizzy would make Tamás a good wife. She'd been raised well, was capable, and pretty enough to guarantee beautiful children. The ghel's mother had been dropping hints for quite some time, and Tsura had noticed Kizzy's shy glances at her son. Whether he'd picked up on them or not was hard to say. Plump, healthy, rosy-cheeked Kizzy was thirteen and already of marrying age. Tamás was a brooding, twenty-seven-year-old who needed to have someone other than his mother take care of him. It was the sensible thing. After the marriage, Kizzy would be Tsura's bori and she would live and work with them all her days.

Rom *(r-AHM)* — Gypsy man, husband
Bori *(BOOR-ee)* – Daughter-in-Law

100

Before she could second-guess herself, Tsura went to Kizzy's family. They were delighted and accepted her proposal on the spot. She tried to tell herself that her son would receive the news without flying into a rage and that he would agree that it was time, but the knot in her belly argued that would not be the case.

With Tamás' future decided, the next order of business was Nadya's betrothal. It all fell upon Tsura's shoulders. And would she receive any gratitude? *"Ha,"* she laughed bitterly to herself. *"Never."*

She was almost home when it occurred to her that if she was going to endure Tamás' wrath anyway, she might as well take care of both issues at one time.

Turning on her heel, she marched to Florica's vardo, where she found her friend bent over the fire preparing the evening meal. Although Florica had approached Tsura about a match between Nadya and her son on a previous occasion, Tsura's unexpected visit took the woman by surprise. Knowing the decision had not been an easy one for Tsura, Florica enthusiastically agreed, the two embraced, and the matter was decided.

It was done, then. Nadya would marry Cappi, Florica's oldest son, on her fourteenth birthday. He would be thirty by then. Florica assured Tsura that they would offer a fine dowry for the chavi, and that planning for the betrothal celebration would begin immediately. Afterall, Nadya was gifted, and when she joined their family, they would benefit greatly from her talents.

The Roma all had to live by the same laws, and Tsura had no authority to grant exceptions. Her business finished, she hurried home to make Tamás' favorite stew and a honey cake with meadowsweet herbs for Nadya. All the way, she prayed to O Del and Balval that her children would not hate her.

$\mathcal{D}$ear, long-suffering Tsura had no idea how dearly loved she was by O Del, that He knew her heart in ways no one ever could, and that she was His instrument more often than not. She also struggled to grasp that His plans would always be better than hers, and that the fates would have their way whether she meddled or not.

Chapter Twenty One
~ Blue Moon ~

"Three things cannot long be hidden...the sun, the moon, and the truth."
Buddha

Tsura had been huddled by the campfire all night, and when Nadya found her there at daybreak, her adoptive mother's eyes were red and swollen from crying.

"Dai Tsura?" She asked tentatively, *"What's wrong?"*

Tsura just pulled her shawl closer, looked at the ground, sniffled and poked one of the logs fiercely.

Knowing better than to pry, Nadya patted her back and kissed her on the cheek.

"I will go start my chores."

Tsura just nodded miserably.

Baro was gone from his tether behind the wagons. Nadya wondered only briefly about this, for Tamás often traveled far out into the countryside to look for work. Payment came in the form of meat, cheese, vegetables, or whatever homesteaders had to barter.

One day, when Nadya was little, Tamás had come home with the gelding and given Nadya the honor of naming him. In awe of the powerful animal, she'd answered *'Baro!'* meaning 'big.' He was magnificent – a jet black Friesian with a long, flowing mane and tail that almost reached the ground.

Baro soon became the caravan's star attraction and every head turned when he pranced into a village with Tamás astride. His size, strength and speed were matched only by his devotion to his young mistress, with whom he exercised great patience, particularly when she braided wildflowers into his hair.

After a while, Tsura rose and went about her duties, but she did not speak a word until she called Nadya to dinner by the fire. Tamás hadn't returned, so the two of them ate in silence. Nadya caught Tsura looking at her a couple of times as though she was going to say something but couldn't.

On any other night, the ghel would have tried harder to find out what was wrong, but not this one. She'd overheard someone say that the caravan might be moving again, and if so, this would be her last chance to get answers about the book. For lack of knowing what else to say, she lovingly kissed Tsura on the cheek, and said, *"I hope you feel better tomorrow."*

Tsura sighed, took a long drag on her pipe followed by a swig of wine, and waved her off. Thankful to be relieved of duty, Nadya retired to her vardo and left the door open a crack so that she could keep an eye on the unhappy woman's whereabouts.

𝒯he girl was disappointed to have found out so little about her mother's book thus far. It was stashed under her mattress and she took it out often, but staring at the writing did not help her decipher the words, and from the way Brother Caesaré had reacted, they were important. Not long after her last trip to see him, she'd overheard one of the grandmothers say that magic would soon be in the air because two full moons were happening close together. Nadya had taken it to be a sign. Since the previous moon hadn't delivered the luck she needed, surely this next one would – and it had arrived.

As soon as Tsura's vardo went dark, Nadya slipped out her door only to be greeted by one of the caravan's dogs begging at the bottom of the steps. She had nothing to give him, nor time to return him to his family, so in hopes he would lose interest further on, she set off toward the forest with him trotting behind. Once outside camp, she threw a stick as hard as she could back in that direction, but he thought she was playing a game, retrieved it, and dropped it at her feet. While she was thankful for his company, she didn't know what she would do if he followed her all the way to the village.

The old woman had been right. The night was heavy with magic. Heaps of shape-shifting clouds in shades of ochre and grey sailed through an indigo sea in a game of hide-and-seek with a giant pearl. It

jook *(jOOK)* – dog

was the brightest moon Nadya had ever seen, and when its shining face peeked out at her now and then, she could see all the way up to Charos.

She had always known there was another world above, with its own mountains, valleys, shimmering waters, cresting waves, and waiting shores. It was even more beautiful than the world to which she was bound. She'd glimpsed it many times and supposed it to be a land of great riches because she'd been finding gemstones that had fallen off its edge since she was little. Were this any other night, she would have wrapped up in blankets, laid by the fire and watched the changing celestial show until stardust put her to sleep.

The Wildwoods did not sleep at night and Nadya knew it. She shouldn't be there, and had her determination not outweighed her common sense, she would have been at home, safe and warm in her vardo, surrounded by her tribe, where no harm could befall her.

Fear kept step behind you in the forest, whispering, crawling down the back of your neck, telling you to turn back. She fixed her thoughts on her destination, walked briskly, and sang her song. For all its otherworldly beauty, this trip felt different than the first one, and not in a good way.

The woodlands were a feast of smells for the fearless little jook. Head to the ground, he ran recklessly in front of her, zigzagging back and forth, stopping only to stuff his nose into a clump of moss or a rotting log and lift his leg to mark the spot. She was worried about what she would do if he didn't go home soon and told him sternly to do so. He paid no attention and a second later, his ears perked up, he barked, and ran full speed around the bend ahead. Next, she heard limbs snapping, and a surprised, painful yelp followed by deadly silence. She stopped in her tracks and stood as still as a statue for several moments. Then, she lifted her lamp high and took a cautious step forward.

"Jook?" She called out softly, praying that the smelly, annoying mutt would come running out of the bushes.

Nothing.

"Jook?" she took another step and called louder this time. There was a rustle and what she imagined to be the shadow of something or someone crossing the path ahead. What now? She was in the middle of the forest with only two choices – to keep going or turn and run.

*"**Courage**."* The inner voice was firm.

She straightened her shoulders and continued on through the forest, past the place where the jook had been taken, across the rushing creek, and through the grove of evergreen giants a hundred times her age and wiser by the same. Finally, the path opened onto the meadow where the road led to town.

Soggy tendrils of cold fog lay in Mirno's deserted alleyways and courtyard. A few windows glowed with candlelight, but not many. The only voices came from the tavern, and as Nadya slipped past, the bawdy laughter and the familiar smell of ale and tobacco were a comfort.

The cold was seeping into her bones and the warmth of Brother Caesaré's hearth dominated her thoughts.

She arrived at the back door of the cathedral and was about to knock when there was a whisper behind her in the cemetery. A chill shot up her spine. Should she pretend she hadn't heard it or turn around and face it? She chose the former and banged on the door loudly in the desperate hope that the friar would answer quickly. To her great relief, he did.

Concern overrode surprise when he saw the look on the girl's face, and he immediately brought her in.

"What is it, child?"

"I heard..." she started to blurt it out but thought better of it. *"I am sorry I wasn't able to tell you that I was coming."*

"You are welcome any time, my dear. Did you bring..."

"Yes, I have it." She patted her skirt.

"Good! Are you hungry? Thirsty? Let's warm you up. I have bread, cheese, and cider." He hastened down the hallway with Nadya following close behind. She was focused on reaching the fireplace and failed to take note of the fact that this time he left his chamber door wide open rather than closing and bolting it as before. She took her place on the hearth as close to the fire as she could get. A kettle of spiced cider hung over the flames and the smell was intoxicating.

When Brother Caesaré had plated the food, he poured her a cup of the steaming brew and sat down. The drink was strong and Nadya was unfamiliar with some of the spices, but it warmed her belly. She handed him her mother's book.

"Can you read it to me now?"

He nodded slowly and began.

She did not interrupt while Brother Caesaré's deep, thick voice droned on and on from within his beard, but as he'd predicted, she could not understand the words and he did not stop to explain them. Something in the cider had made her head fuzzy and she was having a hard time staying awake. She could not bear to think about the trip home. Everything within her wanted to stay.

Suddenly, the friar stopped reading and stood up. *"We're almost out of bread. I'll go fetch more from the kitchen. You'll be alright here alone until I get back?"* He said it like a question, but before she could reply, he left the room. It seemed to her that there was plenty of bread.

He was gone for much longer than Nadya would have expected and as the time passed, her uneasiness grew. When she finally heard footsteps, she was relieved, but Brother Caesaré was not alone.

They were at the door, and she felt trapped the way she had in the cave. She wanted to run, but it was too late, so she drew her knees up under her skirt, pressed her back against the fireplace, and tried to make herself as small as possible.

The friar was accompanied by a younger man in a black robe with a crisp white collar who she recognized as the reading man from the courtyard.

"Nadya, this is Father Vincent. I've told you about him."

The priest nodded his head in greeting. He was very handsome – clean shaven with teeth as white as his collar and beautiful eyes. She felt a little bit better.

"Hello, my child," the priest said, *"Brother Caesaré has told me about you."*

"And about the book," the friar nervously interjected, nodding toward the table.

The priest's eyes seized upon it hungrily.

Nadya's surprise and disapproval were written on her face.

"I know you wanted it to remain a secret, Nadya, but this is more important than just you and I," said Brother Caesaré firmly.

"Indeed so," soothed Father Vincent. *"We will keep it safe for you now."* He took a step toward the table.

"No! It is mine to protect!" Nadya argued. She had no intention of handing over the book, and before the priest could reach it, she leapt from the hearth, grabbed it, and held it behind her back.

Brother Caesaré looked shocked and Father Vincent's pretty eyes changed. A terrifying shriek shook the walls and an icy blast smothered, the fire. The friar fell to his knees, put his face on the floor and began crying out to his mother Mary for mercy.

The priest strode up to Nadya and grabbed her by the arm. His touch felt like burning coals and she screamed. He was not handsome anymore. Her pain seemed to delight him, and as he drank it in, his eyes grew darker and his grip tighter. He spied her necklace and laughed cruelly, *"Oh, my, I see you have a little rock to protect you. Shall we put it to the test?"* His face was within inches of hers and foul spittle was gathering at the corners of his grotesquely twisted mouth. His breath smelled like rotten meat and he snarled, *"Do you think I have time for the likes of you? Do you wish to live, you filthy little creature?"*

Nadya *did* wish to live, and Tamás had taught her how. She pulled back and kicked the priest hard where she knew it would hurt him most, then wrenched herself from his grasp and ran. He recovered quickly and was close behind as she flew down the hallway and out the back door of the church. For a brief second, she contemplated hiding in the cemetery, but considering the evil already at her heels, thought better of it and scrambled around the building toward the courtyard instead, all the time crying out over and over in her mind, *"Dai, help me!"*

Blind with fury and hindered by his robes, the priest was so intent upon capturing his prey that he never saw the old beggar woman step out of the mist. The dagger slid cleanly between his ribs, and with one deft, lethal twist, the job was done.

~

Only a few knew the nature of the knife. The good who had reason to wield it, and the evil who met its edge. It had been forged by a Gypsy craftsman for his daughter in an age when artists held the power to imbue their creations with magic. The handle had been carved from bone not of Earth, and the blade remained perpetually as sharp as a razor.

In the hands of O Del's chosen, it never missed its mark.

~

And so it was that Luciano Cristoforo Abella fell and died on the cathedral steps with a look of utter disbelief on his once-charming face. The waiting abyss claimed his unrepentant soul, and his executioner vanished into the mist.

Oblivious to what had taken place behind her, Nadya continued to run for her life, ducking in and out of shadows, hiding in doorways, and then speeding on through the village as though Beng himself were in pursuit. Not until she was through the gates and up the road did she dare to stop and look back.

The streetlamps were dim and the courtyard was deserted. For a fleeting moment she thought she'd made a clean escape, but then the cathedral bell began to ring. She could imagine Brother Caesaré's beefy hands pulling on the rope and knew he must be alerting the whole town to find her. She slipped her Dai's book back into her skirt pocket, kissed the stone around her neck, and told herself that the man in the moon had his eye on her and she'd soon be back in her vardo with her quilt over her head, safe and hidden from evil.

Had the ghel given heed to the raw intuition of her wildly beating heart, she'd have known better. She was indeed very brave, and could sometimes see and hear what others could not, but she was also headstrong and had yet to learn that sometimes – this time for certain – fear was a teacher.

Chapter Twenty Two
~ The Escape ~

"You cannot go straight when the road bends."
Gypsy Proverb

Ghostly wisps of fog floated over the fields like lost souls, and Nadya wondered if they were the Mulo. An owl hooted to alert her that the path to the Wildwoods was just ahead, but given her experience there earlier in the evening, she didn't know what to do.

Decisions had always been difficult for the ghel. She wished she weren't that way, but it never got easier. All options had to be carefully weighed, and pressure made it worse. Were you supposed to choose by what your heart said, or from experience, or by what you'd been told was wise? How? The answers were all mixed up and never the same!

Nadya had always lived with more than one voice in her head, and since she knew they were all parts of herself, she listened to them. But when two or more were talking at the same time, it was torturous.

"I don't know what to do!"

"Well, you need to figure it out fast."

"Which path should I take?"

"You could hide easier in the forest."

"But the poor little jook met his fate there, and whatever got him could still be hanging around."

"It could also be gone, though. I could make it through, right Dai? I survived in the cave with your help!"

"By the skin of your teeth. Why must you do these dangerous things, Nadya?"

"I have 'The Dook.'"

"Even so, you might not survive. You cannot die yet. You have a lot more to do. Recklessness is not a good trait."

"I wonder where the monster from the cave is?"

"Out hunting."

"No! Don't think about that! He's sleeping in the cave!"

"Probably not. Creatures like that hunt by night."

"**Think**, Nadya! You have to decide which way to go!"

"I'm deciding!"

"If I stay on this road, I'll have the moonlight."

"You'll also be easy to see and catch – especially if they come after you on horses!"

"I could hide in the grass."

"But look around. It isn't tall like it was in the summer, and they've cut down all the corn. There's nowhere to hide."

"You need to get going!"

"They'll be coming. They are not going to give up! You'd better keep an eye out behind you."

"I can't see anyone on the road."

"Wait! What is that red in the sky?"

"Fire?"

"The cathedral is on fire!"

"Oh, no! Those poor people!"

"They were not good people!"

"Still..."

"There's nothing you can do about it now. This road or the short cut? Which will it be?"

"The forest, I guess, but I'm still not sure."

"Are you forgetting that you don't have a lamp?"

"OH! NO, NO, NO! I left it behind!"

"Well, you'll never get through the Wildwoods without it."

"I left it sitting on the table in the friar's room! I liked that room – I wonder if it's all burned up now. That would be so sad..."

"And then you fought with the priest and your lamp got knocked over, and you ran."

"And now the cathedral is on fire..."

"Oh, dear! It's my fault!"

"It isn't your fault, it's theirs!"

"Which way, Nadya? You have to choose NOW!"

"The forest is too dark. It can only be this road."

Relieved that the decision had been made for her, Nadya trudged along beneath the moon and sang her song in a shaky voice, until finally her nerves settled down enough that she was able to think through everything that had just happened.

"Brother Caesaré betrayed me."

"I don't want to think of it, but he must have put something in the cider."

*"He **betrayed** me! How could he do that? I hate that fat old man!"*

"You should feel sorry for him, I think."

"Remember the beggar woman? She warned you but you didn't listen!"

"I didn't understand what she was talking about!"

"But she said she was there because of you!"

"I didn't know why!"

"Well, now you do."

𝒯he pathetic old friar. He'd never been who she thought he was. For all his apparent sturdiness and seemingly caring nature, he was a weak man who was easily controlled. The kind who didn't think for himself. A faithful slave to the rituals and authority of the church and to the priest whom he both venerated and feared. She'd rather think of it that way than to believe that under the surface, he'd always been just as wicked as the priest and that she simply hadn't wanted to see it because she'd been desperate for his help. His violation of her trust and his deceitful actions had almost gotten her killed.

She'd know in the future not to place her trust in such feeble-minded individuals.

And as for the priest, with his superiority and perfect looks – she knew about men like that, and the monsters that hid inside them and watched you from behind their masks. They pretended to be nice but turned horribly ugly and would hurt you if you did not do what they wanted. There used to be one like that in the caravan who often tried to get her alone, and who made her and the other ghels afraid. One day she noticed that he was gone and had asked Tamás about it.

"He's no longer part of us." He said. *"I've handled it."*

His face was rigid and looked very much like when he'd had to kill a rabid dog that had attacked a little chav. When he'd seen the sadness in Nadya's eyes, he'd simply said, *"It had to be done."*

The chav had survived but would wear the marks of the injuries for the rest of his life, and when you see your scars, you remember how you got them, which is a whole different kind of pain.

She hadn't known how important the book was, but the priest and the friar did, and would stop at nothing to get it. She was furious with both of them.

While still young to the world, Nadya had unlimited spiritual potential. She wore her heart on her sleeve, every leaf and flower were cause for sacred contemplation, personal introspection was endless, and the insights drawn up from the well of her soul were far beyond her years. While she generally subjected newly-hatched revelations to a gauntlet of practical tests, that was not necessary this time. A painful, new truth was staring her right in the face.

It announced, without emotion, that she had no right to be angry with anyone but herself.

The priest and the friar were bad men to be sure, but to blame them for her current situation was dishonest. They were merely tools of Beng. This mess was a result of her own bad decisions. She'd plotted and lied and taken every step herself. She hadn't asked O Del about her plan beforehand because she didn't want to hear *'No,'* or even *'Wait.'* She hadn't told Tamás for the same reason.

When an obstacle had arisen, she'd wiggled around it, and when things started to go bad, she'd persisted until they got worse. None of it would have happened if she had not been so stubborn and impatient. No one was free from the consequences of their choices, and this nightmare wasn't over. The priest wanted the book, and everyone in the village knew where the caravan was. He would send riders.

Nadya's legs were trembling from exhaustion and it was getting hard to pick up her feet. Then she heard the sounds. Animals, large and small, domestic and wild roamed the meadows. It could be anything. She peered out over the pasture hoping to spot the silhouette of a cow or a deer's antlers but saw neither.

The sounds grew louder. Something huge, panting heavily, charging through the field. She knew what it was and that she'd never be able to outrun it. To add to her terror, the thunder of horse's hooves arose from the dust behind her. She was caught between the two.

She desperately willed herself to fly. If the magic didn't work, she'd be dead.

The beast was upon her, its jaws open for the kill when her feet left the ground. Then, everything went black.

Nadya was only partly conscious during what followed, but she saw the fire in the horse's eyes and heard the skull-crushing strikes of its hooves, followed by the hideous shrieks of the beast.

When the monster fell silent, the horse reared up on its hind legs and delivered one final, deadly pounding. Then, it snorted with satisfaction and galloped on, sparing her the sight of the bloody, disfigured corpse that would lie alongside the road for days afterward, frightening and mystifying travelers until the scavengers ripped it apart and drug it away in pieces.

The rider uttered a command and the horse slowed to a familiar gait. Only then did Nadya realize who it was. Crying out in relief, she grabbed handfuls of Baro's mane, buried her face in his neck and sobbed. His master lifted her up, sat her in front of him, and put a protective arm around her waist.

Caught in her deceit, she was so filled with shame that she could barely say the words. *"Tamás, I'm so sorry."*

He did not respond and they rode back to the camp in silence. Once there, he dismounted, helped her down, walked to her vardo and began to ready it for travel.

"We're leaving tonight." He said. *"Now."*

"But why? Is it my fault?"

"Shhhh! We mustn't wake Tsura!"

"But where are we going?" Nadya asked anxiously.

"Wherever the road takes us. Do you trust me?"

"Yes! Always!"

"Then pack everything up. Quickly and quietly! I'll tie the crates to the side."

Nadya remained rooted to the ground.

Tamás grabbed her hand and led her away from the wagons where they would not be heard. Then he took her by the shoulders and said, *"We cannot stay here Nadya. They have arranged for our marriages – mine to Kizzy and yours to Cappi. I said I would not accept either and it did not go well. My Dai will talk to the elders tomorrow. There will be no arguing with them. Tradition will stand. Do you want to marry Cappi?"*

"No!" Nadya replied emphatically. *"I...I..."* she stuttered and then exclaimed, *"I don't want to leave you, Tamás!"*

"And I made a promise to care for you," he stated firmly. *"That is why we cannot stay. Now hurry!"*

Nadya was thoroughly shaken. She was waiting for him to ask what she was doing on the road outside the village but he was focused on their departure. They worked for another hour getting everything ready. Nadya tried not to let herself think of the family she was leaving behind, or how much she would miss them. She felt the worst about Tsura, but her adopted Dai's life would be easier without having to tend to the two of them, and the others would bring her to their campfires.

Tamás finished harnessing Baro to the wagon and they left without looking back. She sat close by his side with her head against his shoulder. It was the only place she ever felt completely safe.

116

Later, she would tell him everything she had been keeping secret for months – the dreams, how she had retrieved the book from the cave, and why she'd gone into the village that night.

Although he would be upset that she had done such dangerous things, his love for her would not falter.

"Can we stop at the cave for my Dai's box?" she asked in a small voice. *"The beast is gone for good, isn't it?"*

"Yes. It is gone. We'll get the box and you can put the book back inside where it will stay from now on. Am I right?"

"I promise. I'll never do anything like that again. Tamás! Thank you for saving me! And it's alright if you want to call me 'Princess' again. I like it. I never didn't like it, I was just..."

"Hush, Princess. It's going to be a long ride. Sleep."

☾

The Roma had a saying,

"You cannot go straight when the road bends."

What lay ahead, only One greater than their own hearts knew.

Part Two

☾

Europe
20th Century

☾

Chapter One
~ Together ~

"Love's highest purpose is not always to rescue and comfort us,
but to challenge us, teach us, humble us, and change us."

SGR

*T*amás' and Nadya's devotion to one another and their love of the land through which they traveled were the only things that made the harshness of life bearable. They managed to survive on their own, but it was never easy, and the security provided by a band of brothers and sisters had appeal. Every now and then, they would consider re-joining a caravan, but those they encountered never felt like home. They were subjected to too many questions, and when asked *"Kasko san?"* their answers were by necessity vague. The interrogations that followed were always uncomfortable.

The Roma are a wary lot and for good reason. They did not know what to think of the two, who were fiercely independent, side-stepped tradition and declined to discuss their past. This led to the assertion that mysterious forces followed Tamás and the ghel, which was not untrue. As a result, they would end up staying with a caravan long enough to make a few acquaintances but never to integrate, and after every tribal sojourn, the pair invariably found themselves moving on alone again, never realizing how closely their journey was paralleling that of their beloved Renata before them.

From season to season, they lived on what they could hunt, fish and forage, and occasionally upon the kindness of others with whom they found temporary work. They followed the river south to warmer places – Trieste, on the coast of Italy, and from there back up through Slovenia again and on into Hungary and Romania.

"Wherever," Tamás would often say, *"the road and the river take us."*

Despite the traumatic events in Mirno, there were still occasions on which Nadya followed leadings away from their camp. There was no stopping her, and Tamás spent a fair amount of time praying to O Del about the ghel.

Like her mother, she heard voices that he could not. Her dreams were deep, mysterious, and sometimes frightening, but when she cried out in her sleep, he was close by to comfort her. Nadya felt compelled to seek out the meanings of her dream journeys and would excitedly share what she'd been shown. On other occasions, Tamás would also be given dreams and they would interpret them together. One morning they were amazed to find that they'd both had the same dream, scene for scene. This they believed to be a sign of the strength of their bond. Nadya also came to understand that her growing closeness to O Del had an influence on her dreams, and that even the strange ones were messages once she figured them out.

Nadya felt most at home in the forest, where the soft carpet of moss and fallen leaves welcomed her footsteps and the trees whispered their secrets. One day she had stopped to gather pinecones for kindling when a strange, pitiful sound caught her ear. She followed it and discovered a wolf cub whimpering in the hollowed-out base of an enormous tree. It was white as snow, and the first thing she noticed was that it had one light brown eye and the other ice-blue. She did not want to think that its mother had met with misfortune, but the absence of its siblings and this one's frightened state made her suspect so. They must have wandered off and left the runt behind. Believing that when a need presented itself, she was meant to meet it, Nadya gathered the little creature into her arms, soothed it, and carried it back to camp.

Tamás just shook his head and exclaimed, *"A volk? What am I to do with you, Nadya?"* He put his hand under the pup's chin and lifted its head. *"What's wrong with its eyes? They're strange."*

"Nothing!" She replied defensively. *"He's special! We'll feed him scraps until he can hunt. Please, Tamás? He won't make it otherwise."*

Confident that if the animal survived, it would leave of its own volition, Tamás relented, and Nadya named the cub *'Kesali,'* which is

Kesali (Keh-SAH-lee)

'Spirit of the forest.' Proving his master partly right, the wild in the wolf often took him away, but he would always return, and became a faithful protector, hunter, and companion over many years to follow.

~

𝒩adya grew into an exotic young woman, and she and Tamás were a handsome pair. As Renata had foretold when he was a boy, Tamás became an accomplished gilabno, and spent every evening playing his violin by the fire while Nadya sang and danced to the songs.

Whenever they camped near a village, they would dress in their most colorful clothing, she would braid wildflowers into Baro's mane and tail, and they would ride into town, where they immediately drew the attention of marketgoers. As soon as Tamás began to play, people would gather, and Nadya would dance for coins.

The young woman moved like the flame of a candle, or smoke from a fire. Every graceful move told a story and cast spells that captivated many an unsuspecting heart. She knew her power and how to use it. Her green eyes and long raven tresses attracted the men, young and old, but should one of them become overly attentive, a swift, dark glance from Tamás would send the message that she was off limits.

However seductive Nadya's public performances, at home she was still the same ghel she'd always been, and the two of them were an inseparable team. Tsura had taught Nadya a gypsy woman's responsibilities, and the ghel made many of them more enjoyable by applying her own ingenuity and creative touches. She did not consider it drudgery to take care of Tamás' needs, nor did he feel it burdensome to provide for and protect her.

The only thing they did not share was the marriage union, and this, they had both secretly begun to think about upon their beds at night. Always the bolder of the two, Nadya was the first to confess that she wanted to be his wife.

When they returned from the village that night, they were tired and hungry, but happy to have earned enough to buy provisions for several more days. Tamás tended to Baro while Nadya started a fire to roast meat and potatoes. While the food cooked, they sat back, gazed into the flames, and drank their wine in comfortable silence. It was mating season, and nearby, at the edges of a pond, a multitude of braskis were croaking tirelessly with desire.

Nadya reached into the fire to turn the food, and then moved closer to Tamás. She was no longer the reckless child who had to devise strategies to get what she wanted. She would never deceive this kind, faithful man again.

"Tamás..."

"Yes?"

"I want to be married."

He stopped breathing. He had always known he couldn't hold on to her forever.

He tried in vain to keep his voice from shaking, and asked *"And who is this lucky fellow?"*

She laughed, and he did not understand why.

*"I want to marry **you**!"* she said, turning to face him. *"You! If you want it, too."*

The strong, sensible man's voice broke, and he made no further attempt to hide his emotions. *"I am yours. I have always been and always will be."*

𝒯here were no rituals to be followed, no dowry to be paid, and no wedding ceremony to be planned. It was just the two of them, as it had always been, choosing their future with Balval as their witness. They finished their dinner, retired to the candle-lit vardo, spoke their vows, and became one.

braskis *(BRAH-skees) -- frogs*

Chapter Two
~ Anica ~

"...for the evil one himself masquerades as an angel of light."
The Bible

Nadya kept the box of her Dai's treasures hidden, and only took it out on occasion to wonder, as she always had, over its contents. Then, after a while, she would push her questions aside and tuck it back in the corner under their bunk. Tamás had made her swear never again to put herself at risk for the sake of understanding the book, and she had promised.

The night he rescued her from the beast, she'd had a dream. In it, she was walking beside a stream in a place more beautiful than any she had ever seen. A soft melody was rising from the ground, and the wildflowers were singing along. A man was watching over a small flock of sheep, and a voice said, *"Peace, child. I will lead you. There is no impatience in my kingdom."* She knew who it was and had not worried about the book since.

Tamás and Nadya had been camped alongside the Drava River near Maribor for over a year. The region was rich with vineyards, and the townsfolk were welcoming. The couple had become familiar faces in the village and they earned enough to live comfortably.

One day, when a few extra coins jingled in the posotis of her skirt, Nadya impulsively purchased pigments and brushes with which to paint bright designs on their vardo. She could see them in her mind before she began, and when she touched the brush to the wood, her creations took on a life of their own. She did not know where the ability had come from but enjoyed it immensely and could feel her mother's spirit as the colors flowed. Thus, a new talent emerged that not only brought her great joy but was also a marketable skill. She would often think of the words a seer had spoken over her when she was little: *'Chavi,*

O Del has given you many keys because He knows you will use them.'

Not wanting to disappoint, Nadya eagerly welcomed every creative opportunity that presented itself.

Tamás was an expert craftsman whose metalwork ranged from pots and pans to knives and jewelry. They designed the latter together, and often incorporated the stones Nadya had been collecting from childhood. Those who wore their creations insisted they brought good fortune. The couple received the compliments with humility, and would point upward and state, *"All thanks to O Del."*

Even though they crafted elaborate pieces, Nadya treasured the small stone around her neck the most. Its power had been proven and she would not part with it until she gave it to her own daughter – should O Del choose to bless her thus.

She'd been born with what their people called *'The Dook,'* but had never really understood what that meant. Didn't Balval call everyone away into the silence to be taught, or to see their departed loved ones in dreams, or receive messages? When others did not speak of such things she wondered why. It all came naturally to her, and as she matured, so did her gifts. She was beginning to sense things about people and had begun to receive words of guidance and comfort for them. Tsura had always told her that she was like her mother, and that had Renata lived, she would have played an important role as a seer in the tribe. When the time came, Nadya would be expected to do the same, and for that reason, the young woman was relieved they were not part of a caravan. Telling fortunes on demand seemed like a heavy responsibility. She could not force Balval to speak, and if He didn't, she wasn't going to make things up. She'd learned well that lies led to trouble.

There were times when she dearly missed Tsura, and she knew, without him saying so, that Tamás did, too. There were things that she hadn't had time to learn from her adoptive mother. Things that older Gypsy women knew about the rhythms of their bodies. The men were taught nothing of such matters, nor did they wish to know. They were afforded far more freedom than the women, and a Romni could only hope that her man would be faithful to the marriage bond by choice. There were no reprisals if he was not – none but the tears of his wife for salt in his stew, and the distrust in her eyes forevermore.

Tamás was not such a man.

Romni *(Rom-NEE)* – Romany wife

126

On occasion, young people from the village would visit Tamás' and Nadya's camp in the evening. There, they could play their musical instruments, sing, dance, drink more wine and smoke more tobacco than would be allowed at home. The couple enjoyed the company, and the merriment often lasted late.

On one such night, Nadya noticed a young girl by the name of Anica. There was a sadness in her eyes that told Nadya something was wrong, and if there was any way she could help, her instinct was always to do so.

Anica was not dancing with the others, so when the fiddling was at its height, Nadya pulled her gently to her feet. She coaxed one step out of her, and then another, until Anica began to follow. She learned the moves quickly and the dark cloud began to lift. When the girl smiled, she was quite pretty. The music stopped and the dancers laughed, paired off, and found seats around the fire. Nadya sensed Anica's discomfort and motioned to a spot where the two of them could sit, not far from where Tamás was instructing three young fiddle players who were enthusiastically trying to imitate his style. Nadya turned to Anica and began a conversation.

"You should always dance. You're a natural."

"Do you really think so?" the girl answered shyly.

"I do." Nadya replied emphatically. *"And you have a beautiful smile. I'm Nadya, but your friends probably told you that."*

"Yes, they did, and I've seen you and your husband perform in town. She looked toward Tamás with appreciation. *"I'm Anica."*

"Welcome to our camp, Anica," Nadya said warmly.

"Thank you for this. I mean, for being so kind. The others tend to forget that I'm along. I came tonight because I've been told your people sometimes...know things." She looked hopefully into Nadya's eyes like she expected her to understand.

Nadya didn't. *"What sorts of things?"*

"The future." The girl replied.

"Ah." Nadya answered, *"Well...sometimes. We ask for guidance from O Del and Balval speaks."* Then she laughed. *"I don't read palms or minds."*

Anica did not ask who O Del and Balval were. Her tone was desperate. *"Can you tell me what I should do?"*

"What's wrong?" Nadya asked, taking the girl's hand.

"I have nowhere to live. My father died a short time ago. We can't pay the rent, and my mother and I must move. She's found a job as a housemaid, but she'll be living with the family, and there is no room for me. I don't know what to do or where to go." Her eyes brimmed with tears that spilled over and trickled down her plump, rosy cheeks.

"How soon?" asked Nadya.

"Tonight." Anica answered miserably.

"Tonight!? Well, then you must stay here with us," Nadya offered, immediately regretting her impulsiveness, for such a decision was not hers to make alone. It was too late, however, for Anica's arms were already around her neck and the girl was sobbing with gratitude.

That night, after the others left, Anica slept by the fire, bundled in blankets brought from the vardo by Nadya. Tamás was even more uncomfortable with the situation than he'd been when she'd brought the wolf pup home, and while she tried to plead her case, he expressed it to his wife in no uncertain terms.

He knew how this would go. His concerns would be met with pleas for them to act with compassion, and he knew before the argument was over that he would give in and resign himself to hope – as he'd done with every other stray rescued by his kind, overly trusting wife – that this latest needy creature would quickly find the strength to leave. She was gadje. Not their kind.

𝒜s the days passed, however, Anica didn't leave. There was never a convenient time, or anywhere for her to go, and neither Nadya nor Tamás had the heart to send her away. Furthermore, the girl was more of a help than a hinderance. Extra hands made for lighter work, and Nadya enjoyed Anica's companionship when Tamás was gone from the camp.

Before long, Anica began to take on the role of a daughter. She was sweet, agreeable, competent, attentive, and loving, and she also possessed knowledge about female matters, which benefitted Nadya greatly. She assumed that Anica's mother had taught her these things in the traditional manner, and the girl allowed her to think so. Anica never spoke of the brutal ways in which she had learned them and instead invented a past she had never lived – one in which she had been loved.

In truth, the girl had known nothing but pain. The people who claimed to be her parents had been selling her body since she was small. They took away her first child at birth, forced abortions followed, and by the time she was fifteen, Anica could endure no more. Though her previous attempts at escape had been brutally punished, she had fled in desperation again – this time to the Gypsies, and not for the reasons she had given Nadya, but in fear of her life.

Anica divulged none of these things. Her lies were far less ugly, and it was easier to be treated like a normal girl who had simply come upon hard times.

She had fallen secretly in love with Tamás the first time she'd seen him in the market and fantasized that he desired her also. She was sure that if her abusers tracked her down, he would kill them to protect her, and that she would be safe with him forever after that.

Nadya was not a part of that dream.

When the weather turned colder, they made a place for her in the vardo. It was separated from their bed by a curtain and when all was still at night, Anica would lie awake listening to Tamás snoring softly and pretend that she was the one beside him.

*A*s good as Maribor had been to them, Tamás and Nadya eventually found themselves longing for the road. When they told Anica, she cried, fell to her knees, and pleaded to go with them.

Against their better judgment, they relented. Things were not the same with Anica in their lives and had Tamás been a different sort of a man, he could easily have taken advantage of the situation. To the contrary, he was growing increasingly uncomfortable with her closeness and the way she catered to him while playfully calling him Dati. He was no one's Dati until he and Nadya had a child of their own, nor had he ever desired to be close to any other woman but his wife.

Considering Nadya's intuitive powers, one might think it odd that she could not see what was happening, but this was because her gifts came from a higher place and could only flow through a pure heart, not one prone to pettiness, suspicion, or jealousy. Her openness translated to unhesitating, unconditional love and acceptance of all others, animal and human alike. This was not the typical Gypsy way. The Roma had no reason to trust the gadje, for they had never been shown mercy by them. Conversely, Nadya believed that each person stood on their own before O Del, and He was the only one who could truly read a heart.

Therefore, it seemed right to share their home with a girl who had nowhere else to go. As long as Anica was with them, Nadya was determined to love her unreservedly. Further, she was enormously thankful for Anica's help, especially as she had begun to feel increasingly tired and ill of late. She attributed this to her body not having released its flow for three full moons. When she finally mentioned this concern to Anica, the girl squealed with surprise, *"Nadya! You are with child!"*

The three of them celebrated that night, Tamás and Nadya both wishing they did not have to share such tender moments with anyone else, and Anica keeping a smile on her face while feeling more than ever the outsider.

The girl's thoughts were running wild. If only something could happen to Nadya. With her out of the way, Tamás would be Anica's, and his future babies could grow inside of her instead, where no one would take them away.

She was younger and stronger than Nadya. It would be easy to make it look like an accident.

The Vrag was not looking for a strong vessel that evening. He needed one that had already been broken. One with no purpose nor convictions left. One who had been so deeply scarred that it would not feel repulsed by his proposal. One who was desperate enough to carry it out.

They sat in their usual places around the fire. It was too early for Nadya to feel movement in her womb, but when she glanced over at

Anica, she felt a sharp kick. She looked down at her belly in surprise and covered it protectively with her hands. Tamás instinctively pulled her close.

Across the fire a shadow fell over Anica's face. Her eyes met his, and her pretty features changed. Thinking it to be a trick of the flames in the darkness, he was ready to dismiss it when an unbidden memory leapt to mind. It was of their encounter with the monster in the cave many years before. Phantom pains shot through the scars on his arm and he flinched and rubbed them with his hand.

Nadya looked at him with concern. *"What is it, my love?"*

"Nothing."

"Nothing what?" she knew him well.

"Trick of the fire. And old scars reminding me to be watchful over you."

She knew the scars he was referring to and leaned over to kiss them.

Anica looked away.

Chapter Three
~ Mercy ~

"Darkness cannot drive out darkness, only light can do that.
Hate cannot drive out hate, only love can do that."
Martin Luther King

*W*hile their own lives had been far from stable, there was more to Anica's past than Tamás and Nadya could ever have imagined. The things she suffered had left gaping holes that could not be filled, no matter how hard she tried. She lived in a continual state of loneliness, fear, and desperation, and coped by attaching herself to others and playing any role that was needed to fit in.

O Del knew this and would have healed her, but it was not the protection of His arms she sought. Neither did she want advice. She wanted someone else's life: Nadya's, and everything that came with it.

~

*"H*ow are you feeling today, Dai?"

Nadya cringed at Anica's use of the Gypsy word reserved for her beloved Renata.

"Alright so far." Nadya replied. She wasn't in the mood for conversation. Something felt off.

"I'll go to the river for water, so you don't have to. You shouldn't be carrying it from now on. I'm worried about you."

"There's no need for worry. I'm strong."

"Well, things can happen."

Not knowing nearly as much about childbearing as she wished, Nadya had to ask, *"What kinds of things?"*

Anica evaded the question. *"A lot that isn't pleasant to talk about.*

You should let me take care of the chores from now on. I'll just pretend I'm a Romni," she laughed. *"I'll do the washing when I get back and then I'll start Tamás' dinner. He left early. I packed his lunch and he said he'll be back before nightfall. We didn't want to wake you up."*

At the word *"we,"* Nadya's stomach tightened with suspicion. She wasn't bed-ridden, neither had she given either of them any indication that she was unable to perform her usual tasks, yet Anica appeared to be pushing her aside and stepping into her shoes. Nadya shifted the control and stated firmly, *"We'll get the water together."*

This was what Anica had hoped for. She dropped her head submissively and said, *"Of course, if you want to, but please be extra careful. The river is high and running very fast."*

"I can hear it." Nadya replied in a voice that curtailed further conversation. She picked up two buckets and headed out of camp. Anica grabbed two more and followed.

The Roma depended heavily upon the rivers to supply their needs, so the caravans – or in this case, one lone vardo – camped as near as possible to the life-giving resource. The women did not have far to go, but the embankment along this stretch was steep and cluttered with a tangled jumble of logs, branches and uprooted trees left in the wake of winter flooding. The barricade necessitated climbing down, balancing on a log, lowering the bucket into the river, and when full, hauling it back up. Nadya was agile, and had done it many times on her own, but the task was a great deal easier with two, as the person below could hand the bucket back up to the one above who would then pass down the next one to be filled.

A minimum of six buckets were needed for the day. Gypsies did not allow water to stand long lest it become contaminated. Separate wash tubs were used for different clothing, and certain items were not allowed to contact others. Dishes and utensils were also washed and rinsed separately depending upon their uses. In addition, there needed to be enough water for cooking, personal use and of course, for Baro.

When they arrived at the embankment, something told Nadya not to go down to the river. Such feelings had always proven out in the past, so she did not argue with them.

Anica saw her hesitation and asked, *"Is something wrong?"*

Nadya nodded. *"Would you go? If you don't mind."*

Anica *did* mind. She had been envisioning a different scenario with Nadya precariously picking her way down the slick trunk of a tree that had been torn from its footings the last time storm waters had chewed at the riverbank. Traversing its length took agility, balance, and skill. Chunks of rotting bark were sloughing off, and sharp broken branches made it even more hazardous.

Anica's plan was to watch Nadya's descent, and at the right moment, vigorously shake one of the limbs above, causing her to slip, fall into the rapidly moving waters below and meet her end. She was sweet and good and would go straight to Charos as the Gypsies called it. Anica had no chance of that, but she would at least have a life with Tamás before hell meted out its punishment.

Now she was going to have to think of something else. Fast.

Anica completed the task far less gracefully, and after they had filled all the buckets, she climbed back up to where Nadya stood. It had to happen now. A strong enough shove, and Nadya would fall backwards off the edge of the embankment down through the splintered branches and into the river where the current would sweep her downstream. Her body would never be found and heartbroken Anica would comfort Tamás in his grief. She had tried desperately to save Nadya, in vain. So sad. So very, very sad. And with a baby on the way.

There'd be nowhere for him to turn but her waiting arms.

Yes. It should work.

Anica coaxed Nadya to go look over the embankment at *'something strange'* in the tangle of dead branches. It was the pivotal moment, but suddenly, Nadya turned, saw something behind Anica, gasped, and ran past her crying *"Kesali!"*

Anica spun around to see an enormous white wolf sitting a short distance above them, calmly surveying the scene. The creature had not been there an instant before. As Nadya approached, it rose and ran to her.

The gadje girl had only heard stories about this mysterious animal who was now happily licking Nadya's face. She knew he had not visited them for many seasons, and that this was a happy reunion.

This was no common wolf. It was a great deal larger than the ones hunters brought into town, and its eyes were more human than animal. They locked on Anica's and she put her face in her hands and fell to her knees.

Mistaking the girl's reaction for fear, Nadya reassured her and made the introductions.

"Kesali, Anica is my friend. Anica, he's my protector. You don't need to be afraid as long as I'm here with him."

*A*fter dinner that night, Kesali lay contentedly on the ground between Nadya's and Tamás' feet while his mistress rubbed his ears. The wolf stared at Anica until she became uncomfortable and excused herself to go to bed. After she'd gone, Tamás rolled a cigarette, lit it, drew in deeply and exhaled in a long sigh. Then he addressed his wife in a quiet, but firm voice – the one Nadya knew allowed for no debate.

"She must leave, Nadya. I have known this for some time but allowed it because she has been a help to you. We cannot have a third person in our marriage."

Seeking confirmation of her earlier concerns, Nadya asked, *"Did the two of you decide not to wake me this morning?"*

"She suggested that." He answered defensively.

Nadya nodded sadly, *"I knew it wasn't true. And today, at the river, I had the strangest feeling that she was thinking about doing me harm. I swear, I knew it, Tamás! Then, Kesali appeared."*

They talked more about possible courses of action, and suddenly, as though dropped down from Charos by the hand of O Del, the answer presented itself. It would be an uncomfortable parting, but there were as many of those in life as happy meetings, and you could not have one without the other.

They need not have worried about how to tell Anica. When she'd gone up into the vardo, a tiny field mouse slipped in with her and ran across the floor beneath Nadya and Tamás' bunk. While moving things to shoo it out, she'd came across a metal box hidden in the back corner. Inside was an old book, a dagger, and other mementos. She had received basic schooling earlier in life and opened the book's cover to see what it said. What she read dismantled everything she had ever believed about herself and the world, past, present, and future. In those moments, her heart changed.

Outside, Tamás and Nadya were preparing to come in, so she quickly replaced the box and continued her search for the mouse. Once inside, they joined in the hunt, but the little invader was never found.

*T*he next morning, Anica announced that she was leaving. When they asked where she was going, she had no answer, other than that she believed God would lead her. They looked at one another and said, *"We know a place."*

Nadya and Tamás had never been able to make peace with the fact that when they fled the caravan, they'd left Tsura behind with a broken heart. She now had no children and Anica had no family. They needed each other.

Tamás knew where their old caravan could be found this time of the year. It was a long trek, but they would pack ample provisions and Kesali would lead Anica to the tribe. Once there, she was to ask for Tsura, and deliver the message that her son, Tamás, and Nadya were safe and happy and were sending their love with a girl who needed shelter.

It happened, on rare occasions, that a gadje with the heart of a Gypsy would be welcomed to live with the Roma, and this, they were certain, would be one of those times. Such a thing would never happen the other way around, because while an outsider could choose to embrace Romany culture, a true Gypsy could never change who they were.

Nadya held back tears when Anica left. Things were going to be much harder now, especially as her time grew near. It would have been nice to have someone to share the work – but not at the cost of sharing her husband. This had been a lesson she would never forget, and perhaps she would one day tell the story to others who needed to hear it.

☾

Chapter Four
~ The Protector ~

"The Lord God created all the animals and chose the wolf to be his dog."

Brothers Grimm

Kesali

I took form as a thought in the mind of The Creator, Who dreams us all into being. We trust, reverence, and obey Him, for we were formed by His hand and imprinted with the instincts by which we must live. How else would my brothers and sisters and I have known the way into the world, or where to find our first food? Why was I saved when my mother did not return to the den and my siblings wandered off while I was sleeping? How could I have once been so small and weak and grown to be so powerful and feared?

There is a path and a purpose for every living thing. It is written within, and those who do not rebel against The Creator are able to find it. Our survival depends upon unbroken connection with Him. I feel this more than most, for I was born with a decree inscribed upon my heart.

Her name is Nadya. My father served her mother, Renata, and so on for generations as far back as I know. Their stories are in my blood. We live to serve the chosen ones. We lead them, rescue them, fight for them, and should it be ordained, will die for them. For my kind, there is no higher call.

~

*T*wo moons passed before Kesali returned. Baro spotted him first and nickered softly to alert Nadya, who looked up from her washing to see him walking slowly toward her. Something was wrong, and as he drew closer, she saw the darkened blood on his side. She held out her

139

arms and he collapsed painfully in her lap, where she soothed him and assessed his injury. As she poured water gently over his matted fur, a long, deep gash on his side revealed itself. Blood was still oozing from it, and her mind reeled with imaginings of what or whom could have inflicted such harm on a creature well able to defend itself.

There being no answers other than one which she refused to entertain, she shook off the horrible imaginings and steeled her nerves to tend to his wound.

Tamás had gone hunting on foot that day and she didn't expect him back until nightfall. She couldn't wait that long. Assuring Kesali that she would return, she kissed his head, grabbed a basket, and headed to a nearby field where she remembered having seen bright yellow yarrow among the grasses. Knowing of its medicinal use for humans, she reasoned it would help heal an animal as well and picked a large bundle. Then, supporting her belly with her free hand, she ran back to camp as fast as the child bouncing in her womb would allow.

Kesali had not moved. His eyes were closed, and his breathing was shallow. She went quickly to work pulverizing the plants into a damp mash. Then, she prayed to O Del with all her heart that the wolf would remain asleep throughout the process of her cleaning the laceration and applying the poultice. Once Tamás was there, they could work together to bandage the wolf's body so that the dressing would stay in place. After that, only O Del's will and the strength of Kesali's heart would determine the outcome.

To her great relief, the wolf did not awaken, and after she had finished, she laid down beside him and stroked his fur until she fell into an exhausted dream.

In that other place, all was well. The sun was warm on her face and a soft chirping sound filled the air. Kesali was healed and happily romping about with what she thought were dragonflies. They sparkled with the colors of the rainbow and called her to come play, too. She felt light as a feather, and as she got closer, she saw that they were not insects at all. Then, an involuntary twitch of Kesali's tail awakened her, and the pieces of the dream drifted away like the seeds of a dandelion puff.

When Tamás got home, he was concerned about the severity of

140

Kesali's wound, and together he and Nadya managed to wrap the wolf's midsection securely with bedsheets torn into lengths. Then, they covered him with blankets and left his healing to his Creator.

Three days passed while the wolf lay silent. Then, at a moment when Nadya was tending the fire, a sound caused her to turn and see him on his feet. She rushed to fill a bowl with water, which he eagerly lapped up to the last drop. She refilled it twice, and knowing he needed strength, fed him all the meat on hand, while praying that Tamás would come home with fresh game. O Del answered, and that night, the three of them shared a celebratory feast of wild boar that nourished them for days.

The weeks of Kesali's recovery were happy ones for Nadya. He was her constant companion and knowing that he would leave again made her cherish the days even more. If only he could tell her the story of his brave journey! What demons had he faced? What had he suffered to complete his mission? She knew only that while his enemy had left him for dead, he was alive.

Had the wounding happened on his way back to them? Had he made it to the camp with Anica, first? Nadya felt in her heart that it must have been so. Was Tsura gladdened and relieved by the message Anica brought? Had Anica chosen a new beginning where she could be whomever she chose to be? Would their futures be happier now? Nadya believed it all to be as she and Tamás hoped. Chances and choices were part of this life and you had to be brave enough to make them and take them.

Kesali grew strong enough to return to the wild and slipped away one night when the moon was full. Nadya recognized his howl in the distance and knew he would always find them again.

The couple took his departure as a sign that it was time for them to move on as well. There was no reason to stay in a place where they would be reminded of things they would rather leave behind. Their home was on wheels, the land provided for them, and their old campsite near Maribor would be much easier for Nadya to navigate.

They would go back.

☾

Chapter Five
~ Ema and Maja ~

"For He shall give his angels charge over thee,
to keep thee in all of thy ways."

Psalm 91:11

*T*he couple received a warm welcome upon their return to the Maribor marketplace. Nadya could not dance, so she sold jewelry, sang, and told stories and fortunes instead. She was, however, no typical Gypsy seer. In fact, it had been difficult for her to come to the decision to employ her intuitive skills in this way at all, and she had made a sacred vow that any message she delivered had to come from the heart of O Del only.

She refused to use any of the unscrupulous wiles she had seen from other drabarni before, nor would she employ any typical dukkering tricks or tools of the trade. She shared only the words of Balval, and that was all. If nothing came, she would just hold the person's hands and look into their eyes and say something kind and encouraging. This being the case, she was always surprised when a person reacted excitedly as though they had received guidance. Her only desire was to deliver hope and strength. Everyone desperately needed it, herself included.

Nadya's belly was enormous and tight as a drum now. She had no idea when the baby was coming, or what to expect when it did. Gypsy men were not included in the process, so Tamás knew no more than she. They were going to have to get through it on their own.

One sweltering summer afternoon in the marketplace, a young girl approached her and touched her on the shoulder.

"Nadya?"

"Yes?" Nadya smiled and wondered how the girl knew her name.

"Why are you here in this heat? You're soon to give birth!"

---

drabarni, dukkering (drah-BAR-nee, DOOKer-ring) – fortune tellers, fortune-telling

"Oh, I hope so!" Nadya replied with a little laugh.

"Is there anyone to help you?" A worried little frown puckered the girl's forehead. Her dark eyes held Nadya's. They were wise old eyes, like those that had warned Nadya in front of a church in a different place and time when she had been about the same age as this child.

Nadya was no longer the foolish little ghel she'd been then. She had learned not to dismiss messengers and took this one's words of concern to heart.

"There is a midwife. She lives a short way down there," the girl pointed to an alleyway. *"When it is time, she can help. Come. I will show you."* She reached down to help Nadya up from the rug where she sat.

While Nadya doubted that a gadje midwife would want to tend a Gypsy, she pushed her qualms and questions aside, bundled up her jewelry in her scarf, and took the girl's hand.

The alleyway was a serene reprieve from the dust and noise of the marketplace. The stone buildings and worn cobblestones insulated it from the heat and a welcoming little breeze stirred together notes of geranium, lavender and other herbs that grew in the pots perched on the windowsills. Someone inside one of the houses was playing a flute, and further on down, a woman in an apron was sweeping a stoop.

A charcoal cat with orange spots, ragged ears and a white face and paws looked only mildly interested as they passed, and the girl said, *"That's Boots. Hullo, Boots."*

The cat replied with a polite little, *"Mew,"* and continued grooming itself.

The door they came to next was painted a lovely shade of cornflower blue and stood half-way open. *"Here we are. Would you like to come in and meet Maja? You must be thirsty!"*

Nadya snapped out of her daze. The moment they had turned down the alleyway things had begun to feel strange – as if she'd been there before and had been surrounded by the same sights, smells, and sounds. Memories of Mirno flooded back – a village much like this one. There, she had been invited into the back rooms of a church with the promise

Maja *(MY-yah))*

of receiving help. Considering what that had led to, was it wise to trust this girl with the familiar eyes?

A tiny elbow (or was it a knee?) rolled across the inside of Nadya's abdomen, and she accepted the invitation.

The woman inside was as gentle as the girl and did not appear surprised to see the pregnant young Gypsy. Their kind grew up fast. She invited Nadya to sit down and brought her a large cup of water with a slice of cucumber in it. Then she pressed the wet, cut ends of the vegetable against Nadya's wrists to help cool her.

A moment later, she asked if she might feel Nadya's belly, and after doing so, she said, *"My dear, you will be a mother very soon. Are the women of your tribe taking care of you?"*

Nadya clumsily explained that she and her husband were not part of a caravan, and the midwife nodded with understanding.

"Well, then, I shall be with you. I am Maja, and this is Ema."

"Her name is Nadya," Ema offered.

Maja smiled. *"I am honored to meet you, Nadya."*

"I cannot pay you," Nadya dropped her head. *"But I have this to trade..."* she said, unfolding her scarf and spreading out the jewelry she and Tamás had made, *"...if you are willing. My husband works with silver and I have been collecting the stones since I was small. They fall from Charos."*

Maja's eyes widened with delight. *"Oh! Silver from Earth and stones from Heaven! And your soul dances between the two, doesn't it? We would be delighted. Ema and I will each choose something, and you must keep the rest to sell."*

Against their protests, Nadya added more to what they selected and sipped her second glass of water while Maja carefully instructed her in what she could expect when her time came. Being careful not to frighten the young woman, she also told her that on occasion, things did not go as expected, and that she needed to be prepared for that possibility as well. Maja did not allow her concern to show, but she knew the girl was already past due and in for a difficult delivery. The midwife went to a cupboard, filled a small muslin bag with dried herbs and handed it to her.

"*Drink this tea. It will relax you. At the first sign of pain or tightening in your belly, have your husband come get me. Don't wait, even if it's the middle of the night. Understand?*"

"*I will.*" Nadya nodded and bowed her head in gratitude. Then she thanked the two of them profusely and said she must return to the marketplace.

When Tamás asked where she'd been, she told him what had happened, and showed him the way to the midwife's house. He was unable to hide his relief, and she heard him whisper his thanks to O Del.

☾

Chapter Six

~ Letting Go ~

"There's twice in our lives when we are the nearest to God:
at our birth and at our death.
At those times, surrender is the only option."

SGR

As she'd grown older, Nadya had come to understand that her preferred timing and O Del's were never the same. And so it was with the arrival of her offspring. The miserable days crawled by, and she feared her belly might split open if it grew any larger. She stayed at home in the vardo and faithfully gulped the midwife's tea, believing it to be a magic potion that would hurry things along. She was down to the last of the crumpled herbs.

Every evening while she rubbed oil on her body with the hope that it would keep the skin of her once-sleek torso from tearing, she blissfully sang her love to the infant inside. In other moments the thought of the delivery filled her with extreme anxiety. She would counter the apprehension by reminding herself that this was a normal process for every mother, but then she'd remember that her own Dai had not survived it, and the fear would return tenfold.

"Tamás!" He had been sleeping with one eye open, praying, waiting.

"I'm awake."

"Get the midwife." Her water had broken, and the bedding beneath her was soaked.

The midnight run signaled only one thing to Baro – Nadya was in trouble. They made it to the gates in a fraction of the usual time, and chased by the memory of another such night when he'd run for help and been too late, Tamás leapt from the horse's back and raced to the midwife's house. He was at the mercy of the same forces that had

147

carried Renata away to Charos, and just as helpless as he had been then.

Before he could raise his hand to knock, a light appeared in the midwife's window, and the door opened. Maja was already dressed. She stepped out and closed the door quietly behind her.

He struggled to catch his breath. *"My wife, Nadya..."*

She interrupted him, *"Yes, I know. We must hurry."*

When they reached the camp, Maja climbed the vardo steps and looked back over her shoulder at Tamás. *"Come in."*

Noting his surprise, she said, *"It's right that you should be with her. Put your horse away. We're in for a long night."* She went inside and he heard her immediately begin to comfort and encourage his wife.

It was unthinkable for a Rom to be present at the birth of his child. This and other rules were implanted from a young age. But Tamás and Nadya lived by a higher law, and it took less than a second for him to make his decision. He thanked Baro for his swiftness and assured him *"She'll be alright, my friend."* Then, he hastened to the vardo.

Nadya's labor was long and intense, but Maja knew what to do, and at one point calmly announced that it was not one baby on the way, but two, which explained the size of the poor girl's belly. *"Twins run in families,"* she winked at Tamás and smiled.

He could hardly contain his joy. Maja tirelessly continued to distract and soothe the young woman with stories of brave Slavic Goddesses, and the reminder that because her children's birth sign was that of the lion, no one should be surprised at their strength and the powerful dji present upon their entrance into the world.

Having Tamás by her side saved Nadya, and she said so over and over. These children were not hers alone. She rode the waves of the increasingly painful contractions by softly singing the song her Dai had given her, and although he did not understand the words, Tamás could feel the magic within them. He was amazed when Maja began to sing along with her in a voice more beautiful than any he had ever heard.

Tamás became increasingly worried about his wife's waning strength. It seemed to him that the babies should have made better progress by now. Another day had dawned and passed, and nothing had

dji *(GEE)* – the spiritual energy of life

changed. Perhaps the little ones loved the safety of their mother's womb so much that they did not want to leave. Or maybe their souls already knew enough about the world awaiting them that they were having second thoughts about making the journey.

Tamás hated watching Nadya in pain. She was exhausted and drifted in and out of awareness between contractions. Finally, to hide his tears, he said he needed to leave the vardo for a moment. Maja nodded with understanding.

Stars were beginning to appear outside. Nadya said they were souls piercing the veil. Tamás wondered if that happened on their way in or on their way out. After tending the fire, he sat down beside it, put his face in his hands and uttered a desperate prayer. He was not prepared for the response he received.

"Give your wife and the children to Me."

What did that mean? Why would this be asked of him? He wanted to blame the outlandish thought on his emotional state, but the directive was clear, and he knew the Voice that had spoken. From the time Renata had awakened his spirit in his youth, he'd sought to hear it. Not in the way she or Nadya did, but as a man hears his God.

He raised his eyes to the sky and saw several tall pillars of light hovering above the trees. Both Renata and Nadya had told him of these. As he watched them, he was overwhelmed by peace, and the word **'Trust'** was spoken into his mind. Then the lights shot upward and disappeared, leaving two bright stars in their place.

Tamás rose from the fire and stepped up into the vardo. Maja looked at him as though she knew what he was going to do. He knelt beside the bed, laid his hands upon his wife's body, closed his eyes, and humbly declared, *"O Del, they are Yours."*

They named their sons Ion, meaning *'O Del is gracious,'* and Amoun, meaning *'Trust.'* Nadya asked Tamás to use the knife from her mother's box to cut the umbilical cords, and when he did so, he understood the meaning of O Del's command.

New life demands the severing of the old, and for O Del to take over, Tamás first had to let go.

❨

Chapter Seven
~ Winter Solstice ~

"Were these mysterious happenings going to follow them forever?"

*I*t was all Nadya could do to take care of twin babies on top of her necessary daily chores, and on occasion she found herself wishing for life in a caravan where she would have more help. That, however, was not the choice they had made. Tamás was working harder than ever. He'd taken on many of Nadya's tasks, hunting or fishing in the early mornings, looking for odd jobs wherever he could find them and playing his violin in the marketplace for coins when the weather allowed.

Nadya did not have the strength to join her husband at Maribor's harvest festival, but by the time of the winter solstice celebration, she told him she thought they should make the trip into the village, so they bundled up the little ones, tucked them securely in a sling over Baro's back, and Tamás led his family proudly into town.

The twins drew the attention of many of the couple's acquaintances, and Nadya loved showing them off. She hoped to be lucky enough to see Maja or Ema in the crowd but when that didn't happen, she asked Tamás to watch the babies for a bit so that she could go to the midwife's house.

Festive wreaths of greenery and holly with bright red berries hung on every lamp post and door, and a light dusting of snow on the cobblestones and shingled roofs made the village look like a gingerbread scene in the bakery window. The shutters and doors in the alleyway were all buttoned up tight against the cold, and the flowerpots sat empty, their herbs having all been snipped and dried. There was no sign of Boots. Things did not feel the same as they had before, but Nadya's desire to find Maja overrode her vague uneasiness.

Brimming over with anticipation, she knocked briskly on the blue door.

Heavy, shuffling footsteps approached from inside. The door opened a crack and a large, red-faced woman swaddled in wool scarves peered out at her suspiciously. *"Wot do ye want? I 'aven't got nuthin' if yer beggin'."*

"Oh, no, I'm not begging," Nadya hastened to answer, *"I'm here to see someone…"* She looked at the houses on both sides to be sure she was at the right one and then stood on tiptoe to try to see inside over the woman's head. *"This is Maja's house, right? Maja and Ema?"*

"Never 'erd of 'em. This is my house and my folks' before me. Go away."

Nadya's disappointment was obvious, and the scowling woman started to close the door. At that moment, Boots strolled up and rubbed on Nadya's leg. She looked down and said, *"Hullo, Boots."*

The woman's eyebrows knitted themselves together in surprise and suspicion. *"'Ow do ye know me cat's name?"*

"From when I visited Maja here before," Nadya answered, grateful for evidence of her claim, *"A girl named Ema brought me here. Maja is a midwife and she helped birth my babies last summer."*

The woman's tone was derisive. *"You're remembering wrong. No midwife lives 'ere. Never has."* She held the door open a bit wider so the cat could slip inside. *"There's a midwife on the other side of town but she's old and lives alone. Maybe that's who yer looking for."*

"No." Nadya argued, shaking her head confusedly. *"I sat inside this house with Ema and Maja and drank water with cucumber…"*

"Eh, all you Gypsies are crazy," the woman spit out the words contemptuously, *"Spinnin' yer tales and spells. Liars and thieves! I told 'ye there's no one like that 'ere and never has been. Now off with 'ye! Yer not gettin' in this house!"* And she slammed the door. A movement in the window caught Nadya's eye. Boots had jumped up on the sill and was staring out at her. The cat blinked and its mouth formed a silent, knowing *"mew."*

Nadya returned to the courtyard in a daze. Tamás could see something was wrong, and when she told him what had happened, he just stared at her in bewilderment. Were these mysterious happenings going to follow them forever? He suspected the answer, shook his head, and sighed.

Who (and where) was Maja, then? He'd thought the meeting was fortuitous from the start, but who was he to question divine help? He remembered wondering how Maja had known to be ready before he arrived at her house that night, and how she understood and sang the words of Nadya's song – dared he believe it – in the voice of an angel. When he expressed these things to his wife, she bowed her head.

"I know who they were," she said. *"There's no other explanation."*

$\mathcal{I}$t had been a long day for their first family outing. Nadya had traded for a wreath, and Baro stood still while she hung it on his neck for the trip back.

The little mother was growing stronger, the babies fatter, and Tamás had begun to feel the pull of the river. In the spring, if O Del willed it, they would move on. Sezana, perhaps. Nearer Trieste and the sea. Or Bled. Yes, the town on the lake surrounded by mountains. Nadya would love it there. Balval would lead them and they would walk in miracles.

Tamás no longer just believed in those – he expected them.

Chapter Eight
~The Island~

"...sometimes, when O Del has reasons, laws bend."

When she was to look back upon it, Nadya would say that the years they spent in Bled were her happiest. The place was all her childhood fairytales come true, complete with a castle on a hill. They camped at the edge of a clear blue lake with an island in the middle, and everything they needed was nearby. Tamás procured a small rowboat which allowed for fishing and excursions to the island on long summer days. Their closer proximity to several other towns meant more performing, more money and the availability of goods they would not otherwise have been able to acquire.

The twins grew like weeds and showed an above-average aptitude for physical agility. By age three they could swim, and by four they could climb just about anything that stood still, including Baro. Wild child that she herself had been, Nadya encouraged every activity that interested them. By the time they were five, they were their father's helpers and being taught he skills of his trade.

Nadya had known for some time that she could bear no more children and had settled this in her heart. Still, on occasion she would dream of a little girl with dark hair and big brown eyes. She had no explanation for the dreams, and they left her with a deep longing for a daughter with whom she could share her stories and the secrets of Gypsy womanhood and who would eventually be the keeper of her Dai's box of treasures. Her sons had no interest in such things.

Summer was slowly leaving the lake. Mornings were cooler and twilight came earlier, but the waters had been warmed by months of sun and still invited an afternoon swim. The further from shore you went, the cooler it got, which was when you flipped over on your back and floated for a while before heading back to shore.

Nadya always rose before the rest of the family, partly because she needed time to get all her work done, but mostly because she treasured time alone with O Del. One morning she stepped out of the vardo to see a figure at the water's edge, its head down taking a drink.

"Kesali!" she gasped. Years had passed. Gathering up her skirt, she ran toward the shore. He met her halfway and pressed his head into her body while she rubbed behind his ears and wept with joy.

The boys had heard stories about him from the time they'd been born, and their eyes would widen as they imagined the huge white wolf whom their Dai promised they would meet one day. Just the night before, when they had all settled in around the fire, she'd told them the story of Kesali's birthplace. They'd both looked at their Dati for confirmation and he glanced up from carving a knife handle and said, *"Believe her, my sons. 'Tis true. All of it."*

Nadya wondered, now, if her telling of the tale had summoned the beloved protector.

The Tree of Secrets

Once, when the earth was new, the Creator planted a tree in the middle of a garden near the sea and buried all of His secrets in the ground beneath it. The sun and moon rose and set faithfully over that place and the tree grew bigger and taller. Its roots pushed deeper and deeper downward where they wrapped around the secrets and anchored the tree when the storms came.

Through the heat and the cold, sun, wind, rain and snow, the mighty tree stood firm where it had been planted and lifted up its arms day and night in gratefulness for its life.

Ages went by, and beneath the Creator's watchful eye, the tree kept growing until its branches reached far up into the clouds. It bore countless seeds which fell to earth and many more trees sprang up around it. These, its children, were all connected to it and to one another through their roots below, but even so, the plan was for each of them to be unique. Together, they watched the great tree's example, heeded its teachings, and grew tall and strong themselves, while always remaining connected to the One who had given them life.

Over time, the garden became a forest where peace and patience prevailed, and where many creatures came to make their homes.

Cool mists from the ocean had always hidden the forest from man, but one day those who rode the waves on boats came ashore and discovered it. The trees did not have a way to speak to the men, so Balval moved through their branches and did so. But the men did not listen and instead, claimed the forest for themselves. In a short time, they fell many of the tree's children and drug them away, destroying the homes of the creatures whose cries were not loud enough to be heard over the sound of axes and saws.

The men decided they would wait to chop down the Tree of Secrets last. It would bring them great riches. Then, they would move on down the coastline to claim another forest.

The Creator watched as the men forged paths of pain and sorrow everywhere they travelled. They were His children, too, and it grieved Him that they did not love His gardens and forests as He did. A few of the men with good hearts spoke out, but they were shouted down by those driven by greed.

One night, when He saw that the men were not going to stop their assault, the Creator's pain turned to anger and took the form of a fierce storm. He heaped together black clouds, shouted in the thunder, shook the ground, and split open the sky so that rain and hail pounded down upon the men. They ran to take cover beneath the great tree, and then, in his wrath, the Creator took aim and struck them with a terrifying bolt of lightning, turning them all to ash.

Because anger is not easily controlled, the great tree was also set ablaze. Flames leapt high up its sides, scorching the bark and turning the branches into torches. The fire burned the hottest at the tree's heart, but Creator sent more and more rain until finally, only a few red coals remained. When the battle between the fire and the rain was over, only half of the great tree was left standing.

But that is not the end of this story. To this day, for all it has endured, the great Tree of Secrets still rises far up into the sky, fed by its roots. Children stand at its feet once more and Creator's secrets remain untouched below.

How do I know? I know because I have seen the tree with my very own eyes, and it was within its charred heart that our Kesali was born.

~

$\mathcal{N}$adya knew that Kesali's appearance was never without purpose. He led her back to the shore and they looked out at the island.

"Yes," she replied to his silent question. *"We take the boat there sometimes."* He made a sound in his throat – the one that usually preceded a howl.

"What is it, Kesali?"

He looked at her, then back at the island, and she understood.

Tamás was equally happy to see Nadya's protector, for he knew nothing bad would happen to his family when Kesali was around. When the boys awakened that morning, their mother prepared them. *"Someone special has arrived. I've told you about him."*

They guessed excitedly in unison. *"Kesali?!"*

She loved their keen intuition and smiled. *"Yes, but don't run out there and jump on him. I'm not sure he'd like that."*

"We won't!" They chimed and were through the door before she could restrain them. By the time she got outside, Kesali was licking Amoun's face, and Ion had grabbed handfuls of fur and was pulling himself up on the wolf's back.

She frowned at Tamás, who shrugged and said, *"I tried ..."*

A few moments later, she told him Kesali wanted them to go to the island. He did not argue other than to teasingly ask whether the wolf wished to ride in the boat with them or swim alongside. That question was answered when Kesali jumped in the water and headed across before they could even climb in their skiff. The boys' pleas of *"we want to swim with him!"* were firmly squashed by their mother.

$\mathcal{N}$o one lived on the little island and visitors were few. They'd rowed out to it on many occasions and Nadya had picked berries and collected colorful stones while the boys played. They'd been taught what was safe to eat, and on this occasion, having missed breakfast, they leapt from the boat and quickly found a heavy laden blackberry

158

bush. Tamás stepped onto the shore, helped Nadya out of the boat, and secured the rope beneath a large rock. Kesali shook the water from his fur and was anxious to get on with the adventure.

Nadya looked at Tamás and he waved her off. *"You go…I'll keep an eye on them."*

A trail led from the beach up into the forest and within a minute, Kesali had disappeared, causing Nadya to have to run to catch sight of him again. She'd been on the same path before, but it was different now, as though someone had been tending it. They were almost at the top of the island when the sun broke through and a small clearing appeared before them. It was carpeted with little wildflowers and a beautiful willow tree stood at its center. Nadya did not remember either the clearing or the tree being there before. Kesali sat down, looked at her, cocked his head, and looked back at the tree.

Then she heard the singing. A voice she knew – one impossible to forget – her Dai!

She was sitting within the willow boughs, just as in Nadya's childhood dream. A little girl was on her lap and Renata was rocking her gently back and forth as she sang the same song she'd given Nadya.

"Hello, my beloved," Renata greeted her. *"What a beautiful woman you have grown to be! And you have given me two grandsons, destined to be heroes. Shining stars who shall pierce the veil!"*

Nadya ran to her mother and knelt. *"Dai! It's been so long!"*

"Not really, my child. Ascended souls are not bound to the passing of seasons."

It was true. Renata had not changed, and now, she and Nadya looked the same age.

Light shone from Renata's eyes. *"I want you to meet someone,"* she said, shifting the little girl to face Nadya. *"Your daughter. I've been teaching her our song."*

"Daughter?" Nadya was bewildered.

"From this moment on." replied Renata, *"Katiza is of you, now."*

And in fact, the adorable little chavi looked like she had stepped out of Nadya's dreams.

"You are not dreaming this time," Renata assured her, *"We are here together, all three of us. As for how it is possible, I cannot say, only that sometimes, O Del makes exceptions to the rules."*

"But where...how?" Nadya's voice trailed off. The little girl looked up at Renata to see if it would be explained.

Renata stroked her hair and did not hurry her words. *"All who choose to come here have reasons, and no one can say for another what those may be. There is purpose in every connection, for we are all pieces of the whole, and what one of us does affects everyone. Examples of this are abundant throughout the natural world. They are reminders, should anyone lose sight of that truth."*

The child nodded eagerly as though she already knew this lesson and Renata continued.

"Our spirits are ageless, but we must enter Earth's experience in bodies formed here in this realm. That is why every new life, however small, must be cherished and protected. A soul is arriving within it. O Del's desire is that none should ever perish, so when a little one is not able to stay, their soul is carried to Charos to be nurtured and taught by us there." She kissed the top of the little chavi's head with reverence. *"That is where Katiza has been."*

Renata gave Nadya time to absorb what she had said and continued. *"She's asked for you to be her mother and her request has been granted. She has returned and is of your blood, now."*

Little Katiza had been waiting patiently on Renata's lap and stood to face Nadya. The light of Charos shone all around her and her huge brown eyes sparkled with love and hope. Nadya's heart broke open and her tears flowed as she wrapped the child in her arms and thanked O Del over and over for the gift of a daughter. She was so taken with emotion that she did not feel the shift, and when she wiped her eyes, everything had changed. The hill with the willow was gone, along with Renata, and she and the little girl were alone with Kesali, standing on the trail back down to the shore.

"Dai, Dai, where arrrre you?" Her sons were calling from further on down.

"I'm coming!" she called back, and she took the little chavi by the hand and hurried down to meet them.

☾

Chapter Nine
~ The Chavi from Charos ~

"The only thing I could truly remember about the place I came from was the peace. Here, wars rage in my heart and my blood is on fire."

*B*eing older by a few years, the boys were thrilled to have a little sister to boss around, and they stepped into their big brother roles immediately. Tamás, though he was charmed by the adorable little chavi, did not know what to think. He refused to believe his wife was dinilo because he'd seen the hand of O Del at work so many times – but now, a chavi from Charos? How could such a thing be possible? Wasn't it more probable that the child had been abandoned on the island, and that Nadya had found her and made up a fantastic story? He squirmed to think of such a thing because he loved his wife. The only way he could settle it was to ask O Del to show him, so this he did. But no answer ever came and after a while it didn't matter, because he, too, loved the child as his own.

They acquired a bigger vardo, which Nadya painted with flowers and colorful designs. No surface went undecorated, for nothing was allowed to be drab or ordinary in her world.

As anyone could see, Katiza certainly was, as Renata had declared, *'of their blood.'* She grew up quickly and copied her mother's dances without missing a beat. She was also determined to keep up with her twin brothers' acrobatics and taught herself how to do flips and headstands on Baro's back while he trotted in a circle. From there, she graduated to climbing up on the boys' shoulders until they were stacked three-high. At their parents' insistence, such stunts were practiced in the river where the water cushioned falls. Then, once perfected, they were performed in the marketplace to the gasps and cheers of the crowd.

Katiza was fearless – their third 'wild child' as Nadya laughingly referred to their offspring – but she was also sensitive and artistic. She claimed Baro as her own, and the affection was mutual. The horse was growing older and his joints were stiff, but with Katiza's care, Nadya's healing liniment, and O Del's gift of extra years, the star member of their troupe continued to impress his admirers.

*A*s time passed, the family's performances drew larger crowds. Nadya and Katiza sewed colorful costumes adorned with gold coins, which sent the message that they were a cut above other acts. The strikingly beautiful mother and daughter knew how to charm their audience, and the twins, who had inherited their parents' good looks, captured the hearts of the young women. The troupe of five all played instruments, danced, sang, and performed stunts with Baro to round after round of applause.

Nadya adored her children and could not imagine her life without them, but she also knew that since they were not part of a caravan, the day would come when they would want more than their family. She tried to ready herself but was not prepared for Katiza to be the first.

*K*atiza

*M*y Dai is my world. I watched over her from Charos, loved her, and longed to be with her here. I even visited her in dreams, for we may reach across that way sometimes. We understand more about love in Charos than people do here. It has to do with the veil. The two worlds are close – just a whisper apart – but crossing between them cannot be done in our own power. It must happen according to the will of O Del. He knows all hearts, below and above, so I believe He may have decided I was needed more here than there. For a time, at least.

It is sad, but I have forgotten much of what it was like to live there. I think it must have to be that way, for life in Charos is so wonderful that if we remembered it, the hardships and sorrows of this place would be too much to bear.

When I was small, my Dai would say, *"Tell me of Charos, Katiza!"*

I would wrinkle up my face, try to remember and answer something like, *"It is sooo beautiful and peaceful there,"* or *"the colors are brighter than here, and the animals and trees and mountains talk to you…"* and I could see her painting the pictures in her mind.

Then her eyes would light up with excitement and she would exclaim, *"Let's sing a song about Charos!"* And we would make it up as we went along. No moments were ever sweeter than those

A girl never forgets the day she awakens to womanhood. Everything changed overnight, and I was lost in emotions I'd never felt before. The feeling of blood draining from my body was revolting, and to make it worse, my insides were in painful knots. Dai was sympathetic. She made me special tea, told me it would all pass and said she had something to show me. I waited for her at the table Dati had built for us down at the lakeshore.

Summer was almost over and Balval had scattered a few crimson and gold leaves at my feet. They did not cheer me, but I thanked Him anyway. He is the wind, and although we cannot see Him, we can feel Him. I was sitting with my eyes closed, listening, when my Dai arrived. She was holding a silver box with designs on top and placed it on the table between us. I had never seen it before nor had I heard the story she began to tell.

"Your Dati," she said, *"made this for my mother when he was a boy."* She opened it and I peered inside.

"She saved these things during her time on earth, and I have added some others." She reached up and cradled the round stone that had hung around her neck since she was young. *"This was also hers. Do you remember her?"*

She'd asked me the question countless times before and every time she would search my face in the hope that a memory had surfaced. I shook my head. Try as I might, I could only recall the story as it had been told to me – that my grandmother had brought me here from Charos because I had asked to come, and that I sat on her lap beneath a big tree while she taught me a song, and after that I became part of our family. I had created pictures in my mind but could not remember the actual events.

The same is true of Charos. There was one occasion when it all came back to me clearly, but my brothers said not to talk about it because our Dai would not have let us go fishing alone again if she knew I'd been bitten by a snake and what happened after that.

I know this much: Charos is peace. We breathe it like air and are filled. There is no such thing as danger or worry, only love. Here on Earth, there is no true rest. Peace is hard to find and easily stolen. And as if that isn't bad enough, now my blood is on fire.

Of the various items in the box, I was most curious about the book. I opened it but could not, of course, read the words.

"What does it say?" I asked.

"We don't know," my Dai replied. *"Only that it is important enough that a priest would kill for it. But that's another story."*

I insisted upon hearing it, and when she relented, I was left with even greater respect for my little Dai's determination and my Dati's bravery. I could picture the battle in my mind, and Baro's triumph over evil. I wondered what other escapades this little woman kept hidden behind her veils. She had always protected me. Would I be as strong?

"I will learn to read and tell you what the book says, Dai!" I vowed. *"We must know!"* Where or how I would accomplish such a thing, I had no idea, but I was determined.

"If O Del wills," she said. *"When I am gone, these things are yours to protect. Your Dati knows this, also."* She replaced the items like they were priceless treasures and closed the lid. Then, she took off the stone necklace and gave it to me.

Her voice was heavy with emotion. *"For protection. Your childhood is over, my chavi, but womanhood holds great riches – love being the best. You shall see."* Then she squeezed my hands and walked back to the vardo where she returned the box to its hiding place. I pulled the necklace over my head and the warm stone rested upon my heart.

My precious Dai was right that day by the lake, but neither of us knew how quickly the seasons would pass. I can't bear the thought of leaving her, but neither can I lose my man. He has awakened me and my pulse quickens at the thought of his touch. He is a traveling musician and horseman – gadje. He'll leave the area soon and if I don't go with him, some other woman will.

~

*W*hen Ansel showed up in a village, every warm-blooded female took notice. His easy swagger, good looks and seductive charm made him irresistible. When Katiza first saw him, he was strolling barefoot through the crowd like a pied piper, playing as he went, strands of his long, sun-bleached hair escaping from the hastily-tied knot at the back of his head, his wrists stacked with bracelets of silver and leather and his loose linen shirt open at the front.

The tune was melancholy – the kind that reaches into a person's deepest longing – and he was utterly lost in it. He did not clutch his violin like others did but held it tenderly like a lover tucked beneath his chin, caressing the strings until they cried and then taking them to passionate heights. At the end of the song, when the spellbound spectators exploded in cheers and applause, he would grin sheepishly as though it had all been easy, and humbly bow his head.

As a performer herself, Katiza knew the exaggerated emotions and modesty to be part of his act. He was, in truth, as proud as a lion, and when he looked at her, she melted like chocolate on a hot day.

She gave him no indication of this, of course. Instead, she pulled her veil across her face, took a step backward and disappeared into the crowd.

*B*ack at camp, Katiza wrestled down the temptation to entertain a fantasy romance and lectured herself on how to behave the following day in the village. The crowd surrounding Ansel would make it easy to avoid contact, but did she really want to?

When the marketplace shut down at day's end, the alehouse came alive. It was overflowing with rowdy, half-drunk villagers and easy women, and from across the courtyard, Katiza could hear the unmistakable sounds of Ansel's fiddle and the shouts of *"More! Bravo! More!"*

She told herself it was just casual curiosity. The tavern was off limits and if she were seen there the wrong assumptions would be made. Her Dati and brothers were extremely protective, and if a male made advances, fists would fly. She would just peek through the window for a moment. Part of her hoped she'd witness something so unappealing that it would douse the fire in her heart, but that did not happen.

Ansel spotted her immediately, handed his violin to a friend, ignored the disappointed cries of the crowd, and walked out the door.

Outside, he pulled her close and kissed her passionately. Laughs and wolf calls erupted from inside the tavern, and he steered her around the corner of the building where they could be alone. Her back was pressed against the rough stone wall and his face was so close that she could feel the warmth of his breath as he teased, *"Hello, my little Gypsy, are you done dancing for the day? Shouldn't you be on your way home?"*

Before she could answer, his lips were on her neck and he begged, *"Come with me. I want to play my songs for you and watch you dance to them. What is your name? Not that it matters, for no name could be beautiful enough."* His fingers travelled slowly down the fringe of the scarf draped across her breasts, and playfully twirled the coin sewn at its point.

Katiza fought to keep her voice steady and feigned only casual interest. In truth, her head was spinning and all she wanted was to feel his arms around her and faint into another kiss.

"Katiza. That's my name. Come with you where?"

"Anywhere. Everywhere." His eyes were burning holes in her common sense.

"I have a…"

"Family. Yes, I have seen your family," he interrupted, cupping her chin in his hand, *"You draw a good crowd, but surely you are old enough to know your own mind. Come with me. The world is waiting for us."*

For a fleeting second, her pride returned and she pushed his hand away. She wasn't going to behave like the rest of the women who flung themselves at him.

"I don't know you." She said it coolly with as much dignity as she could muster.

His head and hand dropped simultaneously. *"Of course,"* he said, and abruptly turned to go back into the tavern.

She caved and called after him. *"Ansel! That's your name, isn't it? I didn't say 'no.'"*

"I'm moving on soon." He threw the words carelessly over his shoulder.

"How soon?"

"I haven't decided. Soon. You can find me here or in the marketplace if you're interested." And he strode away.

Katiza knew she would go with him. That's what Gypsies did. They followed their hearts. That's what her parents had done.

The two met several more times, each encounter more passionate than the one before, and although she did not know how to tell her family she was leaving, she secretly prepared to do so.

It was not going to be easy. Dai and Dati wouldn't approve, and deep inside she knew O Del could have a different plan. But she didn't want to wait, and she was convinced that she would bring much-needed balance to Ansel's life.

Nadya had taught Katiza that there was no escaping the scales. The girl, meanwhile, had figured out that she held the power to tip them at will. What she hadn't yet learned was the price she would pay for doing so.

☾
Chapter Ten
~ Changes ~

"But does he love you more than himself?"

*B*alval was restless, and that meant changes were on the way. Whether humans perceived them to be good or bad, there was no stopping them, and they always came with purpose.

Tamás watched as his children's popularity grew. As soon as the family arrived in the marketplace, people would hurry to see what new entertainment awaited them. Katiza and her brothers were natural performers who constantly spurred one another on, but they were outgrowing the little village, and Tamás wanted to provide them with greater opportunities. His job was to lead his family to a place where that could happen. He had been told that there were large, professional attractions called Cirques or Circos that set up their tents on the outskirts of larger towns, and he was sure that was where they belonged.

So, one night he sat everyone down and asked them if they wanted to go in search of such a place. Ion and Amoun literally leapt for joy at the prospect and pounced on Nadya, pleading, *"Please, Dai, please?"*

Her husband's proposition took Nadya by surprise, and she held her sons at arm's length while giving Tamás a disapproving look for not having introduced her to the idea first.

He met the challenge and said, *"You know it's time. We've been here long enough, and they are grown. They need more."* It was true, but his idea would turn their lives upside down.

Katiza sat in shocked silence, frantically trying to figure out how this unexpected turn of events would affect her own plans. Even though Nadya had said it many times, the young woman had no idea how much she was like her Dai at a younger age – keeping secrets, hatching schemes, and strategizing behind her loved ones' backs, if need be.

Katiza's desire for Ansel had brought out the worst in her.

Tamás took his daughter's silence as agreement, so he and his sons opened a bottle of wine, rolled cigarettes, and began discussing what direction to take.

Nadya moved over next to Katiza and put an arm around her shoulders. *"What is it, chavi? He's right, you know. I love this place, but you and your brothers are gifted performers and could even be famous. That will never happen if we stay here."*

Katiza smiled weakly. *"I suppose. But..."*

"It's the gilabno, isn't it?"

Katiza stiffened. How did she know? Had she known all along?

"Any woman could see why you want him." Nadya continued, laughing a little. *"Did you think I wouldn't know my own child well enough to see when she's drunk on love?"* Nadya had lowered her voice but the men were too deep in conversation to care anyway.

Nadya continued in a hurt tone that made Katiza vow inwardly never to hide anything from her again. *"Were you ever going to tell me, or where you just going to run away in the night? Did you think I wouldn't understand?"*

"But Dati won't!" Katiza's tears began to fall.

Nadya took her by the hand, pulled her to her feet and said, *"The moon is full tonight. Look at its reflection on the lake! Have you ever seen anything more beautiful? Let's walk down to the shore."*

At the water's edge, she said, *"You will always seem like our little chavi, no matter what. If we were part of a caravan, you would have been promised in marriage long before now. Your Dati knows that. He only wants to protect you and to give you more time to find..."*

She stopped herself mid-sentence. *"Shhhh!"*

Katiza was startled. *"What is it?"*

"There!" Nadya nodded toward the bushes where two eyes glowed in the moonlight.

Katiza gripped her mother's hand.

"Don't move," Nadya said in a deadly calm whisper. Then the animal stepped out. She gasped in relief. *"Kesali!"* and ran to embrace him.

170

It had been years, and something was different. An aura of quiet dignity surrounded him, like that of a wise old warrior confident in his power, with no more interest in glorifying his battle scars.

Katiza had heard the stories from the time she was small but had no memory of the legendary wolf who had led her family to the island when she came from Charos. Kesali, however, had not forgotten her, and no introduction was needed. He came to her side, nudged her hand up onto the top of his head in a show of trust and that was that.

Like all of them, Kesali had aged. Nadya could see it in his frame and face. She knew he had come to meet Katiza, but she had the feeling there was something more.

The women headed back to camp with Kesali between them.

"Ansel wants me to go with him," Katiza blurted out.

"Of course, he does," Nadya replied. *"And you want to go."*

"More than anything, but I don't want to leave our family either. I don't know what to do!"

"Perhaps there is another way," mused Nadya. *"Would he want to travel with us, do you think?"*

It seemed like the perfect solution, and Katiza desperately wanted to believe it could work. *"Dai! That would be wonderful!"*

"I cannot speak for your Dati, but I believe he might be coaxed."

"Can we ask him now?"

"I think the morning would be better. It's been an exciting night, and now, Kesali…"

"You're right. Tomorrow."

*A*fter breakfast the next morning, Kesali lay contentedly near the family giving no indication that he was going to leave. The moments were peaceful, and after exchanging looks with Katiza, Nadya took the opportunity to approach Tamás about Ansel.

"Katiza has become friends with a young man – a gilabno like yourself and our sons…" she began.

"'Friends', you say," Tamás replied, and Katiza's brothers made rude kissing noises.

"Shut up!" their sister hissed at them. Kesali's ears went up and Baro snorted softly and shook his mane. He was accustomed to their rowdy exchanges when stunts went wrong.

"Chavs! Do not embarrass her!" Nadya narrowed her eyes and they stifled their laughter.

"Well, perhaps more than friends, but please hear my thoughts, husband." Nadya continued.

Tamás sighed. *"I'm listening. But I hope we aren't talking about that arrogant German fiddler who hangs out in the alehouse."*

Katiza looked at Nadya as if to say, *'I knew it would go like this.'*

"His name is Ansel," she said in a small voice.

"Ann-selll" the twins echoed in sing-song voices. Fierce looks from both parents silenced them. Kesali looked around at the various family members with interest.

"He isn't bad," admitted Tamás. *"Reckless, undisciplined and full of himself, but he plays with great passion."* Ion rolled his eyes and Amoun followed suit.

"Yes!" Katiza agreed, but a look from her Dai told her to refrain from showing too much excitement.

Nadya got to the point. *"We,"* she nodded in Katiza's direction, *"thought that perhaps our family could invite him to travel with us."*

Silence fell like a stone and the boys looked stunned. Before anyone could object, Katiza quickly added, *"It would be temporary. He's usually on his own, and I haven't even suggested this to him, but he's leaving the area soon. I knew I needed to ask you first…"*

Tamás interrupted. *"And if I say 'no' to this proposal, you will run off with him?"*

He didn't wait for an answer and addressed Nadya. *"This sounds like your idea. Another gadje, wife? Have you forgotten how that turned out last time?"*

He sighed deeply and all three children looked curiously at their mother. She stared at her shoes and said nothing.

After a long, silent moment, Tamás stood up abruptly, forcefully stirred the fire, and then pitched the stick into the heart of the flames like a spear. *"He'd better pull his weight."*

Katiza jumped up, ran to her father, and hugged him until he was uncomfortable. Her brothers groaned in unison and Ion muttered sarcastically, *"Can't wait to see how **this** goes."*

Nadya was enormously relieved not to be losing her daughter, but the stars were crossed and she knew hard lessons lay ahead.

*A*nsel laughed at Katiza's invitation, but when he mentioned it to a couple of his friends over tankards of ale, they said his chances of finding acclaim would be greater if he traveled with the girl's family to larger settlements where they would draw bigger crowds.

Ansel thought about it and after teasing Katiza about being afraid to leave the nest, he negotiated the purchase of a small wagon and drove with her out to the lake to formally meet her family.

He was on his best behavior and the visit went well. The night even led to the four men drinking wine and playing their fiddles around the fire while discussing the best direction to take when they left. Nadya and Katiza retired to the vardo, made steaming mugs of spiced tea, and sat in bed together under Katiza's tattered childhood quilt.

"Tell me about when you knew you wanted to marry Dati," Katiza coaxed, smoothing the frayed binding of the blanket between her fingers as though her touch could heal the love-worn fibers. She'd heard the story a hundred times beneath the very same quilt, but she needed to hear it again.

"Well, I was your age," began Nadya, *"but it was different. I had been with him my whole life. He loved me, rescued me, and protected me. I cannot imagine life without him."* She paused. *"This young man, Ansel. Does he love you more than himself, the way your Dati loves me? Will he rescue and protect you?"*

Katizar could only answer *"I hope so."* She was sure her love would change him. Nadya did not ask more questions. She did not need to consult supernatural forces about Ansel. Her heart already knew. But she also knew her daughter, and this was the best way to keep her safe.

*K*atiza arose before dawn to fetch the day's water and smiled with relief when she saw Ansel's wagon still there, and him in the back, sleeping off too much wine from the night before. Kesali was on watch and followed her down to the lake. At the shoreline, he made a sound deep in his throat, cocked his head and looked at her intently.

"What do you want to tell me, Kesali? If you were the King of Charos, what would you say?" she asked. She looked into his eyes but could not unlock the message. Her Dai would have, and Katiza was frustrated that she could not. Knowing this, the wolf moved closer to her side and leaned his head against her body while they looked out at the island together for the last time.

A knot of anxiety had lodged itself in her chest. Her Dai said that such feelings were signs that should not be ignored.

"Anything I know, I learned the hard way," Nadya would say, if she had any inkling that Katiza might be questioning her advice. The statement was usually punctuated by the final stirring of a pot, or the biting off of a thread after the final stitch, or the inspection for spiders in the wood pile before she picked up a stick to put in the stove.

It had been so much easier when Katiza was young – holding on to her Dai's skirt, following her footsteps, trying to be like her. But she was not her mother. She did not see visions, had a hard time hearing Balval, did not strike up conversations with the moon, and had never found a single gem from Charos. She was her own woman with her own decisions to make, and she was choosing Ansel above everything else.

She beseeched Kesali, *"Please stay with me."* And from then on, he was never far away.

Ansel was uncomfortable around the family's protector. No matter how many stories they told, he refused to trust a wolf. Kesali made no friendly overtures toward Ansel, either. It was the only thing that Katiza would have changed, for the rest seemed perfect. Thanks to Nadya's intervention, she had everything she wanted.

*T*hey gave one last performance in the village that day, took their final bows, gathered up the coins tossed into their hats and tambourines, and the two wagons headed south to follow the Sava River to where it met the Danube in Belgrade.

☾

Chapter Eleven

~ Brothers ~

"We came into the world brother and brother.
Now let's go hand in hand, not one before another."

Jon

One night I had a dream in which I was desperately trying to escape from the confines of a small, dark place. My brother was there with me, and walls pressed in on us from every side. My body was weak and each move depleted my strength, forcing me to rest before pressing on. Giving up was not an option. My instincts told me that this was a life-or-death struggle and I desperately wanted to live. I did not know what might be waiting for me – only that I had to get out to survive.

Progress was excruciatingly slow, but finally, with one last agonizing push, I entered this world.

People do not believe me, but I remember my own birth. I was first, with Amoun on my heels that muggy summer night. Our Dai was barely conscious and Dati used a knife with a handle of white bone to separate us from her. Someone else was there also. A seraph I'd known in Charos. Light surrounded her and she held me as though I was holy.

I am possessed by insatiable curiosity. I want to see everything proven, including what my parents say. I must put it all to the test, whatever the risk. Dreams and visions were given to me at a young age, though I am inclined now to dismiss them as the fruits of a vivid imagination. I spoke early and could sometimes read my Dai's thoughts. She believes I may have *'the Dook.'* I doubt such things.

Dati's expectations are less lofty. He just wants his sons to be strong, skilled, respectable men.

My brother, Amoun, and I are at best co-conspirators and at worst, combatants. Our closeness is a double-edged sword that keeps us head-to-head in competition and partnership. 'My two lion cubs,' Dai used to say, until we told her that we did not want to be called 'cubs' anymore.

Our inborn talents became evident at a young age and were nurtured by our parents, who expected that their offspring would naturally embody the best parts of themselves. Whether it be music, dance, agility, or a flair for performance, Amoun and I did not disappoint.

There was never a dull moment, but of all our adventures, there is one we will never forget.

*W*e'd ventured into the woods on one of our 'scouts' as we liked to call them. I don't recall what we were in search of, but it was always serious business for two young explorers who were given a great deal of freedom.

It was a cloudy day and the air was heavy with the threat of rain. The forest was dense, and we had taken several turns down animal trails, making sure to stop now and then to break branches as markers for the way back. It was autumn, and yellow birch leaves were showering down like gold coins from Charos. That's what Dai would have said. We collected them, stuffed them in our pockets and pretended we were rich.

We were trudging along, alternately swinging our sticks like swords or as bows to coax songs from invisible fiddles, when we came upon a thatched roof cottage. Smoke was curling from the chimney and an old woman with wild white hair was sitting in a rocking chair on the porch. She was petting a black cat with orange spots and a white face and paws. Upon seeing us, it jumped off her lap, stretched, and walked to the door.

The woman called out, *"I was expecting you sooner. Well, never mind. You're here now. Hungry and thirsty I suppose?"* She stood up slowly, pulled her brown wool scarf closer and reached for her cane.

Amoun and I exchanged baffled looks and each of us waited for the other one to speak. My brother was always hungry, so he finally answered for us both.

"We...uh...well...I guess so."

I hesitated, then shrugged in agreement. We were fast and fearless. We could always overpower her and get away if it turned out that the stories of evil crones who lived in the forest were true.

"Well, come in then," she gestured with her cane and addressed me in particular. *"You've nothing to fear."*

Inside, the smell of freshly-baked scones filled our senses.

"Sit." She commanded, pointing to a bench at the table. *"I know you're fond of blackberry jam."*

I looked at Amoun and his eyes were huge. How did she know that? Was she fattening us up for her dinner? We'd heard such tales.

She read our minds. *"Oh, relax. I am not a witch. Those fables are nonsense."*

"But how did you…?" I asked. Amoun sat speechless, his hands clenched in his lap, his mouth hanging open.

"Better close that," the not-witch said to him. *"There's flies in here."* She gave no indication that she was joking and continued. *"It's difficult to explain, but certain powers can be used for both good and evil, my dears, and I choose only to serve the good."* The cat meowed and rubbed against her leg.

"Here," she placed a platter of hot scones and a crock of shimmering blackberry jam on the table. *"I only have cool water from the well today, but I assure you it's delicious. There is a toad who lives down there. He may be a wealthy aristocrat, but I've yet to figure out how to release him from his spell."* She grinned and winked.

"And Boots is no ordinary cat, either." She bent to pet the feline's head. *"She comes and goes as she pleases. I suspect she's a great deal older than she looks – like me."* She laughed.

The joke was lost on two young boys.

We slathered the scones with jam, wolfed them down, sucked our fingers, and after a cursory check for frog eggs, gulped the water from the pottery cups set before us.

She watched and smiled like an indulgent grandmother. *"There you go. Better now, eh?"*

We nodded and braced ourselves for whatever was coming next. I was the first to speak. *"Thank you, but we best be going now."*

Amoun squirmed. *"Yes. We're a long way from home and our Dai will start to worry."* It was a lie. Our mother never worried and the mind-reading, not-witch probably knew it.

"Stay put. You are here for a reason." She replied in a matter-of-fact voice. *"You realize that don't you?"*

O Del, save us!

"How many times must I tell you that I am not a witch?" She tilted her sharp chin downward, knitted her eyebrows together and looked at me like I should have listened the first time. It was the expression Gypsy women had when they were scolding you and I knew it well.

She sighed wearily, then continued. *"Boys – beloved children of O Del – you have not known me in this life, but I know you. You have not seen me, but I watch over you always. I have been granted this meeting with you to bestow gifts from Charos, if you want them."*

The room grew warmer, and I felt like I was being wrapped in the heavy quilt our Dai tucked around us at bedtime. The air was as delicious as the biscuits and jam in my belly, and as pure as the water from the well. Who was I to turn down gifts?

She walked around the table and laid her hands upon each of our heads in turn, while softly singing a song that sounded very much like the one my Dai often sang.

Then, to me, she said, *"Ion, your gift shall be unwavering bravery in the face of great evil. Seek truth and fear nothing, for O Del's hand rests upon you."*

To Amoun she said, *"You shall be guided, Amoun. Your gift is healing, and to the degree that you yield, O Del's power shall flow through you. You shall be called upon to help many souls."*

She pulled up a chair opposite us then, reached for our hands across the table, and said with great seriousness, *"These are not your only gifts. The others will emerge at their appointed times. You will not forget this meeting, and should it be the will of O Del, you will see me again. In the meantime, please be cautious, whatever you do, as there is a plan for your lives, and O Del desires to see it fulfilled.*

"You shall be given light according to your capacity and capacity

according to your desire. Therefore, chavs, desire much. You came to be of service to this world, but do not think it owns you.

"Beware, for there are foes who disrupt all that is good, and who exist only to deceive and destroy the children of the light. I am sorry to say that you will most assuredly encounter them, and you will need O Del's strength to stand against them."

"This is all," she threw her arms open wide as if to encompass everything in existence beyond the cottage, *"so much larger than yourselves, you see. You are part of a tapestry woven from the dawn of all things and every thread has a divine purpose."*

Her eyes burned with passion. *"Fight **for** one another, not against one another. Love and defend one another always, for your lives are entwined. Grow strong and pursue O Del's will. That shall always be your greatest adventure."*

Then she sighed, released our hands, and said, *"On your way now, dears. I'd have you stay, for I would love the company, but I do not want you to be in the woods after dark."* At the door she embraced us both and kissed our foreheads. I remember that she smelled of the forest itself – like ferns, berries, cedar, moss, and earth.

We didn't talk much on the way back, except to agree that we would keep the encounter to ourselves. I had the distinct feeling that there were spirits around us, and I picked up the pace. Amoun was looking over his shoulder a lot too, so we challenged one another to a race home, where Dai's waiting arms, the campfire, and the vardo would guarantee our safety.

We are grown now and have not encountered the old woman since that day. At times I wonder if it was a dream, but Amoun remembers it clearly, too. I don't know what to think about what she said. I am a seeker of truth, but also of understanding. Things need to make sense.

~

Amoun

My brother and I do not always remember our childhoods the same way. I expect that is true for all siblings.

To a Gypsy, every experience is potential storytelling material, starting when we are young. It's an artform and the best tale-tellers hold absolute power over an audience. Some stories are good for a laugh. Others are based on strange firsthand accounts, and many are imagined.

Everyone has tales to tell, and after enough years go by, most of us settle on the version that keeps everyone entertained, even if that means adding or leaving out a few details. I can always sense when someone is doing that because I do it myself.

I am not an easy person to know, but my Dai understands me. She understands Ion, too, and Katiza and our father. She understands all of us far better than we will ever be able to understand her.

We grew up wild. The world was ours and we gave little thought to the possible consequences of our actions. Our recklessness led us into many situations that could have ended in our demise or at least, in serious bodily harm.

"'Common' Amoun!'" was the battle cry, and I was expected to follow, for mischief and adventure were far more fun with a partner in crime, and Ion was fond of reminding me that because he had shown me the way out of our mother's womb, he was therefore, the rightful leader of our pack of two.

Of course, if he'd left without me, as I feared he'd done once, I would have been extremely unhappy. We'd grown up listening to our Dai tell that story.

She was busy with washing, she says, and I was looking for Ion, who as it later turned out was hiding from me underneath the vardo. We were camped near a forest and often accompanied our mother there to forage. Not seeing my sibling in camp, I deduced he'd gone in that direction, and waited until her back was turned to make my escape.

Shortly after I toddled into the trees, the trail branched off and I became lost. The woodlands are full of dangers, and if not for the intervention of a kind spirit, it is doubtful that I would ever have been found.

She led me out of the forest and pointed me back to camp where my Dai was at her wits end. When she spotted me, she ran to me crying and thanking O Del, showered me with kisses and looked me over to be sure I was unharmed. Then she got down on her knees, held me by the shoulders and asked, *"Amoun! How did you find your way back?"*

"An angel brought me." I replied.

*"An **angel**?"* She said, baffled. *"What did the angel look like?"*

"She was green," I answered. At that point I was done being fussed over and refused to offer any more details.

Therein lies the difference between my brother and me. Had Ion been the one lost and rescued by a supernatural entity, his story would have been every bit as dramatic as it deserved to be, with wild animals thrown in for good measure.

$\mathcal{D}$ati is a musician, a horseman, and an expert Romany metal-worker. Dai is a dancer, singer, storyteller, and painter. She is also a seer when Balval moves upon her, which means she is shown things she couldn't otherwise know. We've all seen it happen, and because of that, Ion and I have never gotten away with much.

I remember my brother standing by one day as I was making up a story to get out of trouble. She looked over at him for confirmation and to my dismay, he just sighed and said, *"You might as well tell her the truth, Amoun. If you don't, O Del will anyway."*

As soon as we could walk, our parents began teaching us their skills. We both took to the fiddle, acrobatics, and horsemanship. When our little sister Katiza arrived, we taught her everything we knew, and although she was too young to learn it all right away, she tried hard to keep up. We rode Baro with her bouncing on our shoulders. We climbed trees and she scrambled up behind us. We swung from branches and so did she. As soon as she was old enough, she became a part of our family's act in the villages, and the crowd loved her. Katiza is special. She came all the way from Charos to be in our family. It's a mystery.

I remember a day when the three of us went to the river to fish. We were still pretty young but had talked our Dai into letting us go alone. She wrapped bread, cheese and apples in brightly colored bandannas and tied them to the ends of sticks for us to carry over our shoulders.

The fishing hole was a long walk from camp for little Katiza, so Ion and I took turns carrying her piggyback while we talked about how we were going to be famous gilabnos someday and own our own vardos and follow the sun.

Katiza asked excitedly, *"Can I go with you?"* and we explained that she would need to stay with our parents until a man came along who wanted to marry her. She pitched a fit and said she would do no such thing and that we were being mean.

As soon as we reached our destination, we baited our hooks with worms caught early that morning and cast our lines out into the river. Katiza was determined to fish, too, but after a short time she grew bored and decided that she wanted to build a sandcastle instead. I pointed out to her that the clay on the embankment would work well, and she happily began gathering her materials.

Neither of us noticed when she ventured into the nearby bushes, and moments later we heard the screams. We dropped our fishing poles and found her on the ground grasping her leg and crying over and over, *"Snake! Snake! BAD snake! Bit me!"*

There were vipers in the area. We could see the fang marks and knew the venom would quickly reach her blood. We were in a panic when a voice spoke from behind us.

"I can help."

We did not recognize the man. He wasn't dressed like a Gypsy or a villager. He didn't wait for us to tell him what was wrong. He just jumped down the embankment and knelt beside Katiza.

"Hello, little one," he said softly. *"Do you remember me? I know it hurts. Be brave. Be at peace."*

She looked at him with great relief and threw her arms around his neck.

"Do you trust me?" he asked her.

"Yes!" she cried.

He lifted her up in his arms and waded down into the river until it was up to his waist and the water could flow over her legs.

We could not hear what else he said, but Katiza stopped crying. He hugged her close and then walked back up out of the river and set her down on her feet.

He stroked her hair and reassured her, *"You're fine now, little one. Be careful where you explore! The snakes here are not like the friendly ones in our world."*

"And you, my young friends," he addressed Ion and me, *"must also be careful. Your sister needs you. She always will."*

Then he looked at the three of us with great kindness and went on his way.

We immediately began asking Katiza questions, but her answers were brief.

Yes, she had recognized him on sight, from Charos. He was the King there. He walked among them, and everyone loved him. She knew when he took her to the river that she would be fine because there is a river in Charos that flows from his castle and brings life to all the land. Nothing bites you or hurts you in Charos. Everything and everyone is good. She loved it there and had only left for a while because our Dai needed her here. Someday she would go back.

"I miss the castle. That's why I wanted to build it in the sand. I'm hungry. Can we eat our lunches now?" And then she said she was done talking about snakes, the King, magic rivers and Charos.

As our sister got older, she remembered less and less about Charos. But I have never forgotten that day by the river and the man who saved her. He did not look or act like a king – not that I've ever known one – but when he looked at me, I felt different, and I wish I would have asked him to stay and share our lunches. Strange as it may seem, I feel I might encounter him again someday.

Chapter Twelve
~ A New Road ~

"Oh foolish heart. That which you desire cannot be caged."
SGR

Life on the move was never easy. They'd been settled near a friendly village for a long time, and now, each new settlement came with unknowns and adjustments.

Would they be welcomed, tolerated, or cursed at and spat upon? Would there be a place to camp and natural resources to meet their needs? Would performances pay enough?

Unless they happened to meet other travelers carrying news, they had no way of knowing, so the twins took turns scouting ahead.

Ansel also had friends who traveled and brought stories from other villages. They'd ride ahead, arrange tavern performances for him, and he'd pay them a few coins with the promise of more if things went well. Ansel would then go to the village, and if he was well-received, Tamás family would follow. Everyone profited, and before long, Ansel was able to purchase a larger vardo that Katiza could make into a home.

The arrangement worked well until Ansel became restless. He did not enjoy sharing the billing with Tamás' family. He did, however, like knowing that clean clothes, a warm meal and a warm woman were waiting for him at the end of the day after he'd drunk his fill of ale.

One night in a tavern, he was approached by a well-dressed man who claimed he could showcase Ansel's talents in Venice. There, he said, Ansel would perform on stage and in ballrooms for the wealthy. He would be assured of fame, fortune, and rich women with plenty of money to spend on whatever gave them pleasure.

After considering the proposition for two sleepless nights, with blissfully ignorant Katiza nestled beside him, Ansel arrived at the conclusion that he'd be a fool to turn down such an offer, and he struck a deal with Monsieur Bonelli the following day.

It was not easy for him to break the news to the family that had brought him into their lives. The expressions on their faces said everything, while Katiza wept and provided all his excuses for him.

However badly she would miss him, she understood that he had to leave for a time so he could make a better life for the two of them. Opportunities like this were rare. It was a miracle. Balval had spoken. Ansel would come back for her as soon as he was established in Venice. It wouldn't take long. In the meantime, she would send her heart with him, for their love was strong enough to withstand a temporary separation for the sake of fame and fortune.

Ansel was enormously relieved and needed only to nod and assure her that everything she said was true.

He held her throughout the night, and the following morning he promised he would find her further on down the road and that they would be together again before she knew it. Then, he climbed into Monsieur Bonelli's carriage and left.

After they were out of sight, Katiza shut herself up in her vardo, stopped eating, and spoke to no one for days.

The family traveled on without the attraction of Ansel, but Katiza was not the same. Her performances remained impeccable but her spark was gone. At night, she would wrap herself in the patchwork quilt she had made for the two of them and cry herself to sleep.

The quilt was a needlework masterpiece of fine fabric scraps that she'd collected since childhood. Satin, velvet, Damask, and Chenille remnants begged at the back doors of dress shops whose goods a Gypsy could never afford, along with linen she'd traded for in the marketplace and dyed by hand in the sun. Every stitch represented countless hours of love and devotion.

Ansel had tossed it aside on the floor when he packed to leave, just as carelessly as he had her heart.

The seasons changed, and he did not return.

As winter's grip tightened and the family performed less often, Katiza made excuses to withdraw. Her heart and bones ached from the

186

cold and she drugged herself with memories of summer days – the taste of her lover's lips, the hunger in his eyes, his damp hair wound around her fingers, the smell of the river on his skin. When she held him, he was hers. Now, she did not know.

While the wind and rain buffeted her vardo, she divided her time between composing melancholy songs and sewing matching clothing for the two of them so that upon his return when they performed together, there would be no question about whose man he was, or to whom she and the child growing in her womb, belonged.

$\mathcal{N}$adya was not one to pry into her children's matters. She trusted that O Del held their lives in His hands just as he did hers. She sensed, though, that there was more going on with her daughter than missing Ansel. She wanted Katiza to be happy, but there had been no word from him, and they all knew the young fiddler was not coming back.

When Kesali was in residence, he made it a habit to lie at the bottom of Katiza's vardo steps, and Nadya was forced to step over him to climb them. He raised an eyebrow but did not move. She knocked softly on the door, and Katiza answered from within. *"Who is it?"*

"Your Dai," Nadya answered.

"I finished my work," was the reply.

"Yes, I know. I wondered if we might talk for a bit. Maybe have some tea?"

There was a pause, and the door opened. *"Of course. Come in."*

The vardo smelled stale. *"I only have mint, I know you prefer chamomile, but I'm afraid I've used it all up."*

"Whatever you have is fine," Nadya smiled. *"I'll give you some of mine tomorrow. Here's more firewood for your stove."* She dropped it in the wood box.

"Thank you."

Then Katiza addressed Kesali, *"You can come in, boy."* The wolf had been hoping for an invitation and took the steps in one easy leap. Inside, he laid down in front of the door, content to be near the two women he loved.

Katiza had not yet met Nadya's eyes and was busying herself by stoking the small pot-bellied stove and checking to see how much water was in the kettle. Nadya sat on the edge of the bed and waited while Katiza measured the tea and poured hot water into the cups. She handed one to her mother and then sat down in a nearby chair.

"Katiza," Nadya's voice belied her concern, *"what is bothering you? Why haven't you told me?"*

"I...I can't." Katiza stammered. *"I'm afraid that..."*

Nadya interrupted her, *"There's nothing you can't tell me. You should know that!"*

Tears immediately spilled down Katiza's face and Nadya put down her tea and drew her daughter over to sit beside her on the bed.

"I don't think he's coming back!"

"Why do you think that?" Nadya knew Katiza's intuition was correct, but she had to allow her daughter to say the words.

"I just know it. In my heart, I know it. I've been a fool. I meant nothing to him. He's found another woman by now. Or several."

No comforting on Nadya's part helped, until she said something that made Katiza feel less alone in her humiliation.

"Oh, my precious chavi, love turns us all into fools. Whether it stays or goes, we are far better off, wouldn't you say, to have taken a risk than never to have tasted it at all?"

Katiza nodded miserably.

Nadya dabbed her daughter's face with a corner of her scarf.

"I know you don't want to hear this now, but I promise that you will find love again, and when you do, it will not be with a man who will abandon you. I have seen it. This man who is waiting in your future will love you the way your Dati loves me. O Del is going to make the match and it will be a perfect one. You will see."

Nadya did not add what she also knew to be true – that when someone was not meant to be in our life, O Del would cause them to leave. She had always known Ansel would not stay.

She reached for her daughter's hands and as soon as she touched them, she knew.

"OH!" she exclaimed, *"A baby!"*

Katiza broke down and her mother held her and rocked her back and forth while she sobbed.

While the news sank in, Nadya immediately began to calculate what needed to happen next. First, they'd have to tell Tamás and the twins. Should they try to find Ansel? Then, major alterations would have to be made to their act. Everything was going to change.

She insisted her daughter rest and covered her with the quilt that Katiza's young hands had made. Then she laid down beside her and held her through the night.

The next morning, it was decided that prolonging the announcement would only make things harder, and that Katiza would tell her Dati and brothers that day. The three men took the news as would be expected. None of them had liked Ansel very much to begin with, and they were glad he was gone.

Comments of that nature just made Katiza cry more, so they told her they loved her and that they would protect her and the child ever after. The vote was four against one when it came to trying to find Ansel. He had broken their trust and she was better off without him.

Tamás ended the conversation by looking at Nadya, shaking his head slowly from side to side, spitting into the fire and uttering one last word: *"gadje."* Then he walked away to harness Baro. He did not need to tell his wife that no outsider would ever be brought into the family fold again.

Chapter Thirteen
~ The Cirque ~

"The sights and smells of a circus turn us all into wide-eyed children."

SGR

*N*ow that Katiza's secret was out and she had the support of her family, her mood brightened considerably. They all talked excitedly about the new addition to their troupe and the baby's uncles-to-be teasingly planned stunts for the little one with the assumption that he or she would charm audiences the same way Katiza had. They wanted a boy, while Katiza and Nadya both believed a girl was coming to balance the scales. Their family would be three men and three women, then.

If everything went as expected, Katiza's child would make an entrance before they reached Belgrade.

When her daughter's time came, Nadya knew what to do, and beneath a full harvest moon beside the Drava River, Aleasa – meaning *'Chosen'* – entered the world. Her crown of raven hair was the only nod to her tribe, for her fair skin and blue eyes were all Ansel.

~

*N*ot far away, evil was giving birth to war, and the cries of innocent blood had reached O Del's ear. Whereas Aleasa was cherished and protected, the souls of other infants had barely arrived before angels needed to be sent to carry them back to places of healing in Charos where they would be loved and nurtured as Katiza had been.

Tamás' and his family knew nothing of the horrors that were brewing, but their ancestors had suffered at the hands of tyrannical forces before. O Del had created their people for laughter, song, and dance, not for hatred and violence. Since the beginning, He had led them away from discord, and because it inevitably cropped up everywhere, the Roma stayed on the move.

Aleasa *(Al-ee-AH-suh)*

This made them a people without a place. They owned no land, possessed few belongings, and had no wish to force their ways on others. They kept to themselves, lived for the day, and tomorrow was the same as yesterday – atasya.

O Del held the world and their lives. He was no respecter of kings over beggars, nor had he drawn boundaries to divide people. That was the work of men, whose pride and greed deluded them into believing they had the right to lay claim to the Earth, to conquer those upon it and to buy and sell both.

𝒯he family camped far outside the city and the men headed into Belgrade in search of the Cirque – Tamás astride Baro, and his sons riding double on Treu, the dependable, but less flashy chestnut Cob that Ansel had left behind.

After asking directions of a small group of Romany travelers going the opposite way on the road, they continued west until they saw the grand tents of Cirque Zeigler rising between the town and the vast forest beyond. Colorful flags flew from the center poles and flapped from heavy ropes staked to the ground. Brightly painted wagons, vardos and modern silver trailers were scattered around the surrounding fields. Corrals and cages held creatures of all kinds, many of which the Gypsies had never known existed. They were astounded by all of it.

Workers were busy feeding and grooming the animals, repairing wagons, painting wood surfaces, and practicing their acts. Several men were polishing a grand carousel, and as a craftsman himself, Tamás was highly impressed by the gleaming brass and the elegant carved detail on the horses, chariots, and mythological animals. He'd never seen such a contraption. Mirrors, masks, and painted scenes of mountains and lakes adorned the upper panels and the whole thing was covered by a red and white striped tent. He hoped for a chance at a closer look. It appeared that people must ride around on it, but he wondered how fast it went and what sort of machinery propelled it. He looked at Ion and Amoun and raised his eyebrows. Their mouths were hanging open.

True to its name, the Cirque was a study in circles and wheels. Everything was round – the corrals, the tents, the arenas, and the grandstands. It was a hive of activity and a feast for the eyes.

A couple of young women walked by dressed in glittering costumes that left little to the imagination. They winked at Ion and Amoun, whispered something to each another and giggled. The young men nodded their heads politely and kept their composure. They were accustomed to female attention and their father had taught them how to manage it.

An old man with a long white beard and an eye patch was bent over working on a back wheel of a royal blue vardo with gold trim and lettering. Nearby, a gypsy woman was painting a picture of an angry bear in a cage on the side of another elaborately embellished wagon.

As always, heads turned at the sight of Baro, who had taken it upon himself to prance – probably because that is what he was expected to do any time he had an audience.

A tall, lanky young fellow carrying a shovel walked toward them. *"That's an impressive animal you got there. Lookin' for somebody?"*

"Thank you," Tamás patted Baro's neck and laughed in response. *"He's a showoff. We're looking for the…"* he paused, not knowing what he should call the man in charge.

"The Boss?" The young man finished the sentence for him. *"You looking for work? If you want this kind of work,"* he gestured around, *"I'd be the one you'd talk to. These your boys?"* He pointed the handle of the shovel at Ion and Amoun. *"We can always use more strong backs around here. Three meals a day and free admission to the shows. No beds, but you can bring a wagon or pitch a tent."*

"Sounds fair," answered Tamás. The twins struggled to hide their disappointment. *"And we appreciate the offer, but it's the owner we need to see."* His sons shifted and sat taller.

"I figured." sighed the man. *"Everybody has to work around here anyhow, you know. Nobody's royalty just because they're performers. Animals need tending, sawdust needs raking, tents need mending, bleachers need painting…"* and his words trailed off, as though he'd worn himself out just listing it all.

"So, where would I…" said Tamás, in an effort to get the conversation back on track.

"That's the boss man's wagon over there," the fellow gestured with the shovel handle again. *"The red one. You got an act?"*

"Yes, we do. We are a troupe of eight." Tamás was including the baby and the horses. The twins kept straight faces. Their father was a smooth pitch man and embellishing the truth was his forte.

"Well, maybe we'll see you around then. Name's Hans." said the young man, *"Hans Bauer."* And with that, he tipped his tattered hat, turned, and limped back to a small corral where several pigs were hungrily snorting and jostling one another. Whether they were part of an act, dinner, or both, was anyone's guess.

Ion and Amoun knew not to interrupt when their father was negotiating work. *"Watch and learn,"* he'd advise, *"I won't always be around, and you'll have to do this yourselves."*

If they had heard it once, they'd heard it a thousand times and maybe more. As much as they respected him, when he turned his back, they would shake their fingers in one another faces and imitate him in serious voices. *"Watch and learn, chavs, this is how it's done."*

Approaching the owner of the cirque was one of the boldest things they'd seen their father do, and they felt privileged to have been brought along. If you thought about it, these dealings were a different kind of stunt work. Such transactions required nerves of steel, perfect timing, intuition, agility with words, quickness of thought, and unwavering confidence. He had elevated self-promotion to an art form over the years, and acrobatics on the back of a galloping horse were probably easier. All you needed was balance and nerve for that. You did not have to convince someone of their need for your services and the transfer of money from their pocket to yours.

Tamás rapped boldly on the black door of the red wagon.

*"**Weristes!?**" ("Who is it?")* a deep voice yelled gruffly in German from within.

Having no understanding of the language, Tamás took a risk and opened the door. On the other side stood a scowling, red-faced mountain of a man in long underwear with charcoal black hair and a matching, impeccably dyed and waxed moustache. Even out of costume, the owner and ringmaster was an imposing character. He was regularly approached by performers of one sort or another wanting to join his cirque, but few made the cut.

"Habe ich gesagt, könntest reinkommen?!" ("Did I say come in?!)

he bellowed, and Tamás got the gist of the words, bowed in apology, and stepped down the stairs backwards.

The angry mountain switched languages and grumbled, *"Clearly you don't speak German. Is this better?"* The three men nodded.

"Well, what do you want?"

"Forgive us, sir." Tamás said. *"The tall young man with the pigs, Hans, said we'd find you here."*

"If you want work, talk to Hans about it. He does the hiring."

"We did speak with him, but we are performers, sir. Musicians, singers, acrobats, dancers. We have stunt horses...and a fortune teller." Tamás had added the last for good measure, though Nadya would not have appreciated the billing. The twins kept straight faces.

"Hah! Gypsies. I don't put much stock in your kind, though I could probably use a back-up fortune teller. The one I have hasn't been here long. Old. Unpredictable. Not very friendly. Scares some folks. Me, I don't put any stock in that sooth-saying nonsense."

He looked Ion and Amoun up and down. Twins were always a draw, and these two were quite good looking. The ladies loved handsome young men performing dangerous stunts.

"Yes, sir, we are Roma," declared Tamás, *"but not like those you may be used to. Our family travels alone. Our horses are outside if you would like to see them."*

The ringmaster poked his head out the door, took one look at Baro – who took the opportunity to whinny, toss his head back and shake his glorious mane – and changed his tune.

"Come in, then." He opened the door wide and stepped aside. The three men entered and quickly took in their surroundings.

"You may be in luck. It just so happens that my last Gypsy act left this morning. Something to do with a 'dark forewarning' about Nazis. Scheisse! Impressive horsemanship and beautiful women, but completely unreliable..." he said, unconcerned about offending the men standing before him. *"Scheisse! The Heer don't bother us! They only come to be entertained! 'Dark forewarning' my hind end!"*

Tamás nodded. He'd heard nothing about Nazis and had no idea who *"the Heer"* were.

The Heer *(Heer)* – The German army

There was a taut moment of silence while the ringmaster twisted the right side of his moustache into a sharp point. *"Tell you what. Come back in two days with the rest of your troupe and show me what you can do. Come early before the afternoon matinee. Yes?"*

"We will be here. Thank you, sir." Tamás bowed in gratitude and Ion and Amoun did the same. The ringmaster turned and walked back to his desk where he sat down, muttered something in German and began shuffling paperwork.

The three exited the wagon and once outside, Ion asked, *"Shouldn't we have asked how much it pays?"*

"Men like that call all the shots," replied his father. *"It's his outfit. You can look around and see that it's well run. It's wiser to show him what we can do, and then see what he offers. I can assure you that it will be more than we are used to. Let's go speak with that fellow, Hans, again. He'll know more, and maybe we can get a closer look at that machine."*

Hans was happy to show them around and explained that while Cirque Zeigler was a traveling show, it had been based in Belgrade for some time. They were doing well there, and Boss said that as long as tickets kept selling and the grandstands stayed full, he'd continue to rent the land.

Hans warned, *"That means that our performers need to stay on their toes, though. We have to make up new routines all the time to keep folks coming back."* He'd been with the Cirque his whole life and knew everything about it from top to bottom and end to end.

Tamás wondered how Hans had gotten the limp.

Upon hearing about the audition, Nadya and Katiza were thrilled and nervous at the same time. Katiza was not yet back in shape. Stunts would have to be modified. They had to put on their best show and two days wasn't nearly enough time to prepare.

Frederich Ziegler was a third-generation Cirque owner who recognized talent when he saw it. He knew what his audiences would pay to see, and had a keen eye for beautiful horses, daring men and exotic women.

Before the family had even finished their audition, he jumped up, waved his cane in the air, and shouted, *"Herrlich! Herrlich! Splendid! You're hired! We practice every day at this hour. You start tomorrow. Both performances. Mondays we're off. Your cut of the gate will be determined by how much the crowd likes you. And call me 'Boss' like everyone else."*

He then promptly turned his attention to the high wire where a petite young woman with blonde ringlets was making her way across while holding a Chinese umbrella. *"Sabella! Bravo!"* He called up to her, *"You're more lovely every day, my dear!"*

That night around the fire, the family celebrated their good fortune in having found favor with Herr Ziegler. They talked about the fact that while it rarely happened, sometimes things just fell perfectly into place, and when they did, it was a sign from O Del. The Cirque signaled the beginning of a new life.

Later, after the others had retired, Nadya saw several pillars of light above the river. She believed they were a confirmation that all was as it was meant to be. She pointed them out to Tamás, and the two of them watched until the lights shot back up into the sky. Then, they went to bed without words.

The twins were in their tent, and Katiza was in her vardo curled up nursing Aleasa to sleep. No other love could compare to what she felt for her child. Certainly not the affection of a man. No. This was higher and deeper – fiercer. More like the way O Del loved His children. She'd forgotten how that felt until now. How blessed she was to have known so many kinds of love.

☾
Chapter Fourteen
~ Fates and Fortunes ~

"The show must go on."

*A*s soon as they moved their camp onto the grounds, the family was swept up in the rhythms of Cirque Zeigler. Hearty meals were served family style three times a day, so it did not take long to meet all the other performers and crewmembers, some of whom were destined to become close friends. Clowns and contortionists, sword swallowers, highwire walkers and fire eaters, little people and large, animal trainers, acrobats and more. All with hearts that needed the same things: love, acceptance, and a home.

'Troupe Balval, ' as the family now called themselves, had been living apart from a caravan so long that being welcomed into the cirque community felt awkward at first. The patriarch was reserved. His wife and children were free to make their own acquaintances, but he had no reason to trust any gadje, and frequently reminded them that first, foremost, and forever, they were Roma.

Practicing their acts did not consume all their time, so when offered the opportunity to learn the trapeze and wire walking, Ion and Amoun enthusiastically accepted. They started out on the lower wire, which, though only a few feet off the ground, presented plenty of challenges, including learning to juggle while riding a unicycle. Fortunately, when a performer lost their balance, the worst they might suffer would be bruises or a twisted ankle.

The high wire was a different story. First, you climbed a rope ladder to a small platform high above the grandstands. If you weren't nervous, it meant you'd never witnessed anyone fall. The twins had suffered enough broken bones in their lives that they approached the training with respect. A net remained in place during practice, but at the Boss's direction, it was removed before performances. Boss knew audiences.

Ion took an immediate liking to a petite, blonde aerial performer named Sabella. The attraction was mutual, and he learned the wires so quickly that they developed an act together. Boss approved it with a wink that made the couple feel uncomfortable and added it to the show, where it was met with vigorous rounds of applause and cheers due to the dangerous aspect of such dual performances, and because audiences liked to believe that artists were romantically linked.

Katiza also became close friends with Sabella. They were near the same age, and the German girl loved taking care of baby Aleasa while Katiza practiced and performed.

While their children were able to handle the rigors of the Cirque schedule, both Nadya and Tamás were being forced to accept the limitations of their aging bodies. Nadya's back and hips were stiff and painful, and her hands ached. She remained a part of the act but performed her scarf dances in the center of the arena instead of on horseback.

The hardships of their life had left their mark on Tamás. Every injury he'd suffered was returning to haunt him, and he did his best to hide a limp when he was in the ring. His children teasingly suggested that he borrow Boss's hair dye but he insisted that the grey made him look more distinguished. Adoring female Cirque-goers proved him right, but Nadya just laughed. She owned his heart and he owned hers.

Having reluctantly relinquished the stunt riding to his offspring, Tamás focused his energies on scoring their performances with dramatic background music. His rousing violin solos dazzled the audiences and made the troupe's act even more exciting. Boss, who'd been relying on organ music and drums up to that point, was greatly pleased, and rewarded him with the title of Music Director, which came with a bonus and a new hat with a gold cord.

Given the center ring in which to showcase their skills, they'd designed a daring new routine, and Katiza was nervous about parts of it. Hans was making last-minute preparations, and as she awaited her cue behind the heavy red curtain, she leaned against Baro's muscled neck, stroked his gleaming coat, and confessed, *"I'm not sure I'm ready for this, old boy. How about you? Are you going to be okay?"*

He turned his head, whinnied softly, and nuzzled her cheek. *"Alright then,"* she laughed. *"Such a glory hog. I'll see you in the ring."*

Hans touched her elbow. *"The torches are lit. You're on."*

While a clown and miniature pony held the crowd's attention in a brightly-lit side ring, Katiza and Nadya slipped into their places in the darkened center arena. The spotlight followed the comedy act until the end, when the pony chased the clown out of the ring, and then, the grand tent went dark and remained silent for several long moments. According to Boss, such pregnant pauses heightened the drama, and Boss knew the business.

Cirques have always been about thrills and chills, laughter, and awe, but the experience goes far beyond entertainment. Ticket holders pay to escape the limitations of the dreary outside world. When the tent flaps close behind us and we find our seats, we become part of a collective fantasy where emotions can run free, and if the artists do their jobs well, we leave filled with wonder, lifted higher, and reminded that human beings really are capable of truly incredible things. The operation of a successful Cirque requires an understanding of psychology, and the scheduling of acts plays a major part in keeping the audience spellbound. Boss knew how to weave that spell.

There was, at Cirque Ziegler, a precise moment when star performers were to make their entrance, and it could not be missed. If they appeared too soon, tension would not have been built. Too late, and the crowd would become restless. Only when the anticipation had become palpable was the spotlight operator given the signal to flip the switch.

In the case of Troupe Balval, Tamás heightened the drama by playing a singular, poignant note that sailed over the stands in the darkness. When it faded into silence, a shaft of light would stream down upon Katiza and Nadya, where they stood back to back, swathed in shimmering gold and red silk, their exotic dance moves creating the illusion of an undulating flame.

The music intensified and the pool of light widened as the women danced and twirled outward, their flowing scarves and skirts spreading 'fire' around the ring. The sensuous dance was a mesmerizing introduction to the family's main act.

201

When the two women slipped away into the shadows, the spotlight moved to the curtain where torches flamed on either side. Hans had placed others, unlit, at points around the ring before the act began. The audience was primed and ready when a deep, disembodied voice announced, *"'Das Feuer!' 'Batpa!'* ***'The Fire!'*** **Troooooupe Balval!"**

 Tamás had orchestrated powerful music to heighten the entrance and when the horses charged through the curtain with Ion and Amoun astride and reared up on their hind legs, the crowd came alive. The twins each grabbed a torch and galloped around the arena lighting all the others. Then, they brought the horses nose-to-nose in the center of the arena and jumped up into standing positions on their backs. This was Nadya's cue to dance into the ring where she began to toss more burning torches up to them one at a time. The heat from multiple fiery clubs could not be tolerated for long, and when each young man was holding three, they began to juggle the fire. As the act progressed, more torches were added until at least eight were in motion at all times. Ribbons of charcoal smoke trailed over the arena as the brothers tossed them high in the air and back and forth between one another. The act ended with each one being dropped back down to Nadya as it fell, while she danced gracefully around the ring returning them to their holders.

Tamás was never able to watch the performance without unconsciously rubbing the scars on his arm.

The second part of the act demanded much more of Katiza. Back behind the curtain, she fiddled with her costume while the usual pre-performance dialogue ran through her head. *"You can do this. Stop doubting yourself. This costume is too tight. You need to lose weight."*

Hans was nearby. *"Anything you need me to do?"*

"I hate the smell of kerosene," she grumbled. *"It gives me a headache."*

"I'm sorry," he said sympathetically, patting her gently on the arm and holding open the curtain. *"Fly high."*

She waited for her opening and danced into the center of the arena where her brothers were riding around the ring while standing on the horse's backs. After a few twirls, she heard Amoun whistle for her to get ready. She calculated the distance and Treu's speed, and when the right moment came, ran to his side, where her brother reached down and pulled her up to stand behind him. Her timing was perfect and she was quickly able to find Treu's rhythm. The stunt was flawless, and the applause confirmed it, but you never dared allow yourself the luxury of satisfaction until the entire performance was over.

Ion signaled from the other side of the arena and Amoun slowed Treu's gait. Seconds later, Baro was beside them. The men reached out, grasped one another's forearms and with mere inches between them, the horses kept pace side by side.

The next move was Katiza's.

She hadn't yet regained her full strength since giving birth, and while her brothers tried to be understanding, they couldn't possibly know what it was like to have your body completely change in a matter of months. She looked fine to them, so they assumed she could do what she'd always done before. That's what made her nervous.

The stunt demanded that she climb up onto Amoun's shoulders while the horses continued to run. *"One more lap,"* she whispered in her brother's ear. Any more than that and an audience would sense fear.

Katiza performed such maneuvers by focusing on one muscle and one move at a time as she talked herself through. *"First, a foot on his waist. Good. Now the other..."* It was best to keep momentum, otherwise things could get shaky or stall. *"Keep going. Hoist yourself onto his shoulders, and he'll put his free hand on your right foot to steady you. Crouch gracefully for a second or two. Keep your head up! Eyes forward! Smile! Believe in yourself, Katiza. No one in the audience can do what you are doing. Show 'em how it's done. Now tighten your gut and* **stand up.***"*

It was just like climbing to the top of a tree, really, except that the tree was moving and the ground beneath it was rolling like a wave in a storm.

Her brothers were incredibly strong. She trusted them completely, and for some crazy reason, when she was standing on their shoulders, she believed she could fly. When that moment came, and she released yards of hand-painted silk that billowed behind her like the wings of a magnificent butterfly, it became a reality.

Thinking it was the highlight of the show, the crowd responded wildly, but Tamás' children had grown up with their father's urging to *"Take it up a notch!"* and they always did.

A look from Ion, and Katiza made small circles with her arms to gather in the fabric. Then she dropped down from Amoun's shoulders onto Treu's back, leapt over to Baro, climbed up onto Ion's shoulders and repeated the stunt. As the butterfly flew, Nadya entered the arena and tossed two large flags to her sons, who held them high while the horses continued to run around the ring.

There was no allowance for a wrong move. Gasps and shouts exploded from the audience, the drums pounded, the cymbals clashed and the fiddlers, led by Tamás, played furiously.

When the horses slowed, Katiza drew in the fabric again and slid down from Ion's shoulders onto Baro's back. Amoun then jumped over from Treu and she allowed the butterfly wings to unfurl again. Nadya led riderless Treu back through the curtain.

The spotlight now shone on majestic Baro as he thundered around the ring kicking up sawdust, with the three siblings standing on his broad back, wings and flags flying behind.

They took a few more laps for the purpose of blowing kisses to the adoring crowd, and it was time for Tamás to cap off the performance. Dressed in black with a shiny red sash and matching bandana, he walked boldly through the curtain brandishing a short whip which the horses knew was only for show. Baro came to a halt in front of him and when his master cracked the whip, he reared up on his hind legs and walked backwards, allowing his riders to dismount one by one – Ion and Amoun doing flips and Katiza sliding off gracefully into their waiting arms with a flourish of scarves and an elegant curtsey. No one knew how badly her legs were shaking from the strain of the stunts.

Next, the troupe lined up to take their bows.

When the applause began to settle down, the brothers looked at one another, whispered and pretended to be embarrassed. Amoun shook his finger at Ion, and Ion looked sheepish. Then, Tamás looked disapprovingly at them both, whistled and they all turned to look at the curtain as Treu pranced out to renewed cheers and applause. This was when Boss strode into the ring and took more bows as though he deserved the glory. Once corseted into his red satin, gold-trimmed suit with its fringed epaulettes, with his top hat and tall black boots, he cut quite a striking, be it round, figure.

Troupe Balval consistently drew crowds and received standing ovations. When the seats were full, Boss was happy, and the happier he was the more generous he became.

*A*s manager, Hans knew the Cirque as well as Boss. Performers came and went, and he'd learned not to form attachments. Even so, he'd taken a liking to Tamás' family and they'd all become friends.

As the only child of a famous husband and wife high wire team, Hans had been trained in the art from the time he was small. He was about ten when Boss – who was determined to recruit the Bauers for Cirque Zeigler – offered them twice their current wage. Audiences loved performing families and he promised them top billing. They accepted on the spot, traveled back with him, and everyone was happy.

*N*othing engages spectators quite like the high wire. A darkened tent and preceding warnings fuel the crowd's nervous anticipation, and as the act progresses, they forget to blink. A shaky step – feigned or real – triggers primal fear, and the fact that a deadly fall could occur at any moment keeps anxiety levels high. No one relaxes or sits back in their seat again until a wire walker's feet are firmly planted on the ground.

At Cirque Ziegler, the drums would roll, the lights would dim, and the peanut vendors would freeze where they stood. Then a somber, commanding voice would boom, *"Ladies and gentlemen, your attention please!"* and the formidable figure of the ringmaster would appear in the spotlight at the center of the arena.

"Thank you for being a part of Cirque Zeigler!" Boss would declare. *"We hope you are enjoying yourselves!"* (He'd say it three times in German, Serbian and English.) The crowd would respond with whistles and applause while he turned slowly in a half-circle and waved his hat over each set of bleachers. When folks grew quiet again, he would continue in a serious voice.

"And now, my friends…" (a low drum roll would add drama to his words), *"our next act is so dangerous that I must ask you to remain absolutely quiet for the sake of our performers. Thank you for your cooperation. And now, ON WITH THE SHOW!"* His pronouncement was followed by a deep bow and another wave of his hat. The spotlight

followed him until he walked back out through the curtain and then switched off, leaving the tent in semi-darkness. The moments of silence were punctuated only by an occasional muffled cough and the scattered whispers of parents hushing the curious chirping of their children. Then suddenly, the spotlight would blaze, lighting up the high wire and the performers as they climbed up to the platform. It was good entertainment when show-goers gripped their kids' hands and pulled them onto their laps so that they could cover the little ones' eyes if a stunt went wrong. One slip of a foot and broken bodies would be strewn on the sawdust like rag dolls. The riskier the acts, the more tickets they sold, and since the performers were paid accordingly, they pushed themselves to the limit and beyond.

*T*he accident was no one's fault. Other stunts were just as dangerous. The whole idea was to put audiences on the edge of their seats. That was what a good Cirque needed, and that's what Boss delivered. In the case of Hans' family, it was just fate. That was the best way to look at it when things went wrong. Had there been a net, the story of his life would have been different, but nets weren't used during performances. Audiences didn't hold their breath when there was a net. You had to be good enough not to need one.

It was the highlight of their routine, with Hans' parents balancing on wooden chairs and their son standing between them with a rope. He'd toss an end to each of them, and they'd begin a game of jump rope, with their son as the jumper. It was fun. Each time he'd jump and land again, the wire would bounce, the chairs would wobble, the cymbals would clash, and the audience would gasp. They'd performed the stunt dozens of times without incident. It was a crowd favorite.

Hans knew only what he had been told. There was a black hole where the rest of the memory should have been. A chair had slipped, and they all fell. When he woke up in the hospital, the doctor broke the news that his parents had both died upon impact and while the resilience of his young frame had spared him the same fate, a crushed hip and splintered leg would prevent him from ever performing again.

Tragedies happened in their line of work and everyone knew the risks. Long months in the hospital taught young Hans to live with pain that would become a lifelong companion. The orphaned child had nowhere to go and when he was released, Boss said the Cirque was home.

(

Chapter Fifteen
~ Dazbog ~

"Then I shall tell you what I know, and whether you believe me or not,
the future will prove me out."

*I*n Boss's operation, everyone cared for one another and no one was left out unless they preferred to be. Such was the case with Dazbog, the fortune teller and sometimes magician, although the magician part applied mostly to his very real and frequent disappearing act.

The fellow used the name Dazbog, after the Slavic god of fortune, though people often shortened it to 'Daz,' which rather diminished his preferred aura of mystery. His celestial blue wagon had been painted under strict direction. Every element had significance. The sun, moon, stars, seasons, and a wolf howling in silhouette – the symbol of the Serbian people. Ornate golden letters proclaimed, *'The All-Seeing Dazbog',* and below that, *'Fates and Fortunes.'*

The fellow kept to himself, seldom joined community meals, and was not in residence much of the time. His door was always locked, and he left no indication of where he had gone or when he would be back. If you wanted your fortune told, you had to be persistent and extremely patient.

People came anyway, for it was said his predictions were uncannily accurate. You would see them standing self-consciously on the top step. They would knock, look around nervously and wait. And tap a toe. And knock again. Sometimes they would lean forward, press their noses against the door, squint, and try to see through the peephole. This was futile as the opening was covered on the inside by a carved crescent moon that swung from a nail. You were either very stubborn or very lucky if you saw the moon move and a wary eyeball peer back at you.

Dazbog *(DAZSH-bog)*

The same tenacity was required of Boss when he needed a wheel fixed, for as aggravating as the old man was, he was also a master at repairing wheels of every kind, both wooden and mechanical, and that's what he was doing the day Katiza walked by. Having not seen him in person before, she stopped to introduce herself.

"Hello."

He did not look up.

"I'm Katiza. We're rather new here. The Gypsy horses act. Troupe Balval. We've not met, and I've been wanting to compliment you on your beautiful wagon. My mother and I also paint vardos."

He did not move.

Fearing that she was bothering him, Katiza said she was sorry for interrupting his work and kept walking.

"Katiza." He stood up and called after her.

She turned and smiled. *"Yes. Katiza. Nice to meet you, Daz. That is what they call you, right?"*

"They do, though I prefer 'The All-Seeing Dazbog,'" he said. The wild mane of wizardly white hair, long beard and eyepatch made his expressions hard to read.

"Oh. I'm sorry," Katiza immediately apologized.

"I was joking," he said with a small chuckle.

"Ohhh." She laughed in relief. *"Well, I like both names."* Everything about him felt incredibly familiar, though she could not remember ever having seen him or anyone even remotely like him before. By the way he was looking at her with his head cocked sideways, she sensed he was feeling the same.

The eye without the patch was fixed upon her with great seriousness. *"This may sound strange, but I would like to tell your fortune soon,"* he said. *"No charge, of course."* Then, not wanting to frighten her, he added, *"It's sort of a tradition with newcomers to the Cirque."* (There had only been a couple.)

The offer took her by surprise, but she heard herself accept, *"Of course! When?"*

"At the full moon, three days hence. That is the best time for me.

But do not come too late. I have other...er..." he paused, searching for the word, and used one that sounded vague, *"enterprises I must tend to."*

"May I come in the evening after my baby is asleep?"

"Yes, of course. Little Aleasa..." He cut himself short but it was too late.

Katiza stared at him. *"You know my daughter's name?"*

"Well, I am the all-seeing Dazbog. I will look forward to our next visit," he said from within his whiskers. Then he vigorously rubbed behind the eye patch, turned his back, and continued his work.

Katiza wasn't sure what to think.

$\mathcal{T}$he family was flourishing in their new environment. Nadya and Tamás were happier and more relaxed than they had been in a long time. Amoun, who never missed a meal, had made a good number of friends that way, and Ion and Sabella were inseparable.

The girl had taken it upon herself to give Ion, Amoun and Katiza basic schooling. The group agreed that it was best to keep the sessions a secret for the time being, so they met in her trailer. When any of them grew frustrated with their studies, she would say, *"You'll get it, darling. Everyone needs to know how to read, write, and do math! Now, let's begin again!"*

Sabella loved the cinema and called everyone *'darling.'* Even though she looked like one of the Kewpie dolls that Cirque-goers won at the carnival games, beneath the surface, Boss's German niece was tough as steel. She'd been born into the world of entertainment and was next in line for ownership when her uncle retired. She had already begun to nurture the dream of marrying Ion and the two of them running Cirque Zeigler together, but for that to happen he could not remain illiterate.

Katiza's motivation for schooling was the promise she had made to her mother about the book. She had considered bringing it to Sabella but knew Nadya would never approve. Her mother had shown her where the box was kept and had emphasized more than once that its contents were to remain safely hidden until the time came for it to be passed down to her daughter, and then, eventually, to Aleasa. Katiza had no idea when that was going to happen but in light of her mother's stories, she knew there was a crucial reason it must be protected.

Maybe Dazbog knew. Several weeks had passed since the meeting in his wagon, but she would never forget it.

*H*e had promptly answered her knock, kissed her hand in a gentlemanly manner, and invited her in. Hot tea was waiting, and a plate of small cakes which she guessed he must have purchased just for her, because it was impossible to imagine a dainty pastry making it past his facial hair. She was touched by his efforts to make her feel welcome.

She surveyed the wagon. There was no woman's touch. Candles sat haphazardly in puddles of wax, cobweb-covered antlers hung from the walls, chairs were draped with hides, and an immense bear skin covered the floor. A worn tapestry at the back of the wagon divided off his sleeping quarters.

It was the den of a hunter and smelled of the wild. When she commented on the rug, he said with a faraway look, *"I still carry the scars from that encounter,"* and patted his side. *"It isn't what you think it is."* He did not elaborate, and she did not want to know. She was barefoot, so tucked her feet up underneath herself to avoid touching it.

She was uncertain about the rugged fellow's motives at first, but as they talked and she heard more of his story, she realized that he had devoted his entire life to the service of others. If someone got lost in life, he tried to point them to the right path. He was guided by strong instincts, which had led him to his present occupation. There had been times, he said, when he did not like what he was shown, but he was faithful to deliver the messages, regardless. He also admitted that he was slowing down these days and enjoyed more time alone.

It was not what one would call a typical fortune-telling session. There was no crystal ball, no reading of palms or the tea leaves left in her cup. The two of them just chatted like old friends. She noticed that he was in the habit of stopping mid-sentence, as though there was more he wanted to say but couldn't, so the next time he did it she asked, *"What are you not saying, Daz?"*

He stared at his fingernails for a long moment, picked up a

210

jackknife from the table next to his chair and began to clean them with the point of the blade. Finally, he said, *"I don't want to frighten you."*

The words put her on guard. *"Why would I be frightened if you are speaking honestly?"*

"Do you believe me to be honest, Katiza?"

"I have no reason not to," she replied.

"Then I shall tell you what I know, and whether you believe me or not, the future will prove me out. I pray to the Almighty that it will be of help to you. Your life must be spared, for there are things of grave importance for you to do."

Their earlier exchange had turned a somber corner and she was not sure how she should feel. Dazbog held out his hands, then, and she took them. They were calloused and cracked, and she mentally determined to bring him some of her mother's healing salve.

"I have seen it coming." He began. *"A great and terrible evil. A beast with a blood red sign on its forehead. Its lust for power is insatiable. It is fueled by…"*

She flinched and he grasped her hands tighter.

"Forgive me, child. You don't need every detail, but you must know that it is building a mighty army which will do its bidding. The ranks will march far and wide inflicting such unspeakable pain and sorrow that even when this beast's reign finally ends," he paused to emphasize the next words, *"the world will never forget."*

He dropped her hands, sat back in his chair, and shook his head miserably. *"It's making its plan, gathering its forces. I can see the wheels turning."*

Katiza had no idea what he was talking about or why he was telling her such terrible things.

He read her expression and said earnestly. *"I am only telling you this, dear Katiza, because they will come for you – the Gypsies – and for others who have committed no crime. Countless innocents will perish. I am forewarning you so that you can be spared when this enemy reaches our door. My heart breaks to say that not all will escape."*

He choked out the last words and angrily brushed tears from his eyes.

Katiza, child of Charos, was accustomed to the supernatural, and knew that O Del and Balval spoke in many ways through many means. So, rather than challenging him, she'd thought it wiser to hear him out and asked, *"What should I do?"*

"Be prepared to flee. Take what you need. Most important is the silver box."

"How do you know about the box?" She interrupted.

"I can see it," he said, closing his eyes. *"There are designs etched in the top. It was first given to your grandmother. You have been shown what's inside."*

She gulped.

"You shall not return to this place, my Dear, and it must not fall into the enemy's hands. He seeks what it contains."

Before she could ask it, he answered her next question. *"Do not worry about your daughter. She is safest with Sabella. They will assume the child is hers."*

Dazbog paused to gauge the impact of his words. *"Do you understand all of this?"* When she nodded, he continued.

"There will be much confusion when this happens, but that will work in your favor. Ride to the edge of the forest where your protector will be waiting. He will guide you from there."

Then, he looked at her with great kindness, and said, *"I am sorry, dear child. I know how this must all sound to you, but I could not leave you in ignorance."*

She walked back to her vardo in a daze and after a sleepless night, made the decision the following morning not to allow fear to govern her days, but to be more vigilant, nevertheless. It was a challenge to balance the two. Daz's warning had come with the promise of safety for her and Aleasa, so she anchored her thoughts in that. But what about the rest of her family? When she'd asked him, he'd replied apologetically, *"I have not seen that yet."*

She struggled constantly with whether to tell the others what Daz had said, but something held her in check – perhaps it was the tenuous hope that the old seer had seen into a different future. Maybe things were going to get better, not worse. It was hard to imagine that Boss,

212

who carried a pistol on his hip, would be unable to protect his Cirque family from such an invasion. But just to be safe, she exacted a promise from Sabella that should something terrible happen, the young woman would raise Aleasa as her own. Sabella argued against her friend's concerns and called them unfounded, but ultimately, she gave her word.

Katiza also started keeping an eye on the soldiers who came to the shows. So far, she saw no change. They were still eating peanuts and popcorn, laughing, applauding, whistling, and having a good time.

She hoped with her whole heart that Dazbog was wrong, and although she felt bad about it, she stopped walking past his wagon.

*H*is appearance at the family's campfire several weeks later took them all by surprise. Katiza made room for him to sit between her and Nadya, which appeared to make him very happy. He declined the offer of tobacco or wine, but thoroughly enjoyed some venison jerky, and complimented Tamás on his meat smoking skills.

Considering his reputation as unsociable, he seemed very comfortable among them. Conversation flowed easily, and at the mens' request, he shared a few stories of his most daring hunting excursions. When the violins came out and Nadya began to sing, he looked as though he might cry.

After a while, Katiza said to her mother, *"Dai, Daz could greatly benefit from some of the healing salve you make for Dati."*

Their guest self-consciously stuck his hands in his pockets and said that while it was truly a kind gesture, there was no need.

"Oh, I assure you, there is a need," Katiza insisted with a laugh.

Nadya replied, *"Yes, of course! I'll be right back!"* She got up, went into the vardo, and returned with a small pot of ointment.

"Give me your hands," she coaxed, and Daz reluctantly offered them. *"Oh my. Katiza is right. Well, this will help."* She slathered them with the salve and began gently massaging it in.

He was embarrassed and looked at Tamás to see if he was bothered. The patriarch was not, and said, *"She knows what she's doing, eh? I could not play this fiddle if not for her magic concoction."*

Daz turned his attention back to Nadya. *"That does feel good. My callouses thank you. You wouldn't want to see my feet!"* They all laughed. *"What is your recipe? Or is it a secret?"*

Nadya replied, *"I've developed it over the years, but Yarrow is the main ingredient, then honey, and some other plants you probably haven't heard of. It's healed worse wounds than these."*

"I am certain it has. Bless you, dear soul," he said with deep emotion, *"for all that you are to everyone."* She did not know how to reply to the tender remark so kept her head down and added more salve. Ion threw another log on the fire.

Melancholy notes from the violins mingled with wayward sparks and disappeared into the darkness above. No one spoke. Daz took the moment to look around at all of them and stated, *"I am here because great change is on the horizon. I have felt it in these old bones."*

He had their attention. Katiza braced herself for what he would say next. Nadya looked into his face and continued to hold his hands. She had known the instant she touched them that he was a true seer.

"Tell, us Daz, she said, *"What do you know?"*

He replied, *"We must be vigilant and listen to the Spirit you call Balval. Our fates depend upon it. You know His voice, as do I. Many don't, but that is not for lack of Him speaking, eh?"*

They all nodded, and Tamás replied, *"'Tis so."*

Daz continued, *"His words are written on everything He has made in this world and beyond,"* he looked upward. *"But only when we seek Him can there be a conversation. Only then can we know the role we are to play in this brave tale. We may do our share of wandering, but we are never lost, for His eye is upon us from beginning to end. Let us be faithful, then. He will supply the strength. Be ready, my friends. We shall all be affected by what is coming."*

Visibly moved, Tamás walked over and put his hand on the old man's shoulder. *"Thank you for this visit, and for your wisdom, my friend. You are always welcome at our fire."*

Dazbog stood to his feet and the two embraced. Ion and Amoun came over to do the same, followed by Katiza, whom he looked at with an expression that said, *"This is the most I could do."*

Turning to Nadya, he took both of her hands, pressed his face into them and kissed them as reverently as if they belonged to an angel.

214

Chapter Sixteen
~ Amoun's Dream ~

"The only thing we can count on in this life is change."

$\mathcal{I}$n the dream, I was standing at the river's edge with a trusted friend. We were skipping stones in a contest to see whose would go the farthest. My stone traveled well beyond what either of us thought was possible, and we were both amazed.

The river was deep and wide. I could see the Cirque tents on the other side, but there was no way to reach them. I looked up and down the river expecting to see a boat or a bridge, but there was neither, and I wondered how we'd gotten there. I was also worried about how we were going to get back in time for the next performance.

Suddenly, the sky grew dark and a cold wind whipped up whitecaps on the water's surface. Thunder rumbled from above. I heard a voice within it but could not make out the words. The ground began to tremble beneath my feet and dozens of snakes slithered out from the bushes and raced toward me with their jaws open. I recognized the riverbank to be the same one from my childhood where Katiza had been bitten and the stranger had saved her.

I tried to run, but my feet were stuck in the clay. There was a great weight holding me down. The harder I fought, the deeper I sank, and I realized my struggle was futile.

In the next instant, lightning split the sky and struck in the middle of the river. A man arose from the water and walked toward me. He held the lightning within his body, and when he stepped onto the shore, the snakes turned and sped back into the bushes in fear. He stretched out his arm to lift me up, and when I grasped his hand, the power in his body rushed through my veins. The charge caused my heart to beat so hard that it woke me up.

I did not sleep for the rest of the night and I can still feel the man's hand gripping mine.

$\mathcal{T}$he following morning, Amoun shared his dream with Hans, who listened, nodded, and said, *"There's someone I think you should meet."*

Jakob Tomich was a Serbian man. He bore no title, nor did he desire one. He was simply a servant of God and a traveler who went where he was led, helping however he could. The Cirque was an occasional stop, and Hans did not think it to be a coincidence that Jakob had just arrived. A small group would be meeting at Hans' camp in the evening after the last performance to hear Jakob's stories.

Amoun accepted Hans' invitation.

The word had spread, and more people than usual were gathered. Conversation was lively and the comradery strong, with much embracing, handshaking, and back-patting. Amoun knew many of the folks casually and his attendance was greeted with enthusiasm.

They'd all come to hear Jakob, who started by giving thanks to God for bringing him safely to the Cirque. Then he shared news about his travels and the things he had witnessed, particularly the miracles.

At one point, he paused, looked at Amoun and announced, *"The God we serve is known by many names. To our Romany brothers and sisters, He is O Del. Why would anyone be bothered by this or any other difference, for that matter, when God Himself is not? He gives grace freely to those with humble hearts and favors no man or woman over another, whatever their heritage or accomplishments may be. I see this in my travels."*

A consensus of affirmative murmurs followed, and Amoun vigorously nodded his head. He was impressed by Jakob's gentle strength and the words rang true in the young man's soul.

After the meeting ended, Hans introduced the two of them, and opened the conversation. *"Jakob, Amoun, has had a dream."*

Hans knew Amoun felt awkward, but he continued. *"I believe it means something."*

Jakob was interested and asked Amoun, *"Would you like to tell me about it?"*

"Well, I've never had such a dream before." Amoun answered uncomfortably.

Jakob Tomich *(YAH-kōb TOE-mich)*

216

"Go ahead," urged Hans. *"Tell him."*

As Amoun recounted the dream, he experienced every moment of it all over again. Jakob's eyes were closed while he listened, as though he could see it playing out in his mind. When Amoun finished, he and Hans waited for Jakob to speak.

The man opened his eyes, and asked Amoun, *"What do **you** think your dream means?"*

Amoun had no idea, but the fact that the riverbank had been the same as the one from his youth seemed pertinent, so he mentioned that.

"And what happened at that riverbank when you were young?" Jakob asled.

Amoun shared the story in detail.

Jakob smiled. *"A miracle, then. Yes, that sounds like Him."*

"Who?" asked Amoun.

"The King of Charos, as your sister called him." Jakob's tone was matter of fact. *"How did you feel when He saved her?"*

Amoun remembered. *"I was amazed and wanted to know Him."*

Jakob replied, *"As do all of us here. That is why He came to you in the dream, Amoun. He has seen the desires of your heart. Right now, I think you may be stuck. This world is teeming with evil – much of it hidden – and there are greater things for you to do. Things you will only be able to accomplish with His power."*

Amoun wanted to believe what Jakob said, but he had questions. Knowing this, Jakob asked, *"And what do you think about the other aspects of your dream? The Spirit – Balval, as you call him – has the answers, Amoun."*

Amoun concentrated. Who had been standing by him on the riverbank? Why it was Hans, of course! Another version of Hans, but the same familiar soul. He shared this realization with Jakob, who smiled and urged him to continue.

Skipping stones for a great distance takes skill and precision. Amoun was a great performer, and liked to show off and be applauded, but what good were his performances other than that? There was no more meaning in them than a stone skipping across the water before it sinks.

The river was deep and wide. There was no way to get back to the Cirque. Perhaps he was not meant to.

He shuddered at the memory of the snakes. In his mind they represented evil in its many forms. They had come out of hiding and were on the attack. Could it mean that something unforeseen was about to happen? The darkening sky seemed to point to that, too.

What had the thunder said? Had it been the voice of Balval? His Dai would have said so.

Suddenly, it came to him! The same way Boss commanded the audience's attention, it had been an introduction of the one who was about to appear.

Rivers were life to Gypsies. The lightning was the mighty power of O Del striking the waters. Did it mean that their lives were going to violently change?

It was the King of Charos who rose from the water, drove away the snakes and reached out to save him. The dream was a rescue, a deliverance, and a quickening.

Suddenly, the prophecy given to him by the old woman in the forest when he was young came back.

And what was he to do with all of this?

"I'll be on my way within a few days," said Jakob. *"Join me, Amoun. There are many people who need our help. I believe your dream was a calling, but you alone can answer it."*

The invitation came as a surprise, and Amoun replied that he must give it more thought, as his family's lives would be greatly affected by such a decision on his part. Jakob said he understood, and that the offer would stand.

Amoun told no one else of his dream or about what Jakob had said.

*T*he young man wrestled with the decision throughout the next day, and that night Daz had come to their campfire. His words had amplified what Amoun had already come to believe, and after the rest of his family went to bed, Amoun sat by the fire alone, asking O Del for guidance. In response, a sudden gust of wind swept across the coals and sent sparks flying in all directions. Balval's unmistakable voice spoke to his heart, and he knew.

The next day he told his family.

Katiza listened, put her arms around him, and said she understood.

Ion accused him of being selfish, his anger masking deeper emotions as usual.

Nadya wept, showered his face with kisses, and said she had been shown long ago that when he was grown, he would make the choice to follow Balval.

Tamás stood in silence, his back to the campfire.

Amoun went to him. *"Dati?"*

Tamás turned, grasped his son's shoulders, and looked into his eyes. *"You are your own man, Amoun. May O Del guide your steps and light your path."*

*W*hen they arose the next morning, Amoun was gone.

The family hastily re-designed their act and braced themselves for Boss's disappointment.

When informed of the change and the reasons for it, he surprised them. *"Don't fret. Each of us must find our way. The only thing we can count on in this life is change. Yah? Too bad he couldn't have stayed, though. We could use a preacher around here."*

☾

Chapter Seventeen
~ The Raid ~

"For last year's words belong to last year's language,
and next year's words await another voice."

T.S. Elliot

On days when there was no afternoon show, many of the Cirque folk went shopping in town. It was a nice day and Tamás and Nadya joined a group in one of the smaller trucks. Later on, when they didn't show up for the return trip, it was assumed they'd found other transportation. Back at the Cirque, everyone was making the usual preparations for the evening show, and the absence of the veteran performers went unnoticed.

Katiza had been on an outing that day with Aleasa and returned just in time to take the wee chavi to Sabella's trailer and get into her costume. She met Ion behind the curtain with only moments to spare.

Their parents were not there.

"Ion? Have you seen Dai and Dati?"

"No. Did they not come back from town?"

"I don't know! They never cut it this close." Katiza peeked out at the audience and saw more grey uniforms than usual. The men looked stiff and serious, and an officer was standing next to the grandstand speaking with Boss. She had never seen such a cold look on the ringmaster's face before. She hurried back to Ion.

"What will we do if Dai and Dati don't show up?"

Ion's tone of voice betrayed his anxiety and he snapped, *"What* **can** *we do? We'll have to put on a show anyway!"*

"We don't have a routine without them!" his sister snapped back.

He grumbled something about Amoun and said, *"Then we'll have to make one up as we go. We've been doing this a long time, my pena."*

pena *(PEN-ah)* – sister

Katiza's insides were churning.

"I'm so worried about them! Where could they be? Something has happened, Ion, I can feel it."

"It's time. We have to go on," said her brother. *"Where's Hans?"* He hastily tied Treu's reins to a tent post, leapt onto Baro's back and pulled her up behind him. The music was thin without their father's violin.

Boss's voice rang out from the arena, introducing Troupe Balval. The siblings plastered smiles on their faces and Baro pranced through the curtain.

Two people and a horse were not a 'troupe,' and the audience's applause was unenthusiastic. The look on Boss's face was troubling, but there had been no time to tell him what had happened. They got through the performance, and after they had taken their bows, Hans met them behind the curtain. Neither of them had seen him all day and Katiza immediately knew that something was wrong.

"Nazi soldiers," he said in a deadly quiet voice, *"It's a raid."*

*E*arlier that morning, Boss's world had been turned upside down. He'd been informed of what was happening in town and was braced for the sharp rap on his wagon door when it came. Since Boss was German, the Nazi officer wrongly assumed that his orders would be met with respect and cooperation, so he took a casual, friendly approach and pretended to be interested in the operations of the Cirque.

The pleasantries ended abruptly when he issued the order that Boss round up anyone within his employ who might be Jewish, along with any *'Gypsy filth.'*

Shrewd man that he was, Boss played along, kept his composure, and said it would be impossible to do so on such short notice, as many of the performers and workers came and went during the day and he did not keep tabs on them.

The officer saw the response for the excuse that it was, but he had been instructed to handle the situation tactfully, as the Cirque provided entertainment for the German troops and was not to be shut down. He informed Boss that he would return and enjoy the evening performance himself, and that when it was over, if Boss had not followed the Feuer's commands, the soldiers would take over. Then, he clicked his heels, declared *'Heil Hitler,'* and saluted.

Boss, who had been holding his pistol behind his back the whole time, did not echo the words or return the gesture.

As soon as the officer was out of sight, Boss went in search of Hans. He found him in the arena inspecting the rigging for the aerial performances. *"Hans! Please come here, my friend. I need your help."* Hans knew by the tension in Boss's voice that something was wrong, and he hastened down the rope ladder.

Boss's tone was grim. *"We have a big problem. We need to think fast."*

Hans had never seen Boss so worried. He put his hand on the man's arm and said, *"What is it, Boss? Whatever it is, we can fix it."*

"Not this, I fear. We cannot fix what is happening within the tide of Fascism. A Nazi officer just informed me that he is coming to the performance tonight. After it is over, his soldiers will be arresting some of our people. He's ordered me to cooperate."

Hans tried to take in what he had just been told.

"Obviously," Boss continued, *"They've crossed the line and we are not going to allow this to happen. But we need a plan, and two minds are better than one."*

Hans offered his first thought. *"We need to warn folks so they can leave!"*

Boss deflected the suggestion, *"There's no time for that. They're scattered all over the place. We would have to find them all and even if we could, where would they run to or hide on such short notice during the day? Their chances of escaping would be better at night when they've had time to prepare. Plus, it will look suspicious if entire acts are missing. No. The show must go on as usual, Hans! I fear there are already soldiers posted, watching us."* He looked nervously over his shoulder and around the tent.

Hans nodded. Boss was right. But if they could at least warn some of the people, then...

"Who, specifically Boss? Who are they going to arrest?

Boss answered reluctantly, *"Our Gypsies, Hans. Among others."*

Hans felt numb. His thoughts were scattered and frantic. Realizing he would be of no help in such a state, he closed his eyes, cleared his head, and silently asked for guidance.

In answer, a picture filled his mind and played out like a scene in a film.

"Boss! What about this! I haven't thought it all the way through yet, but maybe it would work…"

"I'm listening."

"First, I tell everyone I can about the raid, but that we have a strategy. I will explain it and beg them to go through with tonight's performance so that everything will look as normal as possible. I'll also tell them that this way, they will have the time to gather their belongings and plan their escape routes."

Boss nodded. *"And then…?"*

Hans continued excitedly as the plan took shape in his mind.

"Then, the show will go on as it always does. When the main performances have finished, we send the clowns into the ring to create a diversion. We tell them to put on that act where they run around in circles yelling 'Fire!' and ringing a bell, and then pretend to put the fire out by climbing into the bleachers and throwing buckets of confetti on the audience.

*"The soldiers will be in the stands, and then we'll set off a **real** fire alarm. I'll have started fires in a couple of barrels of sawdust backstage and people will see the smoke coming up from behind the curtain. We'll plant a few of our stagehands in the grandstands to point and yell, 'LOOK! THE TENT'S ON FIRE! GET OUT OF HERE!' and the crowd will panic and run for the exits. The soldiers will be caught up in the chaos and by the time things settle down, our people will have escaped."* He caught his breath and waited for Boss's reaction.

Boss frowned, stroked his mustache, looked at his faithful friend, and said, *"It could work."*

"With God's help, it could!" Hans enthusiastically agreed.

Boss was not an outspoken man when it came to his beliefs, but he echoed Hans' words twice – the second time with great emphasis, *"With God's help, Hans. Yes, with God's help! Now we must hurry!"*

*H*ans had seen the truck leave for town that morning, but people came and went at will, and he had no idea who was on it. Later in the afternoon he noticed that it was back and thought nothing more about the matter.

By curtain time, the only people Hans hadn't been able to warn were those he feared for most – Katiza and her family. He believed it to be divine timing that Amoun had left on the mission with Jakob, for they would be far away by now, and safe. When he saw Ion and Katiza ride into the ring without Tamás and Nadya, he thought the worst. He waited behind the curtain until they finished their act and immediately told them what was about to happen. Their horses were swift. There was still time for them to escape.

*D*azbog's forewarning had prepared Katiza, and she knew what to do. She told Ion and Hans about the predictions and was relieved when neither of them argued with her.

"Let's go, Ion!"

But instead of doing as she said, Ion slid off Baro's back to the ground and handed her the reins. *"I can't. I have to find Dai and Dati!"*

She tried desperately to persuade him, *"Dai and Dati are in O Del's hands, Ion. They are strong! They would not want us to be foolish! And Daz promised me that Aleasa would be safe! They won't bother Sabella – she's German and Boss will protect her and the baby!"*

Her brother looked at her lovingly and shook his head 'no.'

"You can't stay here, Ion! They will arrest you! They know we're Roma!"

Though he knew he should be afraid, Ion was not. It was a strange moment for him to remember the words of the old woman in the forest from his childhood, but they were ringing in his ears, punctuated by the last thing Dazbog had said, *"Let us be faithful. God will supply the strength."*

"Go, Katiza! I will find you."

She'd never won an argument with her brother. *"You'd better! Do you hear me, Ion?"*

"I promise. Now GO!"

"Hans!" She cried, *"Don't let him do anything stupid!"*

Hans reached up for her hand and said, *"I won't. We have a plan. Go with God, Katiza."* His eyes held hers. *"I ..."* The loud clown act had begun, and she could not make out the rest of his words.

Baro knew where to go without her telling him. A light was flickering in the window of Dazbog's wagon, so she rode up alongside and rapped on the pane.

"Daz! It's me, Katiza! It's begun, as you said! They've come for us!" There was no answer. She didn't know what else to say, so ended with *"I leave you with my love!"*

The next stop was her vardo. She hurried in, changed out of her costume, threw on her cloak, and grabbed the carpet bag that she'd packed weeks earlier should Dazbog's predictions turn out to be true. Then, she ran next door to her parents' vardo and retrieved the silver box from its hiding place.

Baro bowed so that Katiza could climb back on, and they headed for the forest, leaving the lights of the Cirque behind them. She bent her knees, hunched forward over Baro's neck and within seconds, the jet black horse and his hooded rider melted into the darkness.

𝒦atiza's knock on Dazbog's window had awakened him from a nap. He'd received the knowledge earlier that this was the fated night, and knowing what lay ahead, he'd thought it wise to rest. He had not answered Katiza lest conversation slow her escape.

The old hunter gripped the worn arms of his chair, stretched, and dug his bare toes into the pelt on the floor. He blew out the candle beside him and the waxy tendrils of smoke spiraled slowly upward where they mingled with the odor of animal hides. He pulled the pungent air deep into his lungs and savored its taste as his heart began to beat faster. Then, he reached up and removed the eye patch from his face. Behind it was no blind, milky orb, or black, shrunken socket as everyone imagined, but the calm, clear, ice blue eye of a timber wolf.

He undressed in the darkness and as his body changed, he stifled the howl that began to form deep in his throat. Pulling back the tapestry, he lifted a trap door in the wagon floor, and dropped to the ground. By then, the transformation was complete, and only the moon saw the one they called Kesali speed toward the forest.

*W*ith Ion's help, Hans' plan succeeded. Boss kept the officer engaged in conversation and when the chaos erupted during the false fire alarm, the raid was aborted. Almost all those under threat of capture had been able to flee the Cirque grounds. The few that remained were in hiding until Hans could come up with a way to get them out before the soldiers returned.

Ion was determined to go to the city the next morning to find his parents. Until then, he would stay with Sabella. Aleasa fussed for hours that night. Sabella thought she wanted her mother, but Ion knew it was more. She'd been born with the gift and could sense what others did not.

"See, Sabella," he said. *"Even now, as an infant, her heart knows what is happening."* He picked up his niece and held her close. *"Whatever is to come,"* he whispered into her velvety-soft ear, *"there will be no changing this about yourself, little one. You are Roma."*

*E*very fiber of Katiza's being screamed to go back for her daughter, but Baro was being propelled by a greater force, and she had to trust O Del.

A broken web of silvery fog lay over the fields. Baro was galloping so fast that she had to hold on with all her might. They became one, and if not for the sound of his massive hooves pounding the earth, she would have believed that they were flying above it. It seemed impossible for the old horse too keep such a pace and she was greatly relieved when the silhouetted forest came into view. At the tree line, Baro slowed and stopped. His chest was heaving and his breathing was labored and ragged.

Katiza patted his neck and told him how much she loved him and thanked him over and over. *"We'll be okay now dear Baro. Just rest a minute, boy, you'll feel better…"*

A movement to their right startled her. Baro tossed his mane, snorted, and side-stepped.

"Who's there?" Katiza demanded, and an immense white wolf stepped out of the mist.

"Kesali!" she exclaimed with relief. *"Baro, it's Kesali!"*

Though sweet, the reunion had to be brief. The wolf wanted them to follow him into the woods. Trusting that he knew where he was going, they did so, but at a walk this time, for the path was studded with rocks and roots and Baro had nothing left in reserve.

They travelled for hours until Katiza was so tired that her thoughts became fuzzy. At one point, she slumped over and would have fallen off if one of Baro's back hooves had not slipped on a slick stone, causing his hindquarters to lurch to one side and jerk her awake.

The moon finally appeared from behind the clouds and lit up the side of a high embankment to their right. There was a wide spot beneath an overhang just ahead and Katiza saw it as the perfect place to stop.

When she dropped down off Baro's back, her legs buckled beneath her. Every joint in her body ached and her muscles were in knots. Baro's head was hanging down in exhaustion. She'd never seen him so spent.

"Poor boy," she said, patting his side, *"Sweet, sweet boy. You saved me, my dear old friend. We can rest now."*

Kesali came to her and nuzzled her hand up onto his head. She laughed, rubbed his ears, and said, *"You, too, of course, Kesali. What would I ever do without you?"*

She shared her smoked meat with the wolf but had nothing for Baro. They all desperately needed water, but she would have to wait for first light to find it. Remembering that her Dai's box held a dagger, she took it out and slid it in the sheath on her belt. At her gentle coaxing, Baro laid down. She pulled her cape around her body, stretched out next to him to share his warmth and tucked the bag under her head. Kesali sat on her other side to keep watch. She put a hand on each of their backs and within moments, fell into an exhausted sleep.

*W*ith no idea of how she'd gotten there, Katiza found herself standing barefoot among a cluster of bright pink bleeding hearts at the edge of a forest. The delicate arching stalks were bowing before a flawless pearl chalice atop a glistening jade stem.

The regal Trillium stood tall and whispered, *"I promise."* When it spoke, a melody arose from the ground and filled the air – a lullaby Tamás had played for her when she was small.

"No sorrows are remembered here." The Trillium said.

Just ahead, the golden rays of the sun warmed a meadow. The sky was clear and the lush grass was vibrant green. A graceful willow tree stood beside a crystal clear lake and dragonflies danced among fuzzy cattails at its edge.

Katiza yearned to go there, but when she took a step in that direction, a gentle voice said, *"Not yet, dear one. It isn't time."*

One of the dragonflies flew to her, looked at her sweetly and said, *"We will wait for you."*

She knew this place. She'd been here before but had left for a little while. She gazed out over rolling pastures that stretched as far as she could see in every direction, and then her heart leapt, for there was Baro, grazing on a hill! When she called his name, he galloped to her, threw his head back, and whinnied in greeting. He was young, and his coat was gleaming like it had just been brushed. Little flowers were braided into his mane and it was obvious that he was loved and cared for. She was petting his velvety soft nose when a grey, chilly reality abruptly displaced the warmth of the meadow, and she woke up.

She'd slept far longer than intended. Her body was so cold and stiff that she could barely move. Her cape was damp from the ground and offered no warmth. She had no idea where she was or whether it was morning or afternoon.

Her fingers were still entangled in Baro's mane and she nudged him with her leg and whispered, *"Baro!"*

He did not move.

"Baro! Wake up!" His belly was not rising or falling, and unwilling to believe he was gone, she buried her face in his mane and screamed silently over and over in the vain hope that this, too, was a dream from which she would awaken.

When that did not happen, her screams became sobs, and the sobs turned into convulsions that tore at her aching ribcage until she curled into a shivering ball and soaked the earth with her tears.

She could bear no more loss. Her anguish was not only for Baro, who had given his life for her, but for all those she'd left behind. She had no way of knowing what had happened to any of them or if she would ever see them again. Kesali was gone, too. How could she go on? What was she to do now?

In answer, the dream began to reconstruct itself at the edge of her mind.

When she closed her eyes, she could feel the sun on her skin and the peace that permeated that place. There was no loss, death, or grief in that realm, and she would return to it one day, just as Baro had.

Nothing born of love could die. It just went home. We were not intended to live in this world of sorrows forever. If she was still here, there was a reason. She wiped away the tears and got to her feet.

The path they had followed the night before ended here. The trees were sparse – spindly evergreens and alder that had not yet fully leafed out – so she was able to see through the forest. She had no idea which direction to take, but as she took the first steps, a spot of bright white caught her eye – a Trillium rising from its wintry sleep beneath a blanket of dead, brown leaves. Surely it was a sign!

What came next took her completely by surprise: it was the sound of an engine.

She peered anxiously through the trees in every direction and finally saw a cloud of dust rising from a dirt road. Fearing the vehicle could be military, she crouched down until she could get a better look. When it came closer, she recognized it to be one of the old trucks from the Cirque, and she ran to the road and waved.

The driver hit the brakes, leaned over, threw open the door and cried out with relief, *"Katiza! Thank God, I found you!"* It was Hans.

She jumped in, threw her arms around him, and kissed him on both cheeks. *"Hans! I can't believe this! How did know where I was?"*

He held her tight. *"Dazbog! He knocked on my door before dawn! I'd already been thinking I should take this road, but the chances of finding you…well, I didn't…I mean, I prayed, but…"* He couldn't stop shaking his head. *"This is a miracle! We have to get as far away as possible before the soldiers return."*

"My baby? And Ion?" she asked.

"I spoke with Ion this morning. He is with Sabella and Aleasa. They are all fine. He was preparing to go into the city to look for your parents. I couldn't talk him out of it, Katiza. He'll bring them back to the Cirque and Boss will give him a vehicle. Ion knows where we're headed and will follow. The plan is to get to the coast and from there on a ship to America. It's the only place your family won't be hunted. There are Cirques there also. We can join one. It's going to be a long trip, Katiza."

He pointed under the seat, *"There's apples and sandwiches and water under there. We need to keep moving."* He stepped on the gas.

"But how will Ion manage to find us?" Katiza asked.

"How did I find you?!" Hans smiled at her tenderly. *"We must have faith."*

"You're right." Katiza said softly, as she thought of the many times she'd been rescued – and was being rescued again.

"Baro died, Hans." She said, welling up. *"Last night's ride was too much for him. When I woke up, he wasn't breathing…"* Her tears began to fall, and she felt self-conscious. *"I know I must look awful."*

"I am so sorry," Hans said with compassion. *"He was a noble horse. And carrying you to safety was a grand finale. He is at peace now in a Heavenly pasture, I expect. And do not worry about how you look. You are always beautiful to me."*

"Heaven – that's your word for Charos, right?" she asked.

"Yes," Hans answered, *"Just as your O Del is the same as our God. Amoun and I talked often of these things."*

"The Roma believe O Del speaks to us through Balval. Does God speak to you, Hans?"

He nodded, *"Sometimes, yes. We are really going to need His help now, so I'm counting on it."*

"How do you know when you are hearing from Him?"

Hans thought for a moment. *"For me, it's simple. I mean, when He says something, there's no reason to argue. It just feels right deep inside."* He patted his heart. *"That's the best way I can describe it."*

They rode in silence for a few moments while she chose her words. *"He speaks to me in dreams sometimes. Shows me things. He showed me Baro in Charos – I mean, Heaven."*

"That's wonderful," Hans smiled. *"Just as I said, then."*

She tested him. *"I came from there, you know – Charos."*

He passed with flying colors. *"I don't doubt that. I love you, Katiza, and I'm a fool for not telling you sooner."*

She did not know how to respond, so opted for humor. *"What a charming and brave man you are, Hans. Now that you've said it, I can admit that I've had my eye on you, too. You must have known. Those evenings on the carousel when I sat so close?"*

"Well, aren't we a pair," he laughed with relief. *"Under different circumstances I would take you to a fine restaurant in Belgrade with white tablecloths and we would celebrate with wine in crystal glasses, but for now, it shall have to be liverwurst sandwiches and water. We'll celebrate in America. Would you mind handing me an apple?"*

Katiza reached under the seat, retrieved an apple, and slid the dagger out of her belt. Hans commented on it as she sliced the fruit.

"That's a beautiful knife."

"Romany men are superb knife-makers," she said.

"Did your father make it for you?" Hans asked.

"No. It's a much older, but it fits my hand perfectly. It was among the things passed down from my grandmother."

Katiza reached into the carpet bag lifted out the box and sat it on her lap. *"Her name was Renata. We don't know much about the things she left behind, only that she treasured and protected them, and that we are to do the same. My Dai believes they hold magic. Like this,"* she clasped the stone hanging around her neck.

"My Dati made this box for my grandmother when he was young and...well, it's quite a long story."

She handed him a slice of apple, wiped the blade on her skirt and returned the knife to the box. Sighing deeply, she closed the lid.

"She always said this would one day be mine."

"And that is why you have it now?" Hans asked.

"No. It's because of Dazbog. When he predicted all of this, he made a point of telling me to bring the box when it was time to run. So, I got it from my parents' vardo last night before I left."

"I see. Well, I will guard it with you. There's never been much magic in my life until now."

"What's happened to my parents, Hans? Do you have any idea?" He answered gently. *"I don't know. But Ion will find them."*

Katiza willed herself to stop worrying and tried to imagine America instead. It was a world away and she could not fathom such a radical change. But where else were they to go?

She trusted Hans with her heart and her life. The prophecy her mother had spoken after Ansel left was proving itself true: *"I promise that you will find love again, and when you do, it will not be with a man who will abandon you. I have seen it. This man will love you the way your Dati loves me. O Del is going to make the match and it will be a perfect one. You will see."*

"Thank you, Dai," Katiza whispered, laying her head on Hans' shoulder.

They made camp by a river that night and as they sat together, shafts of jewel-colored lights descended from the stars above them. Hans marveled at their beauty and wondered what they could be.

"I know." Katiza said softly. *"My Dai said they are the souls of those before us and that they appear when destinies are changing."*

Her eyes shimmered with tears in the moonlight and her voice trembled with emotion. Her soul knew the truth. *"I see you, my precious Dai. Who will I be without you?"*

A wolf howled in the distance and Katiza's heart ached even more. *"Devlesa avilan, Kesali,"* she said tearfully. *"Thank you for all of the times you saved me."*

"Kesali?" Hans asked.

"My Dai's protector – and mine. I will never see him again. But that is another story. I have a great many of them, Hans."

Hans did not question her further. He just put his arm around her shoulders and said, *"Dear Katiza, I promise you that we will have the rest of our lives to tell our stories and to make new ones. And I will be your protector now and for as long as I live."*

She sighed deeply, *"Devlesa avilan, Hans. It is God who brought you."*

devlesa avilan *(dev-LAY-sah avi-LAN))* – It is God who brought you

☾

Chapter Eighteen

~ The Hunt ~

"The good cannot seize power, nor retain it;
to do this, men must love power.
And love of power is inconsistent with goodness; but quite consistent
with the very opposite qualities – pride, cunning, cruelty."

Leo Tolstoy

*D*espite Sabella's pleadings, Ion headed into the city the morning after the foiled raid. At her insistence, he dressed in casual street clothes and hid his long dark hair under a hat. Even so, he was Ion, and not the sort of man one passed without stealing a second look. She stood at the threshold of her trailer holding Aleasa, and watched him stride away, his collar turned up against the cold drizzle, head down, intent on his mission. Unstoppable. She was madly in love with him, and terrified that he might not return. He could feel her eyes on his back, and without stopping or turning around, he lifted his right arm high above his head and made the hand signal they used in the ring to confirm to one another that they were in position and ready to perform one of their aerial stunts.

She laughed, choked down her tears, and for a brief second, imagined herself tucking the baby into bed, grabbing a coat, and running after him. The reality, of course, was that his reaction to such an impetuous act on her part would have been far less romantic than such scenes in the cinema, so instead, she straightened her shoulders, closed the door, and spoke reassuringly to the infant, promising her that her mama and uncle would soon return, and that the whole family would be together again and as happy as they were before.

Ion's first stop was a tavern on the outskirts of town, where the best information was usually to be found. There were no grey uniforms in sight, so he went inside, sat at an inconspicuous table, ordered breakfast, and eavesdropped on a nearby conversation. Not surprisingly, four local men were discussing what was happening to their city now that Nazi soldiers were arriving by the truckloads. None of them were happy about it. Ion waited for an opportune moment, picked up his coffee mug to get a refill and casually stopped at their table. *"Good morning, gentlemen."*

They stopped talking, looked at him curiously and tried to place his accent. *"Dobro juto,"* a couple of them replied.

"Say," Ion tried to sound casual, *"I couldn't help but overhear you talking about all the soldiers in town. I'm with Cirque Zeigler…"*

They all smiled and nodded then, and one said, *"I thought I recognized you! Great show you folks put on out there! Troupe Balval, right? My kids are always on me to take them."*

Ion bowed his head graciously and said, *"Thank you. We like to hear that."* Then he launched right in. *"But right now, our lives are in danger. The soldiers used to come to the shows to be entertained, and there were never any problems. But now they are under orders to arrest some of us, and my family is on the list. They came to last night's performance with that intention, but we had been forewarned and were able to cause enough of a distraction that their raid failed."*

The men looked grim. *"It's happening all over the city,"* said a large, bearded fellow. *"They're pulling protestors off the streets."*

His companions looked shocked, and he insisted, *"I have seen it! People are afraid. If you are not German, it could be you…and even then, if you refuse to comply…"*

"Where do they take those they arrest?" Ion asked.

"They've been putting them on trains," said one of the other men *"Not sure where they go."* He shook his head..

"The train station." asked Ion. *"Can you tell me where it is?"*

"Are you sure you want to go there?" Said the first fellow in a concerned voice as he stamped out his cigarette. *"Mighty dangerous for you, I'd say."* The others nodded in agreement.

"My mother and father came into town yesterday and never returned." Ion stated.

A collective groan of sympathy arose from the men at the table.

"Well, if there's no talking you out of it," replied the most vocal fellow, *"it's in the center of the city. Stick to the side streets. You are a*

dobro juto *(DOE-bro JEW-toe)* – Good Morning (Serbian)

236

good son. I hope you find them." The others echoed the sentiment and wished him luck. Ion thanked them, paid for his half-eaten meal, and was almost to the door when a group of Nazi soldiers opened it.

He quickly pulled the brim of his hat down to shadow his face, stepped aside and looked at the floor until they had all entered. Then he slipped out. The luck bestowed on him by the tavern's patrons had paid off. The uniformed men were in deep discussion and did not seem to notice him at all.

It was a long way to the city center, especially when you took the side streets as he had been advised. On his way, Ion looked everywhere for Nadya and Tamás, but after a while it became clear that the search was pointless. There were too many places they could be. His mind wandered to all the possibilities, both good and bad. If they were in hiding, he would never find them. They were too smart. Even as much as he wished it could be true, something told him it was highly unlikely that any gadje would shelter a Gypsy in times like these, so knocking on doors was out of the question.

Ion was a lot like his father. Practical-minded and not given to frequent leadings from the invisible realm like his mother, sister, or brother. Even so, when he got an uneasy feeling about a situation, he took it seriously. He also did not hesitate to ask O Del for help when he needed it.

The drizzle had turned to heavy rain and those on the street without umbrellas were either huddled together under awnings or hunched over, dodging puddles, and hurrying to their destinations. Rivulets of water ran off the brim of Ion's hat but he gave no notice nor did he slacken his pace. He heard a train whistle and knew he was close. Another block, and the depot came into view. The wet platform and slippery ramps were crammed with agitated people.

Ion disliked cities. The only crowds he could tolerate were good-natured ones who came to the Cirque to see their performances. This throng of people was not happy. They were outraged and shouting angrily at the Nazi soldiers who were pushing a long line of bedraggled men, women, and children into empty boxcars. If anyone stepped out of line they were brutally beaten with the stock of a gun.

Ion could not fathom what these defenseless people had done to deserve such treatment. The thought that his parents could be among them filled him with rage. He wanted to charge into the fray and kill every soldier with his bare hands.

A shot rang out, and he watched as a man like himself attempted to do that very thing. He burst from the crowd, grabbed one of the Nazi guards, threw him to the ground, and was strangling him, when the soldier managed to pull his pistol and shoot him at point blank range. The crowd backed up in shock and the rest of the Nazi guards took the assault as justification to accelerate their cruelty toward those they were shoving onto the train.

Ion's blood was boiling. He could not just stand and watch. He had to do something! But he was one man against many, and they would not hesitate to kill him. He'd be no help to anyone, dead.

Suddenly, she was there, standing beside him looking just as she had in the cottage in the forest many years before when he'd been a boy.

"Ion," she said solemnly, *"this is your time. There they are."*

She pointed and he saw them in the line – his precious mother bent over, limping painfully with a frightened little girl clinging to her skirt, and his father, beaten and bloody, holding on to Nadya and shuffling along beside her. Támas stumbled, and a guard barked something in German and prodded him sharply with the butt of his gun.

It was all Ion could take.

Three bounds and he was through the crowd and at the unsuspecting soldier's back. Before there was time for a struggle, he snapped his neck, and when the soldier slumped to the ground, Ion saw with a shock that he was just a youth. It all happened within seconds, and other protesters immediately closed in around him to hide the crime.

"Dai!" Ion called. *"Dati!"*

They recognized their son's voice and were overjoyed. He made his way to them and the three embraced.

Nadya asked, *"Our family?"*

"We are all safe, Dai."

"Thank O Del!" she sighed in relief and raised her eyes to the sky.

Ion looked down at the child, whose face and clothing gave away her Gypsy blood. *"Who…?"*

"I do not know," the expression on his mother's face was resolute as she reached for the little girl's hand. *"Ours, now."*

Tamás' leaned in and spoke fiercely to Ion. He was fighting for breath, and every word took great effort. *"Son, hear me. You cannot change this. You must let us go."*

"NO!" Ion cried helplessly.

Another soldier had noticed his dead comrade's absence and was heading toward them.

"They will kill you, son!" said Nadya. *"Run!"*

Tamás was struggling to keep his thoughts coherent. When he heard his wife's plea, he saw himself back in the vardo where Nadya entered the world and Renata had left it. That was his first lesson in the sovereignty of the One who held all power over both life and death. He remembered Tsura's command and the turmoil in his young mind and he knew that Ion's heart was being torn in two.

Nadya gathered up the little girl and pressed her into Ion's arms. *"Save her!"* she begged. ***"Run, Ion!"***

And Ion obeyed his mother and ran.

☾
Chapter Nineteen
~ The Final Word ~
"Our hearts belong where the songs are."

Tamás' and Nadya found their way to a corner of the boxcar and sank to the floor. Confusion and fear were written on every face of every color. Most did not understand why they had been arrested, but generations of persecution had taught the Gypsies that there didn't have to be a reason.

Tamás was in bad shape. His ribs were broken and every breath was torturous. Nadya feared his lungs were punctured and that he was bleeding inside. She, too, had been brutally beaten and violated. They had both suffered enough injuries in their lives for her to know that there would be no recovery this time.

~

True to his nature, Tamás did not go quietly when the soldiers accosted them in the marketplace. Nadya was shopping for scarves and he was haggling with the seller over price, when a small group of soldiers pulled them out into the street as an example to intimidate the townsfolk.

"The New Order will not tolerate this Gypsy trash!"

Tamás' took their blows and somehow managed to stay on his feet, but when they started on Nadya, he went crazy. There were five of them, all young, and he ended up getting far worse than he could give. Once he was down, they turned their full attention to her. Her clothing was ripped, her jewelry pocketed, and she was viciously raped. She heard her bones and teeth break, tasted blood, and when her head hit the ground, everything went black.

When she regained consciousness, she could not hear out of one ear, there was a stabbing pain deep in her belly, and she was raw and bleeding.

From the street, they were taken to an abandoned, rat-infested warehouse where they huddled together on a crumbling stone floor along with the others who had been captured. Most of the windows had been broken by vandals, and pigeons were nesting in the rafters. Their cooing soothed Nadya's fears, and she imagined everyone being lifted gently on their wings and carried far away to safety.

In the middle of the night, she felt a nudge. A tiny Gypsy ghel, no more than three years old, had curled up next to her. She pulled the child close, covered her with her skirt, and put a protective arm over her. The little fingers grasped her hand and held on tight.

The next day, they were herded to the train station where a miracle took place. It was nothing less in Nadya's mind. By O Del's mercy she and Tamás were able to see their son Ion one last time, and he had saved the little ghel.

~

𝒯he boxcar reeked of animal manure and urine-soaked straw. After everyone was jammed inside, the heavy doors slid closed, and the prisoners were plunged into semi-darkness. The sound of chains being threaded through the door handles ended any hope of escape. Though she was doubled over in pain, Nadya silently thanked O Del that she and Tamás were together and had a spot where she could lean against a wall. Her courageous husband was unable to sit up and lay on the floor with his head in her lap. It was her turn to protect him.

The train lurched forward, and as it clattered down the track, Nadya revisited the sweetest moments of her life. There was not a single one that didn't include the man still by her side. They had overcome everything thrown at them and their love had withstood every test. No evil could tear them apart.

There'd been no food or water since their capture. Very little light and air made it through the slats in the cattle car and the stench was unbearable. People were retching and being forced to relieve themselves where they stood. The frightened weeping had subsided into an occasional whimper and Nadya prayed the children had all gone to sleep in their parents' arms.

Tamás was awake, but when he tried to cough, the pain was so severe that he was unable to stifle a cry. Nadya stroked his head and bent over as far as her injuries would allow so that she could sing her song to him. When she formed the words that she'd been given by her mother beneath the willow, strength poured into her soul just as it had then. She still possessed the power to rise above the terrors of this world. She was still the same brave warrior of the vision in the cave. This was just a different kind of monster, that's all. O Del would make a way of escape. He always did.

She closed her eyes and it appeared.

She could not contain her excitement. *"Tamás!"* She whispered loudly enough so he could hear her.

"Come with me to the river, my husband. Can you hear it?"

A faint smile formed on his lips.

"Do you remember all our happy days there? And your times with my Dai when you were a boy? She's calling us! I can see her! I can hear her!" She continued to stroke the black hair turned silver and the handsome young face grown old.

"She says this is no place for us – that our souls belong where the songs are. We're going beyond the veil!" Her voice broke with emotion.

With his last breath, Tamás answered, *"Yes, Princess. Let's go."*

~

*W*hen the train reached its destination, it was met by another company of soldiers who drug the prisoners out of the boxcars with no regard for their wretched condition. Deaf to the cries for mercy, they tore the families apart and herded the men, women, and children into different groups.

But another ear heard, and another eye saw.

The air began to crackle with static, and an ominous black cloud materialized above the scene. A terrifying whirlwind descended, and caught up the soldiers one by one, crushing them and spitting them back out. When its job was done, the tornado returned to the cloud, taking the wicked with it and leaving the innocent to find refuge with villagers whose hearts had been prepared to receive them.

*W*hen the sky cleared, the station was empty. There was no one there to see the golden rays of the sun reach into a shadowed corner of a boxcar where the bodies of a man and woman lay entwined. No human eyes witnessed their souls rise to become one with the Light.

~

*I*ncomprehensible though it may seem, as many times as Beng tried and failed, he never seemed to grasp that chains, prisons, and graves held no power over the children of YaH.

*T*hese two simply flew away.

Part Three

☾

America

Mid- to late 20th Century

☾

Chapter One
~ Willow ~

"Either I fell under a spell or awoke from one.
I still do not know which."

Even with sunglasses, the setting sun was so blinding that I had to shade my eyes with my hand and squint between my fingers to see the highway. I'd been driving since dawn and the Redwoods were still well over an hour away, so I decided to find a place to camp for the night.

I know now that it was not by chance that the small, weather-worn sign, nearly overgrown by vines, caught my eye.

'Visit the Victorian Village of Willow.'

Other forces were in motion, and when I took the exit, the magic began. I didn't find Willow, it found me.

Two days and five hundred miles earlier, after a garage sale that yielded far less than I'd hoped, I loaded up my old van with what I would need for life on the road and headed south.

I had no idea where to go – only that it had to be somewhere else.

The first night, I dreamed I had a severe chest wound and was being tended by giants with rough, red skin. They were so tall that their heads touched Heaven, and the peace within their temple was being shattered by my cries.

"Shhhh," they soothed. *"You are safe here."*

"But I'm bleeding and it hurts so bad! Can't you make it stop?"

They bowed their heads and said, *"We have not been given that power. In our kingdom, it is understood that pain visits us as a teacher. It does not stay forever, and when it departs, we are left wiser, with greater endurance and higher knowledge. It is a natural part of growth. Only humans wish to eliminate pain."*

As they spoke, they showed me a world beneath my mossy bed, where a colossal battle for survival raged within a myriad of tangled roots. The obstacles were many, but the roots relentlessly fought their way downward, for to have stopped would have meant the end of their growth. Some had forced their way between stones and pushed them aside. Others had either broken through boulders or embraced them as anchors. I saw that the scene was not only a struggle. It was a glorious unseen quest for life, and the picture of persistence, patience, and endurance. The beauty above was the direct result of what was happening below.

*W*hen I awoke the next morning, I knew where to go. I wrote down the dream, headed for the Pacific Coast highway, and left seventeen years of my life and everything attached to them in the rear-view mirror. Every hope and dream. Everything I'd built. It was all debris, now, left in the wake of a storm unleashed by people whose love had been a lie.

I fight to choke down the feelings of abandonment and lostness. The aching hollowness. The scalding shame of betrayal, failure, rejection, and disbelief. I struggle to hold on to my sanity as the unanswerable 'whys and hows' pile on top of one another like frenzied hamsters taking turns on a wheel.

Yet, even as my heart hemorrhages, the Spirit of Truth survives within – an invincible flame burning hotter than any pain or sorrow, shining upon an eternal altar before which all carnal voices fall silent and all souls must ultimately bow.

Truth's light had always been watching through my eyes. It had shone through the bars of every cage, and then, because they were prisons, unlocked the door and hurried me out, leaving me no choice but to find my wings and fly higher and farther to horizons unknown.

Slowly, slowly, I am learning to trust the wisdom of the hands that bled rivers for my sake – that season after season, year after year, reach through my stubborn thorns to prune my proudest branches. The hands that wait in love while I cry myself to sleep, and when I awaken, are there to brush away the dead and call forth blossoms from within my barren bones.

I believe the Voice that whispers, *"You will bloom again, My beloved."*

It tells me that I am the ember smoldering beneath the pale, gritty ashes of the empty hearth where I once held my enemies close to my heart. That I am the spark waiting in the cold darkness, for the merciful breath of grace that will cause me to leap to life again.

It is daring me, now. Challenging me, calling me to rise through the fire and take to the wing. To fly higher than before.

If you are looking for me, I am not a perfect rose anymore and never really was. I am a dandelion taking root in impossible places, releasing my seeds to the wind. I am a tiny violet, trampled underfoot, blooming from the gritty crack in the sidewalk against all odds. My faith has become experiential and the One in whom it rests does not fail.

Spirit cannot die. We came here to live.

Whatever has been and whatever is to come, I shall choose life.

*E*arlier that day I'd pulled into a rest stop. It was deserted except for a dog sitting by the muddy puddle beneath the water fountain.

I asked myself all the usual questions. Had someone left him behind? Did they know he was missing? Would they come back looking for him? Had he run away? How long had he been here alone? Was he hungry?

I rummaged for a container and walked toward the fountain. He immediately rose, wagged his tail, panted, and smiled in greeting.

"Hey fella. What are you doing here?" I filled the bowl with fresh water, which he thirstily lapped up. When I bent down to refill it, he tried to show me his gratitude, and I dodged his slurpy kisses, laughed and patted his head.

Black and white, parts border collie and Aussie, I thought. His eyes were intelligent and spoke words that I understood just as he seemed to understood mine.

He followed me back to the van and I gave him some jerky which he swallowed in one gulp. I waited for an hour just in case someone might come back for him, and when no one did, he and I looked at each other, and I said, *"Well, I guess it's the two of us now."*

When I thought about a name for him, *'Domino'* immediately came to mind and he seemed to like it. I'd had a dream about dominoes several weeks earlier and recorded it my book. The picture I'd been shown had been stuck in my head ever since. I knew it had come from a higher place.

𝕾hortly after you take the exit to Willow, a narrow, century-old bridge arches over a river. In years gone by, the waters were the swiftest means of transport for the region's commodities to the booming cities further south.

The bridge was constructed in 1911 and is a portal to the past. Everyone feels it. I did the first time I crossed it and still do whenever I leave the outside world behind and slip back in time.

On the other side, a five-mile long, two-lane road meanders through pasturelands unchanged for generations – dairy farms neatly divided by white rail fences, sprinkled with gingerbread cows, and studded with stately, heavily embellished Victorian mansions. Erected by the wealthy dairymen of the era, they testified to a far more prosperous era when the land oozed with heavy cream, sweet butter and artisan cheeses craved by the city folks downriver.

The preservation of these monuments is a formidable and costly task, and tragically, quite a number have been left to the mercy of the elements. The farmers and ranchers do not live in the 'butterfat palaces' anymore. Their dwellings are modest, and they lease the pastureland from the new owners – the city folks who migrated upriver, bought the mansions, and turned them into B&Bs.

Regrettable as that is, you can still drive those miles slowly and pretend it's the early Nineteen-hundreds and envision the master, strong and shrewd, overseeing the labor in his fields and barns, and the lady of the manor graciously instructing her cooks and maids, and the children out in the yard playing fetch with their dog.

And you can close your eyes and imagine a horse and buggy waiting in the driveway to carry the crisply dressed family to church in the lovely Village of Willow when the bells ring, which they still do every Sunday morning.

There is no doubt in my mind that I was purposefully led from the highway, over the bridge, through the pastures and onward to Mainstreet where it splits and forms a triangular shaped park. There, an old willow tree stands watch over a small pond, and when I saw it, I either fell under a spell or awoke from one. I still do not know which.

Though I had never been to Willow before, I somehow knew the place. The sensation of familiarity was far stronger than a fleeting moment of déjà vu. I could not shake it off nor has it ever completely left.

Both sides of the street are lined with extravagant Victorian facades wearing thick coats of chipping paint in carousel colors, and at every turn, places, smells and sounds from yesteryear capture the senses.

I have no rational explanation for the feelings it awakened in me. I felt as though I had been gone on a journey of many lifetimes, and upon my return, all the village ghosts were arising to say, *"Welcome Home."*

251

☾

Chapter Two
~ Fred ~

"Be careful, my dear – listen to your instincts.
Women got it over men that way."

Travelers were offered affordable camping at the Willow fairgrounds, which were only used for their official purpose a few weeks in the summer. A clean, cinderblock building housed bathrooms and hot showers for a quarter, so I parked nearby. Dinner was burritos from the convenience store, and after Dom and I checked out the grounds, we called it a day.

We were alone other than a fellow who arrived just before dark in a rusty old red truck. He chose to park directly behind us, where he set up a small tent and started a fire. Something about him made me nervous. I did not want to have to engage in conversation, so abandoned my own plan for a fire. He caught me watching him through the back window of the van, sneered and made an obscene gesture. I jerked the curtain closed and double-checked to be sure all the doors were locked. It was a great relief to have Dom with me. Had there been any place else to go in town, I would have moved, but there wasn't, and ten bucks a night was a bargain.

After trying unsuccessfully to sleep, I took out my book. It had been a gift from my Uncle Ion, with his instructions that I keep it separate for recording what he called *'the higher kintala'* – meaning thoughts, dreams and messages that came from a spiritual place. We are Roma, and he insisted that such gifts were in my blood.

The times in which I live are far different from how he grew up. I was not sure that I possessed supernatural proclivities – or *'The Dook'* as he called it – but out of respect, and in reverence to the Source from which the words and pictures came, I wrote them down. If I did not have anything to write, I read what I had written before, and my heart would be reminded and encouraged.

It was late. I desperately needed sleep, but the other camper was walking in circles around his fire, smoking, downing beers and talking to himself. At one point I heard what sounded like an argument between him and a second voice, but when I peeked out through the curtain, he was the only one there.

My anxiety was growing, and I contemplated leaving again, but he would see me gathering up the things I'd put outside, and I couldn't afford to drive off and leave them behind.

Dom was napping peacefully, and I reminded myself of what Uncle Ion always said: that protectors from Charos were watching over me, and I had nothing to fear.

Exhaustion finally won, and I fell into a restless sleep. A couple of hours later, I was awakened by the sound of someone testing the door handle on the driver's side of the van. I grabbed my flashlight and silently crawled to the front where I gingerly pulled aside the curtain. Just outside, almost touching the glass, a hideous face grinned back at me. I screamed, and it vanished. I dove into my sleeping bag, pulled it up over my head and did not move until I was able to convince myself it had just been a bad dream. This, I based upon the fact that even though I'd screamed out in fear, Dom hadn't stirred.

At first light, a rooster crowed at a nearby farm and awakened me from another dream. While not frightening like the first one, it was unnerving, and had something to do with a procession of strange people in turn of the century costumes who were all coming to ask me questions about the future.

I was thankful for daylight, shook off the remnants of the dream, and mentally reviewed my travel plans. My budget didn't allow for any long detours, so after we visited the Redwoods, Dom and I would continue further on down the coast to towns where I hoped to sell my jewelry.

When I looked at my life objectively, I had to admit that the Gypsy streak did run strong.

I looked out the window and was relieved to see that the adjoining campsite was empty. The guy in the truck must have left before dawn. It seemed strange that I hadn't heard anything.

When I opened the back doors of the van, I was met by heavy fog infused with the smells of the sea and the dairy pastures it had rolled through on its way inland. Dom jumped out and accompanied me to the restroom. A hose lay coiled alongside a faucet at the side of the building, and I determined that I would give my new partner a much-needed bath later when it warmed up.

I had hoped that a good night's rest would clear my head, but my troubled sleep had been anything but restorative and the fog only added to the mystical aura of my surroundings. I could not shake the feeling that my spirit was levitating between this world and another.

Reasoning that coffee and food would help me feel normal, I decided we would walk the few blocks into town. Dom stayed at my heel without a leash. I had the sense that he was guarding me and did not want me to stray, or perhaps he feared I would leave him as his previous human had done.

As we covered the short distance to town, the inescapable sense of familiarity grew stronger, and when I looked down at my feet, I had the oddest sensation that they belonged to someone else who had made the same trip countless times.

The trucks parked on Main Street belonged to dairymen and sheep ranchers who had been up for hours. A little bakery bustled with activity and the irresistible smell of fresh pastries wafted out onto the sidewalk.

An old fellow with a long white beard and a beautifully carved walking stick spoke to me from his seat on the bench beside the bakery door. *"Good looking pup. What's his name?"*

"Dom," I replied, and Dom's ears perked up. *"Short for Domino. That's a fine-looking walking stick you have there."*

"Why thank you, my dear. It's madrona. Been carvin' 'em for many years from branches that come down in storms. I give 'em a new purpose. They sell 'em at the gallery for me." He gestured up the street with his knobby thumb.

"What a wonderful way to preserve their beauty!" I said appreciatively.

"I believe so." Taking the opportunity to share his philosophy, he added, *"Over all my years, I've learned there's beauty in everything. Even in the broken and the fallen. You just need eyes to see it. Then you put your hand to it and carve away what's no longer useful and keep*

what's strong enough to lean on. You keep the natural shape and leave the knots and a bit of the bark for character. When you're done whittlin', you sand the rest smooth and oil it to bring out the natural grain. I liken it to God's work. Takes time and patience, but I've got plenty of both."

"What part of the process do you enjoy the most?" I asked.

He answered without hesitation, *"Oh, my favorite part is findin' the branches."*

"You reclaim them." I said.

"I do. There's plenty needs savin' that can't save itself." He was speaking to my heart.

"Would you mind keeping an eye on Domino while I get something to eat?"

"My pleasure. Come 'ere, pup." Sensing a kind soul, Dom laid down at his feet.

Like everything else in town, the bakery was frozen in time, and other than a shiny new espresso maker, nothing had changed since the Fifties. Not the booths, tables, or chairs; not the worn black and white linoleum tiles on the floor, or the curved glass cases filled with cakes and pies, or the collection of vintage cookie jar clowns, cows, elephants, pigs, Mr. Peanut, and others that marched merrily around the room on a warped shelf below the ceiling. Locals were sitting at their favorite tables sipping steaming cups of coffee and getting their own refills from the pot on the counter where they dutifully dropped change in the dish marked 'Refills.'

I wanted to be one of them. To call the warm, delicious bakery my regular place, too.

I bought a scone and coffee to go, plus a biscuit for Dom from a jar labeled 'Homemade Doggie Treats,' and on impulse, added a 'Bigfoot' chocolate chip cookie for the old timer outside. Then I walked out past the eyes that were sizing me up over their breakfasts. I could read their thoughts: *"...middle-aged, rumpled hippie-type. Probably camped at the fairgrounds and headed for the hills..."* A few whispered to each other and looked at me strangely. I wasn't sure why.

Back out front I sat down on the bench beside the old man, and we introduced ourselves properly. I dunked my scone in my coffee while Dom gnawed on his rock-hard biscuit. My new friend, Fred, could not believe that I'd brought him one of his favorite cookies. He just held it in wonderment and said he would save it for later.

I asked him about the town.

"Well, I came 'ere as a young buck over sixty years ago myself," he said, *"worked on dairy farms and ranches mostly, and yep, yer right about the bakery…"* (I'd said nothing out loud) *"It ain't changed a stitch 'cept after that one bad shaker a couple years back. We get 'em pretty regular here, mostly small rollers, but you never know. They lost some cookie jars, bricks fell off the front here and a couple of windows broke that time. But they fixed 'er all back up and you can hardly tell it happened now."*

According to Fred, most of the small stores were prone to frequently changing ownership. People would come, fall in love with the quaint little village, open a shop, and then find out that the revenues from the short tourist season were not enough to support them the rest of the year. Next thing you knew, they'd boxed up their inventory and their broken dreams, and a 'For Rent' sign would appear in the window to lure the next romantic entrepreneurial soul.

He shook his head and lowered his voice. *"It's the ranchers and dairymen that keep the town alive – them and the weed growers up in the hills. Common knowledge, but nobody talks about it. Them growers, they call themselves 'farmers.' Ha. Some of 'em are decent folk, and some ain't. They don't want nobody sniffin' around their properties, that's fer sure. There's some disturbin' stories, but I'll spare you. I don't know how you feel about maryjawanna, or weed or grass or whatever they like to call it, but I ain't got no use for the crap. Pardon my French. What's wrong with good old beer? I brew my own, and hard cider, too. If you're gonna stick around, I'll give you some."*

"That's sweet of you, Fred," I answered. *"but I'm headed for the Redwoods, and after that, further on down the coast. Places I can sell my jewelry."*

"Oh, you'll be back," he said with a wink.

"You think so?"

"I know so. I'm sorry, my dear, but I've gotta go. Time's up."

I wondered what he meant. *"Where can I find you if I come back?"*

"I'm here, sometimes." he replied. "*Say...*" he paused as though he'd just been reminded of something.

"Yes?"

"Don't go back to the main highway. Stay on the coast. Take the road at the end of town." He pointed. *"There's a sign. It'll take you up into the hills and then down to the ocean and eventually on into the Redwoods."* He made roller coaster motions with his hand. *"It's a little bumpy in spots, but you'll never see anyplace more beautiful.*

"When you get to Bear River there's a country store. Gal by the name of Ema runs it. Give her my regards." The faraway look in his eyes changed and he added a warning. *"Just don't wander off the main road."*

As he was speaking, the red truck from the fairgrounds rounded the corner and drove toward the bakery at a crawl. Fred saw the look on my face and asked if everything was okay.

I pulled myself together and answered, *"Oh, it's probably nothing, but that truck was parked at the fairgrounds near me, and the guy makes me nervous. Something's not right with him."*

"Hmm," Fred pulled on his beard. *"Be careful, my dear. Listen to your instincts. Women got it over men that way."*

"I'll be right back. I'm going to duck in and get a refill," I said, in hopes that the driver of the truck wouldn't spot me.

Fred nodded.

When I came back out, Dom was sitting in the same spot, but Fred was gone.

☾

Chapter Three
~ The Sea ~

*"If I take the wings of the morning,
and dwell in the uttermost parts the sea,
even there Your hand shall lead me,
and Your right hand shall hold me."*
A Psalm

*D*om and I had walked past a small museum on the way into town and I decided to go back and check it out. An elderly woman had just unlocked the door. She introduced herself as a Historical Society volunteer and welcomed us in.

I spent more than an hour pouring over the displays, maps, and a pictorial history of the region. Most charming were the showcased vignettes of yesteryear where chipped hand-me-down mannequins with missing fingers and matted wigs were dressed in dusty vintage clothing and posed stiffly in scenes of every-day activities.

Before we left, I gathered a handful of brochures to attractions in the Redwoods, local Victorian B&Bs, and a self-guided walking tour of Willow. The fog had begun to lift, and there was time, so we struck out on the tour past picket fences, shrubs pruned to perfection, and gingerbread-laden porches. I read the listings taped to the window of the real-estate office and bought a fifty-cent newspaper from a box in front of the grocery store – the things you do when you fall in love with a quaint little town and imagine what it would be like to live there.

Dom and I walked past every church and tavern (there were roughly the same number of each) and peered through every store window. We checked out alleyways and boardwalks where two buildings had been joined by a roof, and discovered hidden boutiques, galleries, and artist studios. Proprietors were starting to move their sandwich boards out onto the sidewalk, and the butcher shop door already stood wide open for business.

I stuck my head inside, saw the huge walk-in cooler and steel tables in the back, and surmised that it must be the place where locals brought meat, poultry and fish for processing and packaging. The two-story high walls were covered with antlers and impressive taxidermy scenes of bobcats, raccoons, weasels, and pheasants. Piles of specialty cheeses from the region, strings of house-made salami, pastrami, hot dogs and sausages filled the glass cases, along with smoked salmon filets, steaks, slabs of bacon, lamb chops, whole chickens, cured hams and everything a carnivore could dream of. Baskets of freshly baked crusty bread from the bakery had just been delivered, and the smells that emerged from the place could have converted even the staunchest vegetarian. Dom refused to walk past, sat down, stared at me, and whimpered.

I went in, ordered a sandwich to save for lunch (smoked chicken and Havarti stacked high on sourdough), and a half-dozen hot dogs, one of which Dom received forthwith as a reward for having waited patiently outside. Then, we headed back to the van. The ocean beach was only a few miles out of town, and I wanted to see it before we left.

Back at the fairgrounds, I treated myself to the luxury of a 50-cent shower and Dom tolerated his cold-water bath with the hose. The van smelled like cheap shampoo and wet dog for the rest of the day, but it was a small price to pay for his company.

The first few sunny miles on the beach road were as idyllic as the rest of Willow's storybook landscape. Buttercups bordered the lane, assorted wildflowers were starting to bloom, and climbing roses were leafing out over mailboxes. Every homestead had a barn, a garden patch, chicken coop, sheep, and goats.

I was feeling envious of those blessed to live in such a place, when we were abruptly swallowed by a dense fog bank and found ourselves in a misty grey realm where the structures were all weather-beaten into a woeful state of disrepair and every growing thing was struggling to stand erect.

Ocean tempests had sandblasted the bark from massive Cypress trees and bleached their naked bodies the color of the dunes, leaving brutally beautiful, monumental works of art. Poseidon's lovers, I thought, sculpted in varying stages of flight, their long hair streaming behind them as they ran toward the arms of the sea.

This was no welcoming beach. It was wild and ruthless, and best appreciated from a cozy table in the 'Beach Shack Café' anchored at the end of the road, where ragged, faded flags flapped crazily on a pole. A sign nailed to the ramp railing read: *'Open in June.'* The actual date was yet to be determined, I guess, and until then, the windows would remain boarded up.

A small parking area had been bulldozed into the low dunes and we had it all to ourselves. I turned off the engine and was about to get out when I heard another vehicle. I glanced over my shoulder and saw the truck from the fairgrounds pulling in. My instinct was to leave immediately, and remembering Fred's advice to heed my intuition, I started the engine and backed out.

Now that I had Dom, I talked to him instead of myself, and I swear, he would perk up his ears and look at me like he understood every word.

"Well, this is not going to happen, Dom. I'm sorry, boy. We'll find another beach, okay? Bark once for 'yes.'"

When he barked in response, all I could do was stare at him. Had he understood me? And who was the guy in the truck that I should have such a fearful gut reaction to him? Was he tracking me?

𝒯his strange Victorian version of Oz was unsettling. Had we been swept into a different reality like Dorothy and Toto? I prayed not, for I didn't own ruby slippers and neither of us had a home to return to, or anyone like Auntie Em who cared that we were gone.

𝒩avigating The Wildcat, as they called the narrow lane of cracked asphalt that prowled through endless hills and pastures outside Willow, was an adventure. Stunning territorial views met me at every turn, and I knew I was fortunate to be there while it was still green. Within a month or so, summer would turn the grasses brown, but for now, verdant vistas spread out before me like a vision of Heaven. At high points, I could see out over the valleys below where the one-lane road lay over the landscape like a slender ribbon dropped from the sky. Ewes and their lambs grazed freely on embankments, and we were challenged several times by living barricades of cattle who stared at the van as if to say, *"Who are you and what are you doing here?"* It took a few barks from Dom to make them move, and they did so begrudgingly in slow motion to make the point that it was *their* road, and they could darned well congregate on it if they wanted to.

It was hard to fathom that a handful of men owned all this land. In my mind, it belonged to the One who creates such beauty and pours it freely into our souls.

But somebody owned the pock-marked road. And some man had given another man a piece of paper, and together they had signed other pieces of paper, and now the guy with the most paper called the Creator's land and everything on it, his own.

This point was driven home when we rolled past a dead coyote nailed to a fence post.

My stomach turned. Was it a bad omen? A warning? To whom? To me? In an instant, I went from feeling like a wanderer in paradise to a trespasser in a murderous land. We hadn't encountered any other vehicles for over an hour. Per Fred's advice, I was fairly certain I had stayed on the main route, but there had been one confusing fork. Had I gone astray?

I weighed my options. There were only two. Keep going or turn around. I straightened my shoulders, gripped the wheel, and continued to drive through the fairytale hills, which, after the sight of the coyote's carcass, felt decidedly less enchanting.

What I did not know was that one of the most spectacular, heart-healing sights of my lifetime lay just ahead. And now that I think of it, isn't life just like that? And isn't that why we should choose to go forward, not back? Down here, we are all walking through the Valley of the Shadow of Death, but you just never knew when the gates of Paradise might be waiting around the next bend.

One more deep curve, and a slow climb up a hill with a lone oak tree at the top, and then, without warning, the earth fell away. Below and beyond, for as far as I could see, stretched the vast, glistening Azure waters of the Pacific Ocean.

Awestricken, I stopped the van and tried to take it all in. If only I were a bird and could drop from my perch to soar over that ancient, undulating kingdom where boundless sky melted into fathomless deep at the distant horizon! Then, to plunge into her depths and discover what treasures the mother of mysteries had been hiding from the time she was formed. With each breath she took, pearl-trimmed waves swelled up and gave their lives to the jagged shore, where they spilled their briny offerings into the tidepools and the mouths of the thirsty creatures waiting there. Seagulls cried out praises as they sailed on the wind currents above, and I swear my heart stopped for the wild glory of it all. I shall carry the memory of that sight and the almighty sounds of creation forever.

I rolled down the windows and the sea air poured in. Dom's nose twitched, his tail wagged, and he looked at me excitedly.

"Yeah, buddy," I laughed, *"**That's** where we're going."*

$\mathcal{N}$avigating the switchbacks down the near-vertical cliff in an old van was a bit unnerving, but when we reached the bottom, the road along the shoreline widened. I pulled over and Dom did not wait for me to open the door. He was out the window and onto the sand before I could come to a complete stop. I kicked off my shoes, rolled up my pant legs and followed him.

The Lost Coast is no place for fancy folks. No one goes there to lay out pretty picnics on red and white checkered cloths. The waves are neither gentle nor warm, and they are not interested in kissing your toes. They are cold and rush in to fling themselves recklessly against the treacherous volcanic rock formations, where they cascade down like waterfalls over the clusters of barnacles, black-shelled mussels and limpets clinging to the storm-worn pillars for dear life. They scour the sand and leave stringy tassels of tangled seaweed and sticky, crackling foam in their wake. Then, they take a long breath, retreat, and pound it out all over again. If you want to climb and explore, you need to watch every step while keeping one eye on the tide. That day, I stayed on the beach and just watched the show.

We ate our lunch there and I filled my pockets with wet shells and stones that are never as pretty when they dry. Dom chased the gulls and they mocked him. My footprints vanished in seconds as though I was a wayward spirit, touching down lightly on the shore of this tumultuous world and leaving no evidence of my passage behind.

A Psalm that David sang to his God came to mind. It was my song, too. I'd put it to music once many years before and could still hum the melancholy tune. At the time, the notes had come so effortlessly that I'd wondered if they had been sent up through the ages by the shepherd boy-king, himself. I was not nearly so brave as he who had slain a giant in the Valley of Elah while an army cowered in fear, but maybe I could dare to hope that a higher plan would unfold after my own outrageous step of faith. It did for him.

"Where can I go from Your Spirit?" he wrote.

"Where can I flee from Your presence?
If I ascend into heaven, You are there.

If I make my bed in hell, behold, You are there.
If I take the wings of the morning,
And dwell in the uttermost parts of the sea,
Even there Your hand shall lead me,
And Your right hand shall hold me."

I decided to call the place 'Shipwreck Cove,' not because there was any evidence of such a thing, or that it was even a cove, but because I'm a hopeless, shipwrecked romantic, and my imagination runs amok in such inhospitable windswept places. I always want to live there in a cottage built of stone (on a cliff overlooking the sea in this case) knowing fully that I would never survive as those of yore had done.

They were tougher than us. Theirs were the days that birthed timeless tales of passion and courage. Someday I would write one. There would need to be handsome explorers and marauding, equally handsome pirates. I could already see their rugged faces and strong bodies, as they staggered ashore, scabbards swinging from their belts. Did their kind sail these parts, I wondered? Doubtful. I would have to find a library when I returned to civilization.

Back at the van, I scribbled the word *'pirates'* on the back of a drive-through receipt so I wouldn't forget.

With the Redwoods still a long stretch of narrow, curvy road away, the time had come to leave. Dark clouds were gathering, and the wind and tide would not have allowed us to stay, anyway.

Chapter Four
~ Bear River ~

*"And then, like the last whisp of smoke from a candle
extinguished at the end of a bedtime story,
she drifted away."*

We followed the shoreline until the road bent inland, and then, as suddenly as the Pacific had unveiled her splendor, she hid herself behind the hills again. Dom curled up on the seat, and I sighed, shivered, turned on the heat and shoved an *Earth, Wind and Fire* tape in the 8-track player.

The Gypsy word for wind is *'Balval,'* which means *'Spirit of God.'* He had spoken to my heart at the ocean, and the door was still open, but I did not have strength for the raw self-analysis that I feared might ensue. In those stark-naked conversations, you could avoid nothing. No secrets remained hidden, and no lies could be told, to Him, or yourself.

My human emotions were as unpredictable as the road through the hills. In one instant I was soaring on wings of hope and in the next I was like the child in the old Dutch story, with my finger stuck in the hole of a dam. The difference was that in my version, a middle-aged woman was not saving a village, but holding back a tsunami of emotions to save her sanity. If I lost this battle, what then?

I could not allow myself to dwell upon the damage that had been inflicted on my foolish, trusting heart, nor could I reason how I was going to navigate the solo voyage ahead. I existed only in the Now, and these moments in the eye of the storm were a blessed gift. I wanted to live at the shore within reach of the arms of mother sea, where my problems would be as small as sparkling grains of sand and just as easily swept away. I wanted to crawl inside the iridescent shell that had once sheltered a different life, to later be discovered and dropped down into a warm pocket by a kind hand that would delight in the beauty of the polished fragment whose once-sharp edges had all been worn smooth.

The tape kept getting stuck, so I took it out and put in another which did the same thing. Cassettes were the new standard, but I couldn't afford to replace what I had. I drove in silence for a while, and then remembered that I could sing my own songs, so I did. Given the space, a new one came unbidden from the place they all came from. It was drenched in melancholy, like the Psalm at the beach.

Lord of the mountain top,
Lord of the sea,
Lord of the valley,
You have never left me.

Lord of the fire,
Lord of the rain,
Lord of my deepest joy,
Lord of my pain.

Conqueror of darkness,
Prince of the Light,
Lover of my helpless soul,
Bring me through this night…

Balval was intent upon reassuring me that I had the power to overcome any circumstance if I chose to be led by a love higher than my own. I spoke my oath out loud for God and all the angels to hear, knowing that having done so, I would be bound to it.

The terrain changed and forests sprang up across the hills. Bridges crossed rivers that had etched out their own courses for centuries. One of them snaked through a deep ravine on my right and before I could wonder at its name, a small handmade sign announced that the settlement of Bear River was just ahead.

I drove past a couple of run-down houses with vehicles parked in their yards, a concrete block building serving as both the Post Office and City Hall, and another bearing the title 'Community Center.' Almost everything looked abandoned, including a little steepled church which stood on a knoll watching over the settlement below.

A handful of trucks were parked in front of a general store, which I assumed was the place Fred had mentioned. A worn boardwalk porch ran the length of it and a black bear chainsaw carving holding a welcome sign stood beside the door. I parked, told Dom I wouldn't be long and promised we would go for a walk when I got back.

A bell tied to the door handle jangled when I entered and drew the attention of local fellows who were playing cards at one of the tables near the snack bar. They looked at me like I was a stray kitten that had wandered into their lair. As I browsed the aisles, scraps of conversation reached my ears: *"huntin', fishin' ranchin'"* and *"...damned if another storm ain't gonna be rollin' in again tonight."*

I put my purchases on the counter. The woman at the register peered intently at me from beneath eyebrows that had never seen a pair of tweezers and spoke.

"You alone?" It was more of a statement than a question, and before I could answer, wrinkles of concern turned her face into a topography map. She raised up on her toes, gawked around past me and tried to spot my vehicle.

"We're headed to the Redwoods," I replied. *"The van. Just me and my dog."*

She glanced around to see if anyone was paying attention to our conversation and lowered her voice.

"Bad idea. I mean, to be up here in these hills by yourself. It'll be getting' dark by the time you get where you're goin', and since the last earthquake, there's some real bad spots in the road. Slides 'n busted pavement. Do-nothin' government doesn't think we're worth their attention 'cept when they're collecting taxes."

Fred must not have been privy to the deteriorating road conditions, or he might not have suggested the route.

She continued. *"Not to mention that there's folks out in these hills you don't wanna run into. People disappear out here, and worse."*

I had no idea how to answer, so I put my head down and dug for money in my purse instead. The sign on the register read "CASH ONLY" and was underlined three times in red.

She wasn't letting me off the hook. *"I don't want you out there. It's gettin' too late."* Her tone was authoritative, and I could feel her eyes on my face while she waited for me to look up. The old gal was tough as nails. Probably had to be to live out here and run a store so many miles from anywhere, but I sensed her concern was genuine.

As I struggled with how to reply, she reached over the counter, put her hand on mine and whispered, *"Ali, please listen to me."* I was shocked that she addressed me by name, and in the next second a terrifying vision filled my mind – the van in a torrential downpour, swerving, sliding off the road onto the shoulder and rolling down the side of a hill into the river far below. I gasped and stared at her. *"How..."*

"You saw it, then." she said quietly.

I nodded slowly, and although I was afraid to ask, I stammered out the question, *"How do you know me?"*

"I was told you'd be comin'. You're welcome to stay here tonight. I have a little place in back. Dinner at six. I hope you like blackberry wine." She grinned and winked. *"I'm Ema, but you can call me 'Em,' or 'Auntie Em' like these guys do. I answer to anything."*

"You're Ema? A man I met in Willow said to give you his regards..."

"Ah, that would be Fred." She interrupted, and a small smile played at the corners of her mouth. *"How's he doin' these days? Still hanging out at the bakery I expect?"*

"Yes! That's where I met him. He's old but seems fine."

"'Old' is a relative term where Fred and I come from," she laughed.

A young man called from the beer cooler on the other side of the store, *"Hey Auntie! You outta Bud?"*

Two of his friends at a table in the front laughed and yelled back, *"We got yer bud!"*

I thought I'd smelled weed when I came in.

Ema shook her head, sighed, and answered him. *"If it ain't there, I'm out. And I told you guys not to bring that stuff in here!"*

268

"Well, hell." He muttered.

Then she handed me a wrapped caramel from the box next to the register, and said, *"On the house. Ignore these fools. See you later then?"*

It seemed to have been decided for me, so I nodded, walked quickly past the men, got in my van, and opened a package of doggie treats for Dom. It was almost four-thirty and he was expecting me to make good on my promise of a walk, so I decided we would check out the old church.

The building looked to have been neglected for decades, but since it was built of the same virgin redwood timber as everything else in the area, I was sure that all it needed was a little tender loving care and a fresh coat of white paint to bring it back to life. I had always dreamed of converting an old chapel into a home. This one's crowning glory was its beautifully crafted stained-glass windows – three on each side – all portraying different scenes from Christ's life.

An adage I'd read someplace came to mind. *"People are like stained glass windows. They sparkle and shine when the sun is out, but when the darkness sets in, their true beauty is revealed only if there is a light from within."*

I'd always wondered why the writer didn't also consider the opposite: how it felt to be alone inside, when the sun streams through and paints you with holy colors.

Small and humble as it was, I could feel that the chapel had been built with great love. I wondered how many sermons had been preached there, how many hymns had been sung, how many baptisms, marriages, potlucks, and funerals had marked the most profound events in the lives of those who established this place. They were pioneers filled with hopes and dreams of how their little town would prosper and grow.

Maybe the bell in the tower still rang on Sunday mornings, and maybe a few folks still came. The neglected grounds and padlocked doors made me think not. The concrete steps were crumbling, and the plumbing pipe handrails were coated with rust. Weeds had choked out any landscaping there may have been, save for a few scattered daffodils and a tenacious old rosebush that stood stalwartly beside the entrance. I thought it was dead until my eyes were drawn to one brave new shoot reaching upward, declaring life.

A female voice with a faint accent spoke wistfully. *"My beloved rose. She traveled a great distance with me to this place. She loves it here, but she's outlived all of us now, and no one's left to tend her."*

Then the voice sweetened with delight. *"Still, look at her determination! And oh, her blooms are the most glorious pink! I wish you could see them! And the fragrance…"* the voice paused and took in a deep breath, *"…it's from Heaven itself."*

I closed my eyes and could see the place as she did. The devotion, the love, the hard work of faithful hearts who had followed the call to this Lost Coast hill and crowned it with a place of worship.

Their labors had not gone unnoticed or unrewarded. Their names were etched into sunken grave markers but their souls had immigrated to a far kinder place without rust or peeling paint, where storms don't rage and winds don't howl. Where the ground doesn't shake, and rich, warm soil welcomes the touch of their hands. Their souls were the kind who sought heavenly labor, and their dreams had led the way.

"What is your name?" I asked her.

"Elizabeth." She replied.

And then, like a whisp of smoke from a candle extinguished at the end of a bedtime story, she drifted up and away.

I probably imagined the shadowy figure that walked past one of the windows. *'It's just the reflection of a passing cloud on the glass,'* I said to myself. And the faint sound of an organ? Just the wind whistling through the steeple. Nothing more. There was no one else there and the doors were chained closed from the outside.

Dom was behind the church inspecting the little cemetery. I called him, and we headed back to the store.

☽
Chapter Five
~ The Stalker ~

"Those trained and tested in the fires of tribulation lose all fear."
SGR

I was a little early, so I parked and went inside the store to see if I could help Em close up. The ranchers had left and Dom elected to stay on the porch. Em thanked me and handed me a broom. The store had the same feeling as a lot of the buildings in these parts. Built of old growth redwood timber, it had soaked up the warmth of the generations it had served, and its floors bore the marks of their patronage. Such places are the keepers of the past and offer great solace to those like me who find no charm in the cheap, throw-away modern world.

A faraway country station was playing on the radio. The signal was weak, but the unmistakable words of *'Your Cheatin' Heart'* made it through the static, and I winced. Em was fiddling with the tuning knob when Dom began to bark loudly on the porch. A man's rough voice told him to shut up, and the door rattled. Em had locked it and flipped over the Open/Closed sign just moments earlier.

I peered out the window between two displays. It was him – the creep from Willow! He'd seen my van and knew I was inside.

"Don't let him in!" I whispered frantically to Em as I ducked out of sight. My terror must have looked irrational, but she did not question it. *"I think he followed me here!"*

"Over there!" she pointed to the storage room door. *"I'll take care of this."*

I hunched down, scurried like a mouse into the tiny room, and left the door open an inch so I could see what was happening. Em rummaged under the counter and then walked slowly to the front of the store with the keyring in her hand. When she saw I was safely out of sight, she made a show of unlocking the door and opened it a crack. *"I'm sorry,"* she pointed to the sign, *"but we're closed."*

"So early?" he whined. *"Dammit. Figured you'd be open later than this."*

Em's tone was brittle. *"We are, in the summer months, but it ain't summer yet."*

"Where's the owner?" He demanded.

"You're lookin' at her."

"Well, guess I'm screwed then," the stalker replied sourly, assuming he was a stalker, which, even in the face of the latest unnerving evidence, I still hoped was not true. I never liked to assume the worst about anyone, but I was learning that I needed to seriously address that tendency.

"Your dog?"

"Yup," Em lied.

He knew darned well whose dog Dom was. He'd been watching us in Willow.

He looked over his shoulder at my van, then back at Em, snorted and said nothing.

"So, like I said," Em repeated herself, *"we're closed for the day. Open tomorrow morning at nine. Have a good evening,"* she said firmly and started to close the door. In a flash he wedged it open with his boot, and Dom began barking aggressively.

The intruder pretended to be worried. *"Geez, quite the watch dog you got here. Does he bite?"*

Then he turned meek. *"Aw, please ma'am, are you sure I can't just come in and get something to eat and drink? Shit, I'm out of smokes, too."* He pulled out a crumpled pack as proof. *"I get that your sign says you're open until six but it's only six-fifteen. I've been on the road all day and I'm hungry and beat."*

The pleading tone did not match his behavior, and he began leaning his body against the door. Another second and he would have been inside, but in less time than that, Em pulled a pistol from her jacket pocket and aimed it at his head. He jerked his foot back in surprise, and she threw her shoulder against the door, slamming it shut. A quick twist of the key hanging in the lock, and the bolt slipped in place.

The guy's mask dissolved and the face that glared back at her was pure evil. Dom barked furiously, lowered his head, and bared his teeth.

"Shut up mutt, or I'll bash your face in!" the guy growled savagely. He drew his leg back for the kick, but Em tapped the gun barrel on the glass and shouted, *"Leave him alone and get outta here! I ain't gonna warn you again! Now GIT!"* She fired a shot into the floor.

He came close to the glass, shouted *"Bitch!"* and flipped her off with both hands. Then he kicked over the carved bear, spit at Dom, and strode back to his truck, screaming curses as he went. After a couple of unsuccessful attempts to start his engine, he peeled out of the parking lot, spraying gravel behind him.

When he was out of sight, Em called to me and said, *"You can come out, dear. He's gone."*

I ran to her like a terrified child, and although she was the one who had handled the encounter, she soothed me while I trembled in her arms.

"Oh, there, there. You're okay. I know his kind. I can smell 'em a mile off. They come around here now and then lookin' for somethin' – in addition to weak souls, I mean. They're not of this world, but they still bleed. You gonna be alright? I can hear your heart."

I nodded miserably. I'd wondered about the holes I'd seen in the floor when I was sweeping. What did she mean, *'not of this world?'*

"Know why he's trackin' you?" she asked.

I shook my head. *"No!"*

"Hmm. Well, there's usually a reason."

Then, cool as a cucumber, she opened the front door again, went out onto the porch, apologized to the Welcome Bear, stood him upright and invited Dom inside. I wanted to comfort him, but he didn't appear to need it and instead went to Em, wagged his tail, and looked to her for praise.

"Well done, soldier," she patted his head. Then, she lowered the shade, pocketed the keys, and said in a cheery voice, *"I'm ready for a glass of wine. What about you?"*

☾

Chapter Six

~ Shelter ~

"Life is a river, Ali, not a well. It's always changing".

I followed Em to the back door of the store. The sky was filled with black clouds and huge raindrops had begun to fall. Lightning flashed in the distance and I mentally counted the seconds until the thunder rolled. Five. We walked to Em's cabin and huddled on the porch while she got the key in the lock. Then she shooed Dom and me inside and said, *"Make yourselves at home, I need to fetch some firewood."*

The place was a homey, earthy dwelling that instantly wrapped its arms around you. Weathered wood paneling, a worn leather couch, river-rock fireplace, rag rugs. Every shelf and tabletop held shells, stones, birds' nests, and other treasures from the natural world mingled with distinctive antique pieces. An old record player and albums with tattered jackets sat on a marble-topped table in one corner, with crooked stacks of books on the floor beneath it. The rest of the space was filled with works of art that begged to tell their stories. Leaning against the wall next to the front door was what looked like one of Fred's madrona walking sticks. It was Gypsy instinct, I suppose, to take careful note of our surroundings. You can tell a lot about a person by what they collect.

The screen door in·the kitchen slammed noisily behind Em as she came in with an armful of kindling and firewood. I hurried to help, but she said, *"It's okay, I've got it,"* and dumped it all unceremoniously in a wooden crate on the hearth. *"Turn on a light, though, will you?"* she asked, as she brushed off her coat.

I crossed the room and pulled the chain on a stained-glass floor lamp. The ruby reds glowed, the green leaves leapt to life, and the mixture of amber and cream glass washed the room in shades of honey.

275

"Much better. Let's warm this place up, shall we? Sit down, dear. Soon as I get this fire goin', I'll pour us some wine."

From the start, there'd been little else to do but obey this fierce little grey-haired woman with the rough hands and commanding eyes. She was bossy, but I felt completely safe in her care.

Anticipating the warmth to come, Dom laid down next to the hearth and watched Em as though the ritual was a familiar one. Then suddenly, his ears went up, he looked toward the hallway, and let out a little bark.

A calico cat strolled casually into the room.

Em greeted her warmly, *"Hello, Beautiful. We have company!"*

The cat meowed so softly that her heart-shaped mouth barely moved. Her snow-white face, bib, stomach, and paws stood out in sharp contrast to the rest of her body, which was black with random splotches of orange. She was a study in whimsy, with one caramel ear and the other black.

Em spoke proudly, *"Ali, this is Boots. Boots, Ali."*

"Hello, Boots," I replied. *"I can see how you came by your name."*

Boots stretched, sat down, and looked calmly at Dom, who stood and happily wagged his tail in greeting. Em didn't bother with introductions.

"It's your dinner time, isn't it?" Em asked the cat. *"Come and get it, then."* She headed to the kitchen.

Boots trotted obediently behind her.

"How's stew sound for dinner?" Em called back to me.

"Sounds wonderful!" I answered. *"Perfect for a night like this! I need to run out to the van, though."*

The rain was coming down hard. I dreaded going out, but Dom had heard mention of dinner, and I needed to go get his food.

Em stuck her head around the corner. *"Move your van around back. There's room next to my Jeep. You know. Just to be safe."* Having issued the order, she went back to dishing up canned tuna.

I pulled my jacket hood over my head, told Dom I'd be right back, and hurried out the door.

By the time I returned, Em was holding a wine glass in one hand and poking at the fire with the other. She'd put some stew in a bowl and said, *"Mix this with his kibble. He'll love it."* Then she pointed to the coffee table where wine and a plate of cheeses, sausage, olives, and crackers waited. I wondered how she'd prepared it so fast.

It was my first real food since the butcher shop sandwich seven hours earlier, and even more delicious. I told her so and thanked her profusely.

"And this wine! I've never had anything like it! Do you sell it in the store? Because if you do, I'll certainly be buying a bottle or two! People would pay a fortune for this in the city."

Em was proud of her brew, and grinned like she'd already known what I was going to say.

"I'm so glad you like it. I don't share it with just anybody, and I don't have enough extra to sell it. Got a secret berry patch – you know, those rare little wild blackberries. It's getting harder for me to pick them though." She held up a hand that could only be described as gnarly, and said matter-of-factly, *"The day will come when this body gives out, but I won't need it then, anyway."*

She saw my puzzled look and said, *"Life is a river, Ali, not a well. It's always changing. But for now, here's to us and the adventures that await!"*

We toasted to that, and to health and strength. Boots wandered back in, sat down next to Dom, and began cleaning her whiskers. Having gobbled his food far less daintily, Dom pretended to snooze while keeping an eye on her.

Em kicked off her shoes and settled into a rocker by the fire. I sank down into the leather couch across from her.

"Wrap up in that quilt until it gets warmer in here," she instructed.

Yes, ma'am.

I couldn't remember the last time I'd felt so safe and content and I prayed silently, *"Thank you, God, for this refuge. And thank you, Em, for insisting I stay. But how do you know me and why are you sheltering me? Who **are** you?"*

☾

Chapter Seven
~ Em ~

*"You are conduits connected to the Source, with the ability
to continually expand and channel greater light, love, and power."*

One glass of wine down, appetizers in my belly, and I was craving answers.

"Em?"

"Ready for dinner?" She asked. *"Let's eat in the kitchen."*

"Sure, but... I have so many questions."

"I expect so," she replied. *"There'll be time for that."*

The stew was hearty and delicious. *"It's always better the second day,"* Em declared, and I agreed. Every time she looked at me, I felt like she was reading my thoughts. If only my own discernment were so acute! I had suffered greatly for lack of it – or perhaps for ignoring or arguing with it.

After we finished, we retreated to the living room, where Em threw another log on the fire. The sound of the storm on the metal roof made me even more thankful that I had stayed. A night like this in the van would have been miserable.

Em poured more wine. It shimmered in the firelight like dark purple juice extracted from some exotic fruit that grows only within the deep caverns of a mysterious planet in a faraway galaxy. If God drank wine (which I was sure He must), this would be it. I thought of communion and toasted Him silently.

Em looked me straight in the eye, raised her glass, and said *"Amen."* Then, she took a long, reverent drink and said, *"Ask away."*

My throat tightened. *"Okay. I'll be brave then."*

"I wish you always to be." She replied.

I blurted it all out. *"Who are you, how do you know me, and how did you make me see what would happen if I didn't stay?"*

"In that order?" she laughed.

"In any order," I laughed with her.

"Well, my dearest Aleasa, I've known you since before you were born. I've seen your joys and sorrows, your hopes, and dreams and I know your calling. I didn't put that picture in your head, I simply shifted my vibration to match yours, and gave your own intuitive abilities a little nudge, so to speak. Like tuning in a tv station until the image forms. The rest was you.

*"And as for who **I** am,"* she paused, seemingly wanting to use the best words, *"People have described us in many ways. We are guardians, sent to aid you. Seraphs in the service of Almighty YaH. Most often, humans call us 'angels.'"*

My mouth dropped open.

She continued matter-of-factly. *"We are hearing the term 'spirit guide' these days, but it must be remembered that YaH wishes His children to look solely to Him for guidance. This is so that no imposters can cause confusion. It also strengthens His bond with you.*

"Our commission is to encourage you on the path your soul has chosen. That means there are times when you must be warned, as you were earlier. There's more than one seraph in this room, by the way." She smiled. *"Some of us take other forms, depending upon the assignment."* She nodded toward Dom and Boots.

I was dumbstruck.

"Yes," she smiled at them affectionately, *"these two, and other creatures of this earthly realm – some gentle and others fierce. They are sent at different times for different reasons – to bring peace and comfort, companionship, protection and to demonstrate unconditional love. They may also arrive as a sign or confirmation. However they choose to appear, they are no less formidable than those of us who take on human form. Even the smallest are tremendously brave. They come and go in human lives because that is their way, whereas we guardians remain close to you from beginning to end. When it is required that we take on flesh, as I have now, we become subject to its laws. Everything*

you feel in your body, we also experience. We grow hungry and tired. We feel pain, we bleed, and we age. I'm proof of that." Em held out her hands. *"In our true form, we are impervious to all of those things."*

I finally managed to speak. *"But you are not..."*

Em finished my sentence, *"...what you would expect of an angel? It's great, isn't it? We walk among humans all the time and nobody suspects a thing."*

Bewildered, I asked, *"But what about all the pictures...?"*

She laughed a little. *"Oh, you mean the wings and halos? The wings only manifest when we need them. Otherwise, they would take up way too much space. And as for the halos..."*

With those words, golden auras began to form around Em, Dom and Boots, and Em's countenance radiated so much light and divine love that I felt compelled to fall at her feet. She knew this, and said, *"No, child. It is only before YaH that we bow."*

As she spoke, pictures began to flood my mind – scenes from a realm made entirely of light. I saw a majestic tree growing at the center of a garden, its lush green branches laden with plump, shimmering fruits of an indescribable color. Beside the tree flowed a sparkling aqua stream. Everything vibrated with life. I also saw creatures of every kind – all coexisting in harmony.

People were strolling through a garden. Their form was human, but their bodies had been transformed so that they were one with the Light. Their garments were made of shimmering fabric which was also alive. Ethereal music and angelic voices filled the air, and every now and then, one of the light beings would step up off the ground, move gracefully through the air, and then come back down.

Four women came toward me, held out their arms and began to sing. The song felt familiar, and I wanted to join them, but before they could reach me, a mist rose between us, and I could no longer see into the garden.

Em had been silent during the vision, and I looked at her in wonder.

"It's our home," she said. *"Yours and mine. When we are not here, we are there. You are able to see it because your soul remembers it. You have work to do there, as here."*

I was overwhelmed. *"The women?"*

"Your heart knows them." She answered and continued.

"This Earth has been struggling in darkness for a long time, Ali, and when you were offered the opportunity to help, you came, just as they did. You are here on this plane now to awaken those who are asleep or have lost their way. You and others are pinpoints of light in the veil between this world and that one."

I tried to comprehend her words but was having difficulty pulling myself back into the present world. *"Why am I being allowed to see this – and to see **you**?"*

There was great compassion in Em's voice. *"The cares and sorrows of this world have pulled you down, child. You are a brave soul, and have sacrificed and emptied yourself for others, but you have been struggling to stay afloat too long and your strength has been drained. When that happens, it can be difficult to see and hear clearly, and there is a chance that the wrong decisions could be made in desperation. No one can tread water forever. You were shown this in a dream – do you remember it?"*

I did. In the dream, I had been pushed overboard far out at sea and was frantically calling for help. Those whom I had trusted were standing on the back of the boat watching as I frantically tried to stay afloat. A bright yellow life ring was hanging within their reach, and I begged them to throw it to me, but they just laughed. Then the boat motored away, and I was left adrift in the ocean.

"So, I'm rescuing you." Em said in a matter-of-fact voice. *"You usually do a pretty good job of that yourself, but on this occasion, you need some help."*

I watched as her brilliance began to fade and the spunky old woman's weathered face returned.

I panicked. *"Don't go!"*

She laughed reassuringly, *"Oh, I'm still me. I just can't sit around looking that other way for too long. It's distracting. Now, my dear Aleasa, you and I must make the most of this time. I have been told that we will not have it in this way again, so, I must impart as much as I can while we are here together."*

282

As she spoke, a blissful, tingling flow of energy began to sweep through my body from head to toe. It pulsed through my veins and every cell was awakened, cleansed, and re-charged. I was overcome by the sensation, and Em explained.

"You are feeling the life force of YaH – the 'dji' as your ancestors called it. As a daughter of the Light, you are connected eternally to the Source from which this energy flows. It moves through your spiritual form the way blood travels through a physical body. It is the invisible substance of creation – the highest vibration – all powerful, all knowing, pure and holy.

"When your soul returns home, you will experience this energy in its fullness. This life-force pours from YaH into everything He has made, circulates, and then returns to Him in the form of praise. That is the song you heard – the worship of His creations in return for His unending love. Animals on earth sing it all the time in their own ways."

I asked incredulously. *"So, the dji is always within us here?"*

"Yes. It is given according to your desire and abides within the cells of those who receive it. You are all created with the ability to continually expand and channel greater light, love, and power.

Em paused and explained further. *"But glorious as it may sound, this process is not always easy. You have all been wounded by the enemy, and this has resulted in bruises, scars, and knots that prevent YaH's light from passing through as it is intended to. You have encountered these shadowed souls. They are easy to recognize. While you can be an example and shine your light toward them, you cannot change, fix, or restore them. You can point the way, but they must seek the companionship of the Light themselves. When they do, it will enter, and healing will begin. YaH longs for this intimacy with His children."*

"And me?" I was almost afraid to ask. *"What does my soul look like?"*

Em replied, *"You are full of light, Ali. There are a few shadows, but they are not as dark as you may think, and if you continue to forgive others and yourself, and keep the vow you made at the ocean earlier, your light will grow brighter until you shine like the sun. This is YaH's promise."*

"You heard my vow?" I asked in wonderment.

"Indeed, I did. It was a life-changing moment." She smiled. *"I am always present for those."*

"Does the past matter, Em? Because it haunts me."

"Yes and no. When a soul seeks redemption and chooses to walk in YaH's light, the record of what they did in the darkness is erased. Not only are those missteps forgiven, but they vanish from YaH's memory just as your footsteps disappeared from the seashore. Then, a new reality begins.

"So, that is the 'no,' and here is the 'yes.' Human choices shape everything in this world. All that has happened and will happen is a result of the decisions you and those before you have made. One of the great mysteries is that YaH gives His children free will while already knowing what their choices will be. Your decision to come into this life was made with full understanding in accord with YaH's divine will. One day, you will look back over it from a higher perspective and see the order in the chaos and the growth within the struggles."

"It doesn't seem like I'm learning very well," I said miserably. *"I've started over so many times, and here I am at square one again. But you're right. I made the choices."* I didn't need to go into details. She surely knew.

She explained, *"It's natural to feel lost when you've never been someplace before. But your soul views all of this as an adventure. Most humans are so weighed down by the things of this earth that when the time comes to fly, they can't.*

"There is another way of looking at losses, my dear girl! They bring freedom! Your soul, like your mother's and those before her, is more adventurous than most. You do not hesitate to hold hands with love and dance fearlessly through this life. This has led to experiences which, whether sweet or bitter, have nourished you with deeper wisdom. When you live within your roots, you cannot see the fruit you are bearing above, but others can, and most importantly, YaH sees it. Earth is His garden. Your soul wished to be part of it, and a wise gardener prunes his trees so that they can bear more fruit."

"So, this is pruning?" It was an oddly comforting thought in terms of my barrenness.

"Only for a season," Em reassured me, *"so that greater beauty and abundance can come forth. You will write about this someday,"* she smiled, *"when you have fruit to offer again.*

*"Within every soul lies a seed of YaH's nature. There are things that can only manifest on earth through **you**, Ali. They are the fruits of your spirit and will always emerge in the right season. It is their nature to do so. From seed to root, root to tree, tree to branch, branch to blossom, and blossom to fruit. Then, the harvest."*

"My life has purpose?" I could not imagine what it would be.

Em was emphatic. *"Yes indeed, and it is a vital one. You were given many keys because YaH knew you would use them."*

I heard my uncle's voice and said tentatively, *"Uncle Ion used to tell me that the women in our family had 'The Sight.'*

"Indeed." Em answered. *"They all possessed the same gift, but they were far more limited in how they could share what they were shown. The days are coming, Ali, when the words given to you will unlock hearts in places and times you could never have imagined. When people hear or read them, the messages will speak to them personally."*

I confessed, *"I can't imagine. A lot of the time, I don't even feel like part of this world, Em."*

"That's because you aren't. Your soul wasn't made for this world, child. It was made for the one you saw moments ago. I am not exaggerating when I say that Earth is in grave trouble. You and others are here for the awakening of souls, but that means you must live on a spiritual battleground which has become more treacherous than ever before. The enemy has succeeded in turning this world upside down and inside out. Lies are the prevailing currency.

"Temptation lurks around every corner. It is easy for souls like yourself to become distracted and forget that they came here for a war, not a picnic. Remember that you are on a tour of duty and just passing through. 'Rest ever lightly, if when weary you must, lest earth's tethers bind you to that which is dust.'"

I'd heard the last sentence before. I'd written it.

Em smiled, *"Yes, they're your words, Ali. Don't forget them."*

☾

Chapter Eight
~ Time ~

*"The Story wouldn't be complete without you…
or without every soul, for that matter."*

"Em?" I asked tentatively, *"Can you tell me more about my family? On the Gypsy side, I mean."*

The angel's face softened. *"Of course. As much as our allotted moments will allow."*

I grabbed my purse and fished out a pen and notepad.

Em re-arranged herself in the rocker. *"Before I begin, would you mind bringing in a couple more logs for the fire? This old body gets cranky when the storms roll in."*

When I returned, Boots was on Em's lap and she was stroking the cat's head with great fondness. *"She's old, too, sweet thing. We've been on quite a few assignments together, haven't we dear? Your ears tell the tale, don't they?"* She ran the tips of her fingers gently over the largest notch in the cat's ragged black ear. Boots blinked and alternately twitched both ears in response.

Em held out her glass for me to refill and began. *"Alright then. Settle in. Here we go."*

I sat back down and got ready to scribble. I didn't anticipate any pauses once Em got started and wasn't sure know how late we'd be staying up.

She began. *"There were others further back, but we cannot take all night, so I will start with Vadoma, one of the chosen. She was so lovely that her husband etched her likeness in stone. Her daughter, Miri, was just as beautiful, and creative, like you. I can see parts of all of you in one another. Vadoma, her husband, and Miri lived in the forest. After her parents returned to Charos, Miri lived in the stone house they'd built until she grew old and ascended also. Nature reclaimed their home, and several lifetimes after that, your Great Grandmother Renata was led to the ruins by a mighty guardian who took the form of a white wolf – a brother to those like our Domino, here."*

She paused and looked lovingly at Dom, who raised an eyebrow and made a wolfish sound deep in his throat.

"Vadoma had hidden something there, and it was awaiting discovery by the next soul called to protect it, which was Renata." She paused as though listening to a voice I could not hear, and then spoke. *"But before I continue, I am being asked to explain something quite important to you first."*

I was ready.

"It's about the notion of time," she stated. *"You see, it doesn't just predictably march along, as humans think. Quite the opposite. Have you ever noticed that some moments, days, weeks, months, and years race by while others seem to crawl? Or that people will say, 'It seems like it was just yesterday that we…' when many seasons have actually passed? Then, there's the expression, 'time stood still.' An entire life on earth can be lived, and people will shake their heads and say, 'Where did the time go?'*

"The answer is that the time went everywhere. It leaps around and flows in different directions, and humans have no control over it whatsoever. What happens at any fixed point effects the whole because it's all one thing. 'Then' was once 'now,' and 'now' will soon be 'then' and you are never the same traveler because you are continually changing, too.

"'Tomorrow' cannot be depended upon, because when and if it arrives, it has changed and become 'now.' It will never be as you expected, imagined, or planned, because it is subject to factors beyond your control. You can neither 'make time,' nor 'kill time.' Those are perceptions, not realities.

"Sometimes, while in the 'now,' you may have the odd feeling that you are remembering or returning to a previous version of the same experience. There is a sense that you somehow belong to both frames. I could go on, but you get the idea.

"Kind of," I said. *"But not really."*

She continued. *"I don't know a human who does. Shifts are subtle and go largely unnoticed or ignored. Even when people agree that something seems off, if there's no obvious explanation for it, they generally dismiss it. For example, when, why and how did that widely quoted line in an old movie change? Or how did it vanish altogether? Why are the maps different from what you remember? How can words that you knew by heart literally change on the page?"*

She saw my frown and said, *"What people cannot see, hear, taste, touch or explain, they denounce. Science denies the supernatural and is determined to unravel every secret, yet their theories are always based upon limited knowledge and are therefore continually disproven. The greatest minds admit that the harder they look, the deeper the mystery becomes. The questions will never end, and YaH is the only One with the answers. So far, most humans aren't ready for them. So, He waits.*

I was completely lost but she was determined to make her point.

"Stay with me, Ali. When a shift is significant, it can lead to great confusion. Some people can clearly see the change while others do not. Arguments ensue and people take sides. Proof may even be presented, but evidence can be manufactured, and even when it is valid, those who cannot see the discrepancies also refuse to see the proof. Anyone who firmly states what they believe to be true is usually accused of misremembering or being delusional.

"It was prophesied long ago that everything which can be shaken will be shaken. Times of great testing and turmoil such as the world has never seen are coming. Confusion is the enemy's stock and trade. It is never YaH who sends it. Whatever you see, remember that all power is His and ever will be. Keep this promise in your heart and your steps will be guided, just as surely as they were when you found your way here to me.

"But back to the subject. You have been taught that time is a straight line to be followed from beginning to end, and that everyone must walk it like a tightrope. The reality is that there is no line, and therefore, no edge. Your soul has always existed and always will. This life you are living now is an ever-evolving experience that offers a

tremendous opportunity for growth. But the concept of time, as humans perceive it, is as much a myth as death, which is actually just another change."

I thought about the unexplainable feelings I'd had in Willow. Em explained further. *"It's wisest just to give yourself fully to the present, for each moment will affect all the others. When you spend that precious drop dwelling on what is behind you or what you imagine is to come, you are forfeiting the moment you are in.*

"Always live in the Now, Ali. There will be days so devastating that you will not be able to see the way forward. And there will be days so glorious that you will wish they could last forever. Surrender to both.

*"Do not ask, 'What will I do with this day, or this hour or this moment?' Ask, 'What will I do with this **breath**?' Be flexible, ready to move and adapt. Your people have always lived by this elemental truth. Did you know that the Gypsy word for yesterday and tomorrow is the same?*

I shook my head.

"The word is 'atasya.'" She repeated it. *"Atasya."*

I wrote it down and underlined it three times.

Confident that she had covered the subject of time to the best of her ability, Em continued, *"Now, let's talk about your family."*

"Your Great Grandmother Renata was a quiet, gentle soul. Like your mother, she was sent from Charos, though the circumstances were different. She had a marvelous imagination and preferred nature to people. She hid many things in her heart and was never understood by those who took her in, except for one young boy named Tamás, your grandfather, who loved her from the start.

"She was lost and wandering, with no memory of her past when she found the caravan. Shortly thereafter, it was discovered that she was with child, and she stayed with them until she gave birth to your Grandmother Nadya. That same night, her soul went home.

Tamás had sworn an oath that he would watch over her child, and he kept his promise unto death. His and Nadya's souls shared an ageless love, and when Nadya reached womanhood, the two of them married. Twin sons were born – your uncles, Ion and Amoun."

"And my mother, Katiza?" I asked.

Em replied, *"I'm getting there."*

"Your grandmother was another multi-talented woman. She and Tamás were performers, and he was also a master silversmith. Like others before her, she was a gifted seer and took her abilities very seriously. She refused to call herself a 'fortune teller.' Instead, she gave only encouragement and hope to those who came seeking guidance.

"I have a precious memory of the dear little thing sitting on a rug in a village marketplace selling knives and jewelry while Tamás played his violin nearby. The day was hot, and her babies were overdue. She had no one to help when her time came, so Maja, a seraph who is highly skilled in assisting human births, and I were put on alert. Boots was there too – weren't you, dear?"

The cat's tail twitched in response and Em reminded her, *"And you appeared to Nadya again months later as a sign to let her know that she had indeed been visited by seraphs. That was so sweet of you."* Boots purred and stared into the fire.

Em turned her attention back to me. *"You will love this part. At that first meeting, when I took Nadya to Maja, Nadya insisted upon giving us some of her jewelry. The workmanship was exquisite, and the gemstones – which she said had fallen from the edge of Charos – were among the most exquisite I have ever seen. I cannot imagine what price such artistry would fetch these days. Seraphs have no need of possessions, of course, but Maja and I still treasure your grandmother's gifts and we keep them where they will always be safe."* She pointed upward. *"You'll see them someday.*

"Now, on to your mother, Katiza."

I interjected, *"I only know what my Uncle Ion and Sabella have told me, and I don't think it was everything. My uncle said they found my mother on an island in a lake when she was little. When I got older, it sounded like a fairy tale. Before he died, things got sort of mixed up in his head."*

Em enlightened me. *"He was telling the truth. Allow your heart to remember him as he was before the illness, and as he is now – full of life and joy among the others of your family who have all completed their missions and have returned to health and youth in their true home."*

She continued. *"Katiza's initial visit to Earth ended abruptly, and her soul was carried back to our realm, where all babies are adored. When she saw Nadya on Earth below, she longed to be her daughter. After the difficult birth of your uncles, Nadya was unable to bear more children, but the face of a little girl often appeared in her dreams and filled her with longing. The desires of Nadya's and Katiza's hearts were heard, and love built a bridge that allowed Katiza to return to Earth. Your grandmother, Renata, accompanied her and gave her a song for strength. Kesali – another guardian whom you have been told about – led Nadya to where Renata and Katiza were waiting on the island, and there, Nadya became Katiza's mother."*

I was captivated.

"So," Em continued, *"Katiza was not born of Nadya and Tamás' blood, but of their spirits. She was 'grafted into the vine.'"*

"So, my mother did not have Gypsy blood?"

"Oh, she did, as do you." Em answered. *"YaH holds the power to change blood, but the secret of this divine alchemy is another of the great mysteries.*

Em paused, and added, *"When a human heart seeks purification, YaH begins a spiritual process of cleansing followed by a transfusion of His own blood. Before His children were deceived by the enemy, pure, undefiled blood ran through their veins, and it shall be so again."*

Em stared deeply into my eyes to see whether I understood the significance of her words. Suddenly the subject of DNA entered my mind, and its vital preservation in the purest form. Seemingly satisfied that I was now at least pondering the subject, Em moved on.

"Katiza possessed a fiery Gypsy soul, and when she was a young woman, she fell in love with a traveling musician by the name of Ansel – your father. They were a striking couple and when they performed together every head would turn. But he was restless and tempted by fame and fortune. They were not destined to remain together, but the world now has you, Aleasa, and you were always meant to be."

"I'm not so sure…" I started to question, and Em frowned, waggled her finger, shook her head, and silenced me.

292

"The story wouldn't be complete without you, Ali," she said. *"or without every soul, for that matter."*

"Throughout her pregnancy and your birth, your mother was supported by the love of her family. I know your Uncle Ion and Sabella have told you how happy you all were during the days in the Cirque."

I nodded. *"Yes. But then, it all changed."*

Em's expression was somber. *"In ways no one was prepared for. When this incarnation of Earth began, one of my kind rebelled against YaH and was banished from the realms of light. Others followed him. They roam here now and seek to invade suitable human hosts. You know, of whom I speak."*

She turned her head in disgust and spit into the fire. Her words dripped with loathing. *"The unspeakable tragedies this traitor causes! He has been given many names, but I personally refuse to dignify him by any of them and refer to him only as 'the enemy.' The enemy of YaH and all creation. Bringer of suffering and death. The thief. The liar.*

"He was once a seraph of the highest order before he courted pride and jealousy. These destructive elements turned him inside out, and bite by bite, he devoured his own heart. Now, only a black hole remains – a bottomless, hungry maw which bleeds evil and seeks to swallow every good thing within YaH's creation."

Em groaned with sorrow, *"We watched in horror and disbelief as he deceived many of our own into following him – seraphs whom I personally knew and loved, for we were all of one heart before the mutiny. They fell to Earth like flaming meteors, where they have been bringing destruction since. Their intention is to transform YaH's jewel into a bleak environment better suited to their own existence. Their efforts to corrupt and enslave Earth continue, but YaH's faithful ones shall not cease to stand against them. The enemy's poison cannot be allowed to spread, so we seraphs who were created for glory in holy realms must now wear armor, keep our swords sharp, and fight."*

Em collected herself and stated, *"But here's the fact, Ali, and it may surprise you. This war was already won long ago, when YaH came down. It's over. Finished. The enemy knows this but pretends not to. Lock-down is coming, and he's doing as much damage as he can before the final hammer of justice falls."*

Chapter Nine
~ The Story ~

"The Children of the Light are here for only one reason.
To embody YaH's nature and shine in the darkness."

Em knew I was familiar with the story she was about to tell. The passionate Gypsy version was written on my heart. But I was coming to understand that there were volumes more to know.

The Guardian began. *"However rebellious His human children can be, YaH loves them above all His creations. This is why the enemy seeks to corrupt, torment, and enslave them.*

"So, long ago, YaH devised a strategy to liberate their souls. There are those who reject it, but I am not here to tell their tales.

"YaH's Son, who was and is one with Him, and whose words brought this world into existence, would take on flesh. He would submit to the laws of His own creation, live a human life and bear a human name. He would feel human emotions – pain, hunger, thirst, joy, sorrow. When wounded, He would bleed. He would demonstrate that YaH is not a distant, angry God. He would show compassion, feed the hungry and heal the sick. He would undo every evil spell and open eyes and hearts blinded by the enemy's deceit. He would show wonders, speak truth, and teach with words the world had never heard before.

"He would do all of this with the foreknowledge that he would be betrayed, abandoned, tortured, and crucified. They all understood sacrifice – their religions demanded it. The blood of a spotless, innocent life to atone for a guilty one. In this case, the Son of YaH's life for theirs. It was the only way to free them from the curse of the accuser.

"Though excruciatingly brutal at its apex, the plan was perfection, and could only have been designed and executed by the One who holds the power of life and death.

"When calculated by Earth time, the incarnation was brief – just thirty-three years. The enemy was suspicious from the time the child was born, and destroyed many innocent lives out of fear, but he never fully grasped where the story was going, and in the end, he played right into YaH's hands.

*"You see, what the enemy did not know was that this man's blood was different than any he had spilled, and this life was unlike all the other lives he had claimed, even those of the saints whom he had personally tortured and slain. **This** life could never be taken, because it was being forfeited for the sake of all humankind.*

"Some of us questioned whether the world would comprehend the magnitude of what was happening, and it appeared, at first, that we might be right. Most people did not grasp it at all, and many still don't. Those at the time who loved YaH's Son were devastated and saw His death as an egregious politically-orchestrated travesty of justice. Others in outlying areas didn't hear about it until later, and just shrugged their shoulders sadly and went on with their lives. Prophets and martyrs were nothing new and the builder-turned-preacher had joined that number. Life would go on and persecution would continue. Why would it change?

"But YaH had foreseen all of this. There was one more move, and He knew that when He made it, souls beyond number would awaken and understand."

Em shook her head incredulously. *"Meanwhile, the enemy was doing a victory dance at his own funeral."*

Her light was growing brighter and filling the room. *"You know, of course, what happened after that. It really is the greatest story ever told, isn't it?"*

She didn't wait for my agreement.

"YaH's Son had promised those closest to Him that He would come back from death, but they did not believe it until His grave was found empty and He stood before them. You should have seen their faces!

"I was there, Ali. What YaH says He will do, He does. Nothing is impossible for Him. His principles operate whether mankind chooses to believe or not. He makes the rules, and when He speaks life, there is

life. It's as simple as that.

"*So, His son kept the promise he'd made and lived among the people of the region for forty more days so that many eye-witness stories could be told. Then, when the time came for Him to return to our Kingdom, He sent The Spirit to continue His work on Earth.. This Holy Spirit, whom your people call Balval, is also one with YaH and The Son, and possesses the same power to teach, comfort and guide those who ask. Your people have long called upon Him for wisdom and direction.*

"*The Children of the Light come here for one reason, Ali. To embody their Father's nature and shine in the darkness. You are one of them.*"

Em's eyes were like coals of fire. "*And now, I am going to tell you something that very few humans know.*"

I stopped breathing.

"*At the instant Yah's son's blood fell upon Earth, all the broken elements of creation that had been drifting in the void came together in perfect alignment, and everything that had gone before and all to come, changed. Oh, if only I could describe that sight!*

"*It is already finished, you see. The enemy has been sentenced to the place prepared for him and those who have chosen to serve him. And as you will ask me why there is still so much evil in this world when YaH has already prevailed, I will tell you that what you are seeing is the end of a desperate ruse. A deception. A lie orchestrated by the 'father of lies,' as he is called.*

"*In reality, the enemy and those who serve him are writhing like a sea of snakes in their death throes. This is a show. A production. The curtain will soon fall, and the audience will walk out. Observe long enough and you will see that the enemy's tactics never change. He sells too hard, lures humans with false hope, hooks them and reels them in. But he always tips his hand and in the long run, his empty promises and smoke screens invariably fail and the truth is revealed. YaH remains one step ahead of him, and so do we. Our ranks vastly outnumber his. We never sleep, and we never lose!*"

Em closed her eyes and took a long, deep breath. "*But where was I? Oh, yes, I was telling you why your family had to leave the Cirque.*

You were with them, of course, but were too young to remember.

"So. One of the enemy's generals is a filthy old demon by the name of Vrag…" Em spit into the fireplace again.

"He was commanded to go forth and search for a powerful article that had long been hidden from evil forces. While on this frustrating, seemingly endless assignment, he came across a man with an insatiable lust for power and an obsession for objects purported to possess supernatural properties. The demon was easily able to invade the man's mind and from there, hypnotize countless souls into relinquishing the common sense given them by YaH. By the time the truth became clear, many of those who had complied with his orders gravely regretted their misplaced allegiance. The enemy has played this same game over the ages. Those who know anything of human history can see it.

"In this case, the possession of this man precipitated what is called World War II. You all know the man's name, but it is another that shall not pollute my mouth. Sad to say, there is a steady stream of ego-driven individuals who are as easily used as he was. They pose as philanthropists, great thinkers, holy men, political leaders and so forth, and are puppets of demons that convince them their causes are righteous. Whatever words may proceed from their mouths, their poisonous fruits always speak louder. The root of their undoing, and the enemy's foothold, is always the same: Pride.

Em sighed wearily but she was not finished. *"The enemy sets snares for brilliant minds, particularly those driven by questionable motives. Multitudes were tortured and murdered during the moustache man's reign of terror – half a million Roma among them. Your people call it the Porajmos – 'The Devouring' – though most decline to speak of those horrors at all. There was a great homecoming when their souls arrived on Charos' shores. Evil can kill the body, but never the soul."*

This was the first time I had heard the word '*Porajmos.*' Uncle Ion had never spoken it. Most likely for the same reason Em had said.

Her voice softened. *"Enough of that, then. It is not a subject I enjoy, but truth is truth. As you know, most of your family escaped the attack at the Cirque, and even in such heartbreaking times, when one would not think it possible, love found your mother again."*

Porajamos *(poora-JAH-mose)* – The Devouring (The Holocaust)

"His name was Hans and if things had gone as he and Ion planned, you would all have been re-united here in America. Despite their best efforts, that did not happen."

I was almost afraid to ask. "And the others? My grandparents, my Uncle Amoun? Uncle Ion and Aunt Sabella would never talk about it."

Em replied, "I will not paint a sad picture, because their brave souls all knew life does not end here, and they carried their songs home with them. No evil could touch them then."

Love emanated from Em's face. "You are all threads in a divine tapestry, Ali. Your souls came to fulfill missions, and you are now fulfilling yours. While in a human vessel, you are only given light for the next step, and strength for the next moment. The unfolding of your purpose takes time, patience, and determination. Think of the difference between the perspectives of the turtle and the eagle. Souls must experience both, here. Those who commit their human lives to the highest objective are always being led, whether they feel it or not. Every individual who came before you in this story was a link in the chain that leads to you, dear child. Your part is that of a receiver and messenger. Whether you believe it or not doesn't matter. It was decided long ago, and at that point in your existence, your immortal self was in full agreement."

I was overwhelmed. It sounded like this life was going to get even harder and take a lot more strength than I possessed. I wasn't sure I was capable of enduring what my family members had.

I asked, "Is there more you can tell me about my mother? I know some things, but…"

Em smiled, "Well, the best word might be 'feisty.'"

I laughed, "I sort of guessed that. I think I inherited her temperament. I don't know what I got from my father. Uncle Ion wasn't fond of him."

Em clarified. "Ansel did not know he was to be a father when he left, and if he had, a different future would have been written. Ansel was not bad, just young, passionate, and driven by a powerful gift.

"I would describe your mother as indomitable. She had the strength and skills to rival any man while charming him at the same time. To watch her ride, sing and dance would have thrilled you. After the escape, when the plan to meet up with your uncle and Sabella failed, her prayers for you never ceased. Mother's and grandmother's prayers are always heard by YaH, for their love is the closest thing to His own.

"No one you love is ever utterly lost to you, Ali. They will be with you again, whether here or there." Em raised her eyes to *"There,"* and my thoughts turned to my little one. I felt my heart slide into the familiar vacuum she'd left behind – the hollow place where none of the questions were ever answered. I wondered if Em was protecting me from truths too painful to bear.

I think she knew what I was going to ask next, so instead of leaving space, she abruptly switched to a sensible mode. *"I suppose that's enough for tonight. It's been quite a day. Let's get some sleep."*

I didn't want the evening to end, and blurted out, *"Is that one of Fred's walking sticks by the door?"*

"You spotted that, did you?" she smiled.

"Is he...are you two..." I didn't really know what to ask.

"Fred is quite another matter. He plays by different rules and is faithful to this world, especially Willow, though I believe he may be falling far behind the times. He doesn't like change. He has a heart of gold, but he is lonely sometimes. Perhaps, if you see him again when you return, you could be his friend?"

"I would, but I have no plans to go back to Willow."

"Oh, you will."

"Fred said the same thing!" I exclaimed.

"Well, he's often right." Em ended the conversation with a chuckle. Boots jumped off her lap and stretched.

"I have a sleeping bag you can use if you're okay with the couch."

"Oh, I can go out to the van and get mine," I said, and the moment the words left my mouth, a gust of wind drilled rain against the windowpane.

"Or...sure, thanks. I'll use yours." We both laughed.

"*I'll get it*," Em declared, and I thought to myself, "she's part angel, part drill sergeant."

Boots followed her down the hallway where she retrieved a sleeping bag and pillow from the closet. She returned, dropped them on the couch, kissed my head in gentle benediction, and said in a soothing voice, "*See you tomorrow, dear Aleasa. Sleep well. You are safe here.*"

I took her hand, kissed it, and pressed it to my cheek. Her skin smelled like the last roses of autumn. I did not want to let go.

She went into her bedroom and I rolled out the sleeping bag. Dom lifted his head from between his paws and I blew him a goodnight kiss. Then I slipped into the downy cocoon, breathed in the warm scents of old leather, blackberry wine and dying embers, and slept more deeply than I had since childhood, when my Uncle Ion would rock me in his strong arms and sing a Gypsy lullaby.

"Hush, hush, chavi of mine,
The forest is sleeping,
and the stars above shine.
The moon is our mother, and the road is our home,
Sleep, sleep, dear child of mine."

I could still hear Sabella's soft laughter, because in true Gypsy fashion, his songs were different every time. They almost never rhymed, but when one of them accidentally did, he'd be extremely proud of himself and would look at her, grin, and wink like he'd planned it that way.

I, like all little children, did not care that much about the words. I only felt the love.

☾

Chapter Ten
~ The Visitor ~

*"In quietness and confidence shall be your strength,
and when you have found it, stand."*

I awoke to sunlight streaming through the windows and followed the aroma of freshly brewed coffee and cinnamon rolls into the kitchen where one of the soft, gooey spirals sat in a puddle of frosting on an old, chipped Blue Willow plate. Em had known the china pattern would evoke heartwarming memories from my childhood. As a little girl, I'd been enchanted by the story behind the design – a sadly beautiful tale of two star-crossed lovers who had turned into doves and flown away. I was a born romantic. It occurred to me in that moment that Romany and romantic were almost the same word. How could I have never thought about that before?

Beside the plate was a hastily scribbled note:

"At the store. Wanted you to sleep. There's more rolls in the freezer. Scramble some eggs. Eat breakfast out back. You'll have a visitor later. Spend the day in peace. Write. The storm has passed, but another one's coming. Please stay again tonight. ~Em"

Through the kitchen window I saw a patio area beneath a vine-covered arbor. Beyond it, empty hills stretched to the sea. I poured a cup of coffee and carried it along with the pastry out the back door to the rough-hewn table and chairs. Boots was lying in a patch of sunlight. She stretched, looked up at me and meowed softly in greeting. Dom heard the screen door close and came running.

The view was incredible. Bear River shimmered like mercury in the valley below, and the Pacific sparkled in the distance. There were no visible roads from where I stood, and it was easy to imagine that none existed.

Everything was drying out from the previous night's soaking, and the silence was broken only by a few noisy crows that were harassing an eagle, above. It was ignoring them, and the lesson was clear. Fly higher. Leave them below and behind, and if they follow you, fly higher still, where the air is too rare for their breed.

I had come to believe that laws and principles are demonstrated to us in the physical world so that we can grasp them in the spiritual. In that sense, everything becomes our teacher. Native cultures understood this. For seekers, the signs are abundant and I relied upon them.

I went inside, poured another cup of coffee, and walked to the van for my book. Like the landscape before me, the pages held the inner mountains and valleys, rivers, and oceans of my life. Some of the knowledge had resided within me since childhood. 'knowings' deeper than such brief life experience could possibly have wrought. Messages too precious to ever be lost or forgotten.

I had always felt compelled to write them down. I used to have an old shoebox full of torn envelopes, restaurant napkins, grocery store receipts and anything else I could find to scribble on at the times when the pictures and words came. When Uncle Ion gave me the book, I transferred them into it.

*I*n obedience to Em, I put pen to paper and laid my heart open. The space was too valuable for anything but truth. There could be no pretense, only honesty. Nothing more, nothing less.

"...Even amid the peace that surrounds me here, and Em's assurances of my value, I am still bleeding. I don't want to feel like this. I want desperately to snap out of it. To rise like a phoenix from the bonfire of the past, my wounds cauterized by the flames. To have no thought about what lay behind or below. To be the eagle above the crows. To live again!

Why am I still limping? Will I stumble and fall forever? The Lover of my soul reaches for me. He says I can walk on water, but as Peter found out, one zealous emotional outburst cannot sustain that level of faith for long. When I look down, I sink. He alone can rescue me. Any other arms would lose me to the tide. I must not forget this fact again.

The pain is stuck to me like my own shadow. It follows at my heels, has burrowed inside and is leaching the life from my bones. Save me,

God! Save us all! You have shown me this world encrusted in layers of hardened sorrow – all the blood spilled since the Fall, black as tar – a scab that must be shed before You can fill the raw hole with new life. I see Your hand, abrading, exposing, stripping the layers one by one so that all can be made new again as it was before the vicious wounding began. How long, oh God? How long?"

My tears were falling upon the page when she arrived.

𝓘 did not hear her footsteps

from my chair in the morning sun
where I was crying for peace.
For an end to Earth's wars, and the one in my head.
Her tawny body glided by, and I thought,
"She doesn't see me. I dare not move."
She paused at the arbor's edge and gazed out over the valley
still as a statue, except for her ears,
on swivels, waiting for the messages.
I shifted and the chair creaked.
She turned her head, our eyes met.
I spoke to her heart, praised her beauty, and said,
"No one will harm you here. Please stay."
She lingered for a thousand breaths, until my own
finally slowed down enough
for me to hear the answer to my threadbare prayer.
It had always been waiting in the calm,
its small, clear voice too often muffled
by the loud cries of my heart.

"𝓘n quietness and confidence you shall find your strength,

and when you have found it,
Stand."

The doe blinked once and bounded down the hill. I wrote the last words and closed the book.

Hush now.

Be still.

☾

Chapter Eleven
~ Dominos ~

"A great dividing is coming and shades of grey shall disappear.
All choices will become black or white."

I don't know how long I sat on the patio. My watch had stopped working the first night with Em. I thought about how lovely it would be to live without having to track minutes or hours. To eat and sleep when the desire arose and follow the rhythms of the sun and moon, the land and the waters. People had done so in times past, and Earth had met their needs.

While a second roll warmed in the oven, I wandered over to the chicken coop past where my van and Em's old Jeep were parked. The fat brown hens clucked their greetings and ogled me to see if I'd brought food. The soil had been freshly turned in a garden patch alongside the coop, and stakes with seed packets on top marked the rows.

I could live happily in a place like this. There was no rush to get to the Redwoods. They'd been standing for over two thousand years. I returned to the kitchen, scrambled a couple of fresh eggs, and looked around for a clock. I couldn't find one anywhere, and it finally dawned on me that supernatural beings have no need for clocks, and while I was there with Em, neither did I.

I soaked up the dappled sun beneath the arbor until it got chilly and dark clusters of clouds began forming above the hills. There was a firepit in front of the patio, and newspaper, kindling and logs by the back door, so I started a fire and pulled my chair close. I sat, hunched into a ball, arms clasped around my knees, collar pulled up over my chin, and stared into the flames. I fed them pieces of my splintered past, and they leapt, danced, and crackled – their tongues eager to tell me primeval tales of their own tumultuous courtship with man.

Everything has a voice when you listen.

After a while, the screen door opened and Em spoke from behind me, *"You made a fire! Wonderful!"*

"So glad you're home!" I started to get up and she said, *"Stay there, I'll be right back."*

I drug the other chair over next to mine, tossed a log on the fire, and before long, Em returned with mugs of hot, thick cocoa with marshmallows on top.

"Oh! My favorite!" I exclaimed.

"I know it is," she said, grinning. *"How's three-day-old stew sound for dinner?"*

"Even better than two-day-old stew!" I said enthusiastically.

"I'll add dumplings."

"I love dumplings!"

"I know you do," she said again, and we both laughed.

I heard myself declare, *"I don't want to leave, Em."*

Her tone reminded me of a compassionate nurse who had tended me once in an ICU. *"I wish you didn't have to. But the rest of your life is waiting. There's a lot of road ahead, Ali. This adventure is far from over."*

Anxiety tightened my chest. For some crazy reason, I'd thought staying would be an option. *"But what if I need you?"*

Em soothed, *"I've always been near and always will be."*

Then, she changed the subject. *"I'd love to hear more from your book later."*

"*Okay, but don't you already know what I've written?*

She clarified. *"It doesn't work quite that way. Guardians don't necessarily hang around looking over your shoulder, but we are beside you when you need us. We can't read your mind, but we know what you're made of and what you are called to. The struggles and suffering of humanity are very painful to observe, and our compassion is great, however, we act only in accord with YaH's will, which means we must sometimes stand aside while lessons are being learned. We fight for you against evil entities, but those battles generally take place in a different* dimension where you cannot see them – nor would I want you to. Sometimes you may sense our presence, and other times you may not, but for your human part, just pray, ask for help, and be assured that you have been heard and that forces have immediately been set in motion on your behalf."

She sighed, then. "No matter how I try to explain these things, they will not all be within your understanding. There are secrets hidden in deep places of the Source where not even we seraphs can go. We are told that when YaH's children ask according to His will, they are given access to realms where all the knowledge they seek awaits them.

"For now, during this brief human experience, just remember that I, and the others who watch over you, remain always concerned with your soul's wellbeing. Do not doubt and do not dismay, for everything that is allowed, no matter how it may be perceived at the time, has purpose. YaH wastes nothing. He turns what the enemy means for harm into good. There is no loss, only gain.

"You are here now because you needed healing and protection, but you are stronger than you think, Ali. Always remember that you are infinitely and irrevocably loved. YaH never forgets, and nothing in all of Heaven or earth can take you from His hand. You are part of a family of countless children born of the Light. They are your brothers and sisters. Your soul knows this."

I bowed my head. "I won't forget."

Em smiled and patted my hand. "I hope not, dear child, but in case you do, I will find a way to remind you."

After dinner, we took our same spots in the living room, with Em in her rocker, Dom, and Boots by the fire, and me on the couch. I read from my book and Em listened, nodded, and murmured now and then, "Yes, yes. That is truth."

When I'd finished one verse in particular, she sighed and said, "Humankind has always relied on visible signs that precede the changing of seasons. So it will be at the end of the age, but only those who are watching will recognize them. YaH reveals His nature in everything He creates, but sad to say, many don't pay attention. They have become blind and deaf to the miracles happening all around them. They call their blessings 'luck,' and take YaH's gifts for granted."

She shook her head sadly, *"Winds of division are stirring and will blow more fiercely than any hurricane. They will separate the wheat from the chaff, and the humble from the proud.*

"YaH's truth is free to all with eyes to see and ears to hear. However, opposing forces work incessantly to cloud it and to create confusion. This shall come to an end. An awakening has begun and hearts are opening."

I hardly dared speak, but hesitantly offered, *"I was shown that shades of grey will disappear, and all will become black or white, good or evil..."*

"Precisely." Em quoted: *"'a knife edge upon which no one can stand.'"*

"You see," she added, *"This world is in a broken state because of countless poor choices. Although people have always been given freedom, they have not understood that every decision defines them and affects others. In the end, their own hearts shall judge them.*

"It is not long from now, which is the reason YaH is sending so many messengers. You are voices in the wilderness. Poets and prophets, musicians, singers, artists, and storytellers – all declaring the same thing in different ways. It has always been so, and human nature being what it is, the messages are not always fully understood until they manifest before peoples' eyes. By then, those who delivered them are often long gone.

"Receivers and messengers must be protected. There is great contention over you. The enemy seeks always to silence you. To break your spirits and to erase your names. But 'the pen is mightier than the sword,' Ali. One of Earth's poets wrote that. He had no idea at the time how powerful those words were or how long they would reverberate. He was simply obedient to record them."

Suddenly, Em's eyes blazed and her voice deepened. *"Woe to those who call evil good, and good, evil – the liars who call darkness light and lies truth. Who spread confusion and lead YaH's children astray! He will not withhold His hand forever, and on that day, every faithful seraph will don their armor and draw their sword."*

The feeling in the room had changed and goosebumps appeared on my arms. Both Boots and Dom were standing at attention before Em. I was struck by how similar the two of them looked, with their black bodies and snow-white muzzles, breastplates, and paws.

Em's voice turned matter-of-fact. *"But that is not our present duty. At ease, my friends."* Boots and Dom both obediently laid down.

"We must wait for orders. Victory is certain, but we bow to YaH's wisdom. When it is time, we will march, and trample the enemy beneath our feet."

If I was reading Dom's eyebrows correctly, he was ready for battle. Boots rubbed her body against Em's leg, meowed and walked casually toward the kitchen in hopes of changing the subject from spiritual warfare to tuna. I gulped the last of my wine and pulled the quilt around me tighter.

Everything Em had said led me to believe that I was in the presence of a high-ranking seraph with great authority.

"I have so many questions, Em! We can't possibly cover them all tonight, and I'm afraid that I'm going to drive away from here tomorrow and remember things I forgot to ask!"

She reassured me, *"All you need to remember is that you are never alone. We are close by, always."* She gestured to Dom and Boots. *"As I've promised, comforters and protectors, both human and animal, will come to you, which reminds me of something **I** wanted to ask **you**. Dom was named after a message you received, right?"*

"How did you know?" I asked.

"He told me, of course. Will you read it to me?"

I nodded and turned pages until I found it in my book. *"Well,"* I explained, *"as usually happens, first a picture appears in my mind out of nowhere…"*

Em corrected me. *"Not from 'nowhere,' dear. The pictures are sent from the Source to capture your attention. Visualization is a powerful creative gift and it was given to you for this purpose. I love the way you use it in everything you do. So many spiritual gifts are left on the shelf."* She shook her head sadly. *"I will never understand why."*

I remarked, *"I used to think everyone could see things, until they said they didn't. Uncle Ion understood, but no one else ever has. So, I learned to be quiet about it. Being laughed at or called crazy is painful.*

When you're young they say you have a wonderful imagination, but as you get older, they put other names on it. So, I started to write things down instead of talking about them.

Em nodded with understanding.

"In this case, I was shown a picture of a long, curvy row of dominoes that stretched as far as I could see. Then, there was one little push and they all began to fall. I didn't know what it meant at first, but I think I'm beginning to understand."

Em nodded. *"Your faithfulness to listen and record what you see and hear is of greater importance than you realize, Ali."*

"Here's what I was given to write," I said. *"While the world watches for colossal signs, know this: like a row of dominoes set strategically on end, all things in Heaven and Earth are moving into position. The pieces have been aligning over centuries, and because many have been placed without human realization of their significance, the whole picture cannot be seen or understood by man. Consider that it may not be a cataclysm, but just one small nudge that will set in motion an unstoppable chain of events."*

Then, she grew quiet.

Having given up the hope of an evening snack, Boots returned from the kitchen and was sitting before the fire. The flickering flames were reflected in her eyes and her tail switched restlessly back and forth.

Having heard his name in the context of my reading, Dom stood, walked over, rested his chin on my knee and looked at me with the devotion of a true companion – one who understood everything I said, and would stand by my side through whatever was to come.

Then, Em spoke again. *"The dominoes you were shown represent those who have exalted themselves to rule over others. They signify kingdoms, nations and empires, governments, systems, institutions, organizations, false religions – everything that has been constructed by those who lust for power and control at the cost of others. It's the game they play. In short, all things not built according to the will of YaH are destined to fall. One after another, they will topple, and then finally,"* she said definitively, *"an end to this long season of oppression and sorrows will come."*

☾

Chapter Twelve
~ The Gift ~

"Remember that for the children of YaH, no good thing is ever truly lost."

Em was finished. I could feel it. Thunder rolled in the distance, and when a drop of sap popped in the fire, I jumped.

She announced, *"It's time for rest. Tomorrow you must continue your journey, and it will demand all your faith and strength."* Then she lowered her voice as though spilling a secret, *"I am told you shall receive a gift in the night. I think you will be pleased."*

"But Em!" I cried, *"I haven't asked you the most important question!"*

"I know," she said, with compassion. *"I was there, Ali. I saw. I heard, as did YaH. You must make peace with it, and you may never have clear answers. YaH has seen your tears and heard your prayers. There is none more merciful and just than He. Restoration will come. If not here, There."*

"My heart aches every day," I cried.

"I know," Em said. *"I know."*

"Why? What happened? What did they say to make her leave? Did I do something wrong? I'll never understand!" My words fell apart.

"No, you may not. That is the hardest thing about being human. But I give you this promise: because your blood runs through her veins, she is overshadowed by the same Heavenly forces, and that includes me."

"Since the first spark of light shone in the darkness, the nature of truth has not changed, and it never will. Those who choose to pursue it, must love it more than they fear their pain. It is a momentous quest. All of your notions will be challenged, and you will shed many versions of

yourself along the way, but when you have laid down all your useless defenses, Truth will make its home in your broken heart, heal you, and fill you with unshakeable peace."

I crossed the room, sat at her feet, and laid my head in her lap. She stroked my hair and said, *"What a gift these moments have been. I've been doing this your whole life while you slept, and only just now, are you able to feel my touch."*

*I*t was decided that I would leave early the next morning before Em opened the store. I cried, and when she went to her room, I saw brilliant golden light pour out from under the door.

As I lay on the couch staring dejectedly into the dying embers, a soft white paw appeared on the edge of the cushion. Another paw followed, and then Boots silently leapt up and stretched herself out on my side. She had never come to me before, and I knew it was an act of love. As her warm body rose and fell with my breathing, all worries slipped from my mind and I fell into a deep slumber.

Moments later my eyes opened, and I found myself in the same realm where the four women had come to me before. This time, there was no mist to divide us. They encircled me and sang the song again. Then, the one nearest me said, *"Dear Aleasa, we've brought you a gift!"*

I knew, somehow, that the soul speaking to me was my grandmother Nadya.

"Listen!" she said with delight, and the song became even more beautiful.

Then I was shown scenes of each of them singing it at times during their earthly lives – in a forest, a cave, in childbirth, and beneath the moon. In every case, I witnessed the song conquer fear, break bondage, shatter barriers, and crush evil. I also saw that the notes were their most powerful when sung in praise.

"We've given this song to one another," she said, *"and now we are giving it to you."* As they sang, the sounds found their way to my center and changed the vibration of my heart. All doubts and unworthiness were swept away and replaced by a reconnection to my own soul as it was created to be – perfect, strong, free, and loved unconditionally.

I was then taken into deeper sleep and shown more of the Heavenly realm of Charos, as my people call it. It was explained that my visit must, of necessity, be brief because humans are unable to fully comprehend that reality.

The last thing I remember is standing on the shore of a vast, silver sea. An exquisitely-shaped opalescent shell lay shimmering at my feet, and when I bent to pick it up, the mist surrounded me and I was sent back to this world.

*M*orning arrived with the sound of Em grinding coffee in the kitchen. I knew I had to leave, but when anxiety tried to creep in, I remembered Boots' solace the night before, the gift of the song, and the wonders I'd been shown.

Em and I didn't talk a lot at breakfast. I just watched her and marveled at the humility and devotion of this powerful angelic being who was serving me in love.

I told her about my dream, and she smiled and said, *"I knew you'd love that. Sing your song often, Ali. It is more powerful than you can imagine. Some have literally moved mountains. Oh, and this is for you. A little souvenir."*

She retrieved something from the breast pocket of her blue flannel shirt and placed it on the table in front of me. It was the shell from my dream.

I gasped.

"It was real, then?" I turned it over and over in my hands. It still held the warmth of her body.

"Of course, it was real. Why wouldn't it be?" She replied. *"That, and a whole lot more that you are soon to discover. This new chapter is only the beginning, my dear, so you need to get on with it."*

I gathered my things and we walked to the van. She stood beside my window and said, *"Remember that for the children of YaH, no experience is wasted, and no good thing is ever truly lost. Take this..."* she handed me a roll of bills and something wrapped in a thick towel.

Before I could argue she said, *"I won't be needing this stuff. The gun is loaded, but that's the last of the bullets. You know how to shoot."*

I did. I also feared my stalker might still be out there somewhere. We hadn't talked more about him.

Em knew what I was thinking. *"Trust YaH, but remember to lock your doors."*

Something else I'd meant to ask leapt to mind. *"Em, this is a strange question, but on my way here, I saw a dead coyote hanging from a fence post. Why?"*

She answered, *"It's a warning to predators who might be thinking of harming the sheep. You, my little lamb, belong to a shepherd like that."* I knew Who she meant.

"Now," she leaned in, kissed me, and tapped on the door. *"Off you go to visit with the Giants. Tell them 'hello' for me. Dom, we shall see one another down the road, old friend."* Dom tilted his head back and emitted something between a bark and a howl. Boots was sitting on the porch and her mouth formed the soft, white heart that I knew was a kiss.

Em had said that courage wasn't something I could muster up. It was remembering the invincibility of my God. Even so, my tears made it hard to see as I backed up the van.

When I got turned around and looked in the rear-view mirror, I expected to see Em waving, but she was nowhere in sight.

$\mathcal{T}$he remainder of the Lost Coast drive was beautiful, but nothing could match the spectacular unveiling of the ocean and the surreal days with Em. I felt as though my old life had ended there and a new one had begun.

$\mathcal{I}$ was lost in my thoughts when the road abruptly narrowed and towering sentinels rose on both sides.

Their voices spoke louder than any manmade sign.

"You have entered our Cathedral. Hush. Slow down. If you have not come to bow and worship, then just quietly pass on through."

I pulled over at the first opportunity. The parking area was empty, and I was thankful that tourist season wasn't yet in full swing. Dom and I got out and entered the forest.

Within a short distance, the trees and undergrowth closed in behind us and I lost sight of the van. Led by dry creek beds and animal trails, we made our way deeper in.

Each step told me I was on sacred ground and I prayed it would always remain so. I could not fathom what these trees had witnessed over the centuries. Their testimony was one of endurance, and they needed no other.

I stretched my arms as far as they would reach around one of the lightening-scarred giants, pressed my ear to its bark and listened to its heartbeat. Beside it stood another towering survivor which had been burned almost all the way through. From the time of the fire until now, it had drawn all its nourishment from one remaining strip of bark that supported it from the ground to the sky. The charred hollow at its base had become a shelter for forest creatures and was serving up a fine feast of smells for Dom. Nothing was wasted here – not even the scourge of fire. Everything constantly adapted and served the whole.

I heard a river and told Dom we should try to find it. On our way, a bright spot of white caught my eye. When we got closer, I saw that it was a flawless newborn Trillium. Knowing that the miniature kingdom at the Giants' feet held its own magic, I sat down beside the sweet little thing, and listened. After a few moments, her petals trembled ever so faintly and a voice like crystal windchimes spoke.

"My name is Faith," she whispered. *"Who are you?"*

"Aleasa," I whispered back, for loud voices would never have been proper there.

There was a long pause while she relayed the information over the network that connects all such spirits. Then, she replied, *"Oh! We remember your mother! I am told she needed a sign from us. But you are so very far away from where and when that was! Are you lost too?"*

"No," I replied, *"But if it meant I could stay here with you, I would wish to be."*

I could be part of this place, and I told the Trillium princess and the Redwoods so. I would be no bother in my little ivy-covered cottage. I would fish in the nearby river, drink from the stream, and eat salads of huckle and salal berries with mushrooms, tart sorrel leaves, and tender fiddleheads. I would live out my days here, send my songs of gratitude up through fragrant branches into the heavens, and when my human life was done, I would sink down into the forest's soft green womb. From there, my soul would find its way into the labyrinth of the Giant's roots, where ancient wisdom awaited discovery in the silent depths below.

☾

Chapter Thirteen
~ The Theft ~

*"With my last breath, I would sing the song I'd been given.
It was all I had."*

I must have nodded off, for suddenly Dom was there, nuzzling my hand and looking anxiously back through the trees.

"What is it, boy?" I asked.

In answer, he turned and began running. Knowing I would not be able to find my way out of the forest without him, I jumped to my feet and followed.

Smoke. The closer we got to the parking area, the stronger the acrid smell grew. My eyes started to burn and Dom was barking frantically. By the time we arrived, the van was engulfed in flames. A thousand thoughts raced through my head simultaneously and I was helpless to do anything but watch in horror.

Then I saw the stalker through the billowing smoke. He was jumping up and down, laughing and bobbing his head in a bizarre, inhuman fashion and my immediate assumption was that he was either insane or high on drugs or both. Em's words came back: *"They're not of this world, but they still bleed."*

He'd found me, broken into the van and set it on fire.

Dom's urgent barking alerted the demon to our presence and he became even more agitated. He cackled and taunted me while juggling the gun and the roll of bills from Em. Then, he shrieked insanely, threw the money into the flames, and watched for my reaction.

I didn't care about the cash or the gun, or even the van. The only thing on my mind was my book.

The creature seized upon my fear, pulled the book out from under his jacket, held it up and pretended to throw it into the fire next.

"NOOO!" I yelled, and ran toward him. Dom was faster. He launched himself through the air and was almost upon the demon when a deadly shot rang out and I saw Dom fall to the ground.

I screamed and the demon laughed maniacally, waving the gun around and firing shots haphazardly into the trees. Then, his face sobered, and he pointed the barrel straight at me.

In that instant, everything stopped. The wind in the treetops, the birds, the buzzing of the insects, and even the river. Within the silence I heard Em's voice, *"What will you do with **this** breath?"*

I knew.

With my last breath, I would sing the song I'd been given. It was all I had.

I opened my eyes, looked straight into the face of my enemy, and opened my mouth. The voice that came out did not sound like my own.

The demon recoiled in shock and the color bled from his face. He took aim and pulled the trigger. I sang louder. The gun in his hand turned red hot. He shrieked and threw it on the ground. He appeared to be afraid of something in my direction, but I didn't dare take my eyes off him to see what it was. A dark, swirling vortex had begun to form behind him and he was in a panic. His eyes were wide with terror as he frantically whipped his head back and forth between whatever was behind me and the jagged black orifice. He was trapped.

I watched incredulously as huge, disembodied claws emerged from the black hole and blindly groped the air. The demon shoved my book back into his jacket and contorted his body obscenely in an attempt to evade the talons, but they found him anyway, sank deep into his flesh, and drug him inside. His blood-curdling screams echoed out from within, and then the hole collapsed upon itself and disappeared.

In the next second I heard the sound of enormous wings taking to the sky behind me, but when I spun around to look, there was nothing there. The forest and the parking lot were quiet but for the pitiful noises coming from my burning van. Something urged me to look down, and I saw a bullet lying in the gravel at my feet. It had stopped just short of my body.

Dom wasn't moving, and I ran to him, fell on my knees, and buried my face in his fur. I was sitting on the ground beside him sobbing when a Jeep veered into the parking lot and skidded to a stop. A fellow in a worn denim jacket and cowboy hat jumped from the driver's seat and ran to us.

"Are you okay? Is your dog okay?" He could see we were not, and laid his hand on Dom. *"Oh,"* his voice echoed my grief, *"poor fella."* He touched my shoulder gently and said, *"I have to get you further away from this fire. The gas tank's gonna blow."*

I reluctantly stood up and he put his arm around me for support. I looked over my shoulder and agonized, *"Dom, oh my sweet boy...I can't leave him here."*

"He's already gone, darlin'. Nuthin' we can do. Right now, we gotta run."

My legs gave out and he lifted me up in his arms and ran back to the Jeep, where he braced me against the front bumper. Seconds later the van exploded, and he pulled me into his chest to shield me from the heat of the flames. When they had subsided, he let me go and reached inside for his CB.

"Come in, Dispatch. Off-duty Crew Boss Bill Hicks reporting a vehicle fire on Mattole, 'bout a mile South of the State Park road at Bull Creek. Gas tank just blew. Still burnin'."

"Roger that, Hicks. Sending them now. Any injuries? Dispatch over."

"Driver's okay – in shock." He looked at me sympathetically and acknowledged Dom. *"Her dog didn't make it. Over."*

The compassionate female voice on the other end answered, *"Aw, sorry to hear that."*

He led me around to the other side of the vehicle and helped me in. *"We gotta stay 'til they get here. Water?"* He reached behind the seat and handed me a bottle. I took it numbly and nodded my thanks.

"I'm Bill. Wanna tell me what happened?"

I shook my head. *"You'd never believe it."*

"Try me."

I did not have the strength. *"Truly, you would **never** believe it. I can't explain..."* I wrapped my arms around myself to control the trembling, *"I'm incredibly thankful for your help."*

A siren wailed in the distance. *"They're comin',"* he reassured me.

*W*hen the flames were extinguished and the smoke cleared, I looked over the smoldering remains of my faithful old ride. The only thing salvageable was the metal tackle box containing my jewelry-making tools and a few supplies.

Then, I remembered the bullet that had stopped short of its mark. It was physical proof, if only for me, of a miracle. I didn't let anyone see me pick it up and dropped it into my jacket pocket where it joined the broken shells from the beach and the perfect one from Em.

Bill and one of the firemen were waiting for me. *"Uh...Miss..."* Bill said, tentatively.

I'd never given him my name. *"It's Ali."*

"They need you to fill out a few forms, Ali. Where to have the vehicle towed and such. Driver's license, Registration, Proof of Insurance. All that stuff. I'm sorry."

"I understand," I said, realizing with a jolt that all my documents had burned with the van. I pointed and just shook my head.

The fireman with the clipboard was sympathetic. He and Bill knew one another, and I tried to answer the official questions as best I could, while keeping it vague. My story was that while Dom and I were in the forest, thieves had broken into my vehicle and then set it on fire. By the time Dom and I got back to the parking lot, the smoke was so thick that I couldn't see anything. When Dom chased them, they shot him. I considered myself lucky to be alive.

When asked the approximate time of the incident, I automatically looked at my watch and was surprised to see that it had begun working again. I checked with Bill to see what time he had, and it matched mine to the minute.

I had no answer for the final question: *"Do you have someplace you can go? Somewhere to stay until this gets sorted out?"*

Where was I to go and how was I to pay for lodgings should I be able to find them? The van, my belongings, traveling money and identification were all gone.

Bill spoke up. *"I'll take care of her, Mick."* His friend was satisfied with that answer and said, *"Good man."* Then, he shook Bill's hand, wished me well, walked back to the firetruck, and they drove away.

Bill put his arm around my shoulder and gave me a gentle, reassuring squeeze. *"Don't worry, darlin', it'll get figured out."*

I cried, *"I can't leave Dom!"*

He agreed. *"Of course not. He deserves a proper burial. We could bring him with us or bury him here in the Redwoods. No place more beautiful than this."*

I suspected that such a thing was against the law, but Bill didn't seem to care. I asked, *"Can we take him further into the forest?"*

"Sure. I have a shovel. Always carry one."

We laid Dom to rest in front of the tree with the hollowed-out trunk, and I laid moss over the mound and placed sticks and stones in the shape of a cross on top. One small rock was shaped like a lopsided heart and it joined the assortment of keepsakes in my jacket pocket.

Bill didn't ask if I wanted to say any words. He just took off his hat, reached for my hand and recited a prayer.

At the end, I repeated his, *"Amen,"* and added Em's farewell: *"I will see you on down the road, old friend."* When I looked upward, I thought to myself, *'Dom will have the tallest, most majestic grave marker on the planet. One befitting a hero.'*

I was deeply grateful to Bill. *"Thank you for that. It means everything to me. Where'd you learn that prayer? It's beautiful."*

He replied humbly, *"Oh, it's mine. I've had to say a lotta 'good-byes'.*

We walked back to the Jeep and Bill started the engine. *"So, where were you headed before all this ruckus, Ali?"*

"On down the coast," I answered, *"on a sales trip. I make jewelry. I used to, anyway. Everything's gone now."*

"Which way'dja come from?"

"I took the Lost Coast road from Willow through Bear River and on down."

Bill looked surprised. *"Willow, you say. I live there. Where'dja stay in Bear River? There's not much left since the big quake a few years back. It was the epicenter. The little church is about the only thing still standing. You probably saw it. Even the old general store's gone. The Wildcat's gettin' way too rough. Not just happy hippie growers up there anymore. Some dangerous dudes. Best to stick to the main highway now."*

☾
Chapter Fourteen
~ Rescue ~

"I was still alive. I would focus on the miracle of that."

 ℬill's words sent me reeling.

What did he mean, the general store was gone? Where had I **been** the past few days? And why had Fred said to take that route?

I turned my head and stared out the window so he couldn't see my face as I lied in answer to his question.

"I stayed in my van."

Then I saw it just ahead. The demon's red truck pulled off on the shoulder. I gasped and immediately coughed to mask the sound.

Bill shook his head. *"Somebody's gonna get ticketed for leaving that piece of crap there. Redwoods State Park. You can't just pull off anyplace you want and walk into the woods. Well, unless you're me."* And he laughed a little.

I did not want to say anything that might lead to more queries about the string of unbelievable events, so I kept my comments brief. *"Well, I sure won't make that mistake again."*

"So, I have an idea, if you want to hear it," Bill said tentatively.

"Okay."

"Well, Willow's about an hour away. What would you say to dinner in town, and we can talk about everything then?"

I sighed. *"Do they have good wine?"*

"The best on the North Coast" He declared.

Not the best, I thought. Nothing would ever compare to Em's.

"That's very kind, and sure, I guess. There aren't enough words to thank you for everything, Bill. I don't know what I would have done

if you hadn't stopped. I think I'm still in shock. Not feeling very good." It was far worse than that internally.

His voice was comforting. *"It's all gonna be okay, Ali. We don't have to talk now. Just rest. There'll be plenty of time. I'm off duty for a couple more weeks and I'll help you get things straightened out."*

I hunched against the door and pretended to sleep while I mentally replayed the events of the prior three days over and over. Every time I got to the end, I was confronted by the horrible truth that my sweet Dom was gone, along with everything I owned. Why would the demon go to such lengths to steal my book? It was an incalculable loss – a lifetime of writings that I would never be able to reconstruct.

I forced myself to take inventory of what was gone. The money. Em had known I would need it. My big box of finished jewelry pieces to sell. All my camping gear, clothes, toiletries, the gun. At that thought, a sickening shock wave spread through my body. I'd completely forgotten about the gun! Was it back there lying on the ground? Had one of the firefighters picked it up? No one had said anything. Had they believed my story? It wasn't very likely that someone would shoot a gun and then leave it lying on the ground. It was all too much to process. There was no rational explanation, and I finally had to force myself to focus on nothing but my next breath. In. Out. I was alive. I would concentrate on the miracle of that, and the sound of wings.

*W*hen we drove across the bridge and into Willow, I felt as I had the first time, safe in an idyllic past where bad things did not happen. Bill parked in front of the Inn and we entered through the historic bar. Shouts of *'Wild Bill!'* greeted us, and beer glasses were hoisted. He acknowledged everyone, waved off their demands that we join them, and steered me to a quiet corner of the adjoining dining room.

After asking my preference, he ordered a bottle of wine, rested his elbows on the table and sighed deeply. I looked at his face, clasped my hands in my lap, and waited for the questions I knew were coming.

"Ali – I don't know your last name – I hope you know that I am, honest to God, only trying to help however I can."

I answered just as honestly. *"I know. Truly I do. And if you mean the last name I wrote on the paperwork, I was about to change it.*

I haven't decided to what, yet, so for now, I'm just Ali. And I do trust you, Bill. You're a godsend."

He looked relieved, and I could see the kindness in his hazel eyes. He was a good- looking man – tall, trim, dark hair, rugged – the type I'd always been attracted to. I'd noticed that a couple of the gals in the bar stopped smiling when they saw me follow him in.

"So," I teased, *"'Wild Bill' is it?"*

He laughed. *"Well, you know how it is. When you grow up in a small town, the sins of your youth follow you forever."*

I didn't know. I'd grown up on the road and was adept at leaving my sins behind me.

A server in a low-cut top brought our wine and gave Bill a questioning look when she poured it.

"Hey, Jen," he said casually, *"How'ya doin'?"*

"Fine, Bill," she said in a flat tone, *"gonna introduce me to your friend?"*

"Of course. Just gettin' ready to." I could feel his discomfort.

"Jen, this is Ali. Ali, Jen. Ali's van burned up in the Redwoods – bad scene. We're tryin' to figure out what to do."

Jen's expression turned moderately sympathetic as she looked me up and down. *"That's terrible! Will you be staying here in Willow?"*

"I have no idea," I replied.

"Well, if there's any way I can help, you let me know. Okay Bill?" She addressed him, not me.

I answered, *"That's kind of you, Jen. Thank you."*

She walked away and Bill looked embarrassed.

I laughed and reassured him, *"Oh, it's fine. Obviously, she's a 'friend.'"* I put the word in air quotes. *"The last thing I want is to create problems for you, Bill. It appears you're popular with the ladies of Willow. I wouldn't have expected otherwise."*

"Well, I won't comment on that." He rolled his eyes and then became serious. *"Right now, you're the only lady I care about. Here's what I've been thinking. I know you don't have any place to go. No vehicle, no money, and I'm guessing, no one to call. I've got a travel*

trailer I use now and then for longer fishin' trips. It's sittin' next to the house I share with my brother. We take care of an old non-working dairy farm just outside town. You're more than welcome to stay 'til you get things figured out.* He drained his wine glass and waited for my response. I had the strong impression he'd be more comfortable with a beer in his hand.

I closed my eyes and tried frantically to sort through my options. I had none. I could sleep on a park bench, but I didn't even own a blanket.

"So?" he asked.

"Are you sure I wouldn't be an imposition?"

"If that were the case, I wouldn't have asked you." His openness was reassuring, but I'd learned the hard way not to lean.

"It's decided, then," the crew boss announced. *"No more worries tonight. Tomorrow's a new day."* He opened his menu. *"What looks good to you?"*

I was still numb.

After dinner, we drove to the farm. Bill explained that their place used to be a bunkhouse when the dairy was functioning. The main residence was a grand, three-story Victorian that stood empty most of the year except for a couple of weeks when the owners visited from San Francisco. Bill and his brother Vic both worked for the Forest Service and maintained the property in exchange for rent.

The trailer was a bit stuffy from having been closed up, but it was dry and sat on a pad with full hook-ups.

"Wha'daya think? Will it work for you?" Bill asked.

"It's perfect, Bill. God Bless you...again."

"Oh, He does. I'll get you some bedding. If there's anything else you need, we've probably got it in the house, so just ask."

Bill turned on the heat, brought out sheets, blankets, and a pillow, and said there'd be coffee in the morning. Then, he wished me goodnight.

I was beyond exhausted, but my mind fought my body, and it was past three before I drifted off into a restless sleep. I tried to believe that Em was there stroking my hair.

Chapter Fifteen
~ Beginning Again ~

"You don't find love. It finds you…"
Anaïs Nin

I was awakened by a polite knock on the trailer door and checked my watch. Ten thirty! I bolted out of the bunk, smoothed my hair and clothes, and sleepily answered. Bill was standing at the bottom of the steps, smiling, and holding a steaming mug of coffee and a little bag from the bakery.

"I hated to bother you," he said apologetically, *"but I've talked to a couple of folks about your situation, and they want to help. There's a community fund for stuff like this and I thought we could go get what you need. The women who run it will be there 'til noon."*

I stepped out into the same smells that had greeted me the first morning at the fairgrounds – that indescribable mix of ocean and farmland that made you feel like you'd stumbled into a fairytale by the sea.

I shivered and rubbed my arms, but before I could go back in for my jacket, Bill handed me the coffee and pastry bag, and said, *"Drink up. I'll be right back."* I watched as he sprinted to his house and went inside. The guy was in good shape, but I supposed he'd have to be to fight fires.

The sun was glistening on the mansion's windows and lighting up the hillside behind it. I wondered who could afford to buy something like this and not live in it. Maybe they had plans to move someday. If this place were mine, I would never leave.

Bill came back with a sweatshirt bearing the Fire Department's logo and held it out to me. *"It's old but its clean. You can keep it."* He reached for the coffee and pastry. *"I'll hold those."* I pulled the shirt over my head and felt like I was being wrapped in his arms.

"Wanna have coffee on the porch?" he gestured.

"Of the big house?" I asked.

"Sure. We have the run of the place when they're not here."

We sat in wicker rockers beneath a latticework of budding Wisteria vines. I nibbled the coffee cake he'd brought and imagined how romantic it was going to look when fragrant purple blooms dripped down over the white 'wedding cake' mansion. I'd learned the names of the various Victorian styles from the pictures in the walking tour brochure. I hoped the owners didn't come back for a long time.

It did not seem possible that less than twenty-four hours earlier, I'd lost everything in an attack from hell itself, yet was now safe and being cared for in this heavenly setting. Maybe I had slipped into another alternate timeline like the one I'd been in with Em. Apparently, anything was possible since I'd decided to trust my life to the fates.

I could not escape the feeling that I'd sat on this porch before. It had been a warm summer afternoon, then, and I was wearing a white cotton dress that felt cool against my skin. Smooth, slender knitting needles rested between my fingers, a ball of yarn lay in my lap, and a calico cat was curled up at my feet. I could hear cowbells clanking as the small herd came in from the pasture for milking and reminded myself that I needed to pick a few apples for a pie and put the bread rising on the kitchen table in the oven before the baby awoke from her nap.

"Ali?" Bill's voice pulled me back into the present.

"We can come back here later, but I don't want to keep the ladies waiting. You're welcome to use our bathroom and shower. My brother won't be back 'til the end of the month. While you're doing that, I want to check the trailer to be sure everything's up and running okay."

$\mathcal{I}$n town, we parked next to one of the steepled churches I'd seen on the walking tour. This one was Gothic style, and unlike the neglected chapel in Bear River, it was freshly painted and impeccably kept. On one side, a concrete staircase led down to an open basement door where two older women were sorting through boxes of donations. They knew Bill and greeted us warmly.

The shorter and stouter of the two spoke up, *"I'm Martha and this is Mary. I know, but it's just a coincidence. We aren't really the Biblical sisters.*" We all laughed. *"The church lets us use this space. People bring things and we pass them on to those who can use a little help. Please don't be shy. Take anything you need. That's why it's here."*

I was deeply touched by their generosity, and with a bit more coaxing, I filled a grocery bag with personal care items, socks, underwear, instant oatmeal, and protein bars.

"Now," said Martha, *"there's a nice thrift store on Lewis. Bill knows where it is. We work together. Just go on down there, pick out anything else you need and tell them the gals from Hands of Love sent you. It'll be on us. Okay?"*

"And last thing," added Mary, *"we know that folks can't get back on their feet without some money..."*

I protested, *"But you've already given me so much!"*

"Hush now," Martha said firmly, *"this all comes from good-hearted folks who've weathered their own hard times. You've heard that it's more blessed to give than receive?"*

I nodded.

"Well then," she smiled, *"Allow us this blessing,"* and she handed me an envelope.

There were hugs all around, along with the offer of continued help should I need it. At their request, we left the basement door open, and when Bill and I got to the top of the stairs outside, we could hear them clucking about how Bill was such a nice young man and it was too bad he hadn't been able to find a good wife. His face turned red with embarrassment, I covered my mouth, and we both stifled laughter.

Back in the Jeep, I reluctantly opened the envelope and peeked inside. It contained ten twenty-dollar bills, which felt, at that moment, like all the money in the world.

I loved thrift stores and found the rest of what I needed there. An old pink bike with a basket on the front was leaning up against the wall outside and on the way in I commented on how charming it was. At the checkout, Bill plunked down thirty-five dollars and said, *"For the bike outside. It's on me."* I gasped in delight and surprise and tried to object, but he insisted, *"How else are you gonna get around? And by the way, I could use some help grocery shopping. I'm not very good at it."*

I doubted the last part, but I knew it was his way of making sure there would be meals to my liking.

That afternoon, we returned to the farm, put everything away, and retired to the porch again. I told Bill over and over how thankful I was for the kindness I was being shown but he brushed all praise aside.

I was relieved that there had been no more mention of Bear River. All of Em's words were locked in my heart, and I knew I hadn't imagined my time with her. Whether it had taken place in another timeline or dimension, I didn't know, and I doubted I would ever have an answer. The events in the Redwoods also remained beyond comprehension. Bill appeared to be a practical guy, and I knew he must be hoping for more of an explanation, but I wasn't ready to provide it. We needed to know one another better first. I didn't want him to think I was crazy.

"So," I said between chips, *"I've decided on a last name."*

"Oh? Well, that's good."

"Yes. Originally, I was going to wait until I was settled down again to change it, but I think that the fire was a sign. Everything with the old name burning up, I mean."

He nodded empathetically and I continued. *"In the Romany culture, people often choose their own names, and when they want to know yours, they ask, 'how do you write yourself?' My mother was Romany and my father was German. I never knew him, but he was a musician, and she was, well, she was everything. A musician, singer-songwriter, dancer, stunt rider..."* I paused to explain further. *"My family performed in a cirque in Belgrade before World War II. I was just a baby then. The Nazis invaded and we were all separated. I was raised by my uncle and aunt.*

"They had a highwire act together, so after we made it to America, we lived many different places. They took whatever work they could find, mostly in traveling carnivals, which were nothing like the Grande Cirque in Belgrade. I was selling popcorn and cotton candy by the time I was eight." I laughed. *"Most people would think it was a hard life, but I didn't know anything different, and I couldn't have asked for a more loving home. They anchored me with wonderful stories from the past that taught me about my roots and who I was.*

"I love being a Gypsy, so I'm taking the last name 'Bihari.' It's been used by Romany musicians and performers and honors my heritage. Ali's short for Aleasa. So, all of that to say, 'Aleasa Bihari' I shall henceforth be." I loved the sound of the name on my lips. A new beginning, a new me.

Bill took it all in. *"Wow. Well, you're a bit less of a mystery now. The name is lovely. You've intrigued me from the beginning, Aleasa Bihari. I'll never be able to compete with that backstory."*

"Nor do you need to," I laughed. *"But tell me yours anyway."*

"Whaaaayl," he faked a drawl. *"What'cha see is what'cha get. Born and raised here, wound up a firefighter, probably for the excitement, if I'm honest, along with the fact that I love the North Coast and want to see it preserved. That's about all. Been chased by a few women but outran 'em. I have a feeling the stories of a blue-eyed Gypsy woman will be infinitely more entertaining than any of mine."*

We stayed on the porch until sunset that night and many nights after while he played his guitar and I dreamed. We understood each other intuitively, and it felt like we'd known one another forever. I wondered if it had been like this in that other time, when I wore white cotton and he was the one herding the cows in for milking.

In Gypsy lore, when a second full moon appears within a month, the events that take place on that night are imbued with magic. Such was the case when Bill and I met, and what we shared was just as rare.

He was an open book, but to my shame, I was hiding secrets on the dark side of our beautiful blue moon.

One afternoon I was in the trailer trying in vain to reconstruct some of the contents of my book when Bill showed up.

I opened the door and he held out a bag. *"I thought you could use some of this."*

It was a soldering iron and supplies – rolls of silver solder, wire, chain, polish and more.

I gasped. I'd told him jewelry-making had been my livelihood. The fire had taken everything but the contents of the tackle box, which weren't enough to create much of anything. I threw my arms around him and buried my face in his neck. It was the first time we'd embraced in that way, and it felt so right that I didn't want to let go.

He acted nonchalant, but I could see he felt it too. *"I gotta leave early in the morning, but Vic will be home later tomorrow, so you won't be here alone. I figured since you'll have time off from story-telling on the porch, you might enjoy getting back to your craft."*

My heart was singing. *"I can't tell you how much this means to me, Bill! I'll have some pieces to show you when you get back!"*

"I'll be looking forward to that, and to more Gypsy tales, I hope." Then he leaned in and kissed me tenderly on the neck. *"I'll be seeing Vic at the Dispatch Station and I'll fill him in. He'll come over and introduce himself when he gets home."*

He'd learned to read my expressions, and laughed, *"Don't worry, he's the quiet type. He's got a girlfriend in Arcata. I told him about us."*

'Us?' His reference took me by surprise, but I wanted to be *'us'* too, so risked a term of endearment.

"How long will you be gone, darlin'?" I asked.

He winked and grinned. *"No longer than I have to. I'd rather be here with you."* He turned to leave and threw a reminder over his shoulder, *"Don't miss that church potluck on Friday night."*

I laughed and called out after him, *"Okay! I do tend to starve myself when I'm in a work tunnel. Don't do anything wild, Bill."*

He yelled, *"Ha!"* and waved backwards.

I went inside the trailer, spread the supplies out on the table, along with the treasures from my jacket pocket, and began to design. My heart was full, the creative juices were flowing, and I couldn't wait to get back into production. Later that night I went to bed feeling hopeful and empowered. The terrible event in the Redwoods had turned my life upside down, but sometimes hurricanes and shipwrecks can wash us up on the shores of paradise.

I was in love with and loved by a good man and was back to work.

The tide was turning for Aleasa Bihari.

☾

Chapter Sixteen

~ Ghosts ~

"As you may suspect by now, this is no ordinary town, my dear."

I immersed myself in work and the days flew by. Bill's brother offered to taxi me anyplace I needed to go, but I loved riding my bike through the countryside into town.

One day I remembered Fred pointing to the place that sold his canes and I decided to check it out. A sign over the door proclaimed, *'Willow Art Gallery, Est. 1935.'* Inside, the original black and white tile floor and freshly painted plaster walls set the stage for a wide array of local art. I glanced around and spotted a barrel of Fred's canes and walking sticks in a corner beneath a grouping of intricately detailed pen and ink drawings of the area as it had looked in times of old.

A distinguished-looking gentleman was sitting at a desk in the back, and after I'd browsed a bit more, I approached him.

"What a wonderful gallery! So many unique pieces. Those are Fred's, right?" I pointed to the barrel. *"I met him at the bakery awhile back, and a friend of mine owns one."*

"Well, hello, and thank you for coming in." He smiled. *"All of our pieces are originals, and yes, the canes and walking sticks are Fred's."* He added in a puzzled voice, *"So, you've met him?"*

"I did. Awhile back at the Bakery."

"Ah, the Bakery, of course. And how long ago was that?"

It seemed an odd question. *"Several months ago,"* I answered. *"He watched my dog for me while I got coffee and told me which route to take to the Redwoods."*

The curator rose, came around the desk, and held out his hand. *"Forgive me for not introducing myself. I'm Alexander McMillan, the grandson of the woman who originally opened this gallery. Please call me Alex. And you are?"*

"I'm Ali. Ali Bihari. Fairly new to town, but I love it here. I'm an artist, myself. A jewelry designer."

"You don't say! Well, welcome to Willow, Ali. The more artists the better. There's plenty of inspiration to go around. My grandmother was an artist herself and campaigned tirelessly to protect the architecture and history of this town. She's the one to thank for its preservation. Those are prints of her work on the wall above Fred's canes. So, who told you about our gallery?"

"Fred, but I didn't have much time to explore when I was here before. I was headed down the coast, but as fate would have it, I never made it past the Redwoods."

Alex wasn't surprised. *"One hears many stories like that when you've been here as long as I have. I can't help but notice your bolo – it's fantastic. Did you design it?"*

I lifted it up so he could see it better. *"I did and thank you. It tells a story. All my pieces do. I could never part with this one, though."*

"Well, I'm impressed. I love the juxtaposition of the bullet and the shell. It begs a question. Bring your work in any time. I'd like to see more."

I held my excitement in check while jumping for joy inside. *"Happy to. I'm working on several new pieces.*

Alex changed the topic back. *"So…Fred. Would you mind telling me more about that encounter?"*

I wondered why he was so intent upon talking about Fred. *"Well, there isn't a lot to tell. We met at the Bakery and had a nice chat. He told me about his craft, watched my dog while I went inside, and I bought him a cookie that he said was his favorite. He said I should take the Lost Coast road because the drive was so beautiful. Sweet old man. He offered to bring me some of his home brew."* I laughed. *"Later on, I took the route he suggested and it turned into quite the…"* I fumbled for a word and settled on *"adventure. And that's about it."*

Alex hung on every word. Then, after a long sigh, he said, *"Well, you may not believe this, but there's something you should know. Fred passed away almost ten years ago. He and my grandmother were dear friends, and everybody in town knew him. He was always ready to lend a hand, and he used to go up into the cemetery on his own to keep things tidy. He said we owed it to the generations of those buried there who had left us the legacy of Willow. Did you notice the memorial plaque on the bench at the Bakery? That's where he always sat."*

I sank into the chair beside the desk and stared at him.

He stared back and said, *"Really. It's true. You aren't the only one to have seen him. I sure wish I would."*

"So, Alex," I said, clearing my throat, *"You're saying I chatted with a ghost."*

"I don't know what to call him, but it sure sounds like Fred to me. I knew him well when he was among the living."

Now I understood why the bakery patrons had looked at me strangely. To their eyes, I'd been sitting outside talking to myself!

I pointed to the barrel. *"That's quite a few canes and walking sticks. His carving is masterful. Why haven't they sold?"*

"Oh, they sell! Extremely well. When the basket starts to thin out, more appear, one at a time. It's never empty. I give all the money to charity…"

I interrupted. *"Hands of Love."*

He was surprised. *"How did you know that?"*

"Just a feeling. Martha and Mary. They helped me when I first got here. My van caught fire in the Redwoods, and everything I owned went up in smoke. Bill Hicks happened to come upon the accident and has been helping me ever since."

Alex's eyes grew large. *"What a terrible thing for you! But Bill's a great guy. I've known him since he was a kid."*

"Well, he's been incredibly good to me," I said. I couldn't stop thinking about Fred the Ghost.

"I wonder if I'll see Fred again." I mused out loud.

Alex shook his head. *"Who's to say? As you may suspect by now, this is no ordinary town, my dear. Folks generally spot him at either the bakery or up in the cemetery. Keep an eye out, and if you do see him, please be sure to tell him we all miss him."*

"I will."

In the words of Wonderland's Alice, things were getting curiouser and curiouser.

"I'll bring in some of my work soon."

"I will look forward to that." Alex said enthusiastically.

On my way out, I stopped briefly at the basket of Fred's canes. When you touched them, you could feel the life within the madrona wood and the love within the hands that had given it new purpose. I wanted my own creations to speak that way – for each piece to carry a message for the soul meant to receive it.

It was the Gypsy blood, I supposed. *'The Dook.'* I'd always been able to see the beauty in things that others passed by. Apparently, that included souls like Fred.

~

*B*y the time Bill returned, the wisteria was in bloom, and so was our love.

We were made of the same star stuff, and even shared autumn birthdays a few days apart. Ask each of us what mattered most and we would say love, peace, harmony, fairness, justice, and truth – or at least the relentless pursuit of them. The only potential hurdle was the difference in our ages. No one thinks twice when the man is older, but in our case, it was the other way around. After long, serious discussions, we concluded that what we shared was too good to pass up and we chose to forget about the years and to live and love one moment at a time, knowing that those moments would add up to forever.

One day while we were working in the garden, we spotted a small white animal slowly making its way down the hill to us. When it reached the yard, we saw that it was a husky puppy. I filled a pot with water and hurried inside to get food.

When I came back out, Bill said. *"Poor little fella's really tuckered out – I don't know how he made it here. He came a long way, though. The pads of his feet are pretty torn up. There's breeders up in the hills. I think he's part wolf."*

338

The puppy eagerly lapped the water and gulped down the leftovers from our previous night's dinner in seconds. Then he pleaded for more. *"Guess I need to make a trip to the market."* Bill said. *"Don't let him run off."*

There was little chance of that. I was already sitting on the ground with the orphan fur ball in my lap.

"Who are you and where'd you come from?" I asked him in the baby talk that humans reserve for infants and defenseless creatures. He wagged his tail weakly. Then, he looked up into my eyes.

Em had said that seraphs like Dom and Boots come and go in human lives. She'd also said no good thing was ever really lost to the children of YaH. Could it possibly *be*? I held the exhausted little fellow, rubbed his black-tipped ears and knew.

"My sweet boy. You're back!"

He replied with a little bark and licked the tears from my face just as Dom had always done.

When Bill returned, I said, *"We're keeping him, right? I mean, he came to us for a reason. I know it."*

"Well sure, unless someone reports him lost. I'll have the vet check him over tomorrow. He's gonna get really big though, Ali, and he'll be a handful. If I'm right and he's part wolf, he'll have a wild streak like me." Bill laughed. *"But we'll be his pack and he'll be protective. I'll feel good about that when I have to be away on duty."*

He looked at me and laughed. *"You've already named him, haven't you?"*

I loved being known so well.

"My uncle told me stories about a white wolf that was with their family for many years. My grandmother rescued him when he was little. He was especially attached to her and to my mother. His name was Kesali. So, I was thinking..."

"It fits him." Bill agreed, *"Kesali it is."*

☾

Chapter Seventeen

~ Confessions ~

"Strange forces really do surround you, don't they?"

*I*n the months that followed, everything fit into place as perfectly as the last pieces of a jigsaw puzzle. Bill and I were simply meant to be, and Kesali made three. The trial by fire had cleared the way for a life more wonderful than I could ever have dreamed of.

Kesali didn't need much training. He seemed to know intuitively what we wanted and asked only for our companionship in return. When I rode to town, he'd run alongside. I'd explained to him that his size and appearance were intimidating to people who didn't know him, so as soon as we arrived, he would sit and wait for the harness. They knew him well at the meat market, and his patient vigil outside while I shopped would earn him a huge bone which he'd carry home like a trophy.

*A*lex happily took every piece of jewelry I made, showcased them, and always wanted more. One day, he introduced me to a friend who was visiting from San Francisco. She owned three galleries in the Bay area and asked if I was interested in branching out. I hid my excitement and answered casually, *"Possibly. What did you have in mind?"*

"Well, like what you're wearing for a start," she focused on my bolo. *"The bullet theme…it's to die for."*

I cringed at the absurdity of the trendy phrase. No physical object was worth dying for. If not for a miracle, the bullet on my bolo would have taken my life.

"Anything with dragonflies, too," she said. *"They're magical, don't you think?"*

Now she was talking my language. I replied, *"They've been*

visiting me since childhood. They're my 'Spirit animal,' or I guess I should say 'Spirit insect.'" We laughed, but I was serious. Dragonflies even appeared in my dreams, and I knew from what Em had said, that they were messengers.

That is how dragonflies became the signature theme of Ali Bihari jewelry. I supplied galleries and boutiques, worked hard doing what I loved, and was paid accordingly. All without having to leave home.

*B*ill and I had been together almost a year when the truth about my stay in Bear River and the Redwoods finally came out. He had never pressured me, but he didn't need to. I was being nagged daily by the sound of Em's voice repeating a verse of Scripture that promised, *'Everything that is hidden will be revealed and every secret will be brought to light.'*

We were sitting in the living room by the fire that night, when Bill abruptly stood up, put down his guitar and said, *"We need to talk about something. I'll be right back."*

His words were loaded, and I was shocked by how quickly the bottom fell out of my world.

"Oh, Cinderella," a mocking voice said, *"your insecurities never really left, did they? You don't deserve a prince. Even after all these months, you still don't trust him to love who you really are. You're a liar and your fairytale is about to end.."*

Bill returned and set Em's gun down on the coffee table.

I froze.

"I picked this up that day in the Redwoods," he said in a matter-of-fact voice. *"I know what a horrible experience it was for you, darlin', and I wish I didn't have to ask. But we're together, Ali, and I need to know your whole story. If we don't talk about it, it's gonna stand between us. I know there are things you haven't told me. I won't judge you. You should know that by now."*

Bill's ounce of grace on top of everything that had piled up before I met him was all it took to crash my emotional scales. I swallowed hard and pressed my hands to my eyes so the tears wouldn't gush. I'm not one of those pretty weepers whose crystal droplets trickle sweetly down while they dab daintily at their eyes with a lace-trimmed hankie. I'm an ugly crier, and after the heaving, sobbing, and nose-blowing subside, I look like I've been in a boxing match.

I used to have plenty of reasons to cry from the abysmal depths of my soul, but over time I'd finally toughened up, and knew better than to let the agony out. I was now able to successfully quell the occasional small leak, and it had been quite some time since my last severe blubbering.

The breaking of the dam was long overdue, and if I were shown even one drop of compassion, flood waters would pour over the hard, dry ground.

Bill held out his arms and I was underwater.

Kesali lifted his head, came over to the couch and laid down on my feet, presumably so that I could not run away.

With no way out, I risked it all and told Bill everything, starting with what had driven me to leave my home, the strange feelings of being led to Willow, and the sense of having been here before. I described the first night at the fairgrounds when the demon showed up, said I'd met Fred the Ghost, went into detail about the days with Em in Bear River, and lastly, relayed the bizarre events in the Redwoods before he had arrived on the scene. All of it.

My tears fell for way too long, but Bill didn't care. He brought me a box of tissue, looked me straight in the eye and took in every word. This was the kind of man who would slay dragons for the woman he loved, and he was determined to slay mine.

"The bullet didn't touch you…" he said, shaking his head.

"It was a miracle. I should be dead." I stated. *"I was protected by angels. The bullet is the centerpiece in the bolo you've seen me wear, so that I never forget."*

"I've wondered about that bolo, but something told me not to ask."

"I know it all sounds impossible, Bill, but it's true, and I'm so relieved that I don't have to hide any of it anymore!"

"Never, Ali. Never again, okay?" He sighed. *"Wow. My Gypsy woman. Strange forces really do surround you, don't they? It's kinda exciting, actually."*

343

"Yes, it's exciting. But not when evil is out to kill you."

"No, definitely not then. But you have me and Kesali now."

I added, *"And my guardian angel, Em. She brought other angels with her that day – and you were one of them."* I held his hands and kissed them.

Bill, being Bill, was uncomfortable with the adulation and said, *"Aw geez, Ali. I'm not nearly as wonderful as you like to think I am."*

𝓜y burden was lifted that night and our bond was stronger. The next day we talked of getting our own place, and what our future could hold.

The homeowners never visited, and Bill had a hunch they might put the place on the market. It was the end of a long dry summer, forest fires were raging, and both he and Vic were on call around the clock.

When Bill was gone, I often drove with Kesali out to the beach at the end of a day. Sunset walks were a melancholy affair for me, but it was his favorite outing, and he'd streak down the shore in unbridled ecstasy, playing tag with the waves. In stark contrast, I would sit on a piece of driftwood and poke around in the sand with a stick as I plumbed the depths of my alone-ness.

The merchants in town were happy to sell their cheese, bread, and wine to the tourists, and everyone smiled indulgently when starry-eyed couples said they were planning a romantic sunset date at the beach. That particular hour almost always coincided with the arrival of a dense fog bank that rolled in and choked the fiery orb until it sank in the sea. After that, any rosy blush that may have been painted upon the dirty waves would pale to gray and the whole show was over before you could finish your glass of wine.

As disappointing as it was, when you are falling in love, you don't care, and I would never forget my first time there with Bill.

It was warm in town, but the wind at the beach was cold. We found a place to sit on a log facing the waves where we could watch a few fishermen knee deep out in the surf. I was shivering, so Bill sat behind me and wrapped me in his arms. I was surprised because we were still only friends at that point.

344

"Better?" He asked.

"A little," I answered, so he unzipped his jacket and stretched it around us both. His strong, warm chest was pressed to my back and his thighs to my sides, and I remember thinking that it was silly to pretend that I could be safe in his embrace forever. It was more likely that a storm would carry him away like driftwood from the dunes in the winter. Time and tides wait for no one.

As it turned out, those first fears were unfounded, but when Bill is gone fighting fires, very real ones keep me praying for his safe return. He blames his nickname on younger transgressions, but his choice of work is telling.

Few people go to the beach in the off season, so it struck me as strange when I arrived one day to see a figure in a long crimson cape standing alone out on the Dais – a rock named for its size and flat top. The platform is accessible only when the tide is out, and you dare not be caught there when the waves return. The woman's face was obscured by her hood, but something about her was familiar. She was singing to the sea, and when the wind carried the notes back to me, her grief washed over my heart. I longed to console her but something told me there was nothing I could do.

The tide turned, and water began pooling around the base of the rock. I was concerned for her safety, so decided to keep an eye on her from a high spot in the dunes. It only took a couple of minutes to climb there, but when I turned around, she was nowhere in sight.

I remained mystified for hours until I finally assigned the sighting to the 'strange unexplainable occurrences' file in my head. It would be another story to tell Bill, who'd come to expect them. I shared everything with him, not just because he'd made me promise to, but so that if something turned out later to have been prophetic, I could say, *'Hey! Remember when I told you thus and such…?'*

My man came home safely but had to leave again within a week. I'd moved into the bunkhouse months before and was using the trailer as a studio. Staying busy served to keep my mind off worrying when he was gone. The fires were getting worse every year. He shared his thoughts about the cause but didn't voice them to anyone but me.

~

October finally brought relief, and the two of us hibernated throughout the winter. Bill welcomed the break to work on his music, and at his urging, I continued to write. I could never reclaim what had been in my book, though. Those words had come from a different place.

☾

Chapter Eighteen
~ The Reunion ~

"Magic happens when you least expect it."

*W*earable art had become all the rage, and my work was in demand. It was my habit to frequent second-hand stores, estate sales and anyplace else I might find little treasures to incorporate into my designs, and I was on the hunt that day, following my instincts.

I've always known, somehow, that whatever we're in search of, be it vital or trivial, and even if we feel utterly lost and powerless, our souls know exactly where they need to go and what they came to do. We think that we would wander less if more were foretold, but even when it is, most people are so distracted by all the carnal static that they run right over the clues.

*A*n old cement lane with crumbling edges ran alongside the cemetery and ended abruptly at the last row of gravestones. There, it dumped us unceremoniously onto a potholed gravel lane. The Jeep lurched violently.

"Sorry, Kesali," I apologized to my companion, who was doing his best not to slide off the worn leather seat. *"You're the one who insisted on riding shotgun, Buddy. I suggested the back seat. Remember?"*

I jammed one foot on the clutch and the other on the brake, downshifted and swerved, but I wasn't fast enough. The front right tire plunged into a deep puddle, and muddy water splashed up all over the windshield.

"Lovely," I muttered sarcastically, flipping on the wipers, and immediately regretting my reflex when they smeared the brown sludge from right to left across the glass. The washer fluid pump groaned to

remind me that the tank was empty – a fact I could never seem to remember before I set out. The blades drug the grit across the dry windshield with a sound akin to fingernails on a chalk board, and I winced and hit the switch before they could make another sweep.

Garage sale tracking took perseverance. Fortunately, that trait served me well, and I was often rewarded at the end.

There it was – an orange square nailed to a tree. Following such signs led you to places you never knew were there. The thrill of discovery was part of the fun.

I drove at a crawl for another half mile before I spotted the *'Sale Here'* arrow. A tunnel of flowering cherry trees sheltered the short driveway, and fallen petals lay in drifts across the driveway like pink snow. It was a fitting entrance to the nostalgic 1940's storybook cottage ahead.

A car and an old black truck were parked in front of the carport and a bearded man was browsing among the items piled on top of and underneath assorted tables. I parked, taking care not to block anyone's departure – garage sale etiquette.

The place basked in a rare early-April 'intermittent sun break,' as the weatherman would have called it – a sweet, though brief dispensation of grace for us coastal inhabitants. A weathered picket fence wrapped around the little, red-shingled cottage and I paused to take in the charming scene.

Lilacs, their branches nubby with pale, fuzzy buds, had gone wild in the corners of the yard, and the peeling arbor over the gate would be covered with climbing roses come summer. Steppingstones meandered from there across the yard to the ivy-covered porch. White shutters in dire need of paint flanked the pane windows, and moss carpeted the old shake roof. Clumps of yellow daffodils stood at attention in the flowerbeds and popped up here and there in the pasture behind the house, where a grassy hill met a forest of cedar, fir, and alder. Water droplets from an earlier shower sparkled everywhere, and the whole place looked like it had been sprinkled with fairy dust.

Regardless of the little house's general state of disrepair, I was utterly enchanted. I also knew that where I saw beauty and history worth preserving, others would not. If the garage sale meant the owners were leaving, it was highly possible that a developer would pick up the

348

property cheap, fill the potholes, cut down the forest, bulldoze the fairytale and turn it into a housing development. I wondered where the city limits were and prayed that Alex was on the planning board.

Kesali knew the garage sale drill and jumped in back to take a nap. I unsnapped the window flap so he'd have air and headed into the carport. The screen door closed behind a woman who I guessed to be in her fifties. She smiled and waved in greeting, but I recognized the stressed aura common among hosts of her age. I surmised that she was liquidating the belongings of elderly parents who could no longer live there alone, or that someone had passed away.

Such sales are painful affairs. Strangers dicker over precious heirlooms, and transactions often come with pangs of loss for those being forced to let them go.

I've never haggled over a reasonable price. I am a rescuer, not a vulture. The treasures I discover were once pieces of someone's life, and someday it will be the same with my own precious keepsakes. No one will ever know what they meant to me, or the miracles and promises attached to them. The shells I'd saved from the Lost Coast beach and the heart-shaped rock from Dom's grave in the Redwoods would no doubt join other nondescript items in a cardboard box, and I could only hope that someone able to feel their magic would rescue them.

I said hello, and smiled at the other shopper, who glared at me with disdain. A rancid combination of body odor, mildew, stale cigarette smoke and liquor surrounded him, and I stayed as far away as I could. Styrofoam cups and a plate of donuts awaited on the checkout table with signs on each that said, '50 cents.' I contributed a dollar to the jar and helped myself to both.

I looked over the offerings – random dishes, chipped crystal, pots and pans, knitted throws, outdated electronics, rusted tools, a well-worn armchair. The smelly bearded guy was examining everything like an archeologist.

The hostess spoke, *"Are you looking for anything in particular?"*

He answered in hoarse growl, *"I'm looking for old books. Got anything else in the house?"* The question, though often posed at such sales, had always seemed intrusive to me.

"No. Sorry." She answered.

He grunted in response, handed her a dollar bill for a cast iron frying pan, and ignored her pleasant *"Thank you."* As he was leaving, he cast a hateful glance in my direction and I wondered what his problem was. Probably down from the hills. I didn't venture up there anymore. It was strange, how some places could be so beautiful yet feel ominous. After the things I'd experienced, I only drove there with Bill.

We are always given warnings, but there were times when I'd been so focused on getting where I wanted to go that I'd ignored red flags and pushed my way through roadblocks. Not anymore. That lesson, like all of them, had been learned the hard way.

Once the bearded guy was in his truck, I spoke. *"Wow. Glad he's gone. Something not right there."*

The hostess let out an audible sigh of relief and agreed, *"No kidding! I'm Beth, by the way."*

"Ali," I replied, *"I live a couple of miles out on the other side of town."*

"Nice to meet you, Ali. I'm helping the woman who lives here. Her husband passed last year, and the place is more than she can take care of by herself. She's going to have to put it on the market soon." Beth lowered her voice and said, *"It's going to be really hard on her to leave. A lot of memories, you know."* She sighed.

"Oh," I said sadly. *"I'm so sorry to hear that. It's such a lovely spot. Like a fairytale. I haven't been out this way before, but I followed your signs. I'm a jewelry designer so I'm always looking for old pieces, trinkets, charms, stones, that sort of thing. Whatever I can work with."*

Beth responded. *"How interesting!"* She scanned the tables and frowned. *"Well, there were some vintage pieces out here earlier, but I don't see them now. Hmm...that's strange. She might have more in the house. I just didn't want that guy coming inside."*

The words had barely left her mouth when a dark shadow fell over the clearing. The billowy cartoon-animal clouds that had been happily sailing through the blue when I arrived were now jostling one another like an angry mob, their dirty bellies sagging, and ready to rupture. A gust of cold wind swept through the clearing, the temperature plummeted and Beth and I both shivered.

An instant later the dark canopy rumbled, and the tempest was unleashed. Hail hammered the roof and bounced off the ground like a million tiny ping pong balls. Gigantic raindrops came next, then more hail, and then both. Sheets of slush raged across the clearing, tearing the delicate petals from the trees, and pounding the faces of the newborn daffodils into the earth. The carport gutter overflowed, Beth let out a little cry, and we both ran to rescue the items beneath it.

And just like that, the warm, pink magic was gone – a harsh reminder that whatever the season, Mother Nature is in control and every living thing is subject to her mood swings. I couldn't help but wonder if the violent outburst had something to do with her dislike for the man who'd just left. You never knew. My antennae were up.

I helped Beth carry the soaked boxes inside and we dried off what could be salvaged. Within a few minutes the rain stopped, and the back door opened. Beth spoke through the screen to the woman inside.

"It's okay, Mrs. Bauer. Just a squall. Say, there's a gal here interested in old jewelry or things of that nature you might want to sell."

A voice with a familiar accent answered. *"I may have something. Invite her in. Let's have tea. Oh, that wind! Balval is speaking!"*

The accent was Romany. Had she said *'Balval?!'*

"I would love that!" I exclaimed.

The kitchen was dim. *"She's saving electricity,"* Beth explained.

A woman with long, silver hair sat in a wheelchair by the table. A fringed scarf covered her shoulders and a knitted blanket lay on her lap.

"Are you warm enough, Dear?" Beth asked her.

"Just fine at the moment. Thank you, Beth." The woman replied.

A teapot sat on the stove and Beth took cups and tea bags from a cupboard. *"It's chamomile,"* she said, *" is that okay?"*

I nodded, *"Of course. That sounds perfect. It's my favorite."*

"Hers, too," She nodded at the woman and introduced me. *"Mrs. Bauer, this is Ali. Ali, this is Mrs. Bauer, who in all the time we've been friends, has never told me her first name,"* she chuckled good naturedly.

Mrs. Bauer's eyes were fixed on my face.

"It's lovely to meet you." I said.

I instinctively reached down to touch her hands. The translucent skin over lavender-blue veins was soft as a baby bird's and the ridged nails were polished crimson to match the lipstick that had crept into the lines around her mouth. Heavy rings on her fingers told me she'd been the flamboyant sort in her day. She grasped my hands with far more strength than I expected.

"I'm glad to meet you, Ali. Devlesa avilan."

Beth explained. *"It's Romany."* Then she addressed the woman. *"English, dear, or Ali won't know what you're saying."*

I spoke excitedly, *"But I do! I'm Gypsy myself! Balval is making His presence known, indeed, Mrs. Bauer!"*

A smile played at the corners of her mouth, and her eyes twinkled. *"The blood speaks."* She said.

In response to my declaration, Beth exclaimed. *"Oh, how wonderful! What are the odds?"*

Suddenly, I felt lightheaded and had to reach for a chair. *"I hope it's okay if I sit down. It's so kind of you to invite me in. I know how taxing estate sales can be."*

I was sincere, but it sounded trite. This was no casual introduction. Mrs. Bauer was a gypsy queen, the wheelchair was her throne, and I was a vagabond peddler. She ruled the kingdom and I felt the compulsion to kneel on the worn linoleum floor before her in respect.

Beth handed me a Blue Willow cup. It was a sign. I inhaled the comforting aroma and the air grew thicker. More thunder rolled and Mrs. Bauer looked up at the ceiling as though she was listening to a voice from above.

"How typical of you, Ali," I thought, *"You're a fallen leaf adrift on the ripples of a dream – a feather lost to the sky."*

Life was intent upon teaching me that magic happens when you're least expecting it, and the lesson was clear. An hour earlier I'd been out scouting for garage sales, and now I was having tea with an old Gypsy woman in a storybook cottage at the edge of a misty forest.

"*Beth…*" Mrs. Bauer said sweetly.

"*Yes, dear?*"

"*Would you mind keeping an eye on things outside?*"

"*Of course. Let me know if you need anything.*"

"*I don't know what I'd do without you.*"

"*Me either,*" Beth laughed.

As soon as the door closed, Mrs. Bauer's parchment tic-tac-toe wrinkles rearranged themselves and her tone changed. Her voice sounded stronger and there was a hint of urgency.

"*Go to my bedroom, Ali. Down the hall to the left. There's a carpet bag. It's hidden at the back of the closet shelf. Bring it to me, will you?*"

"*Of course,*" I replied. I had the distinct feeling she'd dismissed Beth for this very reason.

The door to her room opened into another world. Warm notes of vetiver, amber and musk hung in the air. Fringed scarves were draped over the lampshades, extravagant vintage rhinestone jewelry was strewn on a mirrored dressing table, and velvet needlework pillows were piled high on the satin bedspread. The closet bulged with colorful skirts, ruffled blouses, embroidered vests, sequined hats, coats with fur collars, and shoes dyed in various colors. A long, red cloak with embroidered trim hung on the back of the door. Something stirred within me when I touched it.

At the back of the shelf, hidden behind stacks of yellowed magazines, was a tattered old carpet bag. I took it down and carried it out to her.

"*Here you are,*" I said, as I lowered it slowly into her lap.

Her lips moved soundlessly as she reached inside and pulled out a silver box.

"*This has been waiting for you a very long time, chavi, as have I,*" she said as she held it out to me. "*And today, O Del has finally made the way.*"

The room was filling with tangible energy, something I'd felt before at times when supernatural forces were at work. I looked at her in wonder and took the box.

Tick, click, tick, click. The tail of the old Kit Kat clock on the wall no longer swished, but its eyes still moved back and forth the way God's do over the Earth.

She held up her arms. *"Help me stand, Ali."*

I did so, and when she was on her feet, she straightened up as tall as her bowed spine would allow. Then she placed one hand on the box and the other on my cheek.

"The miracle happening at this moment, Aleasa, is an answer to a lifetime of prayers. I am Katiza."

My head was spinning.

She continued, *"We do not need to question how this has happened, my chavi. We shall tell our stories, and perhaps the mystery will unravel itself along the way. You have 'The Dook,' of course, which is how you were led here. However strange this reunion may seem, you feel it, do you not?"*

I did.

Em had said, "For the Children of YaH, nothing is ever truly lost." She'd also said my mother had never stopped praying that we would find one another again. She'd never said that my mother was gone. I'd assumed that.

I found my voice and repeated the promise.

"Ah, our angel, Em!" Katiza smiled. *"She has comforted me with those words as well."*

The surreal moment was interrupted by the sound of a vehicle driving too fast down the driveway.

I helped Katiza back down into the wheelchair and poked my head out the door. The guy in the black truck had returned and was limping into the carport. Seeing that I'd been invited into the house, he glared at me angrily and took several menacing steps in my direction. I stepped out, closed the door behind me and said, *"They're wrapping it up here. Closing."*

I looked at Beth for confirmation, and she said, *"Yup. Sorry, sir!"* and made a show of busily shoving things in boxes.

Out in the driveway, Kesali had jumped out the window of the Jeep

354

and was walking slowly toward the carport. He sniffed the air and I saw the hair on the back of his neck stand up. Beth spotted him, too, and her eyes grew wide. I turned toward her quickly and whispered, *"Don't worry, he's mine."*

Kesali made eye contact and knew what the subtle nod of my head toward the bearded intruder meant. An enormous crow cawed menacingly from the roof and flew away. The guy dropped his chin and fixed his black eyes on us. He was too focused on his intended assault to sense the presence of the imposing animal standing like a statue three feet behind him.

"Thought you said there wasn't anything for sale in the house," he addressed Beth sarcastically, continuing in a threatening sing-song voice that turned my stomach. *"You lied to me. It isn't nice to lie."* Then he looked at me. *"You got something out of them, didn't you, bitch?"*

Kesali had heard enough, and a blood curdling growl arose from deep in his throat.

The man spun around, saw him, and staggered backwards. *"Uh, nice dog...uh...wolf...whatever you are. I ain't looking for trouble. Hey lady, call off your freakin' animal!"*

I shrugged and said nothing.

*"Well, shit. Okay, can **somebody** call him off!?"*

Beth spoke up, *"He isn't mine."*

Kesali growled again.

"I have a feeling he wants you to leave." I said. *"I don't think he likes how you smell."*

Kesali stood up and bared his teeth.

The man started moving around to the other side of the table.

"Woah, woah, woah! I wouldn't make any sudden moves if I were you," I said. *"Bound to trigger him, and he looks more wolf than dog if you ask me. I've heard there's a breeder up in the hills."*

He stopped in his tracks and I said, *"So, you'll be leaving then?"*

"Hell yes, I'm leaving." He said, not taking his eyes off Kesali.

"And you won't be coming back?"

"Hell no, I ain't coming back." He was almost out of the carport.

I had the upper hand. *"Before you go, pay my friend for what you stole earlier. I saw you shove stuff in your jacket. And give her more for the frying pan. A buck doesn't come close."*

He rummaged in his pocket and threw the stolen jewelry, along with a crumpled twenty-dollar bill, in Beth's direction. Then, checking nervously over his shoulder with every step, he limped to his truck, got in, revved the engine, and spun out in his haste to leave.

Kesali walked to my side and gave me a big wolfish smile.

Beth was dumfounded. *"Thank you!"*

I explained. *"Kesali's my guardian. He has impeccable timing. This is Beth, boy. She's a friend."*

Katiza had heard the truck leave and opened the door. She maneuvered her wheelchair out onto the ramp and the concerned look on her face turned to disbelief as she gasped *"Kesali! Is it **you**?!"*

He ran to her side and when she saw the dark tips of his ears and his blue eyes, she said, *"Oh, my! I thought you were him!"* He put his head in her lap as though they'd known one another forever.

Beth's routine was to go home for dinner with her family and then return later. We assured her we would be fine.

Katiza and I ate chicken soup by candlelight, and she fidgeted the whole time. When we finished, she could no longer contain herself.

"I think it's time you opened the box."

I felt inexplicably nervous. *"Okay, but are you sure you should be giving me something so valuable?"*

"Open it, chavi. You will understand."

I lifted the lid to find the box filled with a variety of keepsakes that included silver jewelry, gemstones, an exquisite hand-carved dagger, and an old book with a leather cover that was darkened and cracked with age. When I lifted it from the box, it felt strangely familiar in my hands, and when I opened it, my heart stopped.

There was my name, written in youthful script, and beneath it, *"For the higher Kintala."*

Chapter Nineteen
~ Restoration ~

"Miracles do not have to be understood to be believed."

I pressed the book to my heart and exclaimed, *"How? I don't understand! This can't be real! Why is it so old now? How long have you had it?"*

Katiza laughed like a child on Christmas morning. *"For a very long time! It truly **is** yours, then? This is the deepest magic I have ever seen! Gypsy women have been protecting this book for many generations even before you and I were born, my chavi! A calling was placed upon our hearts, and we have all been faithful."*

I asked incredulously, *"You all read it?"*

"Oh, I am sure those before me wanted to, but reading was not permitted in those times. When my mother first showed me the book, I promised I would learn to read so we could know what it said. Your Aunt Sabella was teaching your uncles and me, but the invasion ended that. Later, when Hans and I made it to America, he taught me. When I read the inscription inside the cover, I was amazed, and believed it to be a sign that we would be together again one day. As I read each page, it seemed as though the words had been written just for me. I came to understand why the book had to be protected, but I had no one to pass it on to. Today, when you walked through the door, Balval spoke." Katiza closed her eyes and whispered a prayer of thanks.

I looked at her incredulously, then gasped at a sudden realization. *"This is what that guy was looking for earlier today! I know his kind. They're demons in skin. One like him stole the book from me in the Redwoods. He stalked me from the time I first arrived here in Willow. He destroyed everything I owned, killed my sweet dog, and would have murdered me too, if angels hadn't stopped the bullet. Then, he took the book and disappeared. But that was only a couple of years ago!"*

I was struggling to make sense of it. *"How did it get so old? And who got it back, and when and how?"*

Katiza shook her head. She had no answers either. *"I don't know who retrieved it, chavi. Someone with powers we can't comprehend. Remember that time is not what we think. Did Em explain that to you?"*

I couldn't stop shaking my head in wonder. *"Yes, but it was hard to understand."*

Katiza urged, *"Look at the other things."*

I reluctantly put the book down and began to examine the rest of the keepsakes in the box.

"They all have meaning." She said, *"Like this,"* and she showed me the necklace she was wearing. *"The stone was in the box when Tamás, your grandfather, gave it to my mother. He'd found it in a river when he was young. Your grandmother put it on a cord and did not take it off until she gave it to me. I've worn it ever since. Be careful of the dagger. It's as sharp as a razor. Tell me how it feels in your hand."*

The only sign of age on the knife was a dark stain where the handle met the blade. *"Like it was made for me,"* I said.

Katiza nodded knowingly, *"Yes. It feels the same for me."*

"Whose blood do you think this was?" I pondered.

"I wondered the same thing." she said.

As I held each item, I could feel a connection to the woman who had contributed it. I knew the silver jewelry had to have been Nadya's, for the craftsmanship was just as exquisite as Em had described. I'd never seen anything like most of the gems. They had to be very rare.

"Which keepsake is yours?" I didn't know what I should call her.

Sensing my awkwardness, she said softly, *"Please call me 'Dai,' my chavi. For all my longing, I've never heard it."*

"Dai," I repeated softly. *"My Dai."*

My mother dabbed at her eyes with her scarf. *"I have two things of my own to add, but I've been waiting. Let me get them."* She wheeled herself into the small living room and I heard a cabinet open and close. Upon her return, she set two miniature carvings on the table. A horse of Onyx and a wolf of Quartz.

"These are in memory of Baro and Kesali, my beloved companions who saved my life. I would not have survived without them."

Present-day Kesali was lying in front of the door and upon hearing his name, he lifted his head and came to us.

I reached out to ruffle his fur and said, *"I was led to name him that from the stories Uncle Ion told."*

"Of course." Katiza replied. *"The blood remembers. Protectors like him have saved many of us."*

"Yes, they have! Remind me to tell you about Dom!" I exclaimed. *"But first tell me about Baro!"*

"Ah, Baro. Our champion. There will never be another horse like him. He was with our family from the time my mother was little, and lived many long years. In the end, he gave his life to save mine. He's grazing in the pastures of Charos, now, with flowers braided into his mane, waiting for all of us to come home. I have seen him there."

My heart leapt. *"I've seen Charos, too, in dreams."*

Katiza's voice was matter of fact. *"I lived there when I was small, before Earth."*

"My Uncle Ion told me that!" I said. *"I can't wait to hear more!"*

Katiza abruptly switched tracks. *"My brother!"* she exclaimed. *"Where is he? Can I go to him? It all went terribly wrong, my chavi...you know... back in Serbia when we had to flee."*

Her voice was filled with pain. *"A seer warned me of a coming Nazi raid and told me what to do. I didn't want to believe him, especially when he said that you would be safer in Sabella's care than mine. But his reasoning was sound. She, being full German, could say you were her own child. Unspeakable fates awaited Gypsy children.*

"I can only tell you about the parts of the escape that I lived through, and what Hans told me later. Our people suffered beyond belief." She bowed her head. *"Things did not go as Hans and my brother planned. I have not seen any of my family since then."* Her voice was filled with sorrow.

I tried to comfort her. *"But Dai, we are together now! Uncle Ion and Sabella have returned to Charos, but they raised me with great love and told me everything about you. They always believed we would find one another again, and they were right!"*

Katiza nodded her head, reached for my hand and said, *"My daughter. My blood."*

I assured her, *"Yes! Here, from now on. Devlesa araklam tume."*

"All praise to O Del," she said softly.

"Amen and Amen," I agreed.

A cuckoo clock chimed in the living room. I looked out the window and saw Beth's car coming down the drive. *"Beth's back."* I said.

Katiza pleaded, *"Can't you stay?"*

I answered, *"You must be tired, my Dai. It's been quite a day, and there's a couple of fellas I need to feed. This one,"* I patted Kesali, *"and a two-legged one who's probably wondering what's happened to us."*

"Ah," she answered, knowingly. *"I loved cooking for Hans. There's rhubarb in the back. Pick some and make a pie for your man."*

I laughed. *"Oh! He'll love that! May I come back tomorrow?"*

"Oh, I beg you to!" She beamed.

"Is there anything I can bring you?" I asked.

"Just your stories, my chavi. I want to hear them all."

"And I yours!" I pressed my cheek to hers and we stayed that way until Beth came in the door.

The storm had blown through, and by the time I headed home the first stars were winking at me from the twilight sky. The lampposts at the cemetery entrance were on, and a figure was bent over polishing the brass plaque on a large headstone. He heard the Jeep, stood up and waved. I saw the cane and long white beard. Kesali barked out the window in greeting and I tapped the horn and waved back.

Hello, Fred! Good to see you again. You were right when you said I'd be back.

---

devlesa araklam tume *(dev-LAY-sah ara-KLAM TOO-may)* – It is with God that I found you

Chapter Twenty
~ The Impossible ~

"Well, as usual, it's a doozy of a story..."

$\mathcal{D}$ear, patient Bill. Not only was he stuck at home with no vehicle or dinner, but I was on my way back with another story to tell. As crazy as they all were, he'd never once questioned my sanity. I supposed that by now, life with a 'normal' woman would have been boring.

I arrived to see a large *"For Sale"* sign in front of the mansion. Bill was sitting on the porch with a beer in his hand and a lost look on his face. I parked, ran into the bunkhouse, slid the silver box under our bed, grabbed a bag of chips and joined him.

"Sooo...." I sighed as I sat down.

"You saw it," he said.

"Yup. Wow."

"They want us out within the month." He shoved his hand in the chip bag. *"Sooner if the place sells. No explanation. Realtor's a friend. He says there's already bites. Way out of our price range, of course."*

"So, what now?"

"Dunno. We've gotta do some quick figurin'. There's no place to rent in this town, and no place we'd be able to buy. Not sure what we're gonna do." Bill's slang always got worse when he was nervous or worried. It was an unconscious attempt to sound nonchalant, I think.

"Something will present itself. You know a lot of people."

"Maybe..." his voice trailed off. *"It's gonna be a problem for Vic, too,"* he said. *"Not lookin' forward to tellin' 'im, either."*

"I'm so sorry. It's been the perfect place while it lasted. Funny. Just yesterday I was counting how many times I've moved in my life, including the years as a kid when my aunt and uncle were looking for work."

"And?" he asked.

"Twenty-nine times so far. Guess this'll make thirty." I reached for his knee. He always bounced the left one up and down when he was stressed. *"All I care about is that we're together,"* I said. *"It doesn't matter where we live."* I gave the bouncing knee a strong pat.

He grinned and finished his beer. *"You said it, Gypsy woman. There's always the trailer, I guess. Our own little 'vardo.' We could paint it, find a circus and tag along. You could tell fortunes and I could dress like a clown and sell beer."* He lifted his bottle in a mock toast to his idea. *"Well, would you look at that? I'm on empty. How was your day? Find any good stuff?"*

I laughed. *"Indeed, I did, and as usual, it's a doozy of a story. I'll tell you after dinner, okay?"*

"Good plan. Come on, boy." He nudged Kesali and we retired to our temporary home.

An hour later, after Bill had comforted himself with an enormous bowl of chili, he continued the conversation. *"So, you were going to tell me about your day."*

"Well, I met my mother."

"What? The mother you never knew? Or the one who raised you and is dead? No disrespect."

"My birth mother that I never knew."

"Aw geez, you're messin' with me. I'm not in a joking mood, woman."

I raised my eyebrows.

"Oh, common'!" He groaned. *"You can't be serious!"*

*"I absolutely **am** serious. I can't believe it, myself. Oh, and I saw Fred the Ghost again too, on the way home. You know that road that runs alongside the cemetery?"*

"Uh-huh." He was massaging his forehead.

"Well, there was a garage sale sign and when I followed it to the end, there was a beautiful little valley with a forest on one side, and a sweet little cottage in a clearing with pink trees that line the driveway and..."

362

"And…" he coaxed with a hand gesture that meant 'get on with it.'

I continued and told him everything except the part about the demon. It would only have made him worry and Kesali and I had handled it. I also decided to wait to tell him about the book.

Other than one pause to fetch another beer, Bill listened intently.

"Where's the box?" He asked, and I could tell by the tone of his voice that he was forcing himself to remain objective.

"I'll get it."

Kesali escorted me to the bedroom and back, and I set the box on the coffee table in front of Bill.

"Hmm. Solid silver. Man, I bet this'll polish up beautiful."

"Slovenian Romany craftsmanship, well over a century old. They were legendary silversmiths. But wait until you see what's inside."

I opened the lid and took out the jewelry.

"Wow. Incredible work. So intricate! What stones are these?"

"I have no idea. I've never seen anything like them. Can you believe this? It's been protected and handed down by my ancestors for generations. My mother didn't even know how many. This next thing, you are going to find difficult to believe. Are you ready?"

"Well, no," Bill said warily, *"I'm never actually ready, but I've learned to keep an open mind."*

"To be honest, I still can't comprehend this either," I said as I carefully removed the book and handed it to him.

"This looks really old," he noted. *"Must be valuable, right? Is it a Bible or something?"*

A brittle edge of a page broke off and fluttered to the floor.

"Oops!" He apologized, *"Are you sure we should be handling it? They use gloves in museums…"*

"Just be careful. It isn't just any old book, Bill. Open it. Tell me what you see in the bottom corner of the first page."

He did so and looked at me curiously. *"Aleasa."*

I nodded. *"My given name."*

"So, someone had the same name?"

*"No, Bill. It's **my** book! My handwriting! My uncle gave it to me when I was young, to record what he said was the 'higher kintala.' It's the book that was stolen from me in the Redwoods when my van burned – the **same** book!"*

Bill tried to grasp what I was saying, shook his head, and frowned. *"How is that possible?"*

"I don't know! It wasn't old like this then, but there's no mistaking it. I'll prove it. Do you remember me reciting one of the poems that I said would make a good song?"

"Yeah…I liked it. Just a second, let me think…" He handed me the book, picked up his guitar, plucked out a tune and sang a few notes. *"Rest ever lightly if when weary you must, lest Earth's tethers bind you to that which is dust."*

I found the page and handed the book back to him. *"Look."*

"Oh," he said incredulously. *"Well, there it is."*

"It's my book, Bill! My mother said it has been handed down for generations – that our ancestors were all called upon to protect it. I don't know how any of that can be, but miracles don't have explanations, do they? And time isn't always what we think. You can't imagine how it feels to hold it in my hands again!"

"Wow," he said quietly. *"this is really weird."*

"I told my mother I'd be there tomorrow. Please come with me? I can't wait for you to meet her!"

"Of course," he agreed, *"but if we're talking about the same road, I've lived here all my life and it stops at the end of the cemetery. There's nothing like what you're describing…"* his voice trailed off.

"So, you doubt me?"

"Never, lest Balval strike me dead." He joked. *"But there was that time when you stayed with an angel in Bear River…"*

"That happened," I interrupted firmly, *"and so did this. You'll see."*

☾
Chapter Twenty One
~ Justice & Grace ~

"Life is a sad story," she sighed, *"but also a beautiful one."*

*T*hough unknown to anyone but the participants in this tale, the return of the book to its rightful owner was no small news in other realms. While the firmament above echoed with victorious shouts of praise, the Vrag's rage exploded like a firestorm through the caverns of the damned.

The bearer of the bitter news, an unlucky imp by the name of Slack, who had drawn the short straw, bore the full brunt of his master's wrath. The Vrag was sick and tired of having to hopscotch after the stupid human tabloid, and he still had no idea why it was so important to Beng.

The hairy, lice-ridden demon who'd botched the simple task of swiping the book from an old, wheelchair-bound hag, did not survive his punishment, nor did the sticky-fingered bumblers before him, none of whom had managed to hold on to it. The Vrag had zero tolerance for incompetence within his ranks. Knowing that an interrogation by Beng would be forthcoming, he thought it wise to get ahead of it, so sent word to HQ saying that he was personally taking on the assignment. He was a born liar, of course, and had made the same promise before. There would be a record of his blunders, and he was counting on some well-placed bribes and the inaccuracy of the fact-checkers to keep his sins hidden. If Beng were shown the data, the consequences would be unthinkable. Beng never forgot and never forgave.

As has already been explained, the Vrag was a master of the art of deception. He'd been studying his superiors' tactics for eons and acute discernment was needed to detect his presence. Although humans had been granted plenty of power, few of them understood how to activate it. This was because they spent most of their creative energy conjuring up wishful fantasies rather than facing ugly truths.

That same night, in stark contrast with the vile punishments of darkness, Kesali was celebrated in the realms of light and given a steak dinner in the earthly one.

And the human? Well, I had learned an important lesson. Always pray and guard your mind before you go to sleep.

After a night in which I was tormented by a string of terrifying nightmares, I arose early, brushed off the mental spiderwebs and was wiser. The enemy is cowardly. He lurks in the shadows and waits until we are vulnerable to attack. He is not selective and roams around with the intent to torment any soul within striking distance, be it man, woman or child. There is no rationale other than hatred, and no target is off limits.

At dawn I announced loudly to the entities of darkness that by harassing me in their Halloween costumes, they had succeeded only in giving away their positions, and that there would be no mercy.

I would be on guard and would continue to sing my song in the enemy's face, knowing that an army of guardians surrounds me. My soul will wear armor made of light and I will use the sword I've been given. I will finish what my soul contracted to do on this Earth.

Later that morning, Bill and I went to the bakery and from there to Katiza's cottage. When the lane turned to gravel and the valley came into view, Bill was stunned and insisted, again, that he had no memory of it having ever been there.

I enjoyed being able to say, *"I told you so."*

Beth was in the house making coffee, and I introduced Bill. A few moments later, Katiza came into the kitchen, looking years younger than the day before. She'd fixed her hair, put on make-up and jewelry, and was every bit the striking Gypsy woman I'd always pictured my mother to be. She took an immediate liking to Bill and insisted Kesali come inside.

The rest of the day was spent in a hazy state of joy as we shared the stories of our lives. Bill decided to clean up and organize the carport while Beth sorted through things to donate to the charity in town.

At one point, the conversation with my mother took a serious turn, and she asked, *"Did your Uncle Ion ever tell you what happened when he went to Belgrade to find our parents?"*

"Yes," I answered, reluctantly. *"But it is a sad story, Dai."*

"Life is a sad story," she sighed. *"but also, a beautiful one. Tell me, please."*

"Alright. As I was told, he was determined to find your parents – my grandparents – in town, and finally discovered that they had been taken prisoners and were going to be loaded onto a train with others who'd been arrested. They had been badly beaten and there was a little girl with them. He was so angry that he acted rashly and killed a soldier. He said that act haunted him for the rest of his life. The soldiers were cruel and under orders to kill anyone who resisted. Your parents begged Ion to save the little girl and told him to run. He said no heart should ever have to make such a decision, but he obeyed them."

Katiza groaned softly. *"That is just like them. And like my brother. What about the little girl?"*

I continued. *"This part is happy. When he got back to the Cirque, Aunt Sabella recognized her. She was the daughter of other performers and her family had been frantically searching for her. They had refused to leave until she was found.*

"Aunt Sabella and Uncle Ion packed me up, then, and we all left. He and Hans had planned to meet on the road, but too much time had passed for us to catch up with him. Everyone was praying that Hans had been able to find you, but there was no way to know. It was several more days before we reached the harbor, and by then, the boats were all gone. A family sheltered us on their farm until Sabella could get word back to her uncle at the Cirque. He arranged for another boat, and eventually we made it to America."

There was a sad, faraway look in Katiza's eyes as she watched it all in her mind. *"Herr Zeigler,"* she said, *"was a good and brave man. He put his own life on the line and his actions saved us all."*

I added, *"I was just a baby, of course, but I asked Uncle Ion to tell me the story many times because it kept the hope alive that I might find you again one day. And here we are, despite the evils we have battled!"*

Katiza's voice was fierce and she made a hand gesture which I knew accompanied a Gypsy curse. *"Vile tyrants, those of that time, and of this day, and days to come. They serve Beng, the evil one, who gorges himself on pain. Our sorrow is seasoning for his bloody meals. But it shall not always be so, my daughter. Right now, he's being given enough rope to hang himself."*

"I believe that," I agreed. *"Em said so."*

"Remember this, my chavi," Katiza said with grave seriousness, *"No one can silence your thoughts. No one can chain your soul, and no one can lock you out of the sanctuary of your own heart. No matter how many laws men make, or how many oppressors arise, the spirits of those who walk in the light will **always** be free."*

A moment later, Bill and Beth entered the house and poured themselves cups of coffee. Beth asked, *"Can I get you two anything?"*

We declined, and Katiza said, *"Sit down, Beth. There's something I want to tell you."*

Beth sat, and Bill leaned on the counter.

"This is going to be hard to believe, my Dear, and we are still in shock ourselves," she looked over at me, *"but there's no reason to wait for a different moment. As impossible as it may seem, God has brought my daughter, Aleasa, back to me."*

Beth's mouth dropped open, and my mother reached for my hand. *"I have prayed for this miracle my whole life, Beth. We were separated in the escape from Belgrade. I have told you of those terrible days. Now, she is here. Only with God could such a thing happen."*

Beth's reaction was somewhere between incredulity and joy. *"I **do** believe in miracles! It just isn't very often that we get to witness one! I sensed something yesterday but couldn't put my finger on it. I couldn't be happier for you!"* She jumped up and hugged each of us in turn.

Katiza addressed everyone, *"Beth has been such a blessing to me, but I don't feel right about her leaving her family to be here so often. I know I can't stay alone in this house. It's too much for me now. Things are falling into disrepair. Hans was a hard worker and always took such good care of everything. We were so happy when we were finally able to have a home of our own.* " She struggled to hold back tears.

The three of us looked at one another. No one knew where Katiza was headed.

"I realize this is very sudden, but I feel I'm to ask. Ali, Bill, would you be interested in staying with me? I was going to put the house on the market, but if you don't own a place of your own, and would be willing... " She left the sentence hanging in the air.

𝒞lick tick, click tick. The slits in the Kit Cat clock's eyes scanned each face in the room.

I looked at Bill and he answered for both of us. *"We'd be honored, wouldn't we, darlin'? There's plenty to keep me busy. With some repairs, this little house can be like new again, and you two have a lot of catching up to do. "*

I kissed my mother's hands. *"Yes, yes, yes! We'd love to be here with you!"*

It was one of those rare occasions when everyone finds themselves in the right spot at the right time – when things fall into place so easily that you would be foolish to say 'no.'

I believe it's meant to work like that far more often than it does.

☾

Chapter Twenty Two
~ *Let It Be* ~

"Whether happy or sad, blessed, or belittled, we are all just passing through this world.
It's best to keep it simple and sweet whenever you can."

SGR

*I*n the autumn of that year, Bill and I were married beneath the willow tree in the town square. There was a nice turnout, and a half-page writeup in the paper. Katiza was my maid of honor, and Vic was Bill's best man. Our rings came from the silver box. I didn't know whose they had been, but I could feel the strength of the love in them. We had them inscribed *'Now and Forever.'*

I spared my mother the details of my perpetual heartache over the loss of my granddaughter, and she did the same for me by not discussing my absentee father. I suspected that she kept a place for him in her heart and I wondered if it hurt when she saw parts of him in me.

She also refused to talk about her illness and waved it off as though it was an irrelevant bother. Beth was the one who told me in confidence a few weeks after we'd moved in. *"I've watched it take a toll."*

My Dai was not interested in treatments that would degrade her quality of life and I supported her decision. Neither of us were the type to chart our lives by clinical statistics or to put stock in grim diagnoses. When someone tried to impress the worst upon her, she'd get a defiant look on her face, straighten her shoulders, and state, *"Worry is like injecting poison into your own veins. I reject it. I'll be here as long as O Del wants me here. I'm under contract."*

She was, however, annoyed by the pain and frustrated by her limitations. *"Too many failed stunts,"* she'd say. *"I was reckless. But oh, how I wish you could have seen us then, chavi. We were the stars of the show, and had there been no war, you would have grown up on Baro's back, yourself!"*

371

For emphasis she'd show me her hands. *"This wretched arthritis finds every injury you ever had, including the ones you've forgotten about. But it proves you lived, and there are no wheelchairs in Charos! I shall dance, sing, and ride Baro again!"*

Then she'd look up and call, *"Hear me, Boy? I'll be there soon!"*

And I'd look up with her and add, *"Not that soon, Baro! I still need my Dai!"*

𝓗er stories of our family's days in Cirque Ziegler were my favorites. I could see and feel it all in grand, colorful detail – the striped canvas tents, the smell of peanuts, popcorn, and sawdust. The ringmaster and performers in their dazzling costumes. The horses prancing, my grandfather's music playing and the audience captivated by all of it. I loved watching my mother's face as she relived those times. Her eyes would twinkle and she'd be young again.

"Hans and I..." she confided, *"...well, he wasn't good at showing his emotions, but there was a spark between us from the start. On hot summer nights, when the ticket holders had all gone home and everything was shut down, I'd slip out of my vardo and take you to Sabella's so that I could meet him at the carousel."* She laughed at the memory. *"He'd start it up without the music, and we would ride in the swan boat. I remember closing my eyes and dreaming that we were sailing through the stars. It was incredibly romantic. He was too shy, then, to even put his arm around me or hold my hand, but I always wished he would."*

She sighed deeply. *"He was an easy man to love, and my best friend. How blessed I have been – and am. Nothing born of love can die. He's in Charos waiting for me."*

𝓜y Dai's attitude carried her many years beyond everyone's expectations. We were at her bedside when her soul took flight back to Charos, and Kesali howled, which he only did on momentous occasions. She'd given me the stone necklace the day before. I hung it around my neck and said I would never take it off. We didn't need any other words.

I wore the red cape when we gave her ashes to the sea. She'd told me that my grandmother had made it for her when I was born. I could envision Nadya sitting on the vardo steps with the fabric flowing over her lap, meticulously embroidering the floral trim while her heart overflowed with love for her daughter and newborn me. I wondered if she'd known, what lay ahead. *'The Sight'* is a double-edged sword.

When Katiza gave me the cloak, she told me she'd worn it when she escaped Belgrade. She traced her fingers over the frayed trim with reverence and said, "*My Dai brought magic to everything she touched. The magnolia blossoms are a symbol of perseverance, and the heather, protection. She believed that there were deeper meanings to be found within all things, and she was right...*" she laughed softly, "*...for here I am, still persevering and still protected, just as you shall be.*"

I climbed to Dais Rock to scatter her ashes and sing the song. I knew she was with our sister souls in Charos. When the stars came out, she and several others descended, hovered over the waves, and showered dazzling colors upon the water. Then, they shot back up into the heavens. It was a celebration. Someday, when my contract was up, I would sing and shine and celebrate with them.

~

Years passed, and Bill, Kesali and I were content. Bill received commendations for his bravery but no longer had the stamina of his youth and was planning to retire from firefighting to pursue a music career.

We had the items in the silver box appraised, and our future security was assured. Some of the stones were deemed 'of no known origin,' and were therefore, priceless.

~

It's my birthday. I woke up from a delightful dream where I was wandering through small shops and artist booths in a crowded alleyway of a quaint European village.

373

One of the displays was filled with unusual stones and geological specimens. A cluster of blue crystals streaked with silver stood out to me, and when I remarked upon its beauty, the seller said it was very rare and possessed mystical properties, which he proceeded to demonstrate. When he covered the crystal with his hand, it changed form, and when he swiped it across another flat, rock face, gorgeous pictures appeared in its wake. Then, he held it over my heart and announced, *"Oh, you are a strong, loving soul – a daughter of autumn."* I was amazed and called Bill over to see the crystal.

When he got there, I asked the owner, *"What does it say about him?"*

In response, he held the crystal in front of Bill's chest, and after a moment, declared, *"Ah, a master of the scales. Kind, fair, and strong. You belong together."* Bill didn't seem surprised.

Uncle Ion was also in the dream. He'd come with Bill, and soon after that, I saw a man who looked much like him making his way through the crowd toward us. I knew it had to be my uncle Amoun, and I was incredibly happy that we were all there together.

When I awoke, I remembered that blue crystals represent patience, harmony and Heaven. If I ever see one like in the dream, I'll buy it.

~

*I*t's dreary and raining. Something feels off and I can't shake it. I remind myself that there have been other times in the past when this kind of restless melancholy has hung over me, and the reason has been revealed later, so I have learned to acknowledge the feelings and to let them be.

Bill's due home tonight. We always celebrate our birthdays together and I'm making his favorite pie. Every time I gather the tart red stalks from my mother's garden, I think about how many rhubarb pies she must have made over the years for the man she loved.

Kesali is pacing back and forth, so I open the door. *"Go on. Do your business, but come right back in, okay?"* He dashes to the Jeep and looks back at me anxiously.

"Not today," I say. He puts his front paws on the running board and does that howly-barky thing.

"We can't go to the ocean right now. It's raining and I'm baking a pie."

He whines and refuses to move. I'm cold, so I go back inside.

Tick Click. Tick Click. The clock's eyes are moving in sync with the oven timer and the beating of my heart. Things begin to feel surreal. Something's about to happen. I don't know what, so I take a deep breath and close my eyes.

It's real – the gentle embrace, the smell of his skin, the soft, warm kiss on my neck. I hear the words whispered in my ear. They are a holy truth that I've always had a hard time accepting.

"I love you completely and forever, exactly as you are. You will always be mine."

Somewhere far away in the world of broken clocks and piecrusts, a phone starts ringing urgently and I watch my hand pick up the receiver. The connection is poor, and the voice on the other end is breaking up. I hear men shouting in the background.

"Ali, it's Vic. I'm calling because...oh, God...I'm so sorry...I ...I...can't..." He's sobbing.

"I know, Vic. He's here with me. Everything is going to be okay."

I hang up the phone and the tidal wave takes me.

Breathe, Ali. Breathe. Your body knows what to do. You're still alive. Breathe. Deeper. Now do it again.

The timer goes off, adrenalin jumpstarts my heart. I walk to the oven, open the door, take out the pie. It's beautiful. It's real. Sticky red juice bubbles up through the slits in the top. The smell ascends to Heaven. An offering. I put it in the middle of the table.

Love can't die.

It's raining hard now. Everyone's been praying for this. It will put out the fires. It will save lives.

Kesali is howling on the porch.

ℂ
Chapter Twenty Three
~ *The Blood* ~

"Peace I leave with you. Peace I give to you. Not as the world gives."

Yeshua

*B*ill's family wanted a traditional service and burial in the cemetery. Several of them gave heartfelt eulogies at the gathering, but I was too numb to speak. I've secretly kept aside some of his ashes for the ceremony that only Kesali and I will share. This is that day.

On the way to the ocean, I think about us. All the cups of coffee we shared in the café at our table by the window while we watched the storms roll in; our walks for miles while Kesali chased the wind. My husband's strong heart was the open vessel into which I was able to pour my deepest self without reservation. In our years together, he had never once criticized, blamed, judged, or deliberately hurt me. He loved me for who I was. There would never be another Wild Bill.

'Closure' is a word people love to use, but I don't like it. The door to the void in my heart will never close until I am with Bill again.

It's the second time I've worn my mother's cloak to the rock, and as I make my way across the beach, a memory surfaces of the day years before when I saw the woman in the red cape standing out on The Dais. I know, now, why she seemed so familiar. I'd foreseen my own grief. It was always going to be part of my story, and now I was living it.

I was younger when I came to mourn my mother here and it's harder to climb the rock now. By the time I reach the top, my legs are shaking so badly that I can barely stand, and my heart feels like it's going to explode. The sea spray stings my face, and the wind wants to to tear the cape from my body, but once I plant my feet firmly on the rock, my exhaustion is replaced by the realization that the greater our resolve and the more painful our struggle, the holier our offering becomes.

This time, as I cast my song upon the waters, the notes sound different than before. They are drenched with salt and sorrow and they catch in my throat. Kesali is waiting on the beach, his own mournful cries echoing off the face of the cliff behind us.

Were the roles reversed, Bill would be uttering a profound prayer about now, but I am as hollow as a broken shell. I stare out at the undulating horizon and my body starts to go numb. Fragments of old hymns are rattling around in my head. An anchor for the soul. An eternal blood oath. The Rock of ages. All other ground is sinking sand.

A picture of the brave old rose outside the little abandoned church in Bear River fills my mind. Thank you, Elizabeth.

I am deeply humbled by what I have come to accept about Mother Earth. Unlike humans, her programming does not allow for caring or quitting – only for adapting and surviving. Bill died fighting for her, and she's indifferent. Her heart hasn't skipped a beat and she has already forgotten him. Fires will still rage. Hungry creatures within the forests and tidepools will still demand to be fed, and life here, there, and everywhere will continue whether I think it should or not.

I contemplate carrying Bill's ashes into the deepening waters, but Kesali would never have allowed it.

~

Since that day, the beach evokes too much pain for frequent visits. A friend is kind enough to take Kesali there for runs now and then, but I have the excuse of degenerating joints. I'm becoming more my mother every day, but she wouldn't have stayed in the dumps for long. I can hear her voice reminding me, *"There's a reason we're here, chavi. Think of it. If I had shriveled up and died after I lost Hans, you would never have found me, and we wouldn't be together now. We must finish out our contracts. There's far more at stake than our feelings. God will provide the strength."*

Kesali sticks closer to me than ever and our conversations are a great comfort. Early in his life, we jokingly nicknamed him 'The Gatekeeper' due to his habit of stretching himself out in front of thresholds and doorways. Anyone not of his pack who wanted to enter was subjected to a thorough investigation, and if you were pack and wished to leave, you needed to get his permission first.

One day, I asked him the meaning of this routine, and he answered, as always, by sending pictures into my mind and adding a few wolfy words for emphasis.

First, he said that he wore his Gatekeeper moniker proudly and was surprised by the fact that we had no idea of its significance when we gave it to him.

He went on to explain that he was simply following his directive to protect those within his care. Supernatural gateways, portals, vortexes, or whatever one chooses to call them, exist, and while they are invisible to human eyes, our guardians can see them clearly.

These passageways must always be monitored, as they can be rightly or wrongly used. He reminded me of the places I'd seen him position himself when he was in Domino's body. The water fountain at the rest stop where he entered this dimension, and the porch of Em's store when the demon came to call. It was his duty to secure the gates so that only benevolent entities could pass.

I apologized profusely for the times I'd grumbled about him being underfoot. He licked my face and said that there was a great deal humans didn't know, and that whatever form guardians may take, they are patient with us. It is their hope that once we have learned a thing, we will want to share it so that the reasons for their actions might be better understood.

~

$\mathcal{I}$t wasn't long before my faithful companion rejoined my mother and Bill. I put on the red cape, took Kesali's ashes, and we made the trip to the beach together one last time.

~

With my protector gone, I kept the dagger next to my bed. One night I was awakened by an unfamiliar sound. I slid out of bed, grabbed the knife, and crept down the hallway. A light was glowing in the living room, but when I got there, I could not find its source. It seemed to be coming from everywhere.

Inside the locked curio cabinet where my mother kept her treasures, a music box was playing. She'd told me it had been a gift from Hans and that it had stopped playing long ago.

Suddenly, her favorite fragrance filled the room and I knew she was there. I sat down, put my hands in my lap and said, *"Dai. I know it's you. What have you come to tell me?"*

The light grew brighter and I glanced down to see blood on my hands and gown. In my haste to grab the dagger, I hadn't felt the razor-sharp blade graze my palm.

She spoke. *"Follow the blood home, chavi."*

The music box stopped, the light dimmed, and I hurried to the bathroom to tend to the cut. I cleaned the knife, but my blood had already stained the handle.

I did not know until later what her words meant, and I questioned why such communications had to be so enigmatic. I think I know now, though. Seekers who are determined to decode the messages are given keys along the way. Knowledge opens the door to understanding, understanding leads to wisdom, and wisdom unlocks many a mystery.

No one wants beautiful stories to end, but we all know they must. We're all just passing through this world. No one gets to stay, though as in my mother's case, some are allowed to return.

I've noticed that a lot of folks like to spend their time here scattering hopeful imaginings around like glitter, but in my experience, truth is a slender golden vein deep within a mountain and it's the quest of a lifetime to find it. I don't mind the labor.

~

A few months later, I was sitting outside sipping a cup of tea and watching a dragonfly explore a flowerbed, when I caught a movement out of the corner of my eye. I turned, and there she was, casually strolling across the lawn toward me like we'd seen one another just the day before.

"Boots! Is it you?" She meowed in that way that turned her mouth into the shape of a small white heart, and when she got closer, I saw the notches in her ears.

"Em?! Are you here too? Give me a sign!"

A cool breeze brushed the hair from my forehead.

Boots hung around all summer, demonstrating her love by allowing me to feed and pamper her. When September came, her visits stopped, and I remembered Em saying that such guardians come and go and I knew she'd been called away to another mission.

That very same night, I received mine.

*I*n a dream, I was looking out over a beautiful landscape with fields, forests, rivers, and waterfalls. People were milling about on the cobblestone streets of a quaint village and I could hear them speaking in a Slavic language. In the courtyard, colorfully dressed dancers were performing to the lively music of stringed instruments.

Then, the scene changed and I saw myself sitting beneath an immense willow tree beside a lovely lake. Little white daisies were sprinkled on the ground and the tree's roots reached down into the water. My book was lying open in my lap and a loving voice said, *"Come home."*

The message was so clear that I arose the next day and began to research Slovenia at the local library. My attention kept returning to one village in particular which had retained its historical charm. When I saw the picture of a willow tree beside a lake outside of town, I knew.

~

*L*ike my mother, grandmother, and those before them, my belief rested in the healing powers of my Creator. Therefore, when the doctors issued the same bleak diagnosis as they'd given Katiza, I refused it, just as she had. I'd been taught by her example how to make peace with pain, and like her, my decision served to alienate those around me who simply could not understand.

I was quite content with a solitary life. I felt no need to inform anyone that I was leaving town and doubted they would notice.

I made the airline reservations, wrote a letter which I placed on the kitchen table, and started packing. I'd often wondered what I should do with my book when the time came for me to return to Charos. There were only a couple of blank pages left, but I intended to fill them. In the meantime, I couldn't risk it falling into the wrong hands, so decided to take it with me.

☾
Chapter Twenty Four
~ The Way Home ~

"There's nothing like a Gypsy tale," he sighed happily.

I hadn't travelled more than twenty miles outside of quiet little Willow for years and the chaos at the airport was unnerving. I straightened my shoulders and tried not to look like the confused old woman that I was, but even finding the right ticket counter was daunting. My sight and hearing were poor, and I needed to rely on the use of one of Fred's canes. By the time I got through all the lines and made it to my gate, I was exhausted and collapsed into a seat. A young woman looked at me with concern and asked if she could get me anything. I replied that I would love a cup of tea and gave her a few dollars. By the time she got back, boarding had begun, and they wouldn't let me bring it on the plane.

I don't like airplanes and was not looking forward to the length of the flight. I told YaH I would be relying on Him for strength and received the assurance in my heart that He would provide it.

I made it to my seat and managed to stow my bag. I'd just settled in and was glancing over the emergency procedures brochure when he came down the aisle.

The instant I saw him, I was overwhelmed by déjà vu. He was a dashing older fellow around my age, with white hair and an impeccably groomed moustache and goatee. He stashed his bag, hat, and leather jacket in the upper compartment, sat down and greeted me politely.

"Hello. I'm Daz. Is there anything I can do to make you more comfortable? Would you prefer the aisle seat?"

I smiled back. *"Nice to meet you, Daz. I'm Aleasa – Ali for short – and thank you, but this seat is fine. I'm looking forward to the scenery, though I hope it won't be too disturbing if I need to get up and move around now and then,"* I apologized.

He saw my cane and assured me, *"Not at all. Any time you need to do that just let me know. Have you been to Slovenia before? Relatives there? Your name is Romany, isn't it? Means 'Chosen,' if I remember correctly."* He smiled.

My eyebrows went up. *"How did you know that?"*

"Well, I've been around a long time. I'm Serbian, hence my name, Dazbog."

"Serbia…" I said. *"I wish I could have gone there, too, but the trip would have gotten too expensive. I'm visiting Mirno."*

He nodded enthusiastically. *"Ah, my destination as well. It's delightful this time of the year. It can be a bit tricky to find one's way around, though. There is less English spoken there. Why Mirno?"*

Before I could answer, the stewardess asked for our attention, gave her speech, and the engines fired up. We fastened our seat belts, and I found myself feeling a bit anxious. I grasped the armrests and Daz patted my hand to reassure me.

"I always get a few butterflies, too. I'm more comfortable in conveyances with wheels, but we can't get there that way. May I interest you in a glass of wine once we're in the air?"

I nodded and eased my grip a little.

*B*y our second glass, we were talking like old friends. Something about him made me feel like I could say anything. Other than the discomfort of trying to get in and out of my seat for restroom visits, time passed quite pleasantly. I told him of my Gypsy heritage, and that I was widowed. He said he was retired, had never been married (though he'd been in love) and that he travelled when he needed to.

When he asked me again why I had chosen Mirno, I told him about my dream. He found it intriguing and commended me on my sensitivity and obedience to spiritual urgings. That led to us sharing experiences of a supernatural nature, which he thoroughly enjoyed.

"There's nothing like a Gypsy tale," he sighed happily.

"You must have stories of your own." I coaxed.

He chuckled, *"Too many to tell, my dear. And I dare say they would rival your own,"* he added with a twinkle in his eye.

I'd brought a large purse with multiple pockets in which to carry all necessary items and had pulled it out from under the seat several times during the flight. My book bag, however, remained securely over my shoulder.

"Something special in there?" Daz nodded toward it and asked.

The question surprised me. Why was he asking?

He saw my expression and apologized. *"I'm sorry. Forgive my curiosity. I couldn't help but notice how carefully you are guarding it. Please be assured that you have nothing to fear from me."*

I didn't want to give him the impression that I was paranoid and answered honestly. *"I've...well...it's just that it's valuable and it's been stolen from me before. I've been nervous about it ever since. I try not to let it out of my sight."*

"Well, I can certainly understand that. How did you get it back after it was taken?"

"You'd never believe that story," I replied.

"It falls in the supernatural category, then."

"Off the charts," I said. *"I still don't have the answers myself."*

"May I venture a guess as to what it is?"

"I suppose." What harm could there be in that?

"It's a book. Dear to your heart. Ah! A journal of sorts perhaps?"

I looked at him in disbelief.

He laughed. *"I'm not a magician or a psychic. It's just deduction. Watching your face and body language after each comment or question. It's a study of mine. Let's play a game. If my guess was right, you buy the next glass of wine. If it was wrong, I keep buying."* He craned his head up above our seats teasingly. *"Where's that stewardess?"*

I laughed and relaxed. *"Okay, fine. You win."* I removed the book and he beamed.

"I knew it! The writings of a lifetime? Though I wouldn't guess you to be anything near as old as your book." He winked.

"You flatter me, sir," I played along. *"Be advised that the story behind this book is a long one and very, very strange,"* I warned.

"We have plenty of time, and strange stories are my favorites," he assured me, *"especially when told by ageless Gypsy women on journeys to enchanting places."*

The fellow was fascinating and obviously loved women. The wine had lowered my defenses, and I told him the whole tale. At the end I shrugged and said, *"So, that's the truth if you choose to believe it. You can stop staring at me now. Are you reading me again?"*

"No," he said, laughing gently, *"I was counting your smile wrinkles. They're lovely, and I do not doubt a word of your story. Should I? This world was designed by a divine intelligence Who desires our companionship. Some – the seekers and the dreamers – choose to engage more readily than those who fear deep waters."*

He sighed. *"It's their loss. But you, my dear – well, I've never met a Gypsy girl I didn't love..."* His voice trailed off and he changed the subject. *"You're going to allow me to help you find your way safely around Mirno, aren't you?"*

"You'd do that?"

"I feel I must."

"But I don't really know you!"

"Don't you? Good heavens. Shouldn't people of our age be able to trust our discernment by now? There are no accidents, my dear. We are on this plane together for a reason, and this encounter is not a random event. You feel it, of course."

He was right. Where had that young, romantic, risk-taking girl gone? The one who followed her heart and hated the word 'sensible.' I needed to hand her the reins.

"I feel it." I admitted.

"It's settled then," he said. *"May I have the pleasure of reading some of your writings? We've a long way to go, and you need a nap."*

"I do, and you may," I replied, *"though I'm not sure you will find*

them very impressive."

His voice was kind. *"I think you underestimate yourself."*

"Did you read that in my face?"

"I saw it in your heart. But I see in your face that you are tired. There won't be a lot of time for rest once we land. Why don't you try to get some sleep? I'll wake you up in plenty of time."

𝓘 slept more deeply than expected and when I awoke, both Daz and the book were gone.

I panicked and looked frantically up and down the aisle. I buzzed the stewardess and when she arrived, I tried to keep my voice calm.

"Have you seen the man who was sitting here?"

"No," she replied, *"but he can't have disappeared."* She leaned over and teased. *"It's an airplane, dear. No one can leave until we land. Would you like a warm blanket?"*

Her gentle jibe was lost on me. It seemed patronizing. Why did people assume that age led to feeble-mindedness? She had no idea of what I'd seen in my life or the things I knew.

"Oh, look. There he is!" She pointed to the back of the plane. *"It's nice you two have made friends. He's handsome."* She winked.

My heartrate slowed and I scolded myself for overreacting.

Daz arrived at his seat and handed me the book. *"Looking for this? I figured since you don't let it out of your sight, I shouldn't either."*

I took it and thanked him.

"I hope you can trust me now," he said. *"Better me than complete strangers once we get to Mirno. There are those who make their living fleecing tourists in such places."*

I apologized. *"It's just that I was a little disoriented when I woke up from the nap, and..."*

He interrupted. *"It's alright. Truly. I've done nothing to earn you trust, but please give me the opportunity to do so. Your book, by the way, is inspired. It spoke to me. I shall guard it with you."*

$\mathcal{A}$fter we landed, it became clear that I could never have managed without Daz. He took care of everything, and the following day we headed to Mirno. When I asked, he said his own matters could wait.

The village was enchanting, and twice as enjoyable with my gracious escort. We took a tour in a carriage and he booked rooms in an inn that dated back to the 1800s.

"Their claim to fame is that one of Europe's greatest violinists got his start in the tavern," he said. *"I wonder if your family traveled through these parts? Perhaps they knew him. Didn't you say they were performers? There are a lot of old photographs on the walls in the lobby. We should check them out. Perhaps you'll spot a resemblance."*

Before I could engage on the subject, happy shouts and music erupted in the courtyard and we were delighted to find that the timing of our arrival coincided with the first day of a festival. At dinner I told Daz more about my dream and the willow tree by a lake. A look passed over his face that I wished I could have read as easily as he was able to read me. Before I could ask, he masked it and assured me we would locate the park the following day.

Later, at the door of my room he looked at me with great tenderness, and said, *"I hope you won't think the wrong thing, but may I hold you for just a moment?"*

I felt something undefinable – something long-forgotten that was trying to find its way back to me. His emotions were mirroring my own, but I did not want to behave foolishly, so I smiled and answered him with a measure of restraint, *"I suppose so."*

Gentleman that he was, he put his arms around me, held me long enough for the moment to be real, and then let me go.

"See you in the morning, lovely Gypsy." He said softly with a bow and went to his room.

$\mathcal{T}$hat night, I opened my book at random to a fable about a willow tree. Strangely, I could not remember ever having written it. I fell into a deep, peaceful sleep with the book beside me, and in the morning, I could not find the story again. While that seemed odd, it did not trouble me, for I could remember every word.

(

Chapter Twenty Five
~ Forever ~

"They were all part of me and I was part of them."

When Daz knocked on the door, I was ready. He looked at me and his usual composure crumbled. *"Your cloak…"* He could get no more words out.

"My mother's," I explained. *"I wear it sometimes when I'm meant to. The rest of this,"* I gestured to the jewelry, scarves, blouse, skirt and shoes, *"belonged to her, also. I didn't know why I was packing all of it, but I do now."*

I took his outstretched hand and noticed that it trembled a bit. Downstairs, all the windows and doors stood open onto the courtyard and we were offered a table outside in the morning sun. Breakfast was freshly baked bread with marmalade, and little brown birds chirped and competed for crumbs at our feet.

Our waiter was familiar with the lake where the old willow tree stood and told us how to get there. Festivities were beginning and dancers in Gypsy costumes were mingling with the crowd.

One young woman complemented me on my outfit and asked if I'd made it. I told her it had belonged to my mother, who'd been a dancer, and that my family had performed in these parts long ago. She was enthralled and exclaimed that she was part Romany herself.

She handed us a program. *"Here's a list of our performances during the festival. Our troupe is based in the United States – San Francisco, California. We travel internationally, but I like Slovenia best. I feel like I belong here."*

"Me, too," I said, and we marveled at the fact that while we lived just hours apart in the States, we were meeting a world away. We agreed that it would be fun to chat over dinner later, and I told Daz I wanted to be sure to be back in time for her troupe's last show of the day.

"I'll look for you, then!" She called back to us as she danced away.

No sooner had she disappeared into the crowd than I realized I hadn't gotten her name. *"I'll ask her tonight,"* I said to Daz. *"She's lovely, isn't she? Such energy and spirit!"*

"Quite." He replied. *"She reminds me of another girl I knew at that age."*

*W*hether it was jet lag, or all the added activity, by the time we reached the park, I was in considerable pain, and grateful to see an unoccupied bench near the willow tree.

We sat and soaked up the sun and the peace of our surroundings. Every now and then the distant strains of violins and laughter reached us from Mirno, and the moments could not have been more blissful.

"Such a heavenly spot," Daz said contentedly. *"I love being here with you. I'm in no hurry to leave this time."*

I wasn't sure what he meant by *"this time."*

"Indeed," I sighed, and when I laid my head on his shoulder, I was overwhelmed by the marvelous sensation that we were on a slowly turning carousel. Our location did not change, but as we moved, the scenery did, and I was shown the significance of every moment of my life. Love, loss, joy, sorrow, forgiveness, and restoration. Promises given, kept and broken, and always, seasons passing. I could see the ways I'd been challenged and how my soul had grown. Stretching over it all was a divine canopy of grace.

Pictures, places, and people flowed into one another seamlessly. I saw that they were parts of me and I was part of them.

When I came full circle, the willow tree was young again and I saw a girl floating in the lake with her face to the sun. I could feel the silken water gliding over my own skin and was ageless in its embrace.

Dragonflies were dancing among the cattails and one of them flew to me and whispered, *"Remember?"*

I am flooded with feelings of deep contentment. I can remember how it feels to be planted in this place – to stand barefoot by the water's edge, my hair tangled by the breeze, my heart beating with praise. Daz is beside me there, resting in the shade of my boughs, telling me a story about the love that gave birth to all other love.

"You're seeing it, aren't you?" Daz asks in the now. *"You're there."*

"I am." I breathe.

He stands, walks to the willow, and runs his hand over the bark as though searching for something. Then, his face lights up. *"Gypsy girl. Come see this."*

When I rise, all the pain is gone.

He places my hand on the trunk of the tree. *"Do you feel it?"*

"Yes."

"Do you remember?" He's searching my face.

Bark has enfolded the old carving and it's barely visible.

I trace the letters. His name on my heart.

"But you left me!" I say, recalling my tears.

"I was called away, and had I told you the reason, it would have grieved you more. I know this season has felt very long."

He sits, leans his back against the tree trunk, and plucks a tiny daisy. Patting the ground, he reaches for my hand and pulls me gently down beside him. Handing me the flower, he says. *"Press it in your book so that this moment is never forgotten."*

I take my book from its worn leather bag and am astounded to see that it is no longer old and crumbling. The leather has been restored, the ink is fresh, and there are many more empty pages in the back. A white feather falls out from within them.

I look at Daz in amazement. He doesn't know, or maybe he does, that because I had no one to give it to, I had planned to bury it here beneath the willow.

"All things will be made new," He declares. *"This story is not over."*

"But my contract is almost up." I say.

"It's been renewed," he states. *"Charos is not necessarily a final*

destination, my dear. It is also a place of celebration, rest, rewards, and new beginnings. You shall see."

*H*e looks back toward the village. *"There's another reason we are here."*

"Why?" I ask, but he does not say, and instead assures me, *"I'll be back before long. Rest. Dream some more. Your soul had a part in creating this. Everything in existence begins with a spark of original thought. An endless current flows from the Source through souls willing to receive what it brings. All inspirations are seeds that possess unlimited potential. They are sent from the heart of a Creator who gives good gifts to His children. He loves dreamers, and you, dear Aleasa, are an exceptional dreamer."*

*W*hen Daz leaves, I close my eyes and am given a vision of all those whose blood I've been privileged to share. I see the joys that lifted them, their heartbreaks and triumphs, the hardships and obstacles they overcame, and the powerful dji that lived in their bones. I understand that by divine design, these small, vulnerable human hearts are capable of holding more love and enduring more pain than we can possibly imagine.

I want to tell them it was all worth it. That their sacrifices were not in vain and that their lives made a difference. That we are all parts of one another. But they already know, and their tears were dried long ago.

I hear my own song coming from the sky and look up to see living columns of light filled with swirling colors. They descend and beckon me to join them. When I do, every bond to Earth falls away.

*F*rom above, I see Daz returning. With him is the dancer we met in the village. Knowing I've ascended, he asks her to wait on the bench. At the willow, he kisses the old Ali, takes the book gently from her hands, and unties the stone necklace. Then he walks back to the girl.

I know, now, who she is.

Hundreds of seasons have passed since I held her little hand and she named the trees in the yard. Thousands of days since I sewed fairytale dresses and we played make believe. Countless nights since we'd snuggled in bed and I read her favorite stories until she fell asleep. Her big brown eyes were my windows to Heaven.

*D*az is speaking to her. *"You have not known your grandmother since you were small, but your hearts are very much alike. You are a writer, are you not?"*

She nods enthusiastically, *"Yes! It's my greatest joy."*

"It is your joy because it is your gift, as it was hers." Daz states.

He hands her my book and the worn bag. *"Protect this with your life as others before you have done. There is an enemy who will stop at nothing to steal it. He succeeded, once."*

"But you got it back?" she asks.

"I believe you may find that story inside." He replies. *"It's quite the tale, and one of my longest and most challenging missions."*

Her eyes grow large as he continues. *"Add the words you are given, child. They will be vital one day. The story must continue, and there are days ahead that shall try human souls. The world will need encouragement. This is a divine calling. Do you accept it?"*

"I do," she bows her head and holds the book reverently in her hands.

Next, he shows her the necklace and explains, *"The stone symbolizes protection. It has been handed down for generations."*

She lifts her hair so that he can tie the cord. *"But why me?"* she asks. *"How did you know...?"*

Daz smiles. *"In answer to the last question, I've known you since before you were born, Zoa. And in answer to the first one, it's the blood. There are markers visible only to the One who places them there. I also know you feel like a stranger upon this Earth."*

She exclaims, *"Yes! But I don't understand why!"*

"Because this isn't your home." Daz replies matter-of-factly. *"You are only a visitor here – a messenger."*

My granddaughter looks as though she is beginning to understand, but I know very well that the journey will not be easy for anyone who accepts the calling.

"Does she know how much I love her?" She asks Daz. *"I didn't want to leave her! They told me things...said they knew best... I didn't want to believe them because it didn't seem true, but I was too young to argue, and then, so much time went by that I didn't know what to do...I'm so sorry!"*

"She knows." he answers. *"There are many kinds of love, my child. Those who live in the highest kind consider what is best for others first. Rather than see you torn apart, she released you. Her love never changed, her heart never stopped longing for you and she has never ceased to pray for your happiness.*

"To be loved unconditionally is a priceless gift, Zoa. Countless blessings are forfeited when such love is intercepted, taken for granted, or brushed aside."

"May I talk to her now?" She pleads.

"You may always talk to her, but her season on Earth has ended. I came to be with you both. I've left practical information for you at the Inn. Your grandmother's home and possessions shall be yours. She would want that. Oh, and ask the innkeeper to tell you about the famous violinist in the pictures on the wall. He is your great grandfather.

"You must return to the village now, child. Please alert the authorities of dear Aleasa's passing, but do not mention my presence. I shall be gone before they arrive."

*T*he lights gather close around me as the child of my heart slowly walks away, carrying my story with her.

Daz is gone.

I look down upon the willow and see myself on a long forgotten day. It's spring, and the reasons for perseverance and hope are proven in every bud and blade of grass. The sky is deep blue, the water sparkles, and the sun is warming the earth.

The One who gave me life sits beside me, waiting for me to awaken from a dream.

A soft breeze stirs my boughs and my leaves whisper sleepily,

"What time is this?"

He answers me tenderly,
"What time do you wish it to be?"

Overcome with love for him, I sigh,
"I wish it to be Forever."

"My Beloved," he smiles,

"it already is."

*The true
children of God
are those
who let His Spirit
lead them.*

*The Gypsy Bible
Romans 8:14*

Glossary

The Romany/Gypsy words used in this book came from different sources. Dialects vary greatly between regions and tribes, and pronunciation is not always known. In general, most Romani words put emphasis on the next-to-last syllable.

Names

ATASYA *(ah-TOSS-yuh)* – yesterday, tomorrow
Aleasa *(Al-ee-AH-suh)* – Katiza's daughter
Amoun *(ah-MOUN)* – Tamás' and Nadya's son
Balval *(Ball-VALL)* – the invisible Spirit of God, the Wind
Baro *(Bare-OH)* – the black Friesian horse belonging to Tamás' family
Beng *(bENG)* – the devil
Caesaré *(Sez-ah-RAY)* – the Friar
Dazbog (DAZSH-bog) -The Seer/Prophet/Fortune Teller
Ion *(EYE-on)* -- Tamás' and Nadya's son
Jacob Tomich *(YAH-kōb TOE-mich)* – A traveling holy man
Katiza *(Kah-TEEZ-ah)* -- Nadya's daughter
Kesali *(Keh-SAH-lee)* – The white wolf found by Nadya (and later by Ali)
Luciano Cristoforo Abella *(loochee-AHNO christō-FORO ah-BELLah)*
Luci *(LOO-chee)* – The Priest in the village of Mirno
Maja (MY-yah) -- Midwife
Nadya *(nod-YAH)* – Renata's daughter
O Del *(oh-DEL)* – God, The Creator, YaH
Renata *(ren-AH-tuh)* – A gypsy girl
Tamás *(tah-MAHS)* – Tsura's son
Tsura *(ts-UR-ah)* – Tamás's mother
Vrag (vrAG) – a chief demon
YaH *(YAH, as in 'saw')* – God, The Creator, O'Del

Words and Phrases
A-C
Bori *(BOOR-ee)* – Daughter-in-Law
braskis *(brahs-KEES)* – frogs
Charos *(CHAR-os)* – Heaven

Continued…

399

A-C (Continued)

chav *(sh-AHV)* – boy
chavi *(shah-VEE)* – girl

D-F

Dai *(D-eye)* – MotherDati *(DAH-tee)* – Father
darane svatura *(da-RAIN, sva-TOOR-uh)* –
    fairytales and fables of magic and the supernatural
darro *(DAH-roe)* – dowry
devlesa avilan *(dev-LAY-sah avi-LAN)* – It is God who brought you
devlesa araklam tume *(dev-LAY-sah ara-KLAM TOO-may)* –
    It is with God that I found you.
dinilo *(din-EEL-oh)* – crazy
dji *(GEE)*– the spiritual energy of life
drabarni, dukkering *(drah-BAR-nee, DOOKER-ing)* – fortune telling and tellers
dobro juto *(DOE-bro-JEW-toe)* – Good Morning (Serbian)

E-M

gadje *(gah-DJEE)* – non-Gypsies
ghel *(gell, like 'bell')* – girl
gilabno *(gil-AHB-no)* – traveling musician
jook *(jOOK)* – dog
Kasko san *(casko-SAHN)* – Whose are you?
mahrime *(MAH-ree-MAY)* – contaminated, unclean
mulo *(MOO-low)* – lost souls

N-R

paramicha *(para-MEE-cha)* – fables
pena *(PEN-ah)* – sister
Porajamos (poora-JAH-mose) – The Devouring (The Holocaust)
posotis *(poe-SO-tis)* – hidden pocket
pomagaj mi *(pahm-AH-jee mee)* – Help me
Roma *(Roe-MAH)* – Gypsy, Romany, Romani
Romni *(Rom-NEE)* – Romany wife
Rom *(r-AHM)* – Romany man, husband

S-Z

storvandre *(stor-VAHN-dray)* – long distance traveling musicians
vardo *(VAR-doe)* – wagon

.

The Author

Selah Gayle Rose was born in the majestic Pacific Northwest where her love of nature, literature and the arts took root at a young age.

The daughter of a Serbian mother and part Native American father, she feels a deep connection to the courage and spirituality of her heritage. *"It is my belief that we are designed to be channels of light. Whatever form my work takes, my hope is that it will be an inspiration."*

A published multi-media artist and writer of more than forty years, Selah's work has found its way around the world. A book of collected writings, *The Voice of the Spirit,* was released in 1999, and is available on Amazon.

Inquiries may be sent to: atasya.s.g.rose@gmail.com